Crystal Secrets
The Shattered Crystal: Book 2

By
James Funfer

This is a work of fiction. All of the characters, organizations, countries, and events portrayed in this novel are the work of the Author's imagination.

Cover art by D G Baumgart and Megan Seely
Edited by Genie Rayner

to Kathy Funfer

my first editor, critic, and fan

who nurtured in me

the compulsion to tell a good story

Prologue

Blue is the crystal that shines like the stars
Portals and doorways it opens and bars
Shining a path through darkest of night
Blue for Astara, the Goddess of Light

Orange is the crystal that burns like a flame
That only the greatest of Speakers can tame
Heat in the winter, release for the pyre
Orange for Arragus, who first gave man fire

Green is the crystal that looks like the sea
Master of water, plant, flesh, root, and tree
Venoms and poisons, curatives, potions
Green for Neovus, the God of all Oceans

Red is the crystal like old iron's rust
Rock of destruction, entropy, dust
Decay and disruption, metal and ore
Red for Arus, God of Passion and War

Yellow the crystal that glitters like gold
Energy, action, and movement controlled
Speak ye with caution when this gem is flawed
Yellow for Tybal, the messenger god

Purple the crystal of duskblossom hue
Heightens or lessens what all crystals do
A Speaker's best friend, a defence, a boon
Purple for Luna, goddess of the moon

James Funfer

Pink is the crystal that like a pale rose
Charms and delights wherever it goes
Guile and deception this crystal's true duty
Pink for Avari, the goddess of beauty

Brown is the crystal with tones like the soil
And with it in hand, the engineers toil
Building and crafting is this crystal's worth
Brown for Titania, goddess of Earth

Grey is the crystal as silent as stone
For those who would keep all their Speaking unknown
Masking or changing what others perceive
Grey for Saccarus, the god of the thieves

White is the crystal as pale as a wraith
Energy spent up and used in good faith
Whisper no longer, its power has fled
White for Lutias, the god of the dead

Be mindful the crystal that is black as coal
Sucking in light, it will draw out your soul
Take care not to touch, for your life it will keep
Black for Noxanna, the goddess of sleep

Clear is the crystal with powers most varied
Crafted as rings when great Speakers marry
Defending all Novem and heeding the call
Clear is for Jova, the father of all

--A Young Speaker's Mnemonic Rhyme

Crystal Secrets

***

Paulo heard the sound of bells tolling far away. The pealing, brassy tones were muffled by layers of stone and wood. Deep under Crystus Hill, Paulo was surprised that he could hear them at all. He took another shuffling step and ascended a marble stair in complete darkness.

Every time he moved, the pain in his guts stabbed at him. *Ignore it,* he told himself. *You are strong. You are the son of Maximus Longoro, an Emperor of Novem. The crystal can heal you. The nation is counting on you. You're going to marry Racquela and...*

"Ugh," he groaned, clutching at his side. The thought of Racquela gave him strength and he kept moving.

The bells grew louder as Paulo ascended, filling the silence between his grunts and footsteps. He wondered how long it would take for somebody to find his corpse if he didn't reach the top.

A stabbing pain from his wound brought Paulo to his knees. He collapsed on the cold marble stairs and tried not to slip on his own blood. Paulo thought about crying out for help. He didn't know if anybody would hear him, or if the right kind of help would come. A lot of people wanted him dead, and his loyal followers were far away.

"Shatters," Paulo whispered. A cry for help would have taken too much out of him. He was spending the last of his strength keeping a foot wedged on a lower stair, pinned there to stop him from sliding. The steps were steep, treacherous to the unwary. The darkness and Paulo's growing dizziness made it worse.

Paulo pushed himself up and stood on shaky legs, leaning against the central column of the stairwell. He returned a hand to his gut to cover the wound, pushed his sweat-slick hair back from his face, and braved another steep step. He was the heir to the Empire of Novem. He refused to die ignobly in a forgotten staircase, reeking of sewers and viscera.

I am not going to die, Paulo told himself as he took another step. *Shatters, where is that door? This staircase goes on forever.*

Other sounds began to mingle with the ringing bells. Shouting and wandshot were distant but audible. Paulo smiled wolfishly in the dark. He was getting closer, and so were his rebels.

Paulo's forehead struck something abruptly. He nearly lost his balance, steadying himself against the staircase column. He searched frantically for a doorknob or latch, but the surface in front of him was smooth and featureless. His staircase to the temple had been walled off long ago.

"No," he said weakly. The bells replied forlornly. Paulo's legs gave out and he slid against the wall to collapse upon the final stair. Out beyond the walls of the Old Temple, brave men and women were fighting to overwhelm the army and take the parliament building. They were fighting, unaware that their future emperor, the salvation of Novem, was dying.

Chapter 1
Thirteen Years Earlier

The moulded piece of tin was no bigger than Boy's hand, but at that moment it was his entire world. From boots to cap was the shape of a proud man: legs straight, knees together, chest high. Its body was smooth and well-worn from age, but it held a resolute grip on the tiny black longwand in its hands, brought to shoulder level and ready to dispatch any threat. The paint had worn off most of its face, leaving a pair of black eyes that spoke of grim determination, of old battles hard-won.

Its uniform was an old one – not the blood-red of an imperial soldier or the dull grey of the republican army, but a sun-faded New Kingdom blue. Boy didn't know anything about uniforms or Noven politics, but he spotted a tiny painted medal on the tin soldier's left breast, and he knew he was holding a man of exceptional courage.

The tin soldier marched across the warped wooden floor to a drum beat that nobody else could hear. He was drilling, preparing for battle. Boy decided that the soldier's name was Leo. Leo meant lion, Bruno had told him once, and lions were brave.

He could feel the eyes of the other children watching him as he played with Leo. They were talking about him in a gaggle of voices, but he kept his eyes on the tin soldier marching across the floor. He didn't want to look at them, because then they might come over. Boy wanted to play by himself.

Leo was shooting at imaginary soldiers coming up over the crest of the bump in the floor. In Boy's mind they had green-and-mustard uniforms and funny metal helmets, and they yelled threats in a strange gibberish language. Leo remained undaunted. He stood his ground and aimed carefully, shooting them down as they came.

"Oh no, there's more of them." Boy told the soldier. "Better use your crystal grenade. Boom!"

"Hi, soldier," a girl said. Boy froze. Standing beside Leo was a cloth doll covered in dirt smudges, wearing a red summer dress. Most of her hair had fallen out, and the stitching was loose on one foot, letting a bit of puffy cotton stuffing poke through.

Boy stared at the doll for a moment. Since Leo had no mouth, he couldn't reply to the doll. The tin soldier continued shooting at the oncoming adversaries.

"Quick, let's escape to my house," the girl said as she made the doll prod Leo with a filthy, fingerless hand. "You can protect me with your gun."

Boy shied away and pressed his back to the wall. Bad things happened when he spoke to girls.

"Are you going to live here?" the girl asked. Boy bit his lip and chanced a glance at her.

Her round, rosy-cheeked face was dirty, and she wore a patchwork dress. She looked remarkably like her doll, except that she wasn't missing any hair – the girl's dark curls were almost down to her waist. Boy stared at her wordlessly. Leo took a bold step forward on the floor and bowed to the doll.

"What's your name?" she asked.

"Leo," he said. He didn't want to admit that everybody just called him 'Boy'.

The girl's eyes widened suddenly. "Drop the toy," she said.

Boy frowned and tightened his grip on Leo.

"Drop it now," she urged. "Bernardo is coming." A shadow passed over Boy and he turned his head to see a taller, older boy staring down at him.

"That's my toy," Bernardo said as he pointed with a fleshy finger. Boy clutched Leo to his chest protectively. He'd never owned a real toy before. He looked to the girl for support but she was staring at her shoes.

"Give it back," Bernardo insisted.

Boy shut his eyes tightly and an angry moan escaped from his lips as fat fingers dug deep into his wrist. With his other hand, Bernardo tried to pry open Boy's fingers.

"No, it's mine!" Boy screamed. The tug-of-war continued.

"Stop it, Bernardo!" The girl had to shout to be heard over Boy's screaming. "If Renalda hears, we'll all get a beating."

Bernardo sent the back of his fist across the girl's face. She fell to the floor and wailed.

Enraged, Leo lurched forward. Bernardo was caught off-balance and lost his grip as he fell. Boy landed on top of him. Clutching the tin soldier like a weapon, he bludgeoned Bernardo in the face. Bernardo punched Boy in the mouth, but he barely even felt it. All around him, children were screaming, crying or staring – in his peripheral vision he could see them all, an audience to Leo's righteousness. A good soldier protected the weak.

Suddenly adults were yelling and Boy was pulled off of Bernardo as he screamed with wordless fury. As he was lifted up, he looked down at Bernardo and wondered when the other boy's face had become so bloody. Boy only remembered hitting him once or twice.

A large hand pried the battered, blood-slick soldier out of Boy's hand. Boy wailed and thrashed, but Leo was forgotten on the floor like a dying soldier above the trenches.

Some children were crying, others were excitedly relating their version of events to the fat old woman named Renalda as Boy was hauled out of the room. He found himself outside. The din of the children could still be heard through the open window, and a big pair of hands shoved him roughly against the wall. Boy heard flaking paint rustle and crack against his back.

"Shatters, Boy! What the fuck is the matter with you? Your first day here and already you're picking fights."

Boy stared at the grey sky. Nothing he could say would convince Bruno that he was being noble, or defending himself. It was always Boy's fault.

Bruno slapped him across the face. "Well? What have you got to say for yourself, huh?"

Tears welled up in Boy's eyes but he tried not to let them fall. He kicked at the dirt with his toe that stuck out of the end of his shoe to take his mind off his stinging cheek.

"Nothing, as usual. Just as I thought. Godsdammit, you idiot child, I'm doing this for your own good. Samanta don't want you around anymore. They don't let you in here and I have to put you on the street. Is that what you want? Huh?"

Boy bit his lip, but it was too late. Dark spots appeared in the dirt below him. He missed Samanta. She had never hit him, not once. Why did she make him go away?

"Answer me, dammit!" Bruno hit him again. "And stop crying, you baby! You gonna be a crybaby your whole life, huh? It's your own godsdamned fault you're here, Boy. After what you did to my little Catarina, you ain't fit to be around no more, much as it breaks poor Samanta's heart."

Boy crumpled on the ground. He missed Catarina most of all, and he would never, ever get to see her again. Bruno would hit Boy again if he kept on crying, but he couldn't stop the tears from coming.

"Ugh, disgusting," Bruno muttered. "What a little crybaby. When I have a boy of my own, he's never gonna turn out wimpy like you. Get up."

Boy's tears watered the parched grass. He hoped against hope Bruno would leave if he cried long enough.

"I said *get up*." Boy was lifted to his feet. There was nothing soft in Bruno's eyes as they regarded each other. As Boy wondered if he was going to get smacked again, a shadow passed over him.

"Bruno," a deep voice said. "We need to talk in my office. Better bring the boy."

Bruno grabbed Boy's wrist and they followed the most enormous man Boy had ever seen back into the orphanage. Instead of returning to the playroom, Boy was led down the long hallway from the foyer into a small room with a desk, a bookshelf, and two chairs.

"Shut the door behind you, if you would be so kind," the fat man requested. Bruno complied. He and the large man sat across from each other with the desk between them, and Boy was left to his own devices. When adults were talking he knew to be obsequious, so he traced lines of faded pink flowers on the wallpaper. He was sure to use his clean hand. If anybody found bloody fingerprints on the wall he would probably get another beating.

The fat man cleared his throat. "To be quite clear, Bruno, I'm not certain this orphanage is the right fit for...the boy. What is his name?"

"Not rightly sure, sir." Bruno's hat was in his hands. "He never came with one. He ain't one of my own or I wouldn't never give him up, even as rotten...uh, that is, well, I have little girls, and it ain't a good idea having a boy around who isn't a brother, if you take my meaning."

"Mmm-hmm," said the fat man. "You know, there are plenty of widows out there now that the best of a generation is buried in the fields of Nilonne. Where did the boy even come from? Every child has a mother."

Boy tried to watch without making it obvious. Bruno shrugged.

"Don't rightly know. A soldier brought him to the farmstead as a baby, said the boy was a war orphan that he found. I'm not the type to ask questions, sir. Maybe the soldier was telling the truth. Maybe it was a boy that he got on some girl when he had a wife back home. You know how it went in the war. Anyway, seeing as how I didn't have no sons yet, still don't, I thought to myself maybe he could help out around the farm once he got older and stronger. So I took him in. Only as he got older he didn't get any stronger. The wife babied him too much, I think."

The fat man glanced at Boy. Boy looked back at the wall and continued to trace flowers. He was almost at the bookshelf.

"Well, it sounds to me as though you've already adopted him. Why give him up now? Some boys take a while to toughen up."

"It's not that really, sir. He was...well, that is, uh, I caught him...doing sinful things with my daughter."

Boy stared at the books on the shelf, but he was looking past them, picturing Catarina in his mind's eye. It had all been her idea. She'd never seen what a boy looked like down there, so Boy showed her. Bruno caught them before he got to see hers.

The fat man raised an eyebrow. "At his age? I'm sure it was nothing more than curiosity. Sounds to me like he just needs some supervision and guidance."

"Well, maybe that's so, sir, but the wife and me have already decided. We don't want him influencing our sons once we have 'em. He ain't really one of ours anyway, we was just lookin' after him for a while, is how I look at it. So whether we leave him here or with the church makes no matter to me, but I figure he's better off here, 'specially since it's a long way to the city and I got me a farm to look after."

The floorboards creaked and Boy looked up to see the fat man leaning on his desk for support as he stood. He took off his small spectacles and cleaned them with a cloth. In the silence, Boy and the fat man stared at each other. Ignoring Bruno for the moment, the large man leaned down so that he was at eye level with Boy. It seemed to take him a great deal of effort.

"My name is Teddori. Do you read, child?"

Boy shook his head. No. But he liked the pictures.

"Do you want to read?"

Boy shrugged. How could he know what all the fuss was about? Bruno and Samanta and Catarina didn't know how to read, so it probably wasn't so important.

"What do you want to be when you grow up?"

"A lion."

Bruno scoffed, but Teddori merely chuckled. He grunted mightily as he used the edge of the desk to help him to his feet.

"Here's the thing, Bruno. I'm sure you got a good look at the orphanage already. We're overcrowded and underfunded. Orphans are plentiful because of the war, and I have virtually no staff. On top of that, the republic is either too busy rebuilding the capital or it doesn't have the same concern for the forgotten of society as the empire did. The boy was only here for an hour before a fight broke out. I have no doubt the other child was at least partially to blame, but the last thing I need is another...troubled soul. You saw what they did to each other. Every child needs a certain approach, but I don't think I have the time and the resources to dedicate to somebody with the boy's needs. I'm very sorry, Bruno, but I can't take him off your hands."

Bruno stood up and paced the room, wringing his worn old leather hat in his hands. Boy faded into the shadow between the bookshelf and the wall.

"What am I gonna do?" he asked. "It's a two-day journey to the city with a horse and cart, and two days back, plus the day I'll lose taking the boy to the church. It's just the wife at home and the farmhands, and I'm not rightly sure I can trust 'em...we don't pay much and they're soldiers from the war, just trying to help out, y'see, but all them men back at the farm alone with my wife and young daughters..."

Boy wondered why Bruno was lying. There were no farmhands. Bruno was always talking about how he wanted to hire some but he didn't have any money. He didn't even have enough food to keep Boy fed, most days. The fire had wrecked the farm when the soldiers had come through. Bruno was always talking about the soldiers and how he and Samanta hid in the cellar, before Boy had been born. So they had no money because the farm was wrecked, but sometimes old Nanna in her rocking chair would tell Samanta there was money to fix the farm if Bruno would stay away from the inn.

Boy knew if he called out Bruno's lie then he would get the beating of his life. He kept his mouth shut and stared at the books again, wondering if they were the picture kind.

"I sympathize, my good man, but I'm afraid that's out of my control," Teddori said. "For all intents and purposes, this orphanage is full. You'll either have to find somebody willing to adopt the boy, or go to another orphanage or the church. If you must get back to your farm, it needn't be today, but again, the child is currently *your* responsibility, not mine."

He waddled his way to the door and opened it. "I wish you luck," he huffed. He used the same cloth he'd wiped his glasses with to mop his brow. "These are difficult times."

Boy watched Bruno carefully. Bruno's shoulders were drawn in close to his body, and he was still wringing the hat.

"I...yes, I see," he said finally. His face was glum as he looked at Boy. "C'mon, Boy. They don't want you any more'n I do. It's on to the city, I guess."

Boy approached tentatively. He wanted to ask Bruno if they could just go back to the farm and he would promise to be good and he wouldn't even play alone with Catarina anymore, but he knew what Bruno's answer would be: the back of a hand. Boy raised his arm to allow Bruno to take him by the wrist and they walked down the long, barren corridor to the front door of the orphanage.

Bruno waited until they were outside before he let Boy have it.

"You dullard!" he shouted as he swatted Boy across the back of the head. Boy saw spots and was down on his knees. "You fuckin' dull idiot! This is all your fault, startin' fights like that. Here I finally find a place willin' to take the likes a'you in, and you have to go and ruin it. Well, it's no more than I should've expected from the son of some random farm-slut who opened her legs for a soldier...are you crying *again*?"

Boy shook his head *no*, but that was a lie. Bruno had hit him really hard. He choked back the tears and struggled to his feet. Bruno grabbed him by the wrist again and wrenched him toward old Carlos, who was tied up to the darkoak and munching on some dry yellow grass. Boy took a look back at the orphanage and wondered if the girl with the long dark hair was watching him. She wasn't, but Boy could see a big jowly face in the filthy window.

Boy heard a puffing sound as Bruno was hitching Carlos back up to the wagon.

"Bruno." *Huff, puff.* "Wait."

Bruno looked up and scowled. "Yes?"

13

"We...might just have room for him...after all." Teddori was sweating through his brown blazer. He wiped his hands on his knees.

Bruno looked like he was about to say something, but instead he smiled a thin smile and gave Boy a light push in the direction of Teddori. Boy looked back at Bruno.

"Go on," Bruno urged. An odd look crossed his face, one that Boy had never seen before. "Be brave."

Teddori had painstakingly knelt down again so he could talk to Boy, face-to-face. "Welcome to Darkoak Orphanage," he said in a voice that was almost a whisper. "Nobody will hurt you anymore, not if I can help it."

Boy thought of the fae-story Nanna used to tell about the fat old woman who lured children into her cottage so she could eat them. He wondered if Teddori was going to do that, but he figured the orphanage wouldn't be so crowded if that was the case. He didn't know what to say, so he just stared at the giant face in front of him as Carlos *clopped* away down the road with Bruno on his back.

"That's all right if you don't want to talk," Teddori continued. "This must have been a long and trying day for you. However...we're going to need to find a name for you, other than 'Boy.' Is there something else that you're known by?"

"Leo," he said without hesitation. He took Teddori's sweaty hand and they walked back to the orphanage. Boy closed his eyes as he crossed the threshold, and when he opened them, he was Leo, which meant 'Lion'.

Lions weren't afraid of anything.

Chapter 2

"Racquela," Paulo said. He was on one knee, holding her hand in his. In his other hand, a small box lined with velvet cradled a diamond ring. "Say something."

Racquela couldn't meet his dark eyes. She gazed at the trees of Avati Hill Park and followed a blood-red whiteoak blossom as it tumbled to the grass.

"Paulo...I don't know what to say."

Timori would have been daunted by that answer, but not Paulo.

"There's only one thing *to* say. I'll blame your hesitation on shock."

Racquela bit her lip. It wasn't shock, but it was too much, too soon. The world was not ready to know. If Timori found out that she'd cheated on him with Paulo, she could only imagine what he would do in a jealous rage. It had to be kept secret, at least until Timori found somebody else.

She prayed that he would.

"We can't, Paulo. Not yet." She forced herself to look in his deep, inscrutable eyes, and then at the ring. The best things were worth waiting for, she reminded herself.

"Why not? Nothing's stopping us now." He stood up and brushed dirt and grass off the knees of his black-and-white pinstripe suit. "The annulment is done. What more is there to worry about?" He gestured to the tumbling leaves of red, orange, and gold. "Life is fleeting, darling. Every blossom is beautiful, but sooner or later autumn comes and they shrivel up and fall to the ground. We should live life to its fullest while we can."

Racquela went up on her tip-toes to kiss Paulo on the cheek.

"That's very poetic, sweetheart, but what about Timori?"

"What about him? There's nothing he can do about it."

"Nothing *legally*," Racquela said. "If he finds out about us right now, he'll do something crazy. He held a wand to his own head, remember? He's fragile right now. Don't you care about his feelings at all?"

Paulo turned his back to Racquela and threw up his hands.

"Yes. I know. Timori will be upset. But we're in this together. It's not our fault if he can't face the truth, that he was never good enough for you." He turned his head and raised an eyebrow at her.

Another young couple passed by along the park path and Racquela waited until they were gone.

"Don't say it like that," she scolded. "You know I love you in a way I never loved him."

"Then show me. Accept the ring. Please, Racquela. You're all that I want in a wife. Whose feelings matter more to you, mine or Tim's?"

"That's not fair." She folded her arms. "Yours, of course. Look, it's not just about Tim. The betrothals just ended, and so much is going on right now."

Paulo closed the box and put the ring back into the inner pocket of his blazer.

"If you don't want to get married, just say so."

Her heart lurched.

"No! It's...it's not that." She brushed his hair out of his eyes. "I want to marry you. But I don't feel like it's *safe* for us to tell everybody yet. So soon after the annulment...it's not just Timori I'm worried about. What will our parents say? What if...what if we kept it a secret, for now?"

"You really want that diamond, don't you?" Paulo asked. Racquela pulled away from him.

"It's not about the ring."

"I know what it's about. The expectations of high society and Timori's obsession with you. All the dirt we shouldn't give two shards about." Paulo shrugged. "I understand. You're under a lot of pressure from a lot of people." He put his arms around Racquela and kissed the top of her head. "I can keep a secret if you can."

Chapter 3

"Visitor here to see you, kid," the policeman said.

Timori opened his eyes and stared at the concrete ceiling. His back was sore from lying on the stiff bunk for two days straight. He hadn't even summoned the strength to eat the food that had been left for him, congealed oatmeal and a cup of water. He wondered if he had the willpower to starve himself to death.

Timori heard footsteps approaching his small jail cell. He didn't have the courage to roll over on his bunk and see who it was. He was afraid it would be his mother, or worse, Racquela. He'd go crazy all over again if it was Racquela. The only thing he wanted was her love. The only thing he knew she'd offer him was pity.

"Hey, pally," a hoarse voice said.

"Jake." Timori said, surprised. He rolled over and looked at his best friend. Jacoby appeared about as miserable as Timori felt. The boy's eyes were puffy and red, and his hair was a gods-awful mess. He was wearing the same rumpled white shirt and mud-stained slacks Timori had seen him in two days ago.

Timori sat up on the bunk.

"You look like dirt."

"You, too. What are they feeding you?" Jacoby pointed at the cold oatmeal, but Timori couldn't think of a witty reply. They looked at each other through the bars, pining for easy laughter and simpler times.

"How's Racquela?" Timori asked finally.

"She's...dealing with it all surprisingly well," Jacoby said. He shoved his hands into his pockets. "Better than I am."

"Hey, you've got nothing to feel guilty for, dully. You saved my life."

"Crystara did."

Timori raised an eyebrow.

"Pretty sure it was you there on the bridge, telling me to put the wand down."

"No, I mean...Crystara was there behind me, telling me what to say. She knew exactly what to say. And then I...and then she..." Jacoby's face broke down in anguish before Timori. His friend clutched at the bars as tears streamed down his cheeks. "She's dead, Tim."

Timori leapt out of his bunk and rushed over to the edge of the cell. He saw the guard in the corner reach for his wand, but Timori merely put a hand on Jacoby's shoulder through the bars.

"What? Crystara's dead? What happened?"

It took a moment for Jacoby to calm down. He wiped his eyes on a filthy sleeve.

"Not Crys, but she will be soon. Le...Lenara."

As soon as he said her name, he broke into another fit of sobbing. It took a while for Timori to get the entire story out of him. They sat on the cold cement floor of the police station jail, with only metal bars between them. Timori kept his hand on Jacoby's shoulder through the bars and listened as Jaocby related what had happened after Timori had been hauled away for pointing a wand at his own head.

When Jacoby had finished the tale, Timori was at a loss.

"What I don't get, though, is why they both went to the Old Temple," Timori said finally.

"There's more that I haven't told you," Jacoby said with a sniffle.

"Time's almost up, Stravida," the guard in the corner said.

"Damn," Jacoby muttered. "All right, listen. You need to hear this. I don't know what's going to happen to you, but I don't imagine they can keep you here indefinitely when you didn't actually hurt anybody..."

"I had an illegal wand," Timori whispered.

"What? Where did you..."

"Shh! Never mind that now. What did you need to tell me?"

"You're not going to like it."

"Yeah, well, I can't see how things could get much worse."

"Good point. So the reason both the girls were there is because they switched."

"Switched what?"

"Switched places. In the betrothals."

"How? We had visions."

"You're not going to believe me."

"Just tell me."

The guard approached and placed his nightstick between Jacoby and the bars.

"Time's up." He peered down at Jacoby. "You can come visit him again tomorrow, if he's still here."

"Where are you taking him?" Jacoby asked, keeping a wary eye on the officer's club.

"Someplace where he can't hurt anybody...unless he cooperates and tells us where that wand came from."

Jacoby shot Timori an apologetic glance. Tim stared at the floor as his friend was escorted away. Nobody could help Timori now. Nobody knew where the wand had come from, except for Paulo, and Timori wasn't about to betray him.

"Come see me when you get out," Jacoby called out to Timori as the guard prodded him toward the jail's exit. "Mom and Dad want to see you, too."

"What about Racquela?" Timori asked desperately.

Jacoby's pitying look was less than encouraging.

Switched places. Jacoby's words echoed in Timori's mind. *How?* He shook his head and dismissed the thoughts as he returned to his stiff bunk. It didn't matter, in the end. The crystal betrothals were over, about to be annulled by Racquela, most likely. The Great Crystal was just a big piece of rock controlled by the church, and the betrothals were merely a failing Noven tradition. Timori had only cared because the betrothals had worked to his advantage. He'd loved Racquela from first sight, and he'd lost her. It was folly to think a highborn beauty would ever love a miner's son.

With nothing else to do but wallow in misery, Timori decided it was better to sleep the time away. He shut his eyes and tried to banish thoughts of Racquela from his mind.

Timori heard voices down the hallway and peeled an eye open. He followed the crack in the ceiling as he eavesdropped.

"...hear anything interesting?" The voice was gravelly.

"Not really," Timori's guard replied. "They talked about that girl who killed the keeper, but that's nothing we don't already know."

"Inspector Funari would love to have a chat with that boy. The church isn't talking, and she's under their jurisdiction. It's about time that damn law got repealed."

"I dunno, Frank. She was trying to mess with the Great Crystal."

Timori heard Frank snort.

"That damn rock is the reason all these kids were acting crazy in the first place. Arranged marriages are for noble families, and it's an old tradition anyway. It's almost the twentieth century, for Jova's sake. Let me talk to the kid for a minute."

"Suit yourself. He ain't saying dirt."

A middle-aged man in a brown trench coat and trilby walked up to Timori's cell. He held a cigarette between his lips.

His face was stubbly and worry-lined, but his eyes were not unkind.

"Timori Stravida," the man said. "I'm Inspector Franco Martinus. Feel like talking?"

"Not really," Timori replied.

"Suit yourself." Frank shrugged and took a drag from his cigarette. "Maybe you feel like listening instead. Lorenzo tells me you've been pretty tight-lipped about where that unregistered wand came from. Lucky for you we do things differently than we used to when old Max was around, or the boys'd have you squealing within minutes. I'm not a fan of the medieval method, but damn me if it wasn't effective. However, the city has you up on a number of charges, and we can make things very difficult for you...there are plenty of places more uncomfortable than a jail cell. If forced labour in the coal pits is your idea of a good time, by all means, keep your mouth shut about where that wand came from."

Timori rolled away from the inspector so that he was facing the wall.

"My dad was a coal miner. I can handle it."

"Was she really worth it, son? I'm told you're going to school at Central, and that you're pretty bright. You're really gonna throw it all away for some snotty whitehand girl who doesn't even care about you?"

"I might. Why do you care so badly about where that wand came from?"

"Wands are dangerous things," Inspector Martinus said. "They kill people, for one. Plus the government doesn't like unregistered crystals. My superiors are nervous there might be more of them, and they'd like to know where these crystals are coming from and who owns this supply. We all know you're just a victim in this, kid. But you decided to make a spectacle with the wrong weapon. You could be the fall guy while somebody else continues to profit from selling illegal wands, or you could help us and go free. The city will acquit you of the other charges if you tell us where the wand came from. You could be out of here by this afternoon, and try to win back that girl."

"It was my father's." He rolled over and looked the inspector in the eyes.

Inspector Martinus calmly dropped his cigarette butt and ground it into the cement with his boot.

"Do I look like a dully to you, kid? Your dad's been gone for years. That crystal is brand-shiny-new, and so is the wand. But if you want me to be the tough guy, fine. Nobody's gonna scare you into saying anything, and I can respect that. So instead I'm gonna make a threat, and it's not just hot air. Tell us where that wand came from, or..."

The inspector was interrupted by a frantic voice shouting down the hallway.

"What do you mean, I can't see him? He's my *son*, for Jova's sake! Let me through there right now!"

"Your son has already seen a visitor today, Mrs. Stravida," the guard said from around the corner. "You'll have to come back tomorrow."

"*Please*," she insisted. Timori had never heard her so panicked. "He needs help! He's not a criminal, he's sick."

Inspector Martinus looked at Timori and raised an eyebrow.

"Your mother makes a good point."

Chapter 4

Crystara dreamed of deaths and desires, of a mother she never knew, and a lover she once thought she knew. Sometimes her father chased her through the hallways of the Old Temple, screaming and cursing, clutching a whiskey bottle. Sometimes he morphed into Jacoby. Worse were the dreams about Lenara, who merely shuffled after her, saying nothing, staring at her with milky, accusing eyes. In those dreams Crystara's feet were made of stone, laden and heavy. The chase was as slow as a funeral dirge, but Crystara always woke up screaming when Lenara's cold hand clutched the back of her neck.

When she awoke she would find herself back in her dungeon cell. Sometimes the cold tedium was worse than the nightmares. Crystara's gaoler, a mute man with a club foot, took no notice of her cries. A thorough pilfering of his mind revealed that he knew little of what truly went on in the temple and understood even less than that. He was the perfect man for the job.

At least once a night Crystara dreamed about the gallows. Faceless men would lead her up to the wooden platform. She was always naked, and there was usually a crowd gathered to watch her swing from the rope. The mob would throw stones at her as they shouted, so loudly that Crystara couldn't hear the charges being read by the executioner.

She always tried to struggle, but Jacoby was there at the front of the crowd. He had a crystal ring on his finger, and when he pointed it at her she couldn't move. The executioner put the rope around her neck and drew the noose tight. When he pulled the lever and she felt her feet drop out from under her, Crystara caught a glimpse beneath his hood.

It was Keeper Orvin.

In moments of solitude the guilt crept into her heart. Lenara had deserved her fate, as far as Crystara was concerned, but what gnawed at Crystara was the look of shock she'd seen on Keeper Orvin's face. In the nightmare she tried to tell him it was an accident, but she was already swinging from the rope by then.

Crystara reminded herself cynically that Orvin was no less dead just because it was an accident.

She began to lose track of days and nights. From the hunger pangs she assumed they were only feeding her the same cold, bleak gruel once a day, but she'd forgotten to keep track of the first few days since she'd assumed her death was imminent.

The new keeper came to visit after five more bowls of gruel had passed her lips. The dove-white robes of office seemed ill-fitted upon him, hanging off his stooped, wiry frame.

"I took a look at your ring," he said in his raspy tone. There was something about the way he looked at her when he held out the clear crystal band that made her flesh crawl.

"It's not mine anymore," she replied, glaring at him from the far corner of her cell.

"You'll put it on," he said, "or I'll make you."

Crystara didn't budge. The man's smile was sallow.

"Knights," he called. From the shadows came three rough-looking men, dressed in travelling clothes. They appeared more like brigands than knights to Crystara, and as they approached her cell the stink of horses was almost overwhelming. One of them produced a key.

She shut her eyes and focused, rifling through their minds as the cell door swung open. Their task was not to harm her, simply to stop her from escaping and force her to wear the ring. Not even they knew what the ring did, and Keeper De'Cadomus's mind was as iron-clad as it had been the last time Crystara had tried to read him.

The threat of the ring was bone-chilling in a way a death sentence would never be. Without a crystal to defend herself with, Crystara knew her only option was to make a run for it.

She managed to slide under the legs of the tallest one, but as she reached the threshold of the cell she saw one of De'Cadomus's crystal rings glow yellow and she was thrust backward into the arms of the men. Crystara screamed and flailed, but their grips were as firm as shackles.

She squirmed and balled her hands into fists, but the third knight pried her left hand open and forced the ring onto her big finger. The men unceremoniously dumped her onto the deepstone floor and left. De'Cadomus glowered down at Crystara as she stood up and rubbed her wrists.

"You're a powerful speaker, Crystara, but you'll never..."

Crystara clutched the ring and pulled. A crippling shock of pain shot through her body and she was forced to her knees. She bit her lip and tried again. This time the spasms sent her to the floor as she screamed.

"You fucking bastard!" she sobbed.

"Consider this insurance. You're no good to me locked up all the time, but I can't have you..."

Crystara leapt to her feet and threw a wild punch at the keeper. He stood his ground and the punch never connected. When Crystara's fist got close to his face, the ring on her finger glowed deep amber and she was thrown backward.

"There are quite a few things Orvin didn't teach you, it seems. The ring once bound you to a betrothal. Now it binds you to me. You will do as I say, or that crystal will cause you unimaginable pain. If you try to leave the temple, it will hurt you as well."

"Fuck you," she sobbed. De'Cadomus shut the door to Crystara's cell and stared at her through the bars.

"A young mute orphan is going to come to work for the temple. The Church of the Great Crystal looks after the unfortunate of society...even lame mutes can serve the gods." He gestured to the gaoler, who looked on passively. "This dumb urchin might believe she can speak, but all people will hear are disturbing moans when she opens her mouth. Few will choose to even look upon her, for her face is misshapen and hideous."

Crystara stared in disbelief at the ring on her finger. She'd never heard of crystals doing *that* kind of thing. What did De'Cadomus know? She wondered if she could read his mind when he was asleep. Had Keeper Orvin known those alignments, too?

"Should that ugly mute serve the church well, perhaps she will be allowed a small measure of freedom...but she must never forget that she belongs to the Great Crystal." Again, stabbing pains shot through Crystara's body and she writhed on the marble floor in front of De'Cadomus.

"You may prove your loyalty to me with time, but only my death will remove your fetters. You may think yourself a killer, but you do not have what it takes to kill me. Simpering bookworm keepers and young ladies are one thing..."

Crystara strained to hear the word he whispered as he stared at her crystal ring, but it was nothing more than a puff of air to her. She shook spasmodically as the pain coursed through her body, and she tasted the tang of blood in her mouth. When the pain subsided, she opened her eyes. De'Cadomus was gone and she was alone again in her cell.

Chapter 5

"Good morning, Captus Nove. You are listening to Station One, that's one-oh-one-six on your radio dial. I am Marius Ghost, your host with the most to boast, giving you the morning news and post!"

Julio rubbed his one good eye using his only hand. *Weekend*, he thought groggily. *I left the radio on overnight.*

"Our first news at the top of the morning: the mystery of the Great Crystal! Many of you may have seen the bright flash of light several nights past, which came from Crystus Hill, the Old Temple more specifically, on the night of the Reverie."

Julio sat up in bed, dressed only in undershorts and a white undershirt. The sun was spilling in through the open window, highlighting the dust motes that were settling onto the stacks of papers that were strewn across the desk. Atop a stack sat an opened letter, held down by an antique tribal dagger – a gift from Roberto which Julio used as a letter opener.

"Ramona," Julio whispered, gazing at the letter from across the room. It had been months since their last contact, and the letter had come as something of a surprise.

"The official statement from the Church of Jova states that the light from the Great Crystal coincided with the sudden death of its former keeper, His Clarity Keeper Orvin the First. Keeper Orvin was a dedicated servant of the gods, whose admission into the heavens was seen by all Captus Nove, as a reminder of the rewards of loyalty and fealty to those who watch us from above."

Julio pushed himself out of bed, wincing as old wounds and scars protested. The shrapnel in his leg and next to his spine were always the worst. He scratched at his leg with the hook that had long ago replaced his right hand. He'd sharpened a part of the hook for its utility, and it dealt with an itch better than his nails ever could.

"However, Keeper Orvin's death was an act of malice, my loyal listeners! In a further statement given to the public by the new keeper, Keeper De'Cadomus the Second, it was revealed that a sixteen-year-old student of Central School, in fact one of six of last year's crystal betrothed, murdered De'Cadomus's predecessor in cold blood! The student, one Crystara Mita, is being held in the temple prison after an impartial trial has determined her guilt, and she awaits a just execution for the cold-blooded murder, as well as suspicion of conspiracy against the Great Crystal itself."

Julio frowned and looked at the radio. *Crystara Mita. Largo's daughter.*

"There's got to be more to it than that," he said out loud. He trusted the church's honesty less than he trusted the media's.

"In national news, farmers and miners are no longer the only ones feeling the pinch from the floundering economy, and further food stamps have been issued to applicants among the merchant and labourer castes. With factory closures increasing across the country, young men are flooding to the bigger cities looking for labour and finding little. The good men of the Captus Nove police force have stepped up their patrols to decrease tensions, as the jobless fight over food and shelter, and those who are still employed fear for their safety."

Julio growled in his throat and searched the floor for a clean-looking pair of pants. His maid wouldn't be in for another day or two, and he wasn't about to string up his clothes to dry on the line again. His best coat and slacks had been stolen the other week. He awkwardly shimmied into a slightly-wrinkled pair of cream-coloured slacks and hunted through piles of shirts for a pair of suspenders.

"Many families are leaving the cities for homes in the countryside, and the minister of travel reports that emigration is up thirty percent from last year. However, he has cautioned all citizens of our great nation of Novem that the depression is being felt across the globe, and all nations are in a similar state of affairs. There will be no jobs for the good people of Novem elsewhere, and Titania and the world still look harshly upon Novens for the unfortunate events perpetrated by the Second Empire. The Minister of Travel, our good friend Lazarus Di'Motzi, would like to remind citizens that we must stand proud together, and work together, and struggle together to get through this difficult time."

Julio found a set of old off-white suspenders and awkwardly clipped them to his pants as he lay on the floor.

"A young man was talked out of committing suicide at the Memorial Bridge earlier this week, the third such attempt this month alone. The Captus Nove Police Commissioner, Commissioner Saliarus D'Allini, had this to say ..."

A clean white shirt was far more difficult to find than the suspenders had been. Julio knew already that his drawers were empty, devoid of clean clothing of any kind except perhaps socks. He settled on a shirt with a small ink smudge, easily hidden by suspenders or a coat. He tucked the shirt into his pants and hobbled over to his tiny washroom, doing his best to ignore the stabbing sensation in his right leg.

"I would like to remind these young men," said a tinny voice from the radio, *"that many of these problems are temporary. I have been assured by my good friends in parliament that the economy will improve, and until then we are all in this together. Many have left notes, citing being spurned or rejected by a lady,*

or somesuch, and I would like to assert to these young men that there are other fish in the sea, as they say. Not to mention, the incredible selfishness of putting others in danger. To leap from a bridge or lie down on the train tracks...puts others at risk. There are often motorcoaches and stagecoaches underneath these bridges, and while it may seem unlikely, a train could be derailed. Furthermore, attempted suicide is considered an offense punishable by a fine and incarceration...so think twice. There are punishments for these kinds of foolishness. Thank you."

Julio stood in front of the washroom mirror, checking his stubble. It only really grew on the one side. The other was a mess of twisted scar tissue, crisscrossing lividly across the demolished side of his face. His teeth showed through shorn and parted lips on the bad side, and his eye socket was an empty pocket of pale flesh. Even the hair on his scalp refused to grow on that side, other than a few unruly white wisps. He grimaced at his reflection and, pondering what he was hearing on the radio, wondered why a healthy young man would ever kill himself.

"Those words from Police Commissioner Saliarus D'Allini of Captus Nove. Coming up next, news on the rebellions facing the Eastern Empire, as well as an interview with the Guildmaster of the miners' guild. But first! New music by the Wandering Trio. This is... 'The Bridge'"

He pushed the rubber stopper into the sink and turned on the tap, allowing the bowl to fill slowly. The song on the radio was dour, a crooner singing of a beauty more interested in her own reflection than her lover.

His straight razor was where he had left it, in the medicine cabinet. He tested it with a thumb to make sure it was still sharp. A little fleck of skin came off his thumb to land in the sink full of water. Julio put his thumb in his mouth and sucked out the seeping blood.

He looked up at his own reflection and wondered why he still bothered. Ramona didn't care what he looked like...or rather, she cared too much, and that's why he'd failed to retain her love after the war was over. He'd returned to Captus Nove a broken shell of a man, a half-dead prisoner of war, without a centima to his name.

The stubble was thick on the one side of Julio's face. It was a patchy mess of black, grey, and white. He was only forty-two, but he'd gone mostly grey at the end of the war. He was beginning to forget what he used to look like. Sometimes he would gaze at photographs of himself and Ramona when they were young and carefree, and it looked like she was in the arms of a stranger.

Julio opened his jar of shaving cream and applied it liberally to his face with his old bristly brush. He liked to do both sides – there were a few stray hairs that grew on the scarred side, especially under his jaw.

His friends used to ask him why he never bothered to buy a prosthetic mask. They had become quite common amongst former soldiers who had survived the war but returned with disfiguring scars. Julio's situation was far from unique in that regard. He used to think it was a matter of pride, but Roberto would often tell him it was his self-effacing nature. 'You just roll over and take it,' he could hear Rob's voice saying, 'and you never do anything to try and change it. On the other hand, it makes you accept yourself – scars and all...and that's what I've always admired about you, Jules.'

Julio brought the razor up to his chin and held it there for a moment. He looked at his face in the mirror. It was a mixture of the grotesque and the comedic – the scarred and lonely man, face covered in barber's cream that was dripping into the sink. Julio suddenly wondered what it would be like to simply draw the blade across his throat and finish it all off.

The ballad reached a crescendo as the beauty drowned, following her own reflection, and Julio began to laugh. Suicide was for the young and the brave. Cowardice had stayed Julio's hand thus far – surely it would do so for years to come. He eased the razor down, laughing so hard there were tears in his eyes.

"Kids nowadays listen to the most maudlin dirt," he said as he began to shave.

Chapter 6

The motorcoach dropped Racquela off at the front gate of the De'Trini estate as the sun was setting. Racquela opened her purse and withdrew a silver dinari, which she handed to the driver. He offered her some copper centima coins in return, but she shook her head and waved him on his way. He tipped his hat to her as he drove off.

Ordinarily the front gate to her home was open during the day, but her father had taken to keeping it closed ever since Timori's episode at the Memorial Bridge. Racquela had insisted that Timori would never harm *her*, but her father was nothing if not protective of his only daughter. The entire estate, enclosed by a wrought-iron fence, was now patrolled by the new guards Joven had hired. He insisted the additional staff had been hired because of the increased unrest in the valley, but Racquela knew that was only half of the reason.

Racquela carried a crystal key that opened the side gate into the garden. She made her way through the arched hedge and along the stone path among the flowerbeds, taking a moment to admire the autumn colours. The trees bordered the gardens like living jewellery – there were the golden leaves of the whiteoaks, the bronze foliage of the darkoaks, and the silvery branches of the already barren moontrees.

As Racquela traversed the garden, she realized how much she missed its serenity. Whenever she wanted to be alone, she could go there, and as a child she had spent countless hours playing games with her nanny Sarai's children. They had played hide-and-seek in the hedge maze and held tea parties in the gazebo by the fountain. In the summer her tutor taught her history and cultural studies under the blue summer sky. She would snack on sweet cakes and daydream through the boring parts of his lessons, picturing herself kissing a prince on the old wooden bench that sat near the fountain. That was where her fist real kiss had been, Racquela recalled. She'd kissed Ignatius, her nanny's sweet and gentle son, when she was eight and he was ten. A year later he'd been sent off to boarding school.

A lot had changed since then. Ignatius had a girlfriend up north he wanted to marry, a farmer's daughter. Racquela had changed, too, and so had the garden. Lucius, Sarai's husband, chose a new theme every winter, and throughout the spring and summer he would tend to the garden until it was a masterpiece of natural art.

Racquela admired the man's handiwork as she made her way past the guest house. This year he'd chosen an Eastern theme. There were several flowerbeds that had been covered in pebbles. One was a rock garden in the shape of the country of Novem. For each provincial capital, a large rock had been placed in the garden. Captus Nove's rock was a clear crystal the size of Racquela's head. Among the rock cities, pebble pathways had been made to look like roads. On the other side of the footpath, a matching garden shaped like the nation of Novem was sculpted from colourful flowers. For every provincial capital, a carefully pruned miniature tree was placed amongst the blossoms. The garden's flowers had been brighter in the summertime, but the miniature whiteoak on the southwestern tip still boasted bold yellow leaves and blood-red blossoms.

Beyond the guest house on the left were the servants' quarters and the shed. Looming stately and impressive on Racquela's right was the De'Trini house. The three-storey mansion had been built from the wealth of the De'Trini lands: deepstone and marble from the quarries of the Alatine Mountains to the east and wood from the old forests north of Captus Nove.

Gold from property holdings had paid for everything else. Joven De'Trini still owned most of that vast fortune, an amassed wealth that was nearly as old as the De'Trini name. Old Tevici had drilled the De'Trini family history into her head every year during her summer studies until she could recite it in her sleep.

Racquela stopped and put her hand on the ornate brass knob of the back door, staring at the carved ivy woodwork in the darkoak. It was daunting at times, knowing she was the heir to everything her family had built. She always suspected that secretly her parents had hoped for another child, a son who could carry on Joven's work in the Alchemists' Guild. Women weren't allowed to take senior positions in guilds. After all, they had only recently been allowed to vote by the decision of the Fifth Republic.

"Who goes there?"

Racquela screamed. Her father's guard, the lanky one with the crooked nose, shone a crystal lantern in her face. His other hand was on the wand holster at his hip.

"Gods, you scared me," she gasped as she slumped against the door. "It's me, Racquela."

He turned bright red and lowered the lantern. "Ah. My apologies, Mistress Racquela. I heard you walking through the garden, and I thought you might be an intruder."

She folded her arms. "Well, you can blame Father for keeping the front gate locked, then. Why do you have a lantern? It's not dark out yet."

"It will be soon," he said sheepishly.

"Well, return to your duties, then," she said and slipped in through the back door. The rear parlour was empty, but a fire was crackling in the hearth and her father's pipe was sending up a trail of smoke from its place beside his favourite chair. She listened at the parlour door for footsteps. Dinner would be ready soon, and she wanted to avoid Maria until she was safely at the table. Her parents would ask her questions about school. Maria liked to ask where she had been, and it was hard to lie to the old stewardess. Nobody needed to know about Paulo yet.

Racquela opened the door a crack. The hallway was quiet except for the faraway sound of Mario singing to himself in the kitchen. Racquela took the rear staircase to the second floor. Her bedroom was on the other side of the mansion, and she tiptoed her way past the portraits of her ancestors down the long west wing hallway, where beams of golden sunlight were shining in through the windows.

Maria was dusting in the hallway outside Racquela's door. Racquela scowled. The old woman was dusting there *on purpose*. House cleaning was her daughter Sarai's job.

"Mistress Racquela. Welcome home." Her grey hair was done up in a bun, and wrinkles widened across her face as she smiled at Racquela.

"Thank you, Maria." Racquela reached for her doorknob.

"Mistress Racquela."

"Yes?"

"If I might have a quick word?"

Racquela's grip on the doorknob tightened.

"Of course you may, Maria," Racquela said, keeping her voice level. "You are always welcome."

Maria followed Racquela into the room, which was larger than many lower-caste dwellings. Racquela went to her wardrobe to pick out a suitable dress for dinner.

"Your mother and father are worried about time you spend outside the estate, after Timori's incident at the bridge."

"I'm fine," Racquela said as she took out a dress of burgundy silk. She held it up in front of the full-length mirror, but decided it was a better dress to wear for Paulo than it was for her parents. She selected a more conservatively cut green one and went over to the jewellery stand to find something with emeralds.

Maria sat on the divan under the window and folded her hands in her lap.

"Your father thinks that you should take an escort with you, for your own protection."

Racquela nearly dropped the gold and emerald earrings she was inspecting.

"That's silly," she said. She walked behind her changing screen and slipped out of her clothes. "Timori wouldn't do anything to hurt me."

"This isn't just about Timori," Maria said as Racquela slid the evening dress over her head. "There is unrest in the valley, and you could become a target. Your father wants to ensure that you are protected. He will discuss it with you over dinner."

Racquela approached Maria and turned around so the old servant could tie the bow at the back of her dress.

"Thank you, Maria. Is this going to be a discussion, or is Father's mind already made up?"

Maria's hands froze halfway through tying the bow.

"I'm not sure you realize the gravity of the situation, my dear. Another of your father's factories closed down today."

"So?"

"So...the situation in the valley is getting desperate." Maria finished tying the bow and Racquela walked over to her vanity to put in her earrings. She didn't know what to say. It wasn't her fault there was a depression. Even if she sold all her possessions, it wouldn't feed the entire city. She wondered if she would have to tell her parents about Paulo. If they knew, then she wouldn't have to sneak around...but it was still too soon. If she and Paulo were seen together so soon after the annulment, there was no telling what Timori would do.

"Take those earrings, for example," Maria continued. "Somebody toiled in the earth to find that gold and those gems, and more people worked hard to shape them into something lovely for you. Do you know what those are worth? How many people they could feed?"

Racquela missed the hole in her ear and drew blood.

"Ow, shatters!" She spun around in her chair. "I didn't choose to be born a De'Trini," she spat. "Maybe you've forgotten how lucky you are. Father sent your grandchildren off to school, so that one day your descendants won't be servants. And this is how you repay us, for all we've done for your family? By lecturing me about things I can't control? Get out."

Maria stared at Racquela for a long while. Finally she stood.

"Yes, mistress."

Racquela dabbed at the blood with a handkerchief until her ear was dry, then finished putting in her earrings. When she glanced in the vanity mirror, she saw that Maria was lingering. A worried expression was on the old woman's face.

"I asked you to leave."

"Who is the new boy?"

"What new boy?" She said it too quickly.

"The one I saw you with in that motorcoach, before you left Timori."

Racquela's chest tightened.

"Oh, him. Just a friend."

Maria raised an eyebrow.

"Well, you might want to tell your father about this friend. I don't need to remind you it is not befitting a lady to be spending time un-chaperoned with a boy, especially one her parents have never met." Maria shut the door.

"Shatters," she muttered. She tried to ignore the poisonous thoughts she was having about Maria as she finished brushing her hair.

When she was all done up, Racquela left her room for the dining hall. The sun had gone down, and the crystal lamps in the household had been lit. She paused outside the hall doors when she heard her father's voice.

"...getting dire. It's worse than it was during the Fourth Republic. Thank the gods there isn't another Longoro."

"Well, he did fix the economy," Racquela heard her mother reply. "Maybe what this nation needs is some strong leadership. The republic certainly isn't offering much of that...look at the bureaucratic granite your brother has to try and pick through."

"So we should seek the kind of totalitarian leadership that brings us back to war? Hopefully not. No, it's the Rundia accord that's to blame. The Noctra are selling all our crystals underground because the dinari is undervalued. Nobody's getting wealthy anymore but them."

"We'll survive, Joven. If we have to sell a few assets, so be it. The depression won't last forever."

"It's not assets that concern me. Workers are organizing, demanding more pay when there's less to go around. The socialist groups are gaining too much support. The whole city could crash around us. We survived the last revolution because my father threw in his lot with Longoro, but this time the lower castes will try to abolish the caste system entirely, I just know it. When that happened in Nilonne, the nobles were executed."

Racquela decided to enter the discussion. She threw wide the dining hall doors to find that her father was pacing along the length of the table, fiddling with one of his suspenders. Her mother was seated calmly, dressed resplendently in blue silk. Her dark hair was tied into a single braid that fell across one shoulder, almost to her lap.

"Socialism will never take hold in Titania," Racquela said as she took a seat beside her mother. "Senior Tevici told me that every time there's a socialist revolution, it doesn't last for very long."

Joven De'Trini's greying moustache twitched. He sat down across from Racquela and smiled.

"Sweetheart, it's naïve to think the situation will merely resolve itself. Even if socialism doesn't last, we could lose everything in the meantime. This is a dangerous time to be living in the capital."

"Is that why you're sending me with an escort from now on?"

"Maria talks too much," Joven growled. "I wanted to talk to you about it myself first."

The conversation was interrupted as Mario, Maria, and Sarai entered the dining hall bearing covered trays. The servants went around to each member of the family offering different dishes of food. That evening there was a rotisserie chicken, a seafood soup, roasted potatoes and onions, a tomato and olive salad, duck-stuffed pasta, three different caviars, prawn pastries, peppered beans, and, of course, plenty of bread.

Racquela was ravenous. She hadn't eaten since breakfast, so she tried to cram a little bit of everything on her plate. She selected a white wine to drink with the meal, and finally the servants receded to the wall to wait in case anybody required more food or drink.

As much as Racquela wanted to attack her plate with vigour, she had been raised to take small bites and savour every morsel of food on her tongue. Polite conversation was, after all, impossible for those who bit off more than they could chew.

Mario's prepared meal was, as usual, a masterpiece of culinary delights, and there was easily enough to feed ten people instead of three, which was deliberate. Once the De'Trinis were finished eating, the rest of the food was taken away to the servants' quarters, where all those who maintained the household could enjoy what remained. With the addition of Joven's new guards, there were five servants in the household. Most nobles had dozens, at least, but Joven didn't believe in having more servants just to appear wealthier.

"As I was going to say previously," Joven said after a few minutes had passed, "beginning next week I will be sending an escort with you, Racquela. He will take you to and from school, and be with you any time you are outside of the estate."

"But, Father..."

"'But Father' nothing. This is for your own protection." He took a small sip of red wine.

Racquela prodded a potato with her fork. Her appetite had vanished.

"What about my social life? I bet the other girls won't have some guard following them around everywhere."

Racquela's mother was about to say something, but Joven held up his hand for silence.

"The other girls weren't betrothed to a cracked picker's son."

Racquela resisted the urge to pound her fist on the table. She would have been dismissed from the table instantly for that kind of outburst.

"Timori won't hurt me, I told you. This escort idea is embarrassing and pointless. It makes me feel as though you don't trust me."

Jessica looked up from her peppered beans and spoke.

"Sweetheart, we have been speaking with other noble families, and they are doing the same. It is because of the situation in the valley...you need to be protected right now. That is all. We've always trusted you. Is there some reason why we shouldn't?"

Shatters, Racquela thought, *here it comes. Gods damn you, Maria.*

"Of course not." She looked her parents in the eyes, but she could feel the corners of her mouth curling up involuntarily.

Joven's moustache twitched again.

"We still haven't met that boy you've been spending time with."

Racquela wanted to turn around and throw her plate at Maria. There was nothing she could do to avoid the conversation. Her best tactic was to portray things in a way her parents would find palatable.

"Do you mean Paulo?" she said as casually as she could muster. "Well, we've known each other since the betrothals began." That part was not a lie, at least.

"Maria tells me you've been seeing him without a chaperone."

Racquela held her tongue as she felt her cheeks flush. She'd grown so casual about it with Timori – during their betrothal, the chaperoning hadn't seemed as necessary to Racquela's parents. Now that it was all over, things would go back to the old way. She scrambled through her thoughts to find a way she could still sneak around to see Paulo without having someone else watch her every move.

"I...I am sorry. I just got so accustomed to it with Timori."

"Is he courting you?" her mother asked.

We're secretly engaged, she thought.

"No...not yet. I know he will eventually. I really like him, but of course nothing happened because he was betrothed to Lenara."

The mention of Lenara brought the conversation to a halt for several moments. Joven sighed and pushed away his plate.

"What's his family name?" He turned to address the servants. "Maria, coffee, please." Maria left the dining hall. Mario and Sarai followed, presumably to fetch dessert. "Paulo is an unlucky name. Not a lot of parents choose it anymore."

"Why not?" Racquela asked.

"Senior Tevici probably didn't go over Emperor Longoro's family in great detail, my dear, but his youngest son was named Paulo. The baby boy was found with his mother fleeing up the coast, and they were put to death to stop Longoro's lineage. Any name associated with Longoro is considered bad luck now. Your friend Paulo must have been born before the war ended. What's his family name?"

"I..." Racquela's throat felt stuck. It was so hard to distract her father from a question. She didn't want to admit to him she didn't actually *know* Paulo's family name. She knew for certain he was a noble, or at least a wealthy merchant's son. Who else could afford a motorcoach?

"I forget. He told it to me when we first met, but I forget."

Joven and Jessica De'Trini exchanged a glance. It was enough to let Racquela know Paulo was about to be under intense scrutiny.

"You're certain he's a noble?" her father asked.

"He drives a motorcoach, Father. And he dresses and speaks like a noble."

"Yet you don't know his family name."

"Joven, please," Jessica said. Maria returned with a coffee press and cup and set them in front of Joven. Mario and Sarai came in behind her with a tray of desserts.

"Perhaps if we meet this boy, he can answer a lot of those questions," her mother suggested. "We can't allow you to see him if we don't at least know his family name, Racquela. You know that."

"I do, Mother." Racquela selected a small dish of rice pudding from the dessert tray. "I'll invite him for dinner." *Goodbye, exciting romance,* she thought. *Maybe Paulo can help me think of a way around the chaperone problem.*

Chapter 7

Although Teddori never raised his hand in anger against any of the children, he had other ways of exacting justice.

Such punishments were familiar to Leo. He pondered his inability to avoid trouble as he adjusted his legs in the cramped space, scraping at the caked soot and ash with his filthy brush. Chimney sweeping was the worst possible punishment that Teddori would mete out to the orphans, usually reserved for especially bad behaviour. It was harder than any of the work Bruno had ever made Leo do on the farm, but at least Teddori didn't beat him for not working fast enough.

Leo kept his filthy cap over his eyes and braced himself as he re-adjusted the rag over his mouth. He wasn't scared of tight spaces like some of the other children were, but he hated the fact that it was a punishment. It wasn't really all his fault, but he'd been stupid enough to give in to the dare.

"Just picture the look on his face," Antonio had said. "It'll be so funny!"

Leo thought Teddori always had a funny look on his face, but he figured it could always get funnier.

"Do it, Leo," Bernardo goaded. "Unless you're too scared." Bernardo was always trying to tell Leo he was too scared to do something, even though he never picked fights with Leo anymore.

"This is dull, you guys," Sofia said. She was always worried about getting into trouble. The girls only had to peel potatoes when they were bad, but they seemed to fear Renalda in the kitchen more than the boys feared Teddori. Renalda would spank their bare bottoms with a wooden spoon at almost no provocation.

The worst trouble always seemed to happen when Teddori was away in the city. He would pack the wagon, hitch it up to the old nag, and bring along two of the older boys, leaving Renalda in charge. Renalda preferred solitude unless there was work to be done in the kitchen, so the children were left to govern themselves.

When Teddori left, that's when dares happened. Most of the children were perfectly content to play hide-and-seek in the fields around the orphanage or other similar games, but eventually boredom set in. An element of danger was needed to keep things interesting.

It was certainly the most interesting dare Leo had ever agreed to. The girls thought it was disgusting, but that just made it even funnier.

Teddori owned two pairs of shoes. One was his old leather day-to-day shoes. They looked awful and smelled even worse. Like the soul of the man himself, they were unpleasant to the eye, but old and comfortable, soft yet dependable.

Teddori's wore his other shoes very rarely. If someone important visited the orphanage, the black shoes came out. He always kept them locked in the office, but if he wore them to the city, he would leave his other pair by the front door.

Leo knew he would be severely punished, but he couldn't help giving in to the dare. Nobody else had the bravery to do something so terrible, so *gross*. Nobody else was willing to withstand possible punishment. Bernardo swore up and down, like the rest of them, that he wouldn't rat Leo out. They were all in it together.

Leo knew Bernardo would betray him, even as he was squatting over the shoes.

"Quit peeking!" he shouted at Ravi as the boys and girls chortled and giggled.

He pictured Teddori's face as the man eased a foot into a shoe and felt a *squish*. Then Leo started laughing, too, which had made it nearly impossible to complete the dare. He thought about just peeing into the shoes, but it wasn't the same.

"Okay, everybody shut up or Renalda will hear us," he'd said with a grunt as Ravi peeked around the corner again.

"He can't poop!" Ravi squealed, sending all the children into fits of laughter.

"Just shut up and I can," Leo insisted. "And quit peeking."

Leo realized in hindsight he should have waited to complete the dare until he actually *had* to go. Once the giggling finally died down, he'd managed to fulfill his task. It was only in one shoe, but that was enough. The other children came to inspect his handiwork, laugh uproariously, comment on how gross it was, and compliment him on a job well done. Then they ran off to play.

The oddest part, Leo mused as he furiously scrubbed at the bricks of the chimney, was that Teddori hadn't even seemed upset. Nobody knew if he'd actually stepped into his shoe, or if a sight or smell had tipped him off to the shoe's contents. The boys had all been washing up after cleaning out the stables, and the girls had been helping with supper. Teddori had merely appeared at the well carrying a perfectly calm expression, and asked which one of the boys had graced his shoe with a gift.

Bernardo had cracked before anyone else had even uttered a word. Leo had swallowed his fury and promised himself to exact revenge on the boy later.

Leo shuffled up a bit and kept scraping. The work wasn't so bad. It gave him a lot of time to think. The worst part of the punishment was missing supper. Leo reminded himself, again, that it was better than the farm. At least at the orphanage he ate regular meals.

The minutes passed as Leo scraped. When he got bored, he would practice his letters in the soot, tracing them firmly before dusting them away. If it had been up to Bruno, Leo never would have learned how to read and write. Leo was beginning to suspect Bruno had never known how to do either of those things in the first place.

They didn't have any storybooks in the orphanage. Leo didn't know what a storybook was, really, but Sofia had tried to explain the difference to him once. To Leo, storybooks seemed less interesting than the books about other parts of the world. There were pictures to go with them – black-and-white photographs of desert sands and snow-capped mountains, castles and cities, and people with dark skin and strange clothing. Leo wanted to see it all for real, to know what the colours were on those clothes, and to feel the stones of those castles. Reading about them was almost as good. Storybooks weren't the same. They were imaginary, and anybody could imagine things. The books Teddori let Leo read were about real things he could one day see for himself.

The orphanage wouldn't last forever. One day he would grow up, and then he would be free. He wouldn't have to sweep chimneys or stables anymore, or fight over toys with bigger boys, or kick someone in the shins just to keep his heel of bread.

For the time being, though, he was stuck shimmying up a chimney, coated in ash. Once in a while one of the other children would approach the fireplace and holler something up at him, usually just mocking laughter, but other than that Leo was left alone with his thoughts. Mostly he thought of ways to get back at Bernardo.

The sun had set by the time Leo emerged from the top of the chimney. All about him, the countryside was still. He couldn't see the big city beyond the hills, but he knew it was out there. He pictured the bright lights and winding cobblestone streets and big old marble buildings. As he leaned on the bricks of the chimney and removed the rag from his face to breathe in the cool night air, he decided he would wait on the roof until somebody called him down.

***

When his eyes fluttered open he was shivering, and Teddori's deep, calm voice was calling out to him.

"Leo. Wake up. Carefully, now. You don't want to fall off the roof."

Leo vaguely recalled he had fallen asleep beside the chimney. He'd had the chasing dream again, but this time it was through dark and winding streets. The soldiers who pursued him had bright red eyes and no mouths. Their wands were made of fire.

"I cleaned the chimney," he said sleepily.

"I know. Why didn't you shimmy back down? I saved you some soup, but it's likely cold by now."

Leo rubbed his eyes and peered down at Teddori. The master of the house didn't look mad at all. It made Leo feel a little better.

"Can I still have it?"

"Of course you can. Climb back down the chimney, would you? And don't forget the brush. Oh, and Renalda will want you to wash up first so you don't track soot all over the house. She heated some bath water for you earlier, but that's going to be mighty cold, too."

Leo shivered. He didn't relish the idea of a cold bath, but if he whined about it Renalda would give him a swat with her big wooden spoon. He clambered back down the chimney with his brush in hand.

The big washtub was near the hearth, with a bar of soap next to it. Leo started shivering even before he peeled his clothes off. He shut his eyes and imagined it was a summer's day and he was washing in the river. Despite the picture in his mind, the frigid water made him hiss through his teeth when he stepped into the tub. He didn't want to lower himself in right away, but he heard heavy footsteps approaching the door to the big common room. Leo plunged himself into the washtub. If it was one of the older boys, he didn't want them to see how skinny he was.

"Already scrubbing, hmm?" Teddori asked.

Leo lifted his head and arms out to grab the soap. Teddori was sitting in a chair, holding a bowl of soup. Leo smiled at him and started scrubbing his coal-black hands. By the time he moved on to his face, the water in the tub had become an opaque grey.

"So. Leo. What made you decide to do it?"

"They dared me to."

"Who did?"

"Everybody."

Teddori nodded. He set the bowl of cold soup down on the floor and pursed his lips. As he leaned forward, the chair gave a groan of protest.

"But why did you choose to accept the dare? You always have a choice, Leo."

"Everybody else was too scared to actually do it." He lathered up his face and dunked it again.

"Just because you are brave enough to do something doesn't always mean you should do it. Sometimes these things that only you are brave enough to do are foolish, or hurtful to others. Leo...you are not being admired for your bravery by the other children. It is being taken advantage of. Refusing to partake in an action you disagree with is true courage. Do you understand what I'm saying?"

Leo nodded. He could always say no to a dare, but it usually led to fights, which got him into even worse trouble.

"Unless, of course, your intent was to be hurtful to me. Frankly, I was more disgusted than anything, but it gives me an excuse to buy some new shoes."

"You're not mad?" Leo watched him warily. How could anybody not be mad about something like that? It would be like someone taking Leo's favourite toy soldier and melting it on the stove.

Teddori shook his head and smiled. "I would tell you some of the crazy things I did when I was your age, but I'm afraid it would give you too many ideas. Suffice it to say I remember my childhood well. It's hard not to when you work with children every day."

Leo began lathering up his hair with the soap, which still felt gritty despite the cap he'd worn in the chimney. He realized suddenly how much he appreciated Teddori's honesty. Renalda always talked down to him and all the other children.

"How are your letters coming along? Did you practice while I was away?"

Leo nodded proudly. He could read as well as the other children his age already. It hadn't taken him long to catch up.

Teddori spent some time asking Leo to spell out simple words as he scrubbed away in the bath. After a nearly perfect score of right answers, Teddori left the bowl of soup next to the tub and left the room. Bubbles of fat had congealed overtop of the mushy vegetables, but the smell of it still set Leo's stomach to gurgling. He happily slurped away, spilling drops of broth into the bath water.

Teddori returned with a clean pair of pants and a shirt and set them down next to the tub.

"Ted, what's the city like?"

Teddori beamed. "You always ask about the city."

"So?" He downed the final mouthful of broth and pasty carrots. "I want to hear it again." He could remember a time when he was afraid of the city, because Bruno had been.

"It is bigger than you can imagine. The great marble libraries and government buildings, held up by massive white pillars, sit atop the five hills and sparkle in the sun. Old deepstone castles house the noble families who can trace their lineages back to the first empire and beyond. Below in the valleys are winding stone streets with bright shops and people of all trades, and horses and coaches and bicycles going back and forth. Even the most modest apartments would dwarf our home here. At the docks, ships come and go all day. Many even travel up the Avati River to the middle of the city to unload their wares and then return to their travels upon the four seas of Titania, visiting exotic, faraway places like the Eye of the World and the Eastern Empire and the Commonwealth of Faxon. High above it all, the Great Crystal watches over all the people from the Old Temple. It is said the eye of Jova himself sees through that crystal lens."

Leo smiled sleepily. "What does the Great Crystal look like?" Leo had never seen a real crystal before. They weren't very common in the countryside. He'd seen pictures of them in the books, like the dark red ones they fashioned into wand triggers, or the blue ones they put into the streetlamps.

"Well, I've never seen it, myself," Teddori admitted. "Even though I almost became a priest. From what I've heard, it's magnificent to behold. A great big sphere of the clearest crystal, bigger than this house. When the light of the sun comes down and touches it, rainbows dance across the crystal chamber."

"I want to see it someday," Leo replied. His eyes were shutting involuntarily.

"Maybe someday you shall. You could join the priesthood one day, if you wanted. Even a casteless orphan can rise to greatness in the Church of Novem. However, you'll never get there if you die from a nasty cold from falling asleep in the bath. Up you get. It's bedtime."

Leo shook his head wearily. "No. I want to look at a picture book first."

Teddori stood up and the floorboards creaked. "I don't think so. You can't even keep your eyes open, and I've been pretty lenient already to you today, considering the fact that you ruined my favourite pair of shoes."

"I'm sorry," Leo mumbled. He meant it.

He heard a heavy sigh. "Maybe I should take you with me the next time I go to the city. At the very least, it would keep you out of trouble."

Leo's eyes popped open. "Really?"

"If you promise to stay out of trouble until my next trip into Captus Nove, I will take you with me. No dares, no fights, no whining."

"I promise," Leo said without hesitation. He leapt out of the bath and shivered as he put on his pants.

"We won't get to see a lot of marble buildings or castles, though. The hills are for the wealthy."

Leo didn't care. He wanted to see it all one day, and the crowded streets of the valley were just as exciting.

Chapter 8

The room was brick, painted a stark white. The windows were small, protected by metal bars. Outside the sky was grey. A single crystal light hung from the ceiling over a table and two chairs, bathing Timori in a blue glow. His hands rested on the table, bound together by handcuffs. Frank stood behind him, smoking a cigarette.

The door opened with a heavy creak. The man who entered was completely bald and wore large glasses. He was wearing a doctor's shift and a bland expression, but his eyes held a hungry, predatory look. He looked up from his clipboard and shot an empty smile at Timori. The crystal light shot glare off of his head.

"Timori Stravida," he said. His voice carried even less expression than his face. Timori said nothing, challenging the man with a glare. "My name is Doctor Marus. Do you know why you're here?"

"Because my mother sent me here."

Doctor Marus looked down at his clipboard.

"She did request an evaluation, yes, but that's not the only reason. Let's say your mother had nothing to do with this. Why do you think you would be sent here?"

"I'm not sure." Timori scowled. "Is this a prison?"

"The only true prison is the mind, Timori." The doctor smiled again, but his eyes remained cold. "Would you feel more comfortable talking to me if the police officer left the room?"

Timori heard Frank shift uncomfortably behind him. Obviously Timori was considered dangerous enough that the inspector was not supposed to leave.

"No."

"Very well." Doctor Marus sat down across from Timori. "I can tell you exactly why you're here. You are considered a danger to yourself and to others. You threatened to kill yourself and have displayed many violent, unpredictable tendencies. This evaluation has been requested to determine whether or not you need to spend some time here."

"Evaluate away," he said.

"Very good. Let's begin. Why did you hold a wand to your head?"

Timori rolled his eyes.

"Why do you think?"

"It doesn't matter what I think. What matters are your reasons. Was it an empty threat?"

Timori stared up at the crystal light.

"I don't know."

"Would you have turned the wand on anybody else?"

"No."

"What about your betrothed, Racquela De'Trini?"

"I would never hurt Racquela."

"Or anybody else?"

"I don't want to hurt anybody. I just want to go home."

"You wanted to hurt yourself."

"Wrong. I wanted the pain to stop. I was tired of hurting all the time."

The doctor raised an eyebrow and scrawled something on the clipboard with a pencil.

"Have you always had violent tendencies?"

"No. I don't have violent tendencies. I told you, I wouldn't have aimed that wand at anybody else."

"Where did you get the wand?"

Timori narrowed his eyes.

"Are you a police officer?"

"I'm a doctor."

"Then I don't have to answer that question."

Doctor Marus stood up and began to pace.

"You're right, Timori, you don't. But if you're interested in making things difficult for me, then I can make things very difficult for you in return. Why don't you come with me for a moment?"

Timori stood up. He didn't think he had much choice in the matter. The doctor opened the door and motioned for Timori and the policeman to follow him. He led Timori down a long brick hallway, dimly lit by bare crystal lights. Timori passed by heavy metal doors with tiny windows. The rooms were barren, painted white.

"This is a place of healing," the doctor said as they turned a corner. "Many come here seeking solace, or protection from themselves or the scorn of society. An affliction of the mind is a terrible thing, and sanctuary is required for it to heal. The world might claim to understand your pain, Timori, but only you hold the power to true recovery."

Around the corner, the rooms were no longer empty. As Timori passed them by, he saw figures within, all wearing white. The first one was a man with big, wide blue eyes, wearing a straitjacket. He was staring at the floor, laughing and muttering to himself. In the next one, a middle-aged woman with frizzy hair was biting on her fingers. Her nails were completely gone, and her lips were stained with bright red blood. Timori wondered why *she* didn't have a straitjacket. In the following window, an anguished face was pressed up against the glass. He screamed at Timori and threw his body against the door. Timori heard the police officer behind him jump.

"As you can see, Timori, these people are a danger to themselves, or to others. The goal of this hospital is the safety of our society. If these poor, tormented individuals were allowed to roam free, well...there would be pandemonium."

The doctor led Timori to an open sitting area with couches and a radio. There was a wide window overlooking a courtyard. Numerous patients in white wandered about the courtyard garden, under the watchful eye of the hospital guards. A fat, barefoot man was talking to a tree, and an old woman in a wheelchair was yelling at nobody in particular as she smoked a cigarette. A boy who looked no older than Timori was sitting in a corner, pulling up tufts of grass.

Timori shuddered. The sanitorium was the last place in the world he wanted to be. He needed to cooperate with Doctor Marus, but he couldn't betray Paulo.

"So you see, Timori, we give our patients plenty of outdoor exercise, and here in the sitting room we share discussions and focus on healing. You'll be safe and well-treated during your stay."

"And if I tell you where the wand came from?"

The doctor watched the courtyard with his arms behind his back. Frank cleared his throat.

"Well, I'm sure they would drop the charges if you helped them catch an illegal wand dealer," Frank said. "Your cooperation might convince the doctor you're still responsible and rational. I've heard there's a funeral coming up for a girl you went to school with. You wouldn't want to miss that."

The mention of Lenara's funeral gave Timori an idea. He placed a hand against the window and stared at the floor. He wanted his confession to seem convincing.

"I...no, I can't tell you. I promised I wouldn't."

"Promised whom?" the doctor asked as he adjusted his glasses. "It's you or him, Timori."

"Not him. Her. Crystara Mita. She gave me the wand."

58

"A prisoner of the church the city police can't question," Frank said. "Convenient."

"You asked for the truth and I gave it to you. I'll tell you anything else you want to know, just get me the abyss out of here."

Frank shrugged and escorted Timori to the exit as the doctor watched them go, maintaining his eerily passive expression. Frank lit up another smoke once they were outside.

"You think I was born yesterday, kid?"

"Huh?"

"You can't lie to an empath. Where'd the wand come from?"

Timori glanced back at the sanitorium.

"I...can't tell you."

"Fine. Go home."

"I...what?"

"I said go home. Go back to school. Quit digging in tunnels you shouldn't."

Timori took a couple of tentative paces backward.

"I said scram, kid, before I change my mind. Keep your fingernails clean."

"Thank you," Timori said before he ran off.

"Yeah, yeah."

Chapter 9

Julio was at Ramona's doorstep. The house loomed above him, a larger abode than he could ever hope to afford. The shutters on the windows were drawn. Julio stared at the simple oaken door, trying to summon the courage to knock. It always took him a few moments. He raised his cane and rapped three times with the simple brass head.

He was admiring the flowerbed when she answered.

"Julio," she gasped. "I didn't think you'd received my letter."

Julio forced himself to look at her. It never got any easier. Her hair, still long and wavy and lovely, only had a few strands of grey, where Julio's was a tangled mess of silver and white. Her eyes were the same honest green, bordered by crow's feet but no less lovely for all that. Her lips...

"Julio."

He cleared his throat. "Yes, I got your letter." *Stop it, don't look her in the eyes. You'll cry, you'll get lost, you'll...*

"Well. I'm just surprised to see you today, is all. I thought you might write back first, instead of showing up unannounced. Would you like to come in for some tea?"

Yes.

"Hrm. How does Mister Andari feel about that?"

Ramona scowled.

"Are we really going to go through all of this again?"

Stop being an idiot, Jules.

"Sorry. Yes, tea would be lovely." Ramona motioned for him to follow her inside.

It had been months since he'd set foot inside the Andari manor, but nothing much had changed. Ralfi was the frugal kind of rich, only throwing away things that had completely outlived their usefulness. The ugly brown throw-rug was the same and the coat rack was still in need of varnish. Julio wondered if Ralfi's smoking chair still had cigar burns on the arm.

Ramona took Julio's hat, coat, and cane wordlessly as he examined the good side of his face in the foyer mirror. *Would it have mattered, Ramona,* he wondered, *if I'd had a prosthetic mask made?*

He followed Ramona into the parlour, unsurprised to find the same couches as the last time he'd visited. Ralfi and Ramona kept the room sparsely decorated. The only feature other than the drapes was the amateurish portrait of Ralfi's father above the mantel.

Julio accepted Ramona's arm as she led him to a spot on one of the couches. *I'll take what I can get,* he thought. He drank in her scent, pleased to discover some things never changed. He eased into the seat Ramona offered with an ungraceful grunt and wiped his brow with his handkerchief.

"Hot day out there," he remarked.

"Looks like it," she replied. "I've been stuck inside cleaning. Perhaps some water with tea?"

"That would be lovely, thank you."

"Oh, and – have you eaten?"

Julio thought back to his morning.

"I don't believe that I have."

"You need to eat more," Ramona said as she shook her head. "You're always forgetting. I'll bring out some sandwiches and cheeses with the tea." She retreated through a door.

"You really don't have to..." Julio's protest faded to silence. She had already left. Ramona would always dote on him when he came over. It was almost worse than being ignored. He was the awkward friend, the former lover, the one she felt sorry for.

Julio let his eyes wander to the sparsely stocked bookshelf in the corner. He scanned the shelves, seeing titles he'd already read at least once: *The Future of the Motorcoach, A History of the Kings and Queens of Novem, Raffino: Complete Works...*Julio smiled when he noticed a copy of his *Rise and Fall of the Second Empire* on the shelf, the one he'd given to Ramona as a gift. He shook his head when he realized just how many of the titles on the shelves were romance novels.

"Oh, Ramona," he sighed.

"Yes?" She had returned, bearing a large tray full of bite-sized sandwiches, cheeses, crackers, and a teapot. She set the tray down on the table.

"Nothing. You need to fill your bookshelf."

"That's not the only bookshelf in the house, Julio." She made a dismissive wave of her hand as she returned to the door. "Ralfi just feels most of the books I read are...'unsuitable' for guests."

Julio laughed. Ramona left briefly, returning with teacups and a pitcher of water. Julio admired her grace and poise as she poured tea and water for the both of them. He tried to be delicate as he ate his first bite-sized salami sandwich, but he was ravenous. The snacks began to disappear quickly.

"So where are Ralfi and Drago today?" Julio inquired. "Out on some father-son thing?" He tried to keep the bitterness from his voice, but it crept in regardless.

"No," Ramona replied after taking a small sip of tea. "Ralfi is working. Money is tight, given the situation in the city. He's doing everything he can to keep his factory open."

"Admirable," Julio replied. He didn't have to like Ralfi Andari, but he could respect a man who worked on the weekend to help bolster a struggling economy. "What about Drago?"

"He's working, and should be home later. Actually that's..."

"Why the letter?" Julio interrupted.

"What? Yes, that's why I sent the..."

"You could have sent me a telegram. Or come to visit. Why a letter, when we live in the same city?" Julio could see Ramona forcing the irritation out of her features.

"I wasn't sure how you'd react to a visit. It's been a while, and..."

"Not by my choice."

Ramona set down her teacup.

"No, but by your actions." She gazed up at the ceiling and let out a long-suffering breath. "Honestly, Julio, I don't know what the best course of action is with you. I never know. You say you want to maintain our friendship, but whenever we talk you seem upset about something. Even after all this time..."

Julio stared out the window at the street. A boy and a girl passed by on bicycles.

"My feelings haven't changed. I can't help that."

"And I am married. I can't..."

"Yes, you can."

"I *choose* not to change that." Ramona's eyes narrowed. "But you're still my friend and I want you to be a part of Drago's life. This past year, however, you've been irritable and distant...I broke off contact for a while because I thought it would be good for you."

"As usual, you get to decide what's best for me."

"Somebody has to. You certainly don't look after yourself."

"I'm fine. You could have at least told me that's what you were doing." Julio folded his arms. "I get it. Nothing has changed between us. You keep me at arm's length out of some sense of pity, but just close enough to stay within this painful orbit."

"I know it's selfish." Ramona contemplated her teacup. "For both of us. I wish I could just let you go...but you're still my best friend."

"That's not what I want. I want..."

"I know."

He would never accuse her of rejecting him because of his face, but it always hovered between them.

"I'm sorry," he said finally. "I always make this difficult for us."

"Julio." She put a hand on his knee. It was an inappropriate gesture for a married woman to make, but he would never say so. He just imagined he was holding that hand, and looked into her eyes. "I could stop contacting you," she suggested, "if that would be easier."

"No." *This pain is always preferable to the pain of never seeing you again, my love.*

"I want things to go back to the way they were between us." Ramona leaned back in her chair and bit her lip.

"You and I, we never get what we want, do we?" Julio made a sad smile.

Ramona shook her head and a long, pregnant silence followed. Julio ate another sandwich, trying to think of a way to lead their conversation back to pleasant, comfortable territory.

It's all fine, then she goes and touches my knee, and I can still see the love in her eyes. It's just that godsdamned boring twerp she married. And my godsdamned face...

"So I was hoping that you'd talk to Drago," Ramona said finally.

"What about?" Julio said eagerly.

"His...his father."

"Not Ralfi, surely?" Julio raised an eyebrow. "I thought he already knew that Pietro was his father."

"He does. But he's starting to ask more difficult, pointed questions. Actually I'm surprised he waited this long. In any case, I thought maybe you could talk to him. You knew Pietro better than I did, after all."

I thought I did, until he stole you from me, Julio thought.

Although the memory still brought him pain, he had to admit Ramona had a point. Julio had known Pietro better than anybody else, unless he wanted to do some digging and find Pietro's family down in Nalaro, if they were still around. Since Drago had grown up as Ralfi's adopted son, there had been no such contact up to that point. Even Julio's interactions with Drago were frowned upon by Ralfi, who seemed to frown upon everything. Only Ramona possessed the uncanny ability to convince Ralfi that Julio was harmless. Julio used to wonder how she accomplished it, until he remembered Ralfi was just as in love with her as everybody else.

"Julio? Will you talk to him?"

"Of course I will. What..." Julio stopped himself mid-sentence as he heard the front door open and shut.

"What do you want me to tell him?" Julio said as softly as he could. His rasp of a voice must have been difficult to hear. Ramona leaned in to listen.

"I'm sure you can strategically spare him certain details," Ramona replied in a similar whisper.

"About what, Pietro's death, or Drago's conception?"

Ramona's nostrils flared. Julio thought he might get a cup full of tea to the face, but at that moment the door to the parlour opened. He felt like a child with his hand caught in the cookie jar...or perilously close to the jar, at least. Ramona leaned back on the couch, managing somehow to look sublimely not guilty. Julio made a piece of cheese his pretence for leaning forward.

"Mother," said Drago. He walked over to her side of the couch and hugged her, then shook Julio's good hand.

"Master Vellize," he said. "I haven't seen you in a while. How have you been?"

Drago was the very image of his father, right down to the uniform. It was crisp and neatly pressed, and although it was woven in the docile grey-and-blue colours of the republic rather than the aggressive black-and-red of the empire, the face beneath the officer's cap was very nearly the same. He possessed Pietro's boyish good looks, those same lips that always curled into a smirk, and the same eager blue eyes.

It seemed he'd only inherited his hair from Ramona, and they'd forced him to cut off those dark, unruly locks when he'd joined the military academy. The remainder, short-cropped, was hidden underneath his cap.

"I could send you a photograph if it's less strain on your eyes," Drago quipped. Julio suddenly realized they were still shaking hands.

"Ah. Sorry, my boy." Julio released his grip. "Lieutenant, I mean. I've only got the one, so it takes me twice as long to make sure it's you."

"I save the lieutenant stuff for the training yard." Drago filled his hands with cheese and crackers and began snacking as he sat next to his mother. "It's just Drago at home."

"Are you hungry, Drago?" Ramona was speaking to her son, but she was looking pointedly at Julio.

"Yeah," he said, mouth full of crackers. They were spilling onto the front of his uniform. Julio forced back a snicker. You could dress a boy up and give him a title, but dignity took time.

"Why don't you take Julio out for lunch?" Ramona suggested. "It's been a while since you two caught up."

Drago raised an eyebrow, looking first at Ramona, then at Julio.

"Didn't you two just eat?"

"There isn't enough left to feed a growing boy, though," Ramona replied. "I'll give you some money. You go ahead and take Julio to a café. Buy him a coffee if he's full."

Drago shot Julio an inquiring look. He shrugged in reply. *Might as well feign ignorance until we leave the house*, he thought. *He knows Ramona is plotting, but he'll be more likely to open up to me if he believes me innocent.*

"Keep your money," Drago said. "Father will never let me hear the end of it if he finds out you took a few centima out of your purse to feed me when I have my own wages." He stood up and walked over to the parlour door. "I'm just going to go change out of my uniform."

Julio was once again left with Ramona.

"He saw right through you," Julio chuckled.

"Of course he did." Ramona poured herself another cup of tea. "I didn't expect him to be home so early, and I didn't have time to think up another pretext."

"I don't suppose it matters." Julio smirked. "I'll make sure he doesn't spend any money on me."

"Let him. He spends enough on himself."

"Of course. He's a young man with a good job. People are desperate for that kind of spender right now. There's nothing quite so glamorous as the position of a military officer during peacetime."

"Julio, do you suppose that..."

Drago re-entered the parlour, dressed in fine white slacks and a matching shirt and hat. The outfit appeared new and well-tailored.

"I'll look like a bum next to you," Julio remarked. Drago looked down at his clothes as though they were nothing special.

"Well, I was going to put on a suit, but it's too damned hot outside."

"Drago," Ramona scolded. "Language."

"Eighteen, an officer, and still scolded by my mother," he said to Julio as he rolled his eyes. "If it's not her, it's my captain. Let's go before I get a tongue-lashing for wearing white after blossomfall."

Chapter 10

"I just want to know that it's not going to happen again," Timori's mother said. She sucked on her cigarette. The place where she held it between her fingers was stained a dark yellow. "I want to know that you're not thinking of hurting yourself. You're too good for her anyway."

Timori bit his tongue and tried to think of an excuse to leave the kitchen. He was breathing in through his mouth rather than his nose to avoid smelling the mouldy pile-up of dishes that had overflowed from the sink and taken up the entirety of the small counter space.

"Leave Racquela out of it. I'm fine now, anyway." He said it without looking her in the eyes.

"But you're not fine," Coletta insisted. She tried to touch Timori's hand across the table, but he pulled it away. "You've been gone for almost a week, and..."

"And what have you done in that week, Mother?" Timori stood up so quickly his rickety chair fell over. "Anything? It *smells* in here. I can't even make a sandwich. Of course, maybe that's because there's no fucking bread."

Timori's mother pounded her fist on the table.

"You watch your mouth in this house, young man! Do you have any idea how much bread costs right now? Everybody in the valley is starving. Meanwhile I've been worried sick about you."

"So worried that you sent me to that creepy doctor? Yeah, real nice, Mom. Send your son packing to the nuthouse."

He wanted to pick up the fallen chair and smash it into pieces, but he knew it would never be replaced. There were only three chairs left in the house that could stand up.

"And don't fucking talk to me about the price of bread," he continued. "I've been feeding the girls with *my* money that I've been earning at *my* job."

"A job you won't have any more since you've been gone for a week," Coletta accused. Timori saw Nicola poking her head around the corner from the hallway. "Nicky, Lottie, back to the other room," his mother said. She always seemed to preternaturally know when the girls were creeping around. "Timori and I are having a serious discussion. That means now, girls."

Timori rolled up his sleeves. He waited until he heard two pairs of footsteps recede before speaking.

"Where did you tell them I was?"

"I just said you were sick and had to visit the doctor."

"Hah." Timori's laugh was mirthless. He picked up stacks of sticky plates and piled them on the table in order to empty the sink. "Nicky's old enough to know better. You could give me a hand here, you know."

"I would, but my back has really been hurting lately. I..."

Timori let a stack of plates clatter to the table.

"It's always something, isn't it? Do I have to do everything? *I* look after the girls, *I* buy the food, *I* go to school. Would it kill you to *do* something around here when you get home?" He pulled the last of the dishes out of the sink and dumped them unceremoniously in front of his mother.

"Tim, I..."

"I know. I've been hearing the same excuses my whole life. 'My back hurts.' 'I'm tired from working all day.' Well it's no wonder Dad left. Guess what, Mom? I've got some excuses of my own. The love of my life left me because I'm not good enough. I have to work and go to school and I still don't have enough money to look after everybody. But you don't hear me complaining about it."

"How would...what you tried to do to yourself make it any better?"

"At least I didn't make excuses," Timori spat. "And there'd be one less mouth to feed."

"Oh Tim," his mother sobbed. She buried her face in her arms. Timori watched her cry for a moment, then put the plug in the sink and turned on the tap.

Timori's building didn't have hot water – that was a luxury of the rich – but cold water rinsed dishes just fine. All he cared about was getting rid of the mould. He threw plates and cutlery into the sink. Grabbing a rag, he scrubbed furiously.

For a while, the only sounds were the water running out of the tap, the clattering of dishes, and Coletta's soft weeping. Timori stared at the bricks of the wall and wondered what things would have been like if his mother had left instead of his father.

Nicola appeared beside him with their only dishtowel in hand and began drying off plates.

"Leave the tap on," she whispered as he handed her a chipped cup.

"Why?"

"Because I want to know where you were all week. Mom didn't tell us anything." Nicola was only twelve years old, but nothing got past her. Her pale blue eyes gave him a questioning look. "Well, she said you were in the hospital, but when I asked if we could visit she said no. But you seem fine to me."

Timori sighed and handed her a plate.

"Godsdammit, Nicky. Couldn't you at least have looked after the dishes while I was gone?"

Nicola had to stand on her tip-toes to put the plate away in the cupboard.

"I was busy with homework, mine and Lottie's, plus I had to distract her all week with games because she was so upset that you weren't around." Timori could understand that part. Carlotta had clung to his leg babbling at him for an hour straight after he had come home from the sanitorium. "And I had to cook, too. I don't know how you do it all. And don't avoid the question. Where were you? You don't look hurt to me."

Timori turned the tap as far as it would go, to make sure his mother wouldn't hear him.

"I was in jail, and then Mother sent me to an alienist."

Nicola's eyes widened.

"Why?"

"I'm surprised you didn't hear it on the radio."

"You were on the radio? Tim, what happened? Does it have something to do with Crystara going to jail, too?"

"Yes and no." Timori ground his teeth, trying to figure out a way to explain it to his little sister. "It all had to do with the betrothals," he said as he grabbed an exceptionally mouldy bowl. "Racquela...well, you know how she left me. Went to get an annulment. Well, that part's all done. I was upset, and I got angry, so the police took me away. Then I got sent to that head doctor. As for Crystara, well...supposedly she tried to tamper with the Great Crystal. She was pretty upset that Jake cheated on her."

"Well, Jake and Racquela are both dullies."

"Maybe. But so am I."

"But what did you *do*?"

"Nothing, Nicky. It's what I might have done that worried people." Timori decided to change the subject before his sister figured it out. "I might be able to...borrow some money from work for groceries tomorrow. Is there anything you want?"

"Whatever you can get," she said with a shrug. "Lottie wants sausages, but I know they're too expensive. Are you going to be able to afford to feed everybody and go to school? I could...I could maybe find a job somewhere if I have to. Washing windows or sweeping floors or something."

"Don't worry about it." Timori wanted to tousle his sister's hair, but his hands were filthy. "You just focus on school. Between me and Mom, I think we can keep everybody fed, even if prices are getting ridiculous."

Nicola continued wiping the plate in her hands even though it was completely dry. Her eyes had a far-away look.

"You mean she didn't tell you? I thought that was why she's crying."

Timori glanced back at his mother, who was smoking another cigarette. She shot him a sad smile.

"Oh, gods. Tell me what?"

Nicola's voice dropped so low that Timori had to lean in to hear her over the sound of the water.

"The typing pool let her go. People are losing jobs all over the valley, she said."

Timori dropped the bowl. It dashed to pieces between his feet.

"Fuck. Fuck, shatters, fuck."

He knew what he had to do.

Chapter 11

"What do you mean I can't visit her?" Racquela shifted the heavy basket from one arm to the other.

The chubby priest in blue and white robes shook his head vehemently. His jowls kept moving even after his head had stopped shaking.

"I am very sorry, Lady De'Trini, but it is absolutely out of the question. Crystara Mita is a traitor to the republic. Who knows what manner of poisonous ideas she could spread to you, just from verbal contact?"

"Nonsense. The De'Trini family has always been loyal to church and state. I am not leaving until you allow me to see her."

The priest kept most of his bulky frame behind the door. Although he greatly outweighed Racquela, he appeared anxious that she would somehow overwhelm him and pry the heavy whiteoak door open.

"I am afraid you'll be waiting a long time, my lady. Your only option is to petition Keeper De'Cadomus, and he is not a man easily moved, I can tell you."

"Well, bring him here, then. I'm sure he'll see reason."

The priest mopped at his brow with a white silk handkerchief.

"Ah. I said petition, my lady. He is a very busy man and..."

"And what?" Racquela bit her lip and reminded herself that a proper lady never lost her patience. "By the time he reads my petition, my friend will be dead."

Tears fell down her cheeks. Every time she thought about Crystara, she saw a body swinging from a rope. Traitors weren't given to the flames. Their souls were forever doomed to wander the earth.

"Oh," the priest stammered. "Please, my lady...don't cry. Please. I am sorry, but there's...there's nothing I can...oh, just wait here a moment. I hate to see a lady cry." The large man shut the door.

After dabbing at her eyes with a handkerchief and contemplating the roses for a while, Racquela put down her basket. There was no point in carrying it if she was going to be waiting for a long time. She pulled her shawl closer about her shoulders as she watched the pigeons in the plaza. An old woman was seated by the fountain, tossing seeds to them. Once in a while a sea bird would come down and scatter the pigeons, taking the choicest seeds for itself.

"Lady Racquela De'Trini, I presume."

The voice was like a rusty knife scraping across stone. Racquela wheeled around. An old, bald priest stared at her with icy-blue eyes. Stooped as he was, he was tall enough to tower over Racquela. He raised an eyebrow and locked his fingers together. Some of the joints stuck out at odd angles.

"Keeper...De'Cadomus?" Racquela squeaked. She tried not to stare at the deep pockmarks in his cheeks.

"Yes, though most just call me viper." There was no warmth in the man's laugh, and none behind his eyes.

"I wish to speak to Crystara, if I could." Racquela picked up her basket and showed it to De'Cadomus. "I brought her some food, and a letter. Please, I know she's going to be executed as a traitor, but I really want to see her one last time." Racquela could feel herself choking up again, but she chose to let the tears flow. De'Cadomus could not be so cruel as to refuse a final visitation.

"No."

Racquela wanted to fling her basket at him.

"Why not?"

"I'm not sure how familiar you are with the ins and outs of Noven law, Lady De'Trini, but if not I'll enlighten you. Traitors to the republic surrender any right to be treated like a human being, regardless of caste. Your friend murdered two people, in case you forgot. One of them used to hold my office...and butchering a keeper is a step away from deicide. She could have even severed Novem's link to the gods if the guards hadn't arrived in time to stop her from tampering with the Great Crystal. Given the circumstances, I think we're being more than fair to her. She is being fed in a clean cell, and her execution will be swift. Most traitors are humiliated before they die, and in earlier times they were tortured, too."

"I don't believe she did those things," Racquela said. The wind had picked up and the sun was setting behind Racquela. There were few people left in Crystus Plaza, and the pigeons had gone.

"I don't care what you believe. Now leave, before I am tempted to expose to the public the fact that you clumsily bribed your way into the crystal betrothals. Wouldn't that mar the flawless reputation of the De'Trini family, who always serve church and state?"

Racquela's jaw dropped in horror. *How does he know about that?* she wondered.

"No! Don't. I'll leave." She paused. "Will you give her the basket, at least?"

Without expression, De'Cadomus glanced at the basket, then back at Racquela.

"It's just food and a letter?"

"Yes."

"Fine." He picked up the basket and shut the temple door without another word.

Racquela burst into tears. She was never going to see Crystara again. She felt cold drops amidst the warm ones on her face. Soon a downpour was falling on the plaza. Racquela remained under the cover of the portico that sheltered the Old Temple's front door. She'd forgotten her umbrella, just like she'd forgotten that it was no longer summer.

She waited a few minutes to see if the rain would let up, but it didn't. Sighing, she ducked her head down and ran across the empty square, hoping a motorcoach would be waiting for her on the plaza driveway. The bricks beneath her feet were slick, and she had to slow down. By the time she reached the fountain, her hair was plastered to her face and her dress was clinging to her legs in a very unladylike fashion.

"Shatters," she said as she bundled up her shawl and held it over her head. She was still crying, and water was squishing between her toes at the bottoms of her black pumps. "Shatters, shatters, shatters!"

No motorcoaches were waiting at the broad driveway when Racquela approached, sodden and scowling. Only a lone stagecoach waited. Its driver sat hunched under a wide black umbrella, and the paired coffee-coloured horses looked as wet and cold and miserable as Racquela felt. Racquela hated stagecoaches, and horses especially, but she didn't relish the idea of walking home in the rain.

As Racquela stared at the lonely, sombre stagecoach, she imagined Paulo driving up in his motorcoach and saying something suave as he took her away to help her forget about her failed attempt to see Crystara one last time. 'Don't worry about the leather, darling,' he'd say. 'You look cold and wet. There's a blanket in the back seat. Or we could park and slip back there. Let's get you out of those soaking clothes and I'll warm you up...'

Racquela blushed. She'd never entertained such wild fantasies with Timori, but he'd never been the type to be so bold. Romance to him was flowers and dinner. Racquela always met with Paulo at secluded cafés in the slums where he knew they would serve wine without asking his age, or they would steal off in his motorcoach to the countryside or the ocean.

It was silly to imagine Paulo showing up when he didn't know she was going to visit Crystara, so Racquela approached the stagecoach driver. Under the umbrella, the man was younger than she expected, with wide, innocent-looking blue eyes and blonde hair that tumbled to his shoulders under a porkpie hat. Racquela wasn't too surprised to see his straw-coloured locks. Blondes weren't common in Novem, but they were more likely to be found amongst the lower castes. The young man wasn't quite handsome, but he had a childlike quality to his face that reminded Racquela of drawings of the legendary fae folk from her childhood stories. For an eerie moment, he looked a bit like Crystara.

"Where to, m'lady?" he asked in a valley accent. "You look right soaked, miss. Hop in, see you don't catch a chill."

"Avati Hill, please. The De'Trini estate. It's on the west side. Maricola Road."

The coach cushions were tattered and patched, but the seats and floor appeared clean. Anything was better than being out in the rain.

"De'Trini, eh?" the driver called through the coach window as he urged his horses to a walk. "Fancy girl like you shouldn't be out alone. The plaza's safe, sure, but a beautiful noble should always be chaperoned, if you don't mind me saying so, m'lady."

Racquela watched the Old Temple and the other big marble buildings disappear behind the crest of the hill as the coach made its way to Avati Valley. The rain started coming down harder.

Racquela remembered how much Crystara loved to be outside in the rain, and the tears returned.

"You okay back there, miss?"

"I'm fine," she sniffled. "My dress is ruined, that's all."

"An umbrella and an escort, that's what m'lady needs to bring with her next time."

They had descended into the narrow cobblestoned streets of Avati Valley, where Crystara, Jacoby, and Timori had all grown up. All the buildings seemed to be squished together, like they were huddling for warmth. Occasionally motorcoaches passed around her slow-moving stage. When the horses turned down an unfamiliar lane, Racquela looked out the carriage window for a street sign.

"This isn't the quickest way to Avati Hill," she called to the driver. "We should have stayed on Abrus. It goes right up."

"M'lady knows her way around." He kept his eyes on the road as he spoke. "As it happens, so does Dillas. Abrus is crowded and there are too many motorcoaches. This is a shortcut."

Racquela sighed and sank back into her seat. So long as she was out of the rain, she was glad not to be home. She wasn't looking forward to explaining to her father why she'd decided to go all the way to Crystus Plaza alone.

The coach turned down a side street, and then another. Suddenly Racquela had no idea where she was.

"Are you sure this is a shortcut?"

"This is the best way, m'lady. Dillas promises."

Racquela wrapped her shawl around her shoulders, found it to be damp and cold, and took it off again. The horses continued to amble on at their slow gait. Racquela thought about getting out of the coach and searching for a motor-taxi, but a quick glance out the window told her there weren't any to be found in the impoverished back streets of the Avati slums. She wished Jacoby was with her. He was her only remaining friend who knew the streets of the valley, but ever since Lenara's death he'd buried himself in schoolwork and books.

The coach stopped suddenly. Racquela peered out the window to see if there was an obstruction. Ahead, a band of men in ratty coats were blocking the way through.

"Wait here, m'lady," Dillas said. "No need for alarm."

"Turn around," Racquela commanded. "Quick."

"Street is too narrow for the horses to..."

Suddenly the coach door was open and a large man with a bushy black moustache was clutching her arm. She screamed and dug her nails into one of the holes in the cushion, but the man was incredibly strong. Racquela was hauled out of the coach, and for a moment she didn't know if she was more afraid of being killed or being raped. After letting out another shrill scream, one of the men blocking the coach ran up and shoved a filthy rag in her mouth.

"Get her inside," said a gruff voice, "quickly."

Racquela was being hauled toward a nearby building. She looked up pleadingly at the stagecoach driver. He gave her a sad smile.

"I'm sorry, m'lady. This is the best way."

Chapter 12

Crystara,

I've re-written this letter seven times now, trying to figure out what to say to you. It's not easy after all that's happened, but I want you to know I don't blame you for anything. Nobody does, not even Jake, I don't think. He blames himself. I don't believe you murdered anybody, and I don't think anybody else believes it either.

The news says that you're considered a traitor and blasphemer against the nation and the gods. I like to think I know you well enough to know that the last thing you ever cared about was religion.

Seven letters and I still don't know what I'm really trying to say to you. I have to make this the last one because I have to deliver it soon. The news is that you're going to be executed. It took me four letters to even write that word down. I still don't believe it.

I forgive you. I know things haven't been easy for you in life, or Timori, for that matter, and it took me a long time to realize that fact because until I met the two of you I didn't really understand just how different it is. Growing up the way you did. You've had the stars aligned against you, and it's not fair.

I know you said we're not friends anymore, and I guess it doesn't matter now, but I still care for you. That's a small consolation, I guess. I don't know what else to say. Maybe there is nothing I can say that will make it better or that will change the circumstances. Maybe you would have been better off if we'd never met. Maybe it all would have turned out the same. All I know is I wish I could change it, and I wish there was more I could do for you, and that saying sorry is a pitiful way for a friend to say goodbye.

Jova honour you, and Lutias keep your soul. I hope you find peace and happiness, whatever happens after this life. Farewell.

Your friend always,
Racquela De'Trini

***

A high-pitched bell tolled in the tower and Crystara looked up from her scrubbing. She threw a rag and brush into a bucket of soapy water and massaged her sore arms. The light of sunset shone in through the stained glass of Celesta the Prophetess, gleaming brilliantly off the polished marble.

Crystara bet that Celesta had never been forced to perform menial labour.

The small bell meant dinner, however, which was the singularly clear event in a day full of disappointment. True to the keeper's word, Crystara's body experienced gut-wrenching pains if she approached the front door of the temple. Any passing priest, sister, or guard had made an involuntary face of disgust when they saw her kneeling upon the floor, and attempts at conversation were met with confusion, revulsion, or pity. Nobody understood a word she uttered, except De'Cadomus.

Crystara's stomach growled. The viper, as he was often called, hadn't given her any instructions regarding where to find him, or where she would be living, or whether she would be eating like a priest or a slave. She hefted her pail and made her way toward the dining hall.

Many priests and sisters were heeding the supper bell's call and Crystara fell into line with them. Quite a few stared at her.

Some quickened their pace to avoid her. Crystara reached out with her thoughts to see what they saw. She shuddered. She'd been picturing herself as an ugly girl with dirt on her face. The sideways nose and brittle hair were overshadowed by her brown, crooked teeth in a mouth of parched lips and blistering sores. She wouldn't dare approach herself without good cause.

The dining hall was filling rapidly as she entered behind a group of sisters. Crystara wondered if her crystal curse carried a stench with it, as well...the priests and orderlies seemed to take pains to avoid her presence even when they couldn't *see* her directly.

Conversation and the clattering of plates filled the room. Crystara leaned against a wall unobtrusively and scanned the tables systematically, looking for the priest who'd instructed her to clean the floors. As servants hauled in pots of stew and soup, her stomach gurgled a protest at her.

"Well, let's make this quick, then," someone said. Crystara was surprised to discover she was being spoken to. It was August, the high priest with the massive grey side-burns whom Keeper Orvin had never much cared for. Oddly enough, he had volunteered himself to be Crystara's handler. She hadn't yet found the time to pilfer through his mind for the reason why.

"I don't want to miss my dinner," he continued, beckoning to Crystara as though she were a lost puppy.

"I don't give a shard about your dinner," Crystara replied. It felt better to speak her mind, knowing there would be no consequences. Whatever she said came out as gibberish. The downside, however, was that her voice carried more than she expected. The nearest table turned to stare at the strange, misshapen urchin in the corner who moaned eerily at priests.

"Just a new unfortunate soul our new keeper, may the crystal bless him, has brought into our fold," August explained as he scratched at his side-burns. "Pay her no mind. She might make disturbing noises from time to time, but she is harmless."

"I'm the most dangerous person here," Crystara told him. "I've cracked your precious crystal, I've already killed two people, and one day I'll kill De'Cadomus for what he's done to me."

The throng of priests and servants stared at her for a few moments then returned to the important task of dinner. Crystara watched as more and more servants entered, bearing trays of bread and fruit, meats, cheeses, and baked pastas. It looked like more than enough to feed the temple thrice over at the very least. She hoped she would be allowed to scavenge through the leftovers.

"Come with me, young one," her supervisor sighed, beckoning again. He led her through the hallways to the steps of the Keeper's Tower. "De'Cadomus has asked to speak with you," he explained. Crystara heard his surface thoughts clearly: *no ordinary urchin, especially a mute, warrants the attention of the keeper. If I didn't know for an irrefutable fact that Crystara was doomed to face the Crystal Tribunal for slaughtering Orvin...I'd swear that De'Cadomus has transformed her somehow. Those kinds of whispers are myth, though. No, she's more likely a knight in disguise, sent to spy on us. It suits the viper's reputation.*

When they reached the top of the stairs, August rapped loudly on the whiteoak door that led to the Keeper's chambers.

"Enter," said a raspy voice.

De'Cadomus was seated at a small dining table. A fine spread was in front of him: fancy cheeses, a roast duck, and a bottle of wine. Beside the bottle of wine on the table was an empty basket. Crystara scanned the room quickly and tried to remember as many details as possible, in case she needed them for later. Books were neatly stacked on shelves in the far corner, there was a door in the other corner, and a sitting area with a window overlooking the courtyard.

De'Cadomus swallowed his bite of duck before speaking.

"Leave us, August."

August looked at Crystara, then back to De'Cadomus. Crystara could feel the questions he dared not ask. He nodded stiffly and left, shutting the door behind him. Crystara could still feel his thoughts. He projected them loudly. He had remained to listen at the door.

"You may be tongue-tied, but the church was good enough to teach you to read and write...in code, of course. And you have ears, which means you can tell me everything the priests say in your presence. They will treat you as though you aren't even there." De'Cadomus cut a slender sliver of meat off a breast and stabbed it with his fork.

"I'm sure this is all for August's benefit," Crystara said as she folded her arms.

"Some of the priests know me well enough to know an agent when they see one." One of his crystal rings turned grey momentarily. "There, now we should be able to converse freely. August will hear nothing."

"Nobody understands a thing I say anyway," Crystara replied, "just awkward gibberish. You've seen to that." She looked De'Cadomus in the eyes. He returned the glare as he took a small bite of cheese.

"The world has learned not to underestimate my formidable speaking powers."

"Has it learned that you like to waste people's talents?" Crystara asked. She didn't care anymore if she was adversarial. If De'Cadomus was going to hurt her he would do it regardless. A violent person needed no excuse. She had learned that lesson the hard way from her father.

"I spent my whole day wiping clean marble with a rag. You said you wanted me to help you quell this supposed revolution that's coming, but you make me into a cripple and give me a useless task. I was close to Paulo, you know. I know who he really is...and you..."

"You know, this duck your friend Racquela brought for you is excellent," De'Cadomus interrupted. He took a large bite and chewed it slowly for emphasis. "The De'Trini family must have an excellent chef. This was supposed to be your last supper, but seeing as how you're not really dying, I helped myself to it. What a nice friend you had."

Crystara tried to quell her rage, but she couldn't stop herself from slamming a fist on the table.

"You bastard! When was she here? What did she say?"

De'Cadomus didn't even flinch. He reached into the folds of his robe and brought out a crumpled envelope, opened. He tossed it on the table at Crystara. She snatched it furiously and fought back her tears. De'Cadomus took a generous sip of wine.

"You are going to wait, and learn how to be unobtrusive. You are going to learn how to *listen* instead of shouting when you don't get your way. You are going to do as I say, or I will kill you and find somebody else to do what needs to be done."

Crystara couldn't read De'Cadomus' thoughts, but she had a feeling he was bluffing. Nobody else possessed her talents, her speaking ability and her unusual mind-reading power, or De'Cadomus would surely have recruited them instead. Crystara had already shown she was a rebellious enemy of the church, and not willing to be manipulated. No, it had to be her. He needed her, she realized, and although the ring made her helpless, she could still negotiate.

"Good luck finding another reader," she said.

A jolt of pain shot through her body, starting at her hand and working its way up until it felt as though her teeth would shatter. She refused to scream. Instead she fell to the ground, clutching at a leg of the table uselessly.

"If you want to make things difficult I could end it right now," he threatened.

"What good am I to you dead?" she asked. The pain subsided for a moment and she caught her breath. "You're a reader. Keeper Orvin was. He found me by accident, so I'm guessing there aren't any others that you know of. You would just do everything yourself if you didn't need me for something." She knew she would have to let go of the defiance for a moment, to convince him that he'd won.

"You've proved that you've got me by the rocks...so to speak." She grimaced as she stood up. She could lie if she needed to. He was blind to her thoughts, just as she was blind to his. "The ring proves it. So I'll tell you what. Give me something *useful* to do, and I'll work for you willingly. Push me too hard, and death would be an appealing release. I know all the high windows in this godsdamned temple."

De'Cadomus was silent for a long moment. The only sound was the scraping of his utensils on the plate.

"Other tasks will come in time. To the unwary, you must be an innocuous observer. For those like August, who know better, you are there to inspire fear."

"Fine, then. When I'm not working, I want access to the library."

De'Cadomus narrowed his eyes. Crystara forced herself not to smirk. She'd finally found a weakness. There were things in the library he didn't want her knowing about.

"No," he said.

Crystara walked over to the window and looked down. It would be a long plummet to the courtyard below.

"I saw a group of valley kids corner a stray cat once," she said. "One of them lost an eye."

The pain was immense that time. She dropped so quickly she smacked her head against the brick window ledge.

"I admire your boldness when you know you are beaten," De'Cadomus said. He was still sitting, still enjoying the meal Racquela had brought for Crystara. "But I took away your claws."

"Not my teeth," she said. She put the finger with the ring into her mouth and bit down, hard.

"No!" De'Cadomus shouted, but she barely heard him. Pain throbbed throughout her hand and she tasted warm blood in her mouth. Suddenly she was up against the wall, both hands held firm against the bricks. De'Cadomus's face was so close to hers she could smell the meat and wine on his breath.

"No," he whispered. "Do it and you'll regret it."

It was hard to speak through the pain. She wanted to vomit every time her hand throbbed, and she could feel the blood seeping down her arm. If she'd only bitten down a little *harder*.

"Give me what I want or *you'll* regret it."

"What do you want?"

"The library." She scanned his thoughts as she said it, trying desperately to discover something, *anything*. He was guarded and strong, but so was she, and she could tell there was something he didn't want her to discover there.

"The library," he replied. "In exchange for complete obedience."

Chapter 13

Coach Lagheri's office was the smallest on campus, attesting to the coach's professed belief that Central focused more on academics than athletics. It was made even smaller by stacks of papers, old trophies used as paperweights, and bookends that pressed together ripped and rebound sports manuals and almanacs, and here and there a jersey with yellowed armpits.

The coach didn't care much for tidiness, in his office or his appearance. He didn't look much like the svelte, wild-haired and brash football star Timori knew from old newspaper clippings. The football coach of Central School had a paunch that pushed up over his desk, and though he had lost his untamed tresses of hair to male pattern baldness, he had maintained the sense of unruliness, and a scowl that made the young players of his team squirm.

"Stravida," he said. He didn't so much as motion for Timori to take a seat. "I hope you have a good explanation for missing the first week of practice. I would have given your position away to somebody else if my team wasn't full of weak-kneed whitehands who don't know a football from a boil on their ass."

"Thank you, sir, but if there's someone more deserving on the team..." Timori shifted his weight to his other leg and scratched his chin.

"What kind of talk is that? Don't you have any pride? When I was your age I would have killed somebody for a position on Central's football team. Of course, I would have killed somebody for a brick of cheese, too, but food was the only thing other than football that mattered, that's my point. You kids nowadays don't appreciate anything that you have."

"You're right, sir. The reason I say that, though...well, it isn't that I don't want the position. I've dreamed about being a football star ever since I was old enough to kick a ball..."

"Then be one!" Lagheri roared. Timori wasn't sure if the man was trying to show anger or encouragement. "You've got the potential. You could even be like me one day."

Timori looked at Lagheri's gut, his scattered trophies, and stack of old newspaper clippings of himself in the corner and wondered if fame was a double-edged sword.

"That would be...great, sir, but..."

"But what? You want to be called a picker for the rest of your life, or do you want the daisy-chasers to chant your name in a stadium?"

"Well, the latter, but...I don't really have a choice. Sir, I have to leave the team."

That gave Lagheri pause. He stroked his bare chin and shuffled around some papers on his desk.

"You're serious. This better not be about that crystal betrothal dirt. Trust me. Don't waste any more time mooning over that De'Trini girl. You can get plenty of sluts, highborn or otherwise, when you're famous. How do you think I wound up divorced three times?" he laughed.

Timori wanted to strangle his coach for backhandedly referring to Racquela as a slut, but he didn't think he'd be able to get his hands around that thick neck.

"No, sir, this isn't about girls. I have to leave Central entirely. My mother lost her job. I'm going to go work in the mines."

Coach Lagheri leaned back in his seat. Timori heard the wood creak and wondered if the old chair would splinter and send the man tumbling to the floor. The chair protested, but held.

"Now that's a shame. A damn shame." The coach shook his head repeatedly, but he couldn't seem to find anything else to say.

Timori knew how telling that was – his situation was far from unique. Valley boys left school all the time to work in the mines, helping to support their families. It was doubly worse in Timori's case – his father had left right after Carlotta was born, and the depression and miners' strike had left the industry crippled. Workers were being paid next to nothing for dangerous, back-breaking labour. It was doubly risky to cross the picket lines each morning. Timori wasn't looking forward to being called a traitor to his class, or having mud (and possibly even rocks) thrown at him.

"Well, I don't have much of a choice, sir. It's the mines or I starve."

"Sorry to lose you, Stravida," the coach sighed. "I don't think we'll be making it to the championship this year without you. Mariano's decent, but he's a showboat, and Padrona's disappeared on me, too. I have no team without a decent goalie. But I understand."

Timori wasn't sure if Coach Lagheri did understand – he looked like he hadn't missed a meal in a *long* time – but he choked back his bitterness.

"Thank you, sir." He left the office. *One down, two to go,* he thought. He would save signing the official withdrawal papers for last. He had another apology to make first.

From Coach Lagheri's office in the athletics complex, he crossed the football field toward the innermost cluster of school buildings, which were huddled together in a mixture of concrete, adobe, brick and deepstone. Central School was an educational facility built around an administrative building built around an old prison fortress. With every new addition, the campus grew increasingly complex, with narrow alleyways where students would hide and smoke cigarettes, and drab, draughty hallways connecting old buildings with new.

Timori took an obscure shortcut through a narrow gap between buildings near the belltower, heading for Doctor Ruveldi's physics class. He entered the deepstone fortress of Central School through a side door and made his way toward the science wing.

"Timori," a voice called out from a classroom. Timori stopped in front of the open classroom door. Inside, Miss Tricchio was seated at her desk, wiping off a fountain pen with an old, ink-stained rag.

"Miss Tricchio. My apologies for missing your class for a week. You know I would never skip physics without a good reason."

She arched a slender eyebrow. Although her tightly-tied hair gave her a severe expression, Timori could see a ghost of a smile at the corners of her pale eyes, and in the curl of her lip. He never could figure out why she wasn't married.

"I'm starting to think I'm not challenging you enough, if you're willing to forego the class altogether. I'm loathe to dock you marks for participation, Tim, but I have little choice. It's none of my business where you've been, but I hope everything's all right with my favourite student."

"I thought Central forbade the teachers to pick favourites." Timori sat down at a desk and propped his chin on a hand. "Besides, you and Doctor Ruveldi are going to have to fight over me."

Miss Tricchio dipped her pen in the inkwell and started grading a paper.

"Oh, he wouldn't stand a chance." She winked. "Are you coming back to class, though?"

"I have to leave Central," he admitted with a sad smile. A drop of ink fell from Miss Tricchio's pen to spatter on the page she was grading.

"Did you get an offer from an academy?"

"An academy? I'm sixteen."

"It's been known to happen," Miss Tricchio said, shrugging. "I'm not as old as I look, Tim." Timori watched her pale, bare neck as she threw back her head and laughed. "Are you moving schools, then? I know Central can be a pain in the neck, but you won't get the kind of attention you need at another finishing school. You're gifted, Tim. This is where you belong."

"I know," Timori said, staring at Miss Tricchio's black pumps. "That's what makes this more difficult. It's not about school at all, it's about money. I'm sure you make enough that the famine doesn't affect you as much, but for me...it's everything right now. I have to work. I can't let my sisters go hungry."

For a moment, there was silence. There was nothing to be said, nothing to be done about it. Timori had to leave school and that was that. Feeding his sisters was more important than an education, a future in engineering. It was so *unfair*...

Her arms were around him.

"Shh. It's all right." She smelled pure, like soap, and her shoulder was soft. Timori found that it was damp where he'd buried his head. *Am I crying?*

After a time, Miss Tricchio drew back slightly and looked at Timori. Even through the lenses of her glasses, her pale eyes were sharp but warm.

"I wish there was something I could do. I sometimes forget how privileged I am. This nation really is in a terrible state right now." She sat on the corner of her desk and folded her arms.

Timori nodded and withdrew his handkerchief.

"I'm sorry, I must seem like a dully." He wiped his eyes and blew his nose. "I don't know what came over me. It's just...everything."

"You're no dully, Tim. I can't begin to imagine what you've been through. To be honest, I've heard a lot of rumours, but you know how rumours can be. You can talk to me...but you must have friends like Jacoby you can speak to, instead of an old spinster."

The comment made Timori chuckle.

"You're no spinster if I'm no dully. I appreciate it, really, but I should go and speak with Doctor Ruveldi before he leaves for the afternoon."

"Yes, you should," she nodded.

"All right," Timori agreed, leaving before his emotions decided to get the better of him again.

Doctor Ruveldi's classroom was in the same wing as Miss Tricchio's, but up a long staircase on the third level, in the coldest part of the entire school. Although the weather wasn't as uncomfortably hot as the heat wave the previous year, Timori was still grateful for the cool hallways of the old prison complex during the warmer months. There were many things about the school he would miss.

Doctor Ruveldi's classroom, number 313, was closed, but he could hear his engineering teacher's rough, sardonic voice carrying through the door. Timori realized it was *his* class in there, sophomore engineering. He didn't want to embarrass himself further for the day by entering in the middle and making a scene, so he listened at the door.

"...isn't just about crystals. Engineering is the human art of sculpting our world to suit our own comfort. Yes, crystals are a big part of that, but so is stone, and wood, and any other kind of resource we can shape and craft. Engineering is about an understanding of science: physics, alchemy, biology, geology...the more we understand the natural world around us, the more we can manipulate it. For that is what makes us special. We do not adapt to our environment, as all of the gods' other creations do. We adapt the environment to suit ourselves...and in doing so, we become masters of the world around us, up to and including crystals. And should we ever completely unravel their mystery, we will become as powerful as the gods themselves."

"Why would Jova give us the crystals, then," a student said, "especially the Great Crystal, if we could eventually become just as powerful, and potentially overthrow the gods?"

"Good question, Gionta. But this is engineering class. Religion is on the other side of campus, far away from *useful* areas of learning." Timori heard some laughter through the door. "The point I am trying to make is that we are limited only by our own imagination, and that is especially important to engineering. We cannot sprout wings and fly, but once upon a time somebody discovered that certain gases are lighter than air, and thus we can build a *machine* to help us fly. So don't be limited by what you think is impossible...because all of these things we have now – motorcoaches, radios, wands, even crystal lamps, were once considered impossible, magical things."

Timori heard the bell toll from the tower.

"Remember, don't wait until the last minute to do these projects!" Doctor Ruveldi yelled. Timori could hear his voice clearly through the door, even though desks and chairs scraped against the floor as students stood up. "You have all semester, and it should take you that long to get a good grade. Don't be limited by anything but your own imagination...and gods help you if I catch you asking the senior class for ideas."

Timori withdrew from the door as it flew open and students poured out into the hallway. A few gave him odd looks –

he was the only student not in uniform – and others averted their eyes. Timori could only imagine what kinds of wild rumours had been circulating about him, along with the horrible truth. Nobody bothered to stop and talk to him, so he slipped into the classroom as the last student left.

Doctor Ruveldi was smoking a cigarette as he erased notes from the chalkboard. His ponytail wagged back and forth under his tweed cap as he wiped, and Timori had to hide his chuckle under a hand in case the doctor turned around.

"Timori," Doctor Ruveldi said. "You've got some catching up to do."

"I'm still ahead of all these dullies."

Doctor Ruveldi stopped wiping, then turned around slowly. He put the eraser down and stroked his prematurely white beard thoughtfully.

"You are. You're smarter than any of them. But I can't pass you if you never come to class."

"I was...away." Timori couldn't meet Doctor Ruveldi's eyes.

"I know." He sat down behind his desk. "You're a damn fool. Just like Julio. A damn fool blinded by a woman's charms."

"Who's Julio?"

"Never mind. Care to take a walk?"

"Sure."

Timori left the classroom with Doctor Ruveldi, and their outing took them around the perimeter of the campus. Most of the school's border was lined with elm trees, and Timori enjoyed their shade as he strolled silently with his teacher.

"I heard on the radio you had an unregistered wand. Is that true?"

"Yes."

"I'm surprised they let you go, then."

"I told them where it came from," Timori said with a shrug.

"I heard you held it to your own head."

"I did."

"And what would that have accomplished?" Doctor Ruveldi stopped walking.

"It would have solved my problems."

"For a smart kid, you're an idiot." The doctor lit another cigarette with a match.

"What?"

"You heard me. Are you going to be in class tomorrow?"

Timori's words caught in his throat. No, he wasn't going to be in class tomorrow. He was going to be picking at coal deposits in the bottom of a pit.

"That wasn't rhetorical, Stravida. I really think you might pull some dumb stunt over a girl again."

"What do you care?" Timori muttered.

"I should beat you bloody for that." He frowned and put out his cigarette. "You think I'm only concerned because you're my best student?"

"Fuck you. I have to leave Central, and all you can do is threaten me? Abyss take you." Timori began to stalk off.

"Abyss take yourself, kid," Doctor Ruveldi called after him. "Why on earth would you leave this? This is the best opportunity you'll ever have! Is she really worth it?"

Timori wheeled around angrily.

"This has nothing to do with Racquela! I have to work, all right? My mother got fired and my family can't afford to eat! It doesn't matter how many scholarships I get unless I can trade them in for food. My whole life is shattered because somebody would rather keep a few dollars in their pocket than pay my mother. So fuck Racquela, fuck Central, and fuck you. I have no choice but to work." Fallen leaves blew past his feet as he walked away from Doctor Ruveldi.

"What if you had a choice?" the doctor called out.

Timori sighed. Why did everybody care so much? What good had Timori ever done for them?

"'What ifs' won't put food on my table."

"I mean a choice of work. One that would allow you to continue here at Central. This isn't a 'what if,' Timori, it's an offer that I'm making." He walked after Timori. "I was going to wait until you were in an academy, but clearly you need the money now and his current assistant really isn't working out."

Timori shoved his hands into his jacket pockets.

"Who? This seems convenient, bringing this up now."

"This has been in the works since last year, but if it saves you from making the biggest mistake of your life then it needs to happen now. Remember Doctor De'Barus from the conference?"

Timori felt as though his legs were numb. He looked down to make sure he was still standing.

"Doctor De'Barus the theoretical physicist?"

"No, Doctor De'Barus the trash collector, dullard. He needs a research assistant. I was going to send one of my older students for a year or two, but you'll do better. His work might be a bit advanced for you, but you'll pick it up. Mostly you'll be making his coffee, cleaning his office – except his notes, never touch those – feeding his dog, fetching his mail..."

Timori's mind wandered as Doctor Ruveldi rambled on. It seemed too good to be true. An apprenticeship with a world-renowned scientist was something academy undergraduates dreamed of. He threw his arms up in the air, releasing the tension from his body.

"...and writing telegraphs to his mother. Don't hurt yourself," Doctor Ruveldi said. "I understand the jump for joy, but you look like you just strained something. And damn me if that isn't Master De'Trini coming this way. That's odd, he's usually happy to see me..."

Timori didn't notice Joven De'Trini until the man picked him up by the shirt and shoved him against the rough bark of an elm tree. His face was red, his brows knit together in a scowl. Behind him, two large men in suits had their arms folded, watching with muted interest.

"All right, you greasy little picker," Joven De'Trini hissed, "I'll keep this simple so you can understand me. Tell me where my daughter is, or I'll cut you to fucking ribbons."

Chapter 14

The ring sat on Jacoby's desk, next to his only picture of her. Every morning when he awoke, he stared at the picture, and then at the ring.

It wasn't a great photograph of Lenara, or even a good one, but Jacoby had cut it out of the Central School yearbook so he could see her face at least twice a day. He didn't believe he would ever forget what she looked like, but the idea scared him nevertheless. She looked sad in the photo. Her smile was forced and her eyes seemed to be looking at something far away.

Jacoby began leaving a vase of flowers by the picture frame. It summoned her beauty to mind better than a lacklustre picture ever could.

The ring was a different sort of reminder. Jacoby picked up the clear band of crystal and examined it, as he had done every morning since Lenara's death. He'd worn it for Crystara, but his heart had always belonged to Lenara. He'd known it from her secret smiles in empathy class. He'd known since the Great Crystal had granted him a vision.

Jacoby stared at her picture, turning the ring over in his hand, feeling its flawless surface. He'd meant to place the ring on Lenara's funeral pyre, but he never found the courage to open his hand and let it drop into the flames. To Jacoby, the ring represented the sacrifice they had all made, a series of hearts bound together and shattered by choices both selfish and altruistic. The ring was a final reminder of a love that had never bloomed, and the lies that had made it so.

Jacoby slid it onto his finger. The crystal was clear and neutral – it didn't resonate on its own, and only the whispers of a crystal speaker could make it function as anything other than an accessory.

"Jake!" his mother hollered up the stairs. "You'll be late for school if you don't hurry! Come and eat something for breakfast."

Jacoby hurriedly combed his hair in front of the bathroom mirror and dashed back into his room to grab his book bag from beside the bed. He tore down the stairs and into the kitchen.

His mother, Katarina Padrona, was sitting at the kitchen table, peeling an apple with a knife. Jacoby's younger brother Marco wouldn't eat them if they still had skin.

"Anything for breakfast other than fruit?" Jacoby asked as he poked his head into the icebox.

"You're old enough to make yourself something," Katarina replied. Jacoby frowned. There was no meat of any kind in the icebox, or eggs.

"And yet you still peel Marco's apples for him. Why are we out of eggs again?"

Katarina finished peeling the apple and deftly cut it into sections for Marco. She tossed her silvery hair out of her eyes and began peeling a grapefruit.

"Eggs are getting expensive. Have some oatmeal. There's also rice from last night."

Jacoby moaned and rested his head on the lid of the icebox. He saw Marco coming down the stairs and stuck his tongue out at his brother. Marco, who still acted like a baby to Jacoby even though he was going to finishing school in a year, didn't seem to notice he was being made fun of.

"Your apple is ready for you, precious."

"Shiny," Marco said as he picked up a slice. Jacoby made a grimace and grabbed his own apple from the bowl of fruit on the table.

"Still scared of knives, Marco?" Jacoby asked as he bit into the deep red skin of his breakfast. "Or just too lazy to peel your own?"

"Shut up," said Marco, who never had a clever reply. To accentuate his point, he smeared his sticky hands all over the sleeve of Jacoby's shirt.

"You little picker!" Jacoby shouted as he drew back. "My clean school shirt!"

Katarina stood up and walked in between the brothers before Jacoby could give Marco a solid punch.

"Jake! Don't call your brother names like that. You shouldn't call anybody that word. We used to be miner caste, remember. Marco, finish your apple and wash your hands and face before you leave for school. Honestly, I shouldn't have to tell you to keep your face clean at thirteen years old. And leave Jake be, don't ruin his good shirt just to get a reaction."

Marco made a face at Jacoby and marched back up the stairs. "If I'm a picker, you're a bum-picker," he said with a laugh.

Katarina offered Jacoby half a grapefruit to go with his apple. "What is happening to this household? You two used to get along so well."

Jacoby shrugged and popped the whole half-grapefruit into his mouth.

Katarina made a long-suffering sigh. Jacoby giggled, then chewed the big piece of fruit twice and forced himself to swallow.

"Is that your betrothal ring?"

Jacoby grabbed his book bag and apple, heading for the back door. "Gotta go, Mom, I'm late." He shoved the half-eaten apple between his teeth, threw open the back door, jumped onto his bicycle, and tore off down the street, pedalling hard.

The quickest route to Central School from Jacoby's house on Cateli Hill was a series of winding cobblestone streets, shortcuts through alleyways, and an up-and-downhill beeline through Avati Hill Park. Jacoby referred to it as the 'scenic route,' but he'd dealt with enough morning 'coach traffic on the main thoroughfares that he knew his way to be much more efficient. On a clear day, he could make it to the school in less than ten minutes.

That morning, he dawdled. The streets and the park offered more of interest than Central School. Jacoby didn't have speaking, empathy, or history class that morning. He stopped his bike at a secluded patch of shrubs in Avati Hill Park and watched the whiteoak blossoms tumble off of branches.

He let his bike fall on one side. Stretching and yawning, Jacoby lay down in the dewy grass, staring up at the leaves and blossoms. A falling flower landed on his chest. As he breathed in its scent, he thought of Lenara. He released a heavy sigh and shut his eyes, summoning her lovely face in his mind's eye.

"Shouldn't you be in school, rich boy?"

She was peering down at him, and even upside-down Jacoby could discern a look of piqued curiosity on her freckled face. He reached out with empathy, but apart from the sense of mild interest, the girl's emotions were well-guarded. Jacoby grinned. Caution was a telling emotion, in its own way.

"I'm not a rich boy," he said. She obscured his view of the sky and the trees, but as his eyes adjusted to the glare, he was surprised to note that her frizzy, voluminous curls of hair were a gaslamp-flame orange. Redheads were nearly as rare as blondes in Novem.

The thin, slightly pug-nosed young woman pointed at Jacoby's book bag. "That's silver, there. I could sell that and eat for a week."

Jacoby glanced at his book bag, then back to the girl. He sat up to get a better look at her, realizing how wealthy he must have appeared to a barefoot girl with frayed lace on the fringes of her dress.

"I'm a Padrona," Jacoby admitted, sounding guiltier about it than he wanted to. "I was brought into the alchemist caste because of Class Act, but I grew up in Avati Valley. I'm not *rich*."

The girl was examining his bicycle. For a moment Jacoby thought that she was going to hop on and dash off with it, but she merely spun a wheel.

"That crystal ring says otherwise," she pointed out. "Maybe you grew up in the valley, but it don't mean you're poor now."

"Why does it matter?" He propped himself up on an elbow and secretly admired the girl's backside.

She shrugged. "I'd be making the most of my schooling if I was in your shoes. Heck, I'd have shoes, even."

Jacoby raised an eyebrow. She was laying it on rather thick. He reached out with his feelings again and discovered she was experiencing a contradictory mixture of attraction and revulsion, as well as a bit of fear. Jacoby didn't imagine she was afraid of him specifically, which made him wonder if she was planning on stealing something from him.

"I don't have any food," he said as he stood up.

"Didn't ask for none."

"So what do you want?"

She gave a nonchalant toss of her hair and put her hands on her hips. "Just tryin' to figure out why the gods would give a lazy, spoiled boy like you such privilege when so many people in this city are starving."

"The gods have nothing to do with it." Jacoby rolled his eyes. "It was a political decision, and my father worked really hard to be chosen for it. The city is starving because of a drought and a depression. Blame *that* on the gods."

"Some of us are wise enough not to blame them for anything." The girl flashed her teeth in an aggressive grin. Jacoby noticed an odd sheen coming from her mouth when she spoke. *Is that...a crystal tooth?* he wondered. *Whoever this girl is, she's not what she's pretending to be.*

"And some of us are wise enough to see through façades," Jacoby replied. He shouldered his book bag and grabbed the handlebars of his bike. "If you'll excuse me, I'm late for school."

She stood in front of his bicycle and put her hands over his on the bars. Her look was predatory. "And what do you see, when you look at me?"

Jacoby was so startled he completely forgot to examine her emotions, or guard his own. Her eyes were a murky brown, as difficult to read as the rest of her. He decided to try and throw her off guard in return.

"I see a pretty young liar." Jacoby didn't really think she was that pretty, but he figured it was a good tactic.

"We see what we want to see until we learn to look deeper." She let go of his hands and looked at him sideways. "And I think you're just as much of a liar, *Padrona*. Nice to meet you, rich boy." She dashed off through the shrubs.

"Wait," he found himself saying, "I didn't catch...your name." She was gone. "What in the abyss was that?" he wondered out loud.

Jacoby couldn't stop thinking about the strange redhead, all the way to Central School. By the time he parked his bicycle on the rack by the west entrance, he was no closer to deciding what exactly she had been after.

Jacoby avoided the interior of the school, where hall monitors would be watching for students who skipped classes. He cut through the narrow pass between the original deepstone prison and the brick expansion where most of the science classes were held, and into the outer courtyard to check the big clock that had been added to the old bell tower.

He was late for his mathematics class, and trying to sneak into the classroom held potentially worse consequences for him than simply not attending at all. Jacoby didn't care much for math and he wouldn't need it for his academy studies as a crystal-speaker. *One missed class won't hurt me*, he thought. He'd been through enough in the past couple of weeks that he decided he deserved a break.

Jacoby opted to remain in the courtyard, close to the clock, and wait for the bell that indicated the end of first period. He lay down in the grass, using his book bag as a makeshift pillow, and closed his eyes. His mind began to wander, and he daydreamed about an exciting, passion-charged rendezvous with the fiery stranger he'd met in the park.

As he lay there with his eyes closed, he heard footsteps approaching through the grass and caught a whiff of cigarette smoke.

"Get up," a deep voice said. "We have things to discuss."

Jacoby opened one eye and regarded Paulo, who managed to somehow seem collected despite his dishevelled hair and an un-tucked shirt.

"What do you want?" Jacoby asked.

"I asked you to get up." In spite of Paulo's looming, aggressive stance, Jacoby could feel nothing from the boy but the usual chilly demeanour.

"What for?"

"So you can look me in the eye and tell me you haven't been spreading lies."

Jacoby blinked. He'd told Timori his suspicions regarding Paulo and Racquela. Timori must have already confronted Paulo about it. Jacoby stood and smoothed out his shirt.

"I've spread no lies. I mentioned a suspicion to my best friend."

"Well, maybe you should check your fucking facts first before you accuse me of anything." He prodded Jacoby's chest with a finger. "I'll pick you apart if you try something like that again."

Jacoby stood his ground, though he knew he stood no chance against Paulo, who was long on reach and short on fear.

"It was a gut feeling," Jacoby said, "nothing more. No harm done."

"Fine," Paulo said. "Maybe you can use those gut feelings to help us find her, then."

"Find whom? Crystara? She's..."

"You really are a dully, aren't you? How can you call yourself her friend when you don't even know she's been kidnapped?"

"Kidnapped?" Jacoby felt dizzy suddenly. "Nobody told me anything! What happened?"

"I still don't know all the details, but they've been talking about it on the radio all morning." Paulo lit a fresh cigarette. "Tim was accosted by Joven De'Trini just this morning. I guess Racquela's old man assumed Tim was the one who sent the ransom note."

"Why would Tim kidnap Racquela?"

Paulo shot Jacoby another condescending look. "You dully. He almost killed himself over her. It's not a stretch for anyone to believe Tim would crack. However, Joven De'Trini is simply distraught and not thinking clearly. This kidnapping is obviously politically motivated."

"Obviously? What if it's just somebody after the money?"

Paulo shook his head. "As part of the ransom, they're asking Joven De'Trini to step down as head of the Alchemists'

Guild. Plus the sum they're demanding is ridiculous...a fortune. It would shatter the family's clout *and* their finances."

"What's Master De'Trini planning on doing?"

Paulo took a pull from his cigarette and waved his hand about emphatically before he answered. "If I knew, I wouldn't be here, now would I? The man has the resources to find her, but he and I have never met, and now would be an...inappropriate time for such an introduction."

Jacoby eyed Paulo suspiciously. He couldn't help but hear Lenara's warning in his head. *He doesn't care about anything except for his empire he wants to build.* Jacoby twisted the ring on his finger absentmindedly.

Paulo ran a hand through his curls and sighed. "Are you even listening? We have to find her before her father does. He's playing it careful and safe, but men in a desperate situation will do brutal things to her to try and force Joven De'Trini to pay up."

Jacoby's heart sped up. The gravity of the situation was beginning to occur to him. If Racquela truly was kidnapped, it would be all over the news. Her very life was in danger, and she was one of the last friends Jacoby had left.

"Did you say 'we'?" Jacoby looked into Paulo's cold, deep blue eyes. Although Paulo's manner was placid and confident, as always, there was a hint of something there, below the surface. Jacoby couldn't tell if it was concern for Racquela, or a longing for friendship from a boy who didn't know how to behave like a human being.

"Yes. Timori is scouring the slums for clues as we speak, but he's not an empath or a speaker. Racquela will be well-hidden."

Jacoby sighed. He refused to budge for Paulo, but Racquela was a different story.

"What can I do to help?"

"Come with me to the meeting tonight. I've been meaning to recruit you for some time. Speakers are hard to come by, especially considering the laws surrounding registration."

"I'm helping you so that we can save Racquela, not join your political revolution."

Paulo put out his cigarette and smirked. "You may not realize it yet, but the goals are one and the same. It's all linked, these events happening here in Captus Nove. A socialist revolution would be devastating to a wealthy noble family like Racquela's, but if we rescue her we can get the De'Trinis on our side and save the family from ruin at the same time."

"Is her rescue just a political manoeuvre to you?"

Paulo's eyes narrowed. "Once, it might have been. She's a friend."

Jacoby's empathy revealed nothing new to him.

"Where is the meeting?" he asked.

Paulo pushed his hair out of his eyes. "It's in the slums. I can pick you up in my motorcoach."

"The valley."

"What?"

"It's called the valley, not the slums."

"Fine, whatever you say."

"What am I supposed to tell my parents?"

Paulo rolled his eyes. "Really, Jake. You're dabbling in back-door politics and secret rescues and you're worried about a curfew or something? Grow some balls. Tell them you're spending time with Timori. Tell them it's for school. I don't care, just meet me at Timori's house right after dark."

Chapter 15

Racquela struggled, but they held her firmly by her arms and legs. She could not scream. The foul-tasting rag in her mouth muffled any cries.

"Hurry up," someone whispered. Door hinges creaked and boots clomped upon a wooden floor. Racquela saw a rat scurrying across a rafter.

"Get out of my pickin' way," said a deep voice. Another door was opened. Racquela ceased struggling and tried to think clearly. She had been kidnapped. Her father would ransom her back. They wouldn't dare hurt her, or Father and the police would show no mercy.

"Bind her." It was the same deep voice. "And tie that gag proper. Can't have her hollerin' and alert the whole street."

She was hauled into a room and put on her feet. A candlelit table and chairs were in a corner. Leaning against a chair was a longwand with a crimson crystal trigger. Racquela felt her legs buckle, but the men were holding her up by her shoulders as they bound her wrists with rough rope. She winced as the hemp chafed her flesh.

"She'll scream sometime." The voice was right in her ear. She could feel hot breath upon the back of her neck as a knot was tied in the rope. "Gotta take out that gag to feed her."

"Feed her? We're barely eating as it is."

"This plan don't work too well if she dies, Bartus."

A fist came flying past Racquela's face and she flinched. Someone fell to the floor behind her.

"You throw names around like that again, dully, and an empty stomach will be the least of your troubles. 'Sides, she looks like she could stand to go hungry a few days. Fuckin' nobles make me sick. Whole nation is starving and there they are up on the hills getting fat."

Racquela could see the door – it had been left ajar. She wanted to make a run for it but her legs wouldn't move, wouldn't stop shaking. She prayed to the gods they wouldn't hurt her.

"She ain't fat, just looks like she eats regular." The third voice was nasal, almost whiny.

"Shut up and get her snotty, crying face out of my sight. She can scream 'till the Great Crystal shatters down in the cellar."

The gag was tightened so that it pulled at the corners of her mouth and she made an involuntary cry of pain. The hand that pushed her forward was gentler than she expected.

"What if she tries to dig her way out?" The nasal voice was in her ear this time. His question was met with dark laughter.

"With her hands tied? She'll be diggin' a long time. Maybe it'll teach her what it's like to be a picker."

The burly man called Bartus pulled a metal ring on the floor and it lifted a panel. Racquela saw a rotted ladder and darkness beyond.

"Hmm-mmm," Racquela pleaded, shaking her head.

"How's she supposed to climb down there with her hands tied up, boss?"

Bartus shook his head. "Yer all a bunch of dullies." He lifted Racquela by the shoulders, as effortlessly as though he was picking up a sack of feathers, and lowered her into the cellar. Racquela shut her eyes. *Gods no, please, I don't want to die in a hole without sunlight, please...*

As soon as her feet touched the soft earth, the cellar door above her slammed shut.

In darkness, she crumpled to the ground and wept. A distant voice in her mind told her that her dress was becoming dirty. Above, muffled voices spoke in excited tones. When boots clomped above her, she could feel the dirt and grit falling into her hair. She heard a chair being dragged across the floor.

After a time, the voices stopped, but her weeping did not. She cried through innumerable prayers, asking every god she could think of to come and help her, promising to be faithful, promising to make sacrifices to their altars, if they could just send Father or Paulo or Timori and Jacoby to come and rescue her.

Her eyes gradually adjusted to the darkness. Above, the cracks between the beams of the floor allowed tiny slits of candlelight to trickle down into the cramped cellar. She awkwardly pushed herself to her feet and glanced about. The cellar appeared barren except for a series of wooden beams likely once used as shelves.

Racquela tried to pull her wrists apart. The knot in the rope held, but felt somewhat loose. She could still pivot her wrists. She didn't suppose her captors would be pleased with her if she unbound herself, but she didn't relish the idea of being constantly uncomfortable, either. She struggled with the rope until it chafed, then stopped and slumped down again against the wall of hard-packed earth, defeated. She could think of no way to escape her predicament that didn't involve a direct confrontation with her captors. She didn't know how to fight, or even shoot a wand. More tears streamed down her cheeks. She wondered what Crystara would do and sobbed even harder. She would have traded all of her wealth just then to be a crystal speaker.

Moments passed. Boots clomped upon the floor upstairs and muffled voices spoke in harsh tones. Racquela's bonds held, and she curled up in a corner.

**

Racquela awoke shivering. She didn't know what time of day it was, but she certainly didn't feel well rested. Above, she could hear her captors speaking.

There was a loud creak and light spilled into the cellar from above. Bartus poked his head down and shot Racquela a greasy smile. Racquela screamed and backed into the opposite corner from the cellar door.

"Evening, m'lady. I've your supper here." He waved a heel of bread at her. It looked as though it had been chewed already. "But 'round here, kids sometimes gotta beg for their meals. This ain't the fancy hill yer from. So if you want it, yer gonna hafta get on yer knees and ask real nice."

"Stop it," a voice said from the room above. Racquela didn't recognize the tone. She thought perhaps it was someone new. "Just give her the bread already."

Bartus stood up. "You gonna make me?"

"She's not here so we can torment her."

"Is that what you think?"

"She needs to be fed. Or you can find out what happens when we try to ransom a corpse."

"She ain't gonna die if we don't feed her fer a day." Bartus casually dropped the chunk of bread into the cellar. Racquela didn't dare approach for fear of drawing his attention.

"No, but it will likely take De'Trini a while to gather the funds."

"And she'll beg eventually. Even a noble's daughter ain't stupid enough to starve to death instead of asking for bread."

"If we treat her like dirt, then we're no better than they are."

"And them treatin' us like dirt for thousands of years...I guess that means nothin' then, huh?"

The voices grew quiet. Racquela crept forward by inches, perking her ear toward the cellar door.

"The longer you continue to fulfil their expectations, behaving the way a 'dirty picker' is seen to behave, the longer our climb out of the pits will be."

"How dare you..."

There was an explosion of shouting as boots clomped and scuffed across the floor. They were all yelling over each other to be heard. There was a loud crash, and it sounded as though the table had been knocked over. A hush fell over the room, just as suddenly as the din had begun.

"So you're going to shoot me, now?" It was the unknown speaker. Racquela could hear his voice quavering.

"Bartus, put the wand down," the whiny voice said.

"No. You all need to see. You can talk 'em to death an' still they won't give. This is the only thing those daisy-chasers will ever unnerstand. Crystals an' gold an' gems. The stuff we pick out of the earth and they take. You can shout at 'em in the forum all you want. The only things they'll ever respect are caste and crystal."

A pair of boots clomped across the floor and Racquela heard a door slam. Above her, a collective sigh of relief released itself.

"You okay, Ramus?" the nasal voice was wondering.

"Y-yeah. Just irked. Resisting the urge to sock him one."

As they spoke, Racquela examined her meagre dinner. The chewed end had a light coating of dirt. Racquela was contemplating the indignity of eating with her hands tied behind her back when someone started coming down the ladder. She squeaked like a mouse and retreated to the corner.

"I apologise for his behaviour," he said, adjusting his glasses. "My name is Ramus." Racquela couldn't see his face too clearly, but he seemed young. She was relieved it wasn't Bartus, but that didn't stop her heart from pounding like a marching band drum. "There is no need for such uncouth behaviour, even though you are still technically our prisoner. The rest of us here intend to treat you with dignity and respect."

"Thank you," Racquela said. It was a breath above a whisper. She flinched as he approached her. To Racquela's surprise, Ramus began untying her bonds. She was evaluating whether or not she could overpower Ramus and flee before Bartus returned, but then she remembered the longwand leaning against the table, and the third man with the nasal voice.

"We really don't have anything else to offer you to eat," Ramus continued as he coiled the rope in the palm of one hand. "But I should probably get you some water. It really is the other essential thing."

As he climbed back up the ladder, thoughts of water made Racquela realize she had to pee. *Gods,* she thought, *of all the degrading things. Please let them have plumbing.*

Not knowing when her next meal would be, she took a tentative nibble from the clean side of the bread. It was so stale her teeth had trouble biting into it. When she finally tore off a nearly tasteless chunk, her mouth was so dry she began to cough. Suddenly she was hacking up the morsel in a most un-ladylike fashion.

A raised voice upstairs made her stop mid-cough. Her eyes began to water.

"What is that? A mug of water? And you untied her? Well, aren't we just a fuckin' hotel now."

"The rope is pointless," Ramus countered. "She can't escape. And she'll die a lot sooner without water than food." A hand reached down into the cellar, holding a big metal mug. "Plus it's cheaper than wine."

Racquela furtively grabbed the mug of water, gulping it down. It was warm and had an odd aftertaste, but it soothed her throat. She left a little bit in the bottom of the cup to help her wash down the rest of the horrible bread.

"Oh, we were going to offer her wine? Well, why don't we just escort her home while we're at it?" The cellar door slammed shut.

"Shatters," Racquela muttered. She'd forgotten to ask Ramus about the water closet. She wouldn't dare knock on the cellar door and ask for anything for fear of Bartus's belligerent retribution, but she really did have to pee. She didn't have the guts just then to wonder what she was supposed to do when *other* problems arose.

Racquela stared at a vacant corner of the cellar. It did seem to slope down in that direction, and she supposed there was a lot of dirt around.

"Gods, let this be the last indignity," she prayed quietly. She reminded herself she still had all her fingers, and she hadn't eaten any rats yet, and her father was coming to rescue her.

Chapter 16

"Have you thought about moving out?" Julio asked Drago. They had passed several foreclosed properties on their way to the Southron Market.

"Thought about it, yes," Drago said, nodding. "But it's not a good time. I'm staying for now, to help with work around the house and the rising cost of...well, everything." He laughed. "I was going to buy a motorcycle, have you seen those around? Cheaper than a 'coach, faster, they look really shiny. It's pretty much just a bike with a crystal motor. I could afford one on an officer's wages, but it'd be pretty selfish when Mother and Father are struggling to make ends meet."

Julio shrugged out of his coat and folded it over his arm.

"I didn't realize Ralfi's factory was having trouble."

"He doesn't talk about it, but he's almost had to shut it down twice. Nobody's buying clothes, except for the rich."

"You're lucky you went into the academy when you did."

As they approached the market, Julio could hear shouting. His heart sped up and he hoped it wasn't another riot breaking out. Beside him, Drago appeared either blissfully unaware or completely unconcerned. It sounded as though people were chanting in unison. Not a riot, then, Julio decided, but a demonstration of some sort. He wondered which political faction was organizing it.

In Fishmonger's Square, where Wharf Street met the Southron Market, Julio and Drago discovered the source of the chanting. A great crowd had gathered about the statue of Adolpho Bosso, the famed Noven explorer, and were chanting together:

"Cast down the castes! Cast down the castes!"

As they walked by on the fringes of the crowd, Julio noticed a number of police officers posted at each roadway. Many of them shuffled nervously from foot to foot, playing idly with their batons or their wands. Julio shook his head. If a riot erupted, there weren't nearly enough of them. A few were probably considering the wisdom of the chant.

"Glad I'm off duty," Drago yelled into Julio's ear. Julio shot Drago a look of surprise.

"They call in the army to deal with demonstrators?"

"We're on standby. In case the pickers riot."

A lone figure had climbed onto the base of the statue. In his hands he held up a large plank of wood, painted with a bright red pickaxe. Julio instantly recognized it as the adopted symbol of the Labour Party.

"The republic promised us real change after the fall of the empire," the handsome, aging man on the statue was shouting above the crowd, "but what have they done? They sat by as the depression swept through this country, and we the so-called 'lower' castes were the first to suffer! But up there on the hills, they still eat their fill as we sweat and break our backs and fight each other over the scraps they leave us. Jobs and food are getting more and more scarce, but they have us all blaming each other! They are just like the imperial opportunists they overthrew! But we will stand together, and when the time comes to elect change, the Labour Party will ensure that all are equal!"

"Thoughts on Labour?" Julio asked once they had left the square.

"Angry shovellers asking for handouts," Drago remarked.

"You don't think any of their grievances are legitimate?"

"What the shard is the government supposed to do? Ask the sky to start raining and end the famine? Ask the Council of Nations to reverse the Rundia Accord?"

"You don't suppose the root issue is a disparity of opportunities between the upper and lower castes?"

"No. People are given options to change their caste. You got an education. Mother married into the merchant caste. I became an officer. If you don't want to dig in the dirt, you'll find a way not to. Why, you think a bunch of socialist pickers should be running our country?"

"No, I believe the republic is doing the best that they can. However, if the Labour Party rallies around Barto and he earns legitimate seats in Parliament, it means the people are being properly represented."

"Bah." Drago turned down a side-street, hoping to find a shortcut through the crowds to the market. "They should do it like the military. Leadership based on aptitude, not popularity."

Julio cast a sidelong glance at Drago.

"The upper echelons are all nobility," Julio remarked. "In politics *and* the army. They happily sent us off to die, you know...the nobles had a whole lot to profit and very little to lose. If Novem ever goes to war again, it's men in your position who pay the price."

"Better a war than us fighting each other," Drago countered.

Julio didn't know what to say. *Did you forget your father died fighting a war? Have you noticed I'm a deformed cripple because of scattershot? Why did you join the military, Drago? Do you see your father as a hero, or did you do it just to piss off Ralfi? He tried so hard to make you like him, but you're the spitting image of Pietro, inside and out.*

The streets grew more crowded as Julio and Drago approached the Southron market. The motorcoach traffic ended as they reached a boardwalk, and shopkeepers eagerly shouted offers to anyone who would listen.

"Can't think of a tactful way to disagree, can you?" Drago said as his eyes darted about the crowds and storefront signs.

"You and I have different thoughts about the military."

"Do you think our nation would fare better without one?"

"No, national defence is necessary, but..."

Drago stopped in his tracks and pointed a finger at a series of empty patio tables on the boardwalk. "This is the place." He led Julio over to a table and held out a seat for him. "I'll go inside and order. Do you want anything?"

"A coffee would be nice."

Drago disappeared into the café. Julio leaned back in the wicker chair and watched passers-by with disinterest. Reaching into his inner jacket pocket, he withdrew a crumpled pack of cigarettes and lit one with his crystal lighter, an old gift from Roberto. He was amazed the tiny orange sparker crystal still functioned perfectly after so many years.

Drago returned with two cups of coffee and set them on the table.

"I thought you ordered food," Julio remarked.

"Takes time to make it, dully."

"Dully? How many books about Noven history have you published, hmm?" He sipped tentatively at his coffee, but it was too hot.

"How many crystal-speaking exams have you taken? They don't just hand out that extra bar on my epaulettes."

Julio took a long drag on his cigarette and held the pack out for Drago. Drago accepted one with a smile and borrowed Julio's lighter from the table.

"You know, it's funny." Julio scratched the bald side of his head with his hook. "Your father used to tell me that speaking was just a knack, that it had nothing to do with study." *There, that's an easy segue into a touchy subject,* Julio thought.

"You really do think I'm a dully." Drago played with the lighter, making the crystal spark by tapping it with a finger. "I figured it out a long time ago, you know."

"Figured what out?" Julio took another small sip of coffee.

"That you're my father."

The coffee in Julio's mouth ended up all over the table. He coughed and sputtered as Drago leaned back in his chair, a smirk of satisfaction on his face.

"What?" Julio wheezed.

"Hey, I know Pietro was a real guy. But it doesn't make any sense. I've seen the old pictures of you and Mom. I know you were together before the war."

"And during most of it," Julio added.

"Exactly," Drago said before finally lighting his cigarette. He waved it about excitedly as he spoke. "She never knew Pietro. There's no evidence to suggest it. He was a part of *your* company. He came from down south."

Julio scratched his chin. *You could use this. Better your influence than Ralfi's. Pietro has been gone for years and you've been as much a father figure to Drago as anybody else...probably more than Ralfi in some ways.*

"See, you're not even trying to deny it. I pieced the rest of it together. You were here on leave, and then she thought you died when the Commonwealth rolled through Nilonne. So she married Dad...my foster dad."

"Well, there's actually more to it than..."

A wide-shouldered young man in a white apron emerged from the café, carrying a loaded tray. He set down a bowl of tomato soup, a salad, and a grilled sandwich in front of Drago, as well as cutlery and a napkin.

"Thanks, Ben," Drago said. "Got a minute to sit?"

The young man named Ben shrugged and took a seat next to Drago. He looked over at Julio several times as Drago began to attack his meal. Julio offered Ben a cigarette and watched as the boy's eyes darted to his hook no fewer than five times. Ben lit his cigarette and continued to stare.

"So, Ben..." Julio began.

"Ah, sorry," Drago interrupted. He wiped his mouth with his napkin. "Beneto, this is my father, Master Julio Vellize. Julio, this is my friend, Beneto Di'Costa."

Before Julio could correct Drago about his lineage, Beneto offered his right hand and just about grabbed Julio's hook. "Whoops," he said, and switched to his left hand. Julio found the boy's handshake somewhat limp.

"So," Beneto said as Drago went back to his soup, "it's nice to finally meet you." He seemed to be trying to look Julio in the eye, but his vision wandered to the burned side of Julio's face several times. "I didn't realize you were a scholar as well as a factory owner."

Julio shot Drago a reproachful look, but the young officer was busy devouring his salad and didn't look up. "Ah...you must be thinking of Drago's legal father, Ralfi Andari. He owns the clothing factory. I'm the scholar. I teach history at Central School."

"And you write books," Drago added, his mouth full of salad.

"Quite right," Julio said. "So, Beneto...do you own this café?"

Beneto scratched his neck and flushed slightly. "Um...no. I run it, I suppose. My family owns it....that is to say, my mother."

Drago chuckled. "But she lets him do all the work. I'm telling you, pally, you should come to the academy. Let her run this place again."

Beneto's eyes flashed back to Julio's scarred face, then his hook. "Thanks, Drago, but I don't think the military life is for me. My father died in the war." He continued to stare at the pronged piece of metal protruding from the sleeve of Julio's jacket.

Drago shrugged and pushed away the empty salad bowl. "There's no war right now." He started on his sandwich.

"That doesn't necessarily mean the peace will last forever," Julio reminded him. As Julio finished the last of his cigarette, a woman in a wide-brimmed hat who sported more than a few jewels on her fingers and wrists wandered past their table. Drago found something to look at other than his sandwich, and his eyes followed her posterior as she walked into the café.

"Excuse me," Beneto said as he left the table.

"Why did you tell him I was your father?" Julio asked.

"Because you are, you said so just a minute ago."

Julio could feel his eye twitching. "You didn't let me finish. Why would your mother lie to you about something like that?"

Drago shrugged. "Probably because it was easier for her." His mouth was full of bread when he spoke. "Abyss, I mean, she didn't even tell me anything about Captain Garus until a few years ago, when I started asking questions. She didn't have a lot to say about him, though. Then I started wondering about why you were always coming around, wanting to spend time with me."

Because you're the last little piece of him left, and he was still my friend despite it all. Because it's an excuse to stay close to Ramona. Because I didn't want you to turn out like that weasel Andari.

"Your silence says it all, Dad." The last of Drago's sandwich disappeared in two quick bites.

Julio stared at the pigeons that were pecking at the crevices among the cobblestones. *Ramona doesn't have to know. And why*

123

not? I've been closer to the boy than anybody else except for his mother. Pietro was just a biological father. With Drago's talents, maybe I could convince him to go to a real academy for crystal-speaking instead of a military one...

"Master Vellize? Gods, don't go opaque on me or start crying just because I called you 'Dad'."

Julio shook the string of thoughts away and came to a decision. "I'm fine, Drago. Just...struggling with the truth, is all." He regarded Drago levelly. "Your mother cannot know about this."

Drago's expression was a study in nonchalance. "Fine by me. She lied to me about this for my whole life."

"Well, then," Julio said as he pushed himself to his feet with his cane, "let's be off."

Drago stood and brushed the bread crumbs off of his clothes. "Hang on, I need to say goodbye to Ben and get a better look at that dame. Where are we going?"

"Wherever the wind takes us, my boy." Julio took in a deep breath and paced about in a circle, twirling his cane. The pigeons scattered. "Life is too short to spend sitting around a café smoking."

Julio's smile must have been infectious because one was creeping onto Drago's lips.

"Hey, want to go look at motorbikes?"

Chapter 17

The wind whipped through Jacoby's hair as he sped down the cobblestoned street in the chilly autumn twilight, and he realized he should have brought a jacket. It was far too late to return home and grab one. He needed to make it to Timori's house by dark. He didn't care so much if he disappointed Paulo, but his worry for Racquela overrode all other possible concerns.

His parents had discussed Racquela's disappearance with him over dinner – apparently the story on the radio was all they could talk about – and Jacoby forced himself to be strategically tight-lipped. Paulo remained unmentioned, of course, but Jacoby's parents were more concerned that Timori was somehow involved. Jacoby assured them Timori was as worried as anyone.

It occurred to Jacoby as he turned onto Corti Street and continued on into the valley that he was lucky his parents had even let him leave the house. The implications of his acquired nobility were still playing themselves out, and it had taken all of Jacoby's charm and subtlety to convince his parents there was nothing dangerous about taking his bicycle down to Timori's in the dark.

The stars were out by the time Jacoby veered his bicycle onto the narrow street where he had once lived, right next to Timori. In the dim crystal lamplight, the drab green of his former abode seemed grey, and he shivered. Crystara's father still lived there.

Timori was exiting the door that led to his family's apartments just as Jacoby approached the front steps. Jacoby carefully leaned his bicycle against the brick wall and shoved his hands into the pockets of his slacks.

"Hey, pally," Timori said as he buttoned up his trench coat. "Didn't expect to see you here."

"I thought Paulo might have told you," Jacoby whispered. "I'm coming to help get Racquela back...and to keep my promise to you."

A look of relief played across Timori's features. "I could use you at my back, pally. Being at these NSP meetings is like being put into a cage with a bunch of bears."

"Why did you even join?"

"It was the money, at first," Timori admitted. "It still is, but now it's also about equality. It's like my eyes have been closed my whole life, shut tight because I refused to see the fact that the world treats us – miners, that is – like dirt because they know how important we are, and how much things would change if we were all on equal footing. The nobles have been living off of us for centuries."

"What would that mean for Racquela's family, though?"

"Her father is still the head of the Alchemists' Guild." Timori strolled toward Corti Street. "They'll be fine."

Jacoby raised an eyebrow but said nothing. He heard the guttural hum of a crystal motor at the end of the narrow lane, and hurried to catch up with Timori. As they stepped into the soft blue lamplight, Jacoby noticed a motorcoach parked across the street. He could make out Paulo's hard-cut jaw outlined above the steering wheel. Paulo waved a black-gloved hand at Timori and Jacoby and rolled down the window. A fresh cigarette was between his lips.

"Good of you both to come," Paulo said out of the corner of his mouth. Smoke billowed about his face as he spoke, and with his eyes shadowed by a dark felt fedora, he looked altogether sinister.

Timori said nothing, but opened the passenger door and stepped inside to sit beside Paulo in the front, which left the back seat to Jacoby. Paulo began to drive. Jacoby let his thoughts

126

wander as he watched the crystal streetlamps pass him by, and tried to keep his heart calm.

"No sign of her, I imagine?" Paulo inquired. He was still speaking out of one side of his mouth, and the cigarette smoke was filling the interior of the motorcoach.

"I don't know what else I should do," Timori admitted. Jacoby's heart went out to his friend. Timori sounded desperate. "Unless I want to start knocking on every door in the valley asking if they're hiding a kidnapped noble. Besides which, if we find out where they've taken her, I'm going to need another wand."

Jacoby's ears perked up. *So he got the first one from Paulo?*

"Relax, Tim, I have wands aplenty. I'm loathe to part with another one, considering how the last one ended up in the hands of the authorities..."

"I gave them a dead end," Timori replied. "I told them I got it from Crystara, and she's in the hands of the church. The inspector let me go."

"Even so," Paulo replied, "that was a pretty casual abuse of the trust we've built."

Jacoby clenched his jaw and maintained his silence.

"It was a mistake, I agree," Timori said. They were driving on a narrow street close to the docks. The scent of the sea intermingled with the smoke in the vehicle.

Paulo shifted in his seat. "I just don't get it. What's the use of holding a wand to your own head? Take that frustration and *use* it." He gestured with one hand while he held his cigarette in the other. Jacoby watched the steering wheel with wide eyes, but the motorcoach drove straight despite the indifference of the driver. "A wand is power. It's the ability to change your situation, tip the scales. We're on the brink of a social revolution. All of these troubles you're having now will change once the party is in control and this antiquated system is torn down."

"That doesn't magically win Racquela back." Timori stared out the window.

Paulo sighed and tossed his spent cigarette out onto the road. "We're here," he announced as he pulled the lever to shut off the engine. He withdrew a crystal key from the dashboard and pocketed it.

Jacoby exited the motorcoach. They were parked in front of a large dockside warehouse on a dirt street. The dim glow of gas lamplight peeked through the boarded-up warehouse windows, and Jacoby heard the muffled sounds of voices over the nearby roll of ocean waves. Paulo strode casually up to the unmarked door and knocked, slowly, five times in succession.

"Password?" a voice called from the other side of the door.

Paulo cleared his throat. "Minor nobles, major miners."

"That was last week's," said the voice.

"Just let me in, Sal. It's Paulo. I don't have time to remember the godsdamned password every week."

The door creaked open just over a finger's width, and the barrel of a wand poked through the crack, gleaming in the moonlight.

"Password's there for a reason, Paulo. Who's that?"

"A friend," Paulo replied as he shoved open the door with no regard to the wand. The short, sallow-eyed man named Sal stepped back with an appalled look, but allowed Paulo entry. Paulo beckoned for Timori and Jacoby to follow him inside. Jacoby eyed Sal warily, who seemed to be eyeing him up in return.

Within the warehouse, a table and chairs had been arranged in the dead centre, and a cluster of nine men huddled about an old gas lamp, muttering over some papers. Many of them were smoking, and the haze drifted above them in lazy tendrils like a fog obscuring their hushed rendezvous. Unmarked crates were stacked neatly in the corners of the vast room. Jacoby could only guess at their contents, but judging by the smell he surmised that many of them were filled with fish.

The men had a ragtag, rugged appearance, and many of them were bald or had graying hair. Jacoby felt uncomfortably young all of a sudden.

Paulo lit a new cigarette and approached the table. Timori walked alongside him, seemingly comfortable with the warehouse and its occupants. Jacoby could tell from an empathic reading that Tim's confidence belied a deeper nervousness, but there was a good deal of mistrust circulating about the room, and Jacoby was trying to keep his own hesitation in check. He pictured a pack of wolves clustered about the table, jaws slavering as they sized him up like a piece of meat.

"Who the fuck is that guy?" somebody muttered as Jacoby approached.

"Jova's sake, it's another one of his schoolyard pallies." The man pinched a cigarette between his thumb and forefinger. His yellowed smile did not reach his eyes.

"Actually, Dante, he's a crystal-speaker," Paulo replied. Somehow he had made his voice sound deeper – it seemed to reverberate off the walls. Although Jacoby could feel varying degrees of emotion – some were respectful, some felt nothing but loathing – nobody seemed unaffected by Paulo. Even as a boy of sixteen, he exerted his presence well.

Paulo gestured for Jacoby to approach, and he could feel all eyes upon him. Jacoby timidly stood on Paulo's other side and tried his best to look assertive, but not *too* assertive. How odd it must have seemed, he thought, for a trio of finishing school boys to be so involved in underground politics. More inscrutable still was Paulo's involvement with the group. *Do they know who he really is,* Jacoby wondered, *the way that Lenara knew?*

Dante blew smoke at Jacoby's face. "He's a kid, just like you. No way he's a pickin' speaker yet."

"Not a registered one, no," Paulo admitted. He seemed perfectly relaxed as he leaned on the table and stared at Dante, challenging him with his eyes. Jacoby was amazed at Paulo's placidity. His own heart was pounding in his chest.

"Which works to our advantage," Paulo continued. "Only a registered speaker can be traced."

"The school will have him registered." It was an older man who spoke, his voice calm and level. Beneath a tweed cap, his eyes were hard and shrewd.

"Registered, yes." Jacoby was surprised to hear himself speaking. His voice was shaky, but he knew he was in far too deep to simply make a run for the door and pretend he hadn't seen anything. "But speakers are traced through their resonance pattern, and mine hasn't fully developed yet. I won't pretend I'm as skilled as a fully licensed speaker, but if you need one, I'm familiar with the basics."

"It's better than nothing," a man agreed. He adjusted his glasses and peered at Jacoby. "Unless someone can convince a registered speaker to help us after the crackdown, which I highly doubt."

"So what, we're trusting the revolution to a bunch of schoolboys? Shatters, I'm about to join the Labour Party if this is where we're headed."

"By all means," Paulo replied. "We'll all miss you, Dante." He pointed at the door. "Sit around with a bunch of miners with no political or military expertise and talk about how you're going to *outvote* them."

Dante leaned in, but Paulo, who was a good few inches taller, seemed unthreatened.

"Oh yes, please, let's hear about how a sixteen-year-old boy knows everything about staging a coup," he challenged.

"I think I've already proved my mental capacities far exceed yours," Paulo replied. "And in case you've forgotten, my uncle is bankrolling all of this. His interests are mine, and this revolution goes nowhere without his help, I'm sure you can all agree." He gestured to the other men about the table. "We have age and experience here. I bring money and ideas to the table, and so far they've worked out well. If I happen to bring other young minds, eager to share their thoughts and skills, who are you to say otherwise? There's the door, if you've decided the National Socialist Party should be exclusionary..."

One of the men coughed in the silence as Dante and Paulo stared at each other across the table. The man with the glasses broke the silence.

"Paulo has a good point, Dante. We need all the help we can get, and the very foundation of socialism is strength through unity."

"Right, we should all just let him do what he wants because of the banker," Dante spat. "Without even voting as to whether or not to let in a kid nobody knows or can trust."

"This is a brotherhood," the old man in the cap said. "All are welcome. Besides which, we could use a speaker, and I'm sure we can ensure his loyalty. Paulo has provided invaluable resources to this endeavour, and he's careful enough not to bring a spy into our midst."

The last part sounded like a threat to Jacoby, but again Paulo appeared unfazed. *So he's not their undisputed leader,* Jacoby mused.

Dante sat and folded his arms, defeated. He glowered at Paulo, but said nothing more.

"It looks like nobody else will be joining us tonight," the old man continued. "We might as well get started with the meeting, then. There's a lot to cover, and we must initiate the newcomer."

Jacoby winced at the mention of 'initiation,' but there was no hint of malice or deviousness in the older man's voice.

"Start us off then, General," the man with the glasses suggested.

General? Jacoby thought. He wondered if it was merely an NSP title, or some kind of honorific made in jest.

"We might want to ask this young lad if he has a name, first," the General replied as he looked pointedly at Jacoby. Jacoby pulled up a chair.

"I'm Jacoby Padrona," he said. Several eyebrows were raised at the mention of his surname. "Thank you for allowing me to be here. I hope I can help your...our case. Novem could use some changes."

"A Padrona?" Dante muttered. He glared at Paulo. "You brought a 'Class Action' kid here?"

The man with the glasses rolled his eyes. "Enough already, Dante. If he's a Padrona it means he grew up in the valley. Besides which, his father might have influence that could assist us."

"It's an issue for later," the General cut in. "Let's just get to the meeting for now."

Jacoby settled into his chair and tried to calm his heartbeat using slow breaths. Timori glanced over at him several times with a reassuring smirk as the meeting got under way.

Jacoby expected raised voices and chants of freedom, coupled with intense discussions of how best to take Parliament by storm, but instead most of the meeting centered on finances, philosophy, and the printing of manifestos. Paulo added his voice liberally, but Timori and Jacoby remained silent. As the talk moved from a list of wand and crystal inventory to spies' reports from around the nation, Jacoby began feeling out with his empathy to try and discern the dynamics among the members of the National Socialist Party.

The General appeared mostly dispassionate, even when voices were raised over matters of socialist philosophy. The man with the glasses, whose name was Faustus, appeared to vehemently support the ideas of brotherhood and compromise within the group, and more than once steered the discussion back on track when arguments began. Dante spent most of his time sulking, and when he did speak up it was usually to protest something someone else had said. Paulo seemed to speak when it suited him, adding his voice when the discussion merited input. Jacoby could feel his tension, knowing he was waiting to bring up the subject of Racquela's rescue. Mostly Paulo raised his voice when the castes or money were being discussed, and Jacoby got the distinct impression he and the general were in unspoken agreement about many things.

Once Faustus had run through his stack of papers, the General leaned in and looked at Jacoby. "Well then, let's get to that initiation. The oath must be taken." One of the younger men brought two bottles of wine up from under the table and began uncorking them.

"Not just yet," Paulo interjected. "I have one more item to discuss. But let's pour the wine, certainly. I have an idea that could bring us a lot of influence."

"Gods, another opaque scheme," Dante groused.

"Is this why you brought the speaker?" the General inquired.

"Yes and no," Paulo replied. He lit a cigarette and grabbed one of the bottles of wine, drinking straight from the bottle. "I've been meaning to bring him in, regardless. No, this is a delicate matter that, handled properly, will set us up nicely, adding to our influence and wealth...and quite a bit of an edge when the time comes to move."

"Just spill it," Dante said.

"Very well." Paulo grinned. "I'm sure you've all heard about how the Labour Party kidnapped the heir to the De'Trini fortune and has made demands of Joven De'Trini."

"There's no proof it was the Labour Party," the General countered. "What exactly are you suggesting, Paulo?"

"It doesn't matter if there's proof." Paulo leaned back in his chair and put his well-polished shoes upon the table. "What matters is that if we rescue her, we can frame whoever we want and discredit the party. They're gaining influence daily. If we can bring them down a peg *and* garner the favour of one of the most influential men in Captus Nove – not to mention one of the only nobles sympathetic to the lower castes – it will put us much farther ahead of schedule, and keep an important man in our debt. He owns a good share of this city, and I shouldn't have to mention that his brother is a member of Parliament. Gentlemen, this could be the swing that shatters the rock, so to speak."

"*If* we can rescue her," the General said. Despite the reservations, Jacoby could feel a palpable sense of excitement floating about the room.

"I'm thinking this could get us all thrown in jail, or worse," Dante said. "Besides which, how in the abyss would we even find her if the authorities haven't managed it yet?"

"Leave that part to me and my friends," Paulo replied. He took another generous swig from the bottle of wine. "If it makes you feel secure, General, the NSP doesn't have to devote many resources to this...maybe just a few crystals...and if we fail, we'll disavow any link to this group."

The General scowled beneath his cap, but Jacoby could discern a sense of intrigue building between him and Paulo. "There is no guarantee this will make Joven De'Trini a friend to the NSP, even if you succeed. Which I doubt. Wherever she is, she's hidden well, and I'll bet you five dinari De'Trini will break before the kidnappers do."

"You're on," Paulo said with a smirk.

Chapter 18

After Teddori's promise to take him to the city, Leo's behaviour became as clear as crystal. He performed his chores without reservation or complaint. He offered to do extra work in order to stay on Renalda's and Teddori's good sides. He didn't pick any fights.

Bernardo and the other boys didn't make that part easy for him. They all knew he wanted to go to the city, and they were jealous because Teddori wasn't supposed to pick favourites. Bernardo called him 'fatty friend' and teased him mercilessly. Many of the boys refused to play with him.

Leo put up with it. No matter how badly he wanted to squish Bernardo's nose in, he was certain that would ruin his chances. Every time Bernardo walked by and punched him on the arm or stole his toys, Leo reminded himself of Teddori's advice: 'true courage is the ability to overlook the pain in order to achieve something greater.'

Or so he'd interpreted the words.

Spring was giving way to summer at the orphanage. In the sunny south of Novem, nestled in the hills and far away from the ocean breezes, the little valley of farmland along the dirt road that led west into Captus Nove would bake. The younger children liked to run around naked in the fields, screaming and hooting as they played kick the can or tag. They would wrestle in the dry heat until they wore a second skin of dirt, and it would be washed away in the evening to reveal flesh turned a livid lobster-red by the sun.

Leo was too old to run around naked. He didn't know his exact age, but Teddori figured he was somewhere around eight years old. In the summer, the older boys worked the farmland fields about the small orphanage and fed the chickens and goats, and the older girls tended to the vegetable gardens and the orchard. The children around Leo's age were given all the odd chores, keeping the house clean, and carrying tools or buckets full of water.

Sometimes they got to pick fruit and berries. It was everybody's favourite chore, because they knew they could stuff themselves on olives and strawberries if they were stealthy about it. It was an exciting exercise in subtlety – the older girls were always supervising, and a telltale smear of red around the mouth could lead to getting smacked. Food at the orphanage was always rationed out carefully, and the lion's share was taken to the market in Captus Nove to be traded for other necessary goods, such as fabric for clothing and coal for the stove.

That day, Leo steeled himself and vowed not to eat a single thing until dinner. The other children could gorge themselves on whiteberries or plums all they liked. Leo would be travelling with the first orchard harvest to the summer festival in Captus Nove with Teddori and the older children. It was worth more to him than all the fruit in the world.

Dona, the oldest girl in the orphanage, told Leo he'd be picking juniper berries for the day. Leo smirked to himself. Juniper berries tasted awful. He couldn't imagine why grown-ups would ever eat them, but Teddori took them with him to the market every year. Leo's task meant there would be virtually no temptation. He happily skipped over to the juniper bushes that lined the low stone wall bordering the orphanage and the next farm over.

All about him, the orchard was a bustle of activity. The smaller children chattered excitedly as they picked berries from the smaller bushes that framed the trees of the orchard. The older girls were up in the trees, sending the younger ones to the smaller branches to collect plums, peaches, apples and olives. Dona stood at the edge of the orchard with her hands on her hips and watched the children like a bird of prey, ready to swoop in and strike if she caught anybody sampling berries. There were baskets all about in the grass, and once they were full the bigger boys would carry them off to the house to be prepared for the journey by wagon.

Leo's heart skipped a beat as he approached the bushes. One more day and he'd be off to the city.

Leo began stripping the bushes, and he let his mind wander into imaginative scenarios of big adventures in Captus Nove. His thoughts turned to wild chases through the streets – soldiers were attacking and Leo had to stop them with a special crystal wand he'd found – and the plot grew more and more grandiose until he was proclaimed the new Emperor of Novem for saving the city singlehandedly.

"How come you get to go?"

Leo looked up from the branch he was stripping. It was Bernardo, standing before him, arms folded. Leo turned his attention back to the bushes, standing protectively between Bernardo and the half-full basket of juniper berries.

"How come you get to go and I don't? I've been here longer than you and I'm older. You're just a rock-kissing dully."

"You're supposed to be helping," Leo said as he picked a berry and dropped it into the basket.

Bernardo shoved him and the berries in his hands scattered across the grass.

"Tell me, you dully." Bernardo's fists were balled up and his face was red. "Why do you get to go?"

Leo shrugged. "Teddori invited me. You have to ask him why."

"Teddori's a big fat dirty dully!" Bernardo exclaimed as he gave Leo another shove. This time, Leo nearly tripped over his basket. He turned to face Bernardo, and he could see out of the corner of his eye that a few of the children were watching them, including Dona.

"No he's not," Leo said as calmly he could manage. "I'm not going to fight you. So go away."

Bernardo pushed him again, with greater force. Leo's arms flailed like spokes in a wheel and he fell. He tried to grab onto the bushes for support, but his hand slid roughly along the branches and he twisted as he fell, landing face-first into the basket of berries.

He'd smashed his head against the corner of the basket and his eyes were stinging from the juice, but what hurt the most was that when he pushed himself to his feet, face drenched and coated in crushed berries, the other kids burst into laughter. A smug smile was widening upon Bernardo's lips.

Before Leo could walk away, Dona stalked over with a reproving look on her face.

"You two were fighting," she accused, "and you wrecked the berries and a basket. Do you know how much those are worth?"

"Bernardo did it!" Leo shouted. He could feel his face heating up under the pungent juice that had stained it. "I didn't even touch him. He just pushed me until I fell over."

"I don't care who did it," she said, "you're both in trouble."

Leo let out a pathetic squeak. "Do I still get to go to the city?"

Dona rolled her eyes and threw up her hands. "I don't know and I don't care. Probably not. Go wash your face, you horrible child, and stop being such a whiny little monster."

"I am *not* whiny." Leo insisted. He bit the inside of his lip to stop the tears from coming out as he stormed off toward the river to clean up.

"I'm telling Teddori that Leo ruined the berries," Leo overheard Bernardo say to Dona.

"I don't give a shard," Dona replied. "Do it and then get back to work, you lazy good-for-nothing."

Leo turned his head to see Bernardo dashing off in the direction of the house. Leo rushed off as fast as he could go in the direction of the river, then circled around once he was out of sight of the orchard.

Bernardo was a little bit taller and had a longer stride, but Leo was flying like a wraith out of the abyss and had nearly caught up with his quarry just outside the back door of the orphanage. Bernardo threw open the door and began shouting Teddori's name. When Leo came up the steps, Bernardo slammed the door in his face. Leo was moving so fast he didn't see it coming.

Everything went red. There was a ringing noise in Leo's ears, and his head, chest, and knees were all throbbing. He opened his eyes to see Teddori swinging open the back door. Then the red at the corners of his vision turned to black, swallowing everything in sight.

When Leo awoke, he was abed in the boys' common sleeping room, and bright light spilled in through the windows of the room to warm his bare chest. There was a cool cloth upon his forehead and his pants had been rolled up past the knees. Deep purple and green bruises were forming above his kneecaps.

There were voices outside his door. Leo sat up and winced as the pounding in his head grew stronger. He pushed down the nausea, removed the cloth from his head, and crept across the floor, avoiding the creaky boards and the pain in his knees. He pressed an ear up to the door.

"It's your own fault, Ted. Playing favourites with the children like that." The voice was unmistakeably Renalda's.

"Well, I certainly didn't mean to. I thought maybe a trip to the city would inspire him. He's bright, you know. He could be a priest one day if he wanted. Think about how few opportunities these children have to make something of themselves. Dona still believes some nobleman will sweep her off her feet, and the boys who don't stay to work the farm won't even be welcomed into the miner caste. They'll be treated like the *Dori*."

"You're too soft," Renalda accused.

"Well, what am I supposed to do? This month I witnessed a complete transformation in him."

Renalda snorted. "I don't know why you have such a blind spot for him. He's bloodied up more than his share of noses since he got here."

"Boys fight."

"Not like him they don't. That farmer beat the kindness out of him, and everyone but you can see it. If you really care about the boy, you need to punish him properly when he's bad."

Teddori uttered another sigh. "He's going to pitch a dirty fit if I renege on my promise."

Leo's heart sped up. They couldn't do this to him. He'd been so good, and then Bernardo wrecked it all, and Renalda hated Leo. She'd always hated him.

"Of course he will. But you have to be firm or he'll be walking over you for as long as he lives here. And then he'll get out into the real world and learn what happens when he tries to take advantage of someone with money or status. He'll earn his trip to the city, same as everybody else."

"You treat me as though every choice I make is foolish."

"Only the ones you make with your heart."

Leo heard Renalda's footsteps clunking down the hall, and he dashed back over to the bed. As the door creaked open, Leo pretended he was just waking up.

"Leo...how are you feeling?" Teddori was wringing his hands.

"My head hurts," he said. He briefly considered feigning amnesia, but then he wouldn't be able to defend his own innocence.

Teddori walked up to the bed and knelt down, despite the obvious difficulty it caused him. "You took quite a fall there. Why were you chasing Bernardo?"

Leo took a deep breath.

"He was going to tell you that I crushed the berries, but the only reason I crushed them was because Bernardo pushed me and I fell into the basket and I didn't even push him back because I was being good, and I've been good for the whole time like you told me so that I could go with you to the city, and ..."

Teddori held up his hands in an attempt at a calming gesture. "All right, Leo. Slow down. The trouble is most of the other children are saying you pushed Bernardo first. Except for Sofia."

"That's because they all hate me." Leo folded his arms and looked away. He wouldn't cry, he told himself, he *wouldn't*. Crying was for babies and girls.

"They don't hate you," Teddori insisted, "but perhaps their resentment of you lately has been my fault. That being said, for the sake of peace in the household, we might have to hold off on taking you into the city."

Leo sat up in bed, red-faced. "But I've been good! I was good that whole time and you said! You said if I behaved that I could go, and you can't go back on a promise!" He was crying then, tears spattering the old yellowing linen sheet. "I didn't do anything bad! Bernardo was trying to get me into trouble because he hates me, and everybody is ganging up on me, and you promised, Ted, you promised..."

He couldn't bear to be seen, wailing the way he was. Leo buried his face into the sheet on his bed and sobbed. Teddori put a hand upon his back but he shrugged it away.

"What a crybaby," said a sneering voice from the doorway. "Shatters, Leo, it's just a visit to the city."

"You've caused enough trouble today, Bernardo," Teddori said in a voice Leo hadn't heard him use in a long time.

"Leo's the troublemaker," Bernardo insisted.

Leo was off the bed like wandshot, charging at Bernardo. Bernardo had braced himself against the wall and put his knees and arms up defensively, but Leo didn't care if he hurt himself, so he barrelled into Bernardo with all of his weight, taking an elbow in the eye and a knee in the gut. He didn't feel a thing save for his own fury, and as Bernardo toppled to the ground, Leo landed atop him.

Teddori was shouting at them to stop, but Leo drowned out the voice with his own wordless screaming. He had Bernardo by the hair and was slamming the side of his face into the floorboards. Bernardo punched and kicked, desperately trying to gain leverage, but the blows felt like soft glancing shots to Leo.

"Renalda!" Teddori shouted. "Help!"

"Ted, get him off me, he's cracked," Bernardo pleaded just before Leo knocked a tooth out of that sneering face with a downward blow of his fist. Bernardo made a coughing, sputtering sound as dots of blood speckled the floor. Leo refused to let up, pounding on Bernardo with a flurry of hammering punches. After a few more hits, Leo wondered why Bernardo had stopped fighting back. He sat up, panting, and looked down at Bernardo's bloody face.

Streaks of red were smeared across the floor, and a pair of incisors were lying side-by-side near Leo like two downed soldiers, immobile and drowning in blood. Bernardo's eyes were shut, but he was breathing. Satisfied with his victory, Leo stood and looked at Teddori.

A look of pained horror was written on Teddori's face, and he clutched at his chest with his right hand. His left arm appeared to have gone limp, and Teddori's face was so white he looked like a puffy mallow-sweet in clothing.

"Lee...Leo," he gasped. He seemed to be having trouble speaking.

"Ted?" Leo said in a small voice.

"Geh...get...guh, guh, get reh..." His face became a rictus of pain and he collapsed upon the floor. Leo rushed over to his massive form, unable to discern any possible way to assist the man. He wasn't bleeding and nothing was broken, at least on the outside.

"Renalda!" he shouted. "Renalda, Ted fell down! He's hurt real bad!"

Leo didn't know if Renalda could hear him or if she was too far away somewhere, helping with the summer harvest. He didn't hear any footsteps coming down the hall. He locked eyes with Teddori, but the man seemed unable to respond. All he could do was gasp and clutch at his chest. Leo gripped Teddori's blazer with his bloodied hands and wept.

"Be brave," he whispered. He didn't know if he was saying it to Teddori, or to himself.

Chapter 19

Crystara walked up to her mother's bed. It was taller than she remembered. She could barely see over it. The whole thing was draped in blankets upon blankets, all white. A candle was burning on the bedside table, bathing the room in a solemn glow. A hand was on her shoulder. Father's. She shrugged it off and climbed up onto the bed.

It didn't smell like Mother at all. It smelled like vomit and rotten flowers. Crystara curled up her nose when she hugged her mother, burying her face in brittle white hair that was once gold and flaxen. She could feel the bones in Mother's neck.

"Crystara, my darling little girl," Mother said. "You're getting so big. I can't even lift you."

"And you're getting smaller, Mama," she remarked. "Maybe I will be bigger than you someday."

Mother coughed when she laughed. Crystara spied some green mucous on the bed sheets.

"You will be so many wonderful things," her mother agreed.

"Should you be holding her so close?" Father rumbled. "We still don't know why you're sick."

Crystara bounced on her mother's knee. "We know damn well why. Why do you have to take the pleasure out of everything?"

"You're not going to die, Maria." His voice was thick with emotion, insistent.

"Largo," she replied. Her voice sounded frail but there was an edge to it, the sound of something defiant and proud. "The doctor can do nothing. My crystals can do nothing. You need to face it."

Largo hit the wall so hard Crystara thought his arm would go right through it. It didn't, but he'd left a deep crack where his fist had been.

"Face what?" he demanded. "That you're giving up? On yourself, on us? On Crystara? You need to fight back."

Maria played with Crystara's hair, threading her bony white fingers through it. "Can we not fight in front of her, please? With you it's always about conflict. I'm dying, Largo, and there's nothing you or I or anyone else can do. I just want to spend some time with my little girl while I still can."

"Fine," said Largo. "You always cared more about her than me anyway."

Maria's mouth narrowed into a thin line. "If you were any kind of father, you would feel the same way."

Largo was up next to the bed quicker than Crystara expected. She was between them as he held Maria's throat in his hand.

"Go ahead, Largo," she wheezed. "Hit a dying woman. I'm sure it'll make you feel *much* better."

Crystara heard her father begin to cry, which made *her* start to cry. Father never cried, ever.

"I just...feel so *powerless*," he said. "And I don't know what to do."

"Shh," Maria replied. She was stroking Crystara's hair as she kissed Largo on the forehead. "There's nothing you *can* do, Largo."

Largo stood up and looked away. "Fuck," he said as he wiped away tears. "I'm weeping like a woman. Weak. I have to go, Maria."

"Where are you going?"

"Working. Somebody has to feed her."

"Working the mines?"

"Working." He slammed the door.

The room was silent except for the sputtering of the candle and Largo crashing around downstairs.

"Crystara, my sweet," Maria said. "Be a dear and fetch that light crystal from the drawer, would you?"

"Okay, Mama."

Crystara clambered off the bed, letting her legs slide down until she touched the floor. The drawer in the bedside table was level with her eyes, and she had to pull with both hands to open it. Standing on her tip-toes, she could just barely peer into the opened drawer. It was cluttered with papers, and a bottle of ink had broken and spilled, staining an entire corner of the drawer blue. Near the back of the drawer, a sleekly carved piece of darkoak sat, with a trigger fashioned from a crimson-coloured crystal. Crystara knew better than to touch *that*, so she grabbed the light blue crystal that sat beside it.

She climbed back onto the bed and presented it to her mother.

"Very good, my dear. Can you activate it all by yourself?"

Crystara closed her eyes tightly and whispered the old Noven word for 'light.' She opened her eyes to behold a shining light crystal in her palm. Mother kissed her hair.

"You are such a gifted little girl. I wish..." Tears started to stream down Maria's face.

"Mama, why are you crying?" Crystara asked. She wiped the tears away with her hands and gave her mother a kiss on the lips. "Is it because Daddy was yelling?"

"No, dear. It's because I won't get to see you grow up to be the beautiful, talented, and strong woman I know you will become." Maria withdrew a crystal pendant that hung from a chain around her neck, round and polished and deep indigo, and held it out for Crystara to look at. "This will be yours when I'm gone, Crys. You must keep it safe. Someday you may need its secrets."

"It's very pretty."

"Yes, it is. But it's not for you to show off to people, understand? It's a secret, just between you and me."

"Okay, Mama."

Mother began coughing again, hacking until she was curled up, blankets pressed against her face. When she pulled the sheets away, Crystara could see they were stained with blood and mucous. Her vision began to swim.

***

When Crystara awoke she was alone and sunlight spilled in through the window. Her face and arms were warm despite the lack of blankets. Her ring finger was bandaged, and it pulsed with a dull throb. She vaguely remembered being brought by De'Cadomus to the temple infirmary after they had sealed an agreement regarding the library.

The muffled sound of footsteps came from beyond the infirmary door and Crystara froze. She let out a breath as quietly as she could and searched outward with her thoughts. All she could feel was a guarded presence. Crystara shot up to her feet just as De'Cadomus entered the room.

The pockmarked old priest stood in the doorway and narrowed his eyes at her.

"I see you made it through the night," he said.

Crystara crossed her arms. "You sound disappointed. But if you really wanted me dead, you would've left me in that cell."

"I can put you back if you miss it."

"I dare you," Crystara shot back. "You need me for something, or you wouldn't bother with the cursed ring or anything else. You've made sure I can't leave the temple or communicate with anybody other than you, so why all the secrecy?"

De'Cadomus smirked. "You're bright, but you're impatient," he said. "We've only just started working together."

If you can call it that, Crystara thought. *I'm your prisoner, not your employee.*

"You know, I can hear you when you project like that. In any case, we..."

De'Cadomus stopped himself mid-sentence as the din of a commotion outside came to his attention. Someone was shouting very loudly. Crystara peered out the window, but the noise was coming from beyond the outer wall of the temple.

"Stay here," he said in a gruff, urgent voice. "Until I return."

Make me, Crystara thought, but she didn't dare say it. The pain the crystal ring could cause her was still very fresh in her mind. To her surprise, De'Cadomus dashed out of the room without even shutting the door. Crystara walked tentatively up to the doorway, and heard De'Cadomus shuffling down the hallway faster than a man his age had a right to.

Crystara hesitated. She didn't want to be punished for following the keeper. However, he was moving so quickly Crystara doubted he would spare a glance backward. In the end, her curiosity won. If something had De'Cadomus excited then it could prove to be important. With trepidation, Crystara padded along on bare feet, swift and silent like all the times she'd visited her mother's room while her father had been passed out on his old armchair.

A pair of priests came down the hallway behind Crystara and she fell in step with them. She left her mouth hanging ajar, deciding she might as well play the part of the idiot mute. Nobody would pay her any mind, and De'Cadomus wouldn't *dare* activate the ring with witnesses around.

By the time Crystara reached the Great Hall, a large crowd of priests and sisters had gathered in front of the main foyer of the Old Temple. De'Cadomus had made his way to the big whiteoak doors and was blocking them, along with several familiar-looking men in their traditional armour. Their white robes were topped by a steel breastplate set with crystals of varying colours along the shoulders, close enough to whisper at. The knights flanked De'Cadomus, and although their ornate (and horribly outdated) swords were still within their jewel-encrusted scabbards, it was clear they were there to stop the members of the temple from investigating the commotion.

Through the whiteoak and marble, Crystara could hear the muffled sound of angry shouting, then the din of someone banging a fist on the door. Incredibly, whoever was on the other side was shouting so loudly his words could be heard clearly, even through the thick planks of whiteoak.

"Give me back my daughter, you fucking rock-kissers!"

Crystara's chest felt tight. She knew her father's booming voice anywhere.

"Call the city guard, Your Clarity," one of the priests suggested.

De'Cadomus shook his head vehemently. He scanned the crowd and his eyes rested upon Crystara. She felt her dread double.

"I do not want an incident right outside the temple when the city is in such a state of fervour," De'Cadomus insisted. "All it would take is the blood of one dead miner on those steps for the pickers to go into a frenzy. We're treading the red. I will deal with the man and his dull followers just as soon as you all disperse back to your duties." His words began to spill out frantically. "Leave a keeper to his tasks and look to your own. A whisper or two and he'll forget why he was even here."

Crystara's stomach churned and her legs were shaking. For as long as she could remember, Largo had convinced her she was worthless, yet there he was at the door.

"It must be Crystara's father," a nearby priest muttered to a Sister of Solitude. It was odd for Crystara to hear her own name, but her friendship with Keeper Orvin had been well-known within the temple.

"He can yell until he's hoarse," the sister replied. "That brat murdered the good keeper in cold blood and cracked the Great Crystal. Her soul must have been spat back out of the abyss – she's not even worth the rope we'll hang her with. Curse her once for her blasphemy, and twice for leaving us with De'Cadomus."

Crystara bit her cheek and clenched her fists. *It was an accident,* she wanted to scream, but she knew drawing attention to herself at that moment would be tremendously foolish. She forced herself to remain calm as Largo Mita continued to rail upon the doors with his fists and the priests and sisters milled about, refusing to disperse.

So why aren't the knights just going out there and dealing with Father? she wondered.

"I said disperse!" De'Cadomus shouted. "This is the Church of the Great Crystal, not a democracy! I speak for the gods."

Mumbles and grumbles were heard, but the gathered crowd began to leave the Great Hall. Crystara felt a hand grip hers.

"Come along now, young one." Crystara looked up to see a pudgy Sister of Solitude. From a scan of her thoughts, Crystara discovered the woman's name was Florenza. "We'd best do as he says."

Reluctantly, Crystara left the hall. She was desperate to know what kind of confrontation would occur between De'Cadomus and her father.

I hope they kill each other, she told herself.

Crystara resigned herself to following along silently, content for the moment to be away from two people who made her sick to her stomach. They walked through the Crystal Hallway where the portraits of the keepers were kept. Crystara stared at the floor as she walked. She could only imagine the reproving look she would see on the face of Keeper Orvin as he looked down from his portrait.

Crystara... It was a whisper, barely audible, right when she passed by Keeper Orvin's smiling face. She looked up at Florenza, but the older woman plodded along humming a tune. Crystara wondered if she was finally cracking from all that was happening.

Crystara...come to me. The whisper had become stronger, and was unmistakeably reverberating in her mind. Crystara didn't know how to reply, or if she even could. *Who are you?* she thought. She tried to project it outward, away from herself. Beside her, Florenza continued to walk down the hallway, oblivious.

Crystara. The voice had become more insistent, and a shiver ran up Crystara's spine. With a sense of dread, she realized where she'd heard a voice like that before. As she passed by the great whiteoak doors that led to the innermost chamber of the Old Temple, she scowled.

Glaring at the doors that led to the Great Crystal, Crystara promised herself she would finish what she had begun.

"Come along now, young one," Florenza said as she squeezed Crystara's hand tightly, "that room is not for the likes of you and me."

De'Cadomus appeared before them so suddenly that Crystara suspected he'd used a yellow whisper.

"There you are. You're supposed to be cleaning the floors, not listening to the hens clucking. Come with me." He grabbed her arm. Crystara roughly shrugged him off.

"Be nice to the poor girl," Florenza scolded. "She's just a simple thing. There's no need to be forceful."

"If I wanted advice from a lowly sister," De'Cadomus said with a huff, "I would ask for it." He turned to Crystara. "Follow me, if you can manage that much."

Crystara let go of the sister's gentle hand and followed De'Cadomus wordlessly back to the Keeper's Tower. She warily entered his sanctum.

"Close the door," he commanded. She did so. He stood and grabbed a large set of keys from his desk. "I have a new task for you. Before you protest, it's one you won't mind so much." He grabbed a crumpled set of papers and handed them to Crystara. "And here is the letter from your friend Racquela."

Crystara tensed. De'Cadomus' shift in attitude was alarming. She began to wonder what sort of game he was playing at. Did he realize now how much he required her cooperation?

Crystara held the letter protectively to her chest. "What happened to my father?" she asked.

"I told you not to follow me."

"Too late for that now. What happened to him?"

"He was subdued and placed in prison for disturbing the peace. If there are no more questions, we have work to do."

Chapter 20

Interrogation Transcript
Sexta 21, 1895
Subject: Largo Mita
Interrogators: Inspector Franco Martinus, Detective Captain
Caius Mazotti
9:34 A.M.

D.C. Mazotti: Who do we have next, Ariela? (unintelligible; cannot hear Ariela from typing booth) Mita? (expletive deleted) You ready for this one, Frank? He's dangerous, even tied up. But he knows stuff, he's got

Inspector Martinus: I've read Mita's file before, sir.

DC: Right. Ok. Tell the boys to bring him in, Ariela. And tell them they have to stay for this one. Wands trained on the back of his skull. Got it? (speaking to IM again) Think he might know anything, then? Since you're apparently an expert already.

IM: About the De'Trini case? Tough to say. His ties to the Labour Party are strong, but we don't know it's them that took her, yet. There's a loose connection to the family through the daughter, Crystara, the one the church is hanging. The one the miner kid said gave him the wand he just about blew his brains out with.

DC: I don't buy it, but she's untouchable right now. Maybe Mita knows something. His Noctra connections, possibly?

IM: Maybe. But there's no motive to give that kid a wand. Plus De'Trini's been paying off the Noctra for years. They don't chip away at the whitehands without a good reason.

DC: Maybe he gave them a reason. Him or the Noctra could have had a political shift.

IM: Not De'Trini. He knows how to always come out shiny, and the Noctra wouldn't risk losing their connections through him. Could be motivated by politics, money or personal reasons...but I don't think the Noctra fit. Sir.

DC: Fine, so I guess we have to ruffle Mita enough to get it out of him.

IM: If he even knows anything. He don't squawk easy when you pull his feathers, though. Regardless, if he ain't connected to this case, he might know something about the Labour Party's plans. Or the NSP.

DC: I told you to cut out the NSP dirt, Inspector. You're chasing ghosts.

IM: If you say so, sir. But I have (interrupted by Ariela)

DC: Better step back a bit. Bring him in.

Officer Valachi: Sit in the chair.

Largo Mita: (expletive deleted) you.

DC: Have a seat, Largo. We can do this the easy way or the hard way.

LM: I'll take the hard way, 'Liza.

IM: Cigarette, Largo?

LM: Sure. Just (expletive deleted) the routine, clear?

IM: You willing to cooperate?

LM: Didn't say that.

IM: Fine. Just tell us what you were doing on Crystus Hill the morning of the 20th.

LM: (expletive deleted) dullards, I already told you what I was (expletive deleted) doing there. Cut the dirt and tell me what the (expletive deleted) you want to know.

IM: You were there to try and retrieve Crystara. (Martinus waits for a reply from Mita. No answer.) Who is scheduled to be hanged in...three days? What I don't understand, Largo, is why you went alone and banged on the front door. Why call attention to yourself when you could have spoken to De'Cadomus directly? Or asked your Noctra pals to.

LM: (expletive deleted) check your file again, bright guy. Noctra don't (expletive deleted) with the church, the viper ain't no friend of mine, and sneaking in would have sent both me and the kid through the orange.

IM: But you know De'Cadomus.

LM: Oh, is that what it says on my file? Well, why don't you let me see it so I can (expletive deleted) enlighten you?

IM: You had ties to him through your wife.

LM: Mention her again and I'll (expletive deleted) your (expletive deleted) face before you can say pull.

DC: Ok, give us a minute, Frank.

IM: Fine. (Inspector Martinus leaves the room)

DC: Not trying to tread the red with you, Largo. The inspector is digging in the wrong tunnel there. I get it. You wanted your daughter back and none of your connections were willing to cross the church. You thought that if you made a scene, the Labour Party protestors would riot and you could storm the church while they loot it. Am I along the right alignment there?

LM: I said to (expletive deleted) the (expletive deleted) routine, didn't I? You 'Liza act like this is the first time I've been in here. Tell me what you want to know, and tell it clear. Your cells are looking full down there, Cap, what with all the protests. So I'm guessing you're keeping me here because you want info. I want out. So tell me what the (expletive deleted) you want to know and quit wasting my time.

DC: Ok, you got a deal. Tell us what you know about the De'Trini kidnapping and we'll get started on negotiating your release.

LM: (expletive deleted). Is that what this is about? Yeah, she was friends with my kid, but that's it. I was in here when I heard about it, dullard. Some Labour Party protestor was going on about the whole thing, so maybe you should bring him in here. Or bring in those boys who knew her, that whole stupid betrothal group. It was one of them or it's someone trying to squeeze dinari out of De'Trini. Or a vote, but probably the dinari.

DC: But you were seen in the same plaza where it happened, a mere day later.

LM: Because nobody spends time on Crystus Hill, you (expletive deleted) dullard. I told you why I was there. Now let me go, or you'll find out what happens when you dig in the wrong tunnel and piss off a miner.

DC: Just one more question, Largo.

LM: Fine.

-------Section Deleted-------
As Per: Detective Captain Caius Mazotti
Badge #3357
Crystus Hill District Police
-------Section Deleted-------

```
DC: Bring Frank back in here.
IM: So?
DC: No connection to the De'Trini case,
but I'm going to hold him a while longer.
You missed quite a show, Frank.
IM: Yeah, I saw Tony's nose. Did you
ask him about Noctra and Labour movements?
DC: Nah, he was too worked up. I'm
saving him for you.
IM: Think I should bring either of
those kids in? Stravida or his friend?
DC: Don't bother, Frank. They're just
kids, doing stupid (expletive deleted). I
don't think they're involved in any of this.
```

***

"So what's our plan, exactly?" Timori asked as he sifted through the contents of the crate. Jacoby peered over his shoulder and tried not to blow cigarette smoke into his friend's eyes.

Paulo blew a perfect smoke ring and flicked his cigarette into the river. "We find out where Racquela is being kept. We paralyze their crystals and get her out of there. The authorities take care of the rest."

Timori pulled out several large, clear crystals and laid them down on the bank of the river in the dark.

"Oh, sure," he said. "It's all that simple. We don't know where she is, and have no idea where to start looking if the police haven't found her yet. We have a student-level crystal-speaker, and we could go to jail if we get caught using crystals without a license. Oh, let's not forget that this plan could fail outright if Jake can't align these properly."

"Thanks for the vote of confidence," Jacoby muttered.

"Jake will be fine," Paulo insisted as he leaned up against his motorcoach. "He just needs some practice with this particular alignment. In the meantime I'll be contacting some informants to see if they've discovered anything."

"Doesn't the NSP have the same informants?" Timori asked.

"Hah!" Paulo's grin was mirthful, but his eyes looked black in the dim moonlight. "The NSP is just one part of this revolution...it's so much bigger than just them."

Timori rummaged around in the bottom of the crate and withdrew the remaining few crystals, each small enough to fit within a closed fist.

"That's it?" he asked. "No wands?"

"Not yet," Paulo said. "We'll have them when we need them."

Jacoby shivered as the autumn breeze passed over the Avati River. He'd never even held a real wand before. He couldn't imagine pointing it at somebody.

"When we need them?" Timori echoed.

"After what happened to the last wand I lent you, the NSP is nervous about any kind of distribution. I have other sources, however."

"Your uncle?" Timori asked as he began carefully placing the crystals back in the crate.

"Among others. I have my own collection, you know."

Jacoby helped Timori load the crate into the back of the motorcoach, then he clambered in beside it.

"How soon can we do this?" Timori asked as he climbed into the passenger seat and shut the door.

"As soon as we know where she is," Paulo replied as he fit the crystal key into the dashboard to start the engine. "I'm expecting results within a day or two...I have some very reliable informants in the slums."

"Let's hope we're not too late," Timori muttered darkly. Paulo said nothing in reply, but backed the 'coach away from the riverbank and onto Corti Street to take Timori home. Jacoby let his thoughts wander as the 'coach made its way down the silent, lamp-lit street.

She could be anywhere, he thought. *How are Paulo's 'informants' going to know? Are there really people like that out there, spies who play both sides just to make money?* It felt too much like something out of a radio play. Jacoby was getting pulled into a world beyond his meagre experience. Paulo seemed to have all the answers and no reservations. Not for the first time, Lenara's prophetic words rang out in Jacoby's mind: *You need to understand who Paulo is. He's Emperor Longoro's son.*

"Jake," Timori said.

"Huh?" He looked up from his thoughts to discover they were parked outside of Timori's house.

Paulo chuckled. "I said I can give you a lift home if you want to grab your bike. It should fit in the back."

"Oh. Sure." Jacoby left the motorcoach to fetch his bicycle. Timori followed.

As Jacoby leaned down to pick up the bike, Timori whispered quietly, "Jake, are you sure you can do this alignment?" Jacoby felt no challenge in the words, merely concern.

He looked into his friend's pale green eyes. "No. We've practiced it in class, but it's not easy to do. I'm not the prodigal speaker that...that Crys was."

Timori's eyes wandered to the little bungalow next to his apartment building, where Crystara used to live. "We don't really have any other options, do we? If the police find Racquela first and go in, it could be chaos."

"We'll rescue her, Tim."

"Her father thought it was me," Timori said. "Without even asking...he just assumed it. He walked right up and threatened to kill me if I didn't tell him where she was."

"He was probably just scared, Tim," Jacoby suggested. "She's his only child, she matters more to him than anything, I bet."

"He used to be so nice to me. And then all of a sudden it was like I was the dirt underneath his fingernails."

"Well, you have to remember that..."

Jacoby was interrupted by the blare of a motorcoach horn.

"I don't have all night, dullies," Paulo called out. Jacoby rolled his eyes.

"See you tomorrow in school, Tim?"

"Yeah. I'll be there."

Chapter 21

De'Cadomus led Crystara down the stairwell from the Keeper's Tower and into the courtyard. It was bracing. Crystara felt the sunshine on her face and arms for the first time in a week. She smiled despite herself. A warm seaside breeze was blowing across the hill and she turned her face toward it.

They crossed the bell tower, heading in the direction of the priests' quarters, on the opposite side of the grounds from the sisters' abbey.

"Why is the library in the priests' quarters?"

"It's underneath," De'Cadomus replied in his raspy tone. "It was moved secretly during the anti-crystal rebellion to protect the archives from being burned by an angry, ignorant mob. There are books in that library that survived the sack of Avati Hill. Also, the priests don't have to go far to access information. There is another way in, through the underground passages, but I'll show you those later. You'll need a way to come and go from the temple without being seen...eventually."

"What about the sisters? What if they want to access information?"

De'Cadomus snorted. "The abbey was added fairly recently, and the sisters are a foolish distraction. For centuries the priests and monks operated alone, without the temptations of the flesh, and the sisters had their own abbeys, far away from the world of men. The keeper who changed those rules was a womanizing fool."

They passed under the shadow of the flat-roofed, adobe set of houses belonging to the priests of the Old Temple. De'Cadomus opened a door and ushered Crystara through into a simple, tidy foyer. A straw mat was beneath her bare feet, and an idol of Cami, the goddess of the hearth and home, had been placed upon a small table by the door.

"Why is it so bad for priests and sisters to be in the same place?" she asked as De'Cadomus wiped his sandals on the mat. She noticed that he paid no mind to the idol.

"I told you, it's a distraction. Leave the breeding and fornicating to the pickers and whitehands. The members of the church made a vow to serve the Great Crystal and nothing else...not that such an oath means anything anymore."

Crystara followed De'Cadomus down a hallway. She couldn't believe she was having a civil conversation with him, but so long as he was willing to offer information, she would continue to ask questions.

"Wait, so you're saying the priests and sisters here...?"

De'Cadomus barked a laugh but didn't crack a smile. "Don't be naïve. Of course they do. In secret, of course. Make something forbidden and it only becomes more of a temptation. The crystals the sisters use to protect themselves from...embarrassment and excommunication only make it worse. This is a place of debauchery, and crystal lore is slowly being lost to laziness and hedonism."

"Is that why you want me to spy on them?"

De'Cadomus stopped at the door on the left and withdrew his key ring. Crystara took note of the large brass key he used to open the door. Beyond was a set of deepstone stairs, leading down. Bright blue light crystals in sconces lit the way.

"No. There's not much I can do to stop it now. I'd have to completely cleanse the Old Temple and bring in devout followers from all over Novem, and that's more effort than I'm willing to commit when there are bigger things at stake." He walked down the steps with a practiced calm, as though the entire world waited on him before it turned.

164

The stairway was long, and Crystara surmised they were deep underneath Crystus Hill by the time they reached another unremarkable door. This one had no lock, and it opened to reveal a vast underground space.

The first thing to greet Crystara's senses was the smell. The musty scent of dust and old paper was nearly overwhelming. It reminded Crystara of the Avati Hill Library, but underneath the Old Temple the scent seemed many times stronger. Although the library was underground, Crystara was surprised to discover the air felt incredibly dry. Other than the deepstone ceiling, every conceivable space was filled with books. Old wooden shelves stretched on into a dim blue crystal lamp-lit distance, stuffed with tomes and volumes.

There were so many books it appeared the underground library had run out of space. Neat stacks had been placed upon the floor in front of each shelf, most of which were taller than Crystara. Ladders of various lengths were leaning against the wall to her left, and to the right was a small desk, where an ancient man with thick round glasses and a lengthy white beard was fiddling with a crystal desk-lamp.

Crystara tried to contain her excitement. If she had to be a prisoner, at least it was within a prison of knowledge.

"Lagarus," De'Cadomus said loudly. He rapped on the desk, trying to get the archivist's attention. Lagarus looked up only when De'Cadomus's shadow passed over the lamp.

"Eh?" He adjusted his glasses and studied De'Cadomus for a long moment. Then he examined the keeper's robe sleeve. De'Cadomus looked affronted, but said nothing. "Oh, it's you, Orvin. Welcome back. Feels like I haven't seen you in a week."

"I'm not Orvin," De'Cadomus said coldly. "Orvin is dead. I'm the new keeper. De'Cadomus."

"What?" Lagarus opened a drawer in his desk and withdrew a brass horn. Attached to the tapered end was a grey crystal. Lagarus held the horn up to his ear and leaned in toward the keeper. "De'Cadomus, did you say?" Lagarus grimaced. "Filthy snake, that one. Ehh, what did you say you were here for again, Orvin?"

De'Cadomus pounded his fist against the desk and turned to Crystara. Lagarus seemed not to notice and returned to fiddling with the flickering lamp.

"As you can see, he's senile," De'Cadomus groused. "Just do as he asks. It won't be much. I doubt he can even read large print, so if you take it upon yourself to put books away properly, you'd be doing the priests a favour."

The keeper looked at Lagarus and snarled. "Lagarus." No answer. "Lagarus!"

"Oh. Hehe." Lagarus put the horn against his ear again. "Orvin. Sorry, I thought you were just here to say hello and get some books. Ehh, what can I do for you? Who is that behind you, anyway? Is that the girl I keep hearing about? What was her name...didn't sound like a traditional Noven girl's name. Crystal-something. Crystini, Crystalia, something along that alignment. Anyway. She must be that young speaker you've been working with, hmm? Pleasure to meet you, girl. I hear you were selected for betrothal by the Great Crystal, too. It must be quite the..."

De'Cadomus cleared his throat very loudly. "Lagarus. This is not Crystara and I am not Keeper Orvin." Lagarus had put down the horn and was fiddling with the lamp as De'Cadomus shouted in his ear. "Keeper Orvin was murdered by Crystara." Crystara felt a pang in her chest and stared off at a stack of books, forcing back tears. "I am Keeper De'Cadomus. This girl is a mute who will be helping you keep the library clean since you're too old to do it yourself. She will be staying in the spare room adjacent to the south stacks. She is simple, so don't expect too much from her."

A look of confusion crossed Lagarus's face. He glanced from De'Cadomus to Crystara and back again. Crystara picked at his thoughts to discover they were a jumble of confusing and conflicting information – the old man's memory was a frail and fleeting thing. He'd certainly *heard* De'Cadomus tell him about Orvin's death, but he didn't seem to know what to do with the information, and Crystara had the distinct impression he would forget what he'd been told within a few minutes.

"Well," he said finally, "Simple or no, I've always said speaking had nothing to do with intelligence. So she's staying here now? Good, good. She can help me put away books. And make me tea. Cecelia doesn't bring me tea anymore, and I can't make it up those stairs so well. Back and legs aren't what they used to be, eh, Orvin? You know what I'm talking about, unless you've got some kind of crystal that does the same trick as duskblossom. Come to think of it, wasn't there some old green alignment you were talking about a while back that..."

De'Cadomus turned around to look at Crystara and let Lagarus continue to ramble. "You can ignore him for the most part." He didn't bother to lower his voice. "You don't even have to assist him so long as you can keep up the illusion that you're here to dust and sweep between the stacks. It won't seem out of place. A sister brings him meals and tidies his room, even. I will order her to bring you food, also. You will report to me every evening after meals and tell me what you've seen, heard, and read...and then you will train. I'll expect your first report tomorrow."

"Wait," Crystara said. "If you want me at my best, I want a couple more things from you."

"What?" He folded his arms. "This is a temple, not a place of creature comforts."

"A washtub would be nice. Just because I look like a dirty urchin doesn't mean I have to smell like one. And more than one set of clothes. The sisters will talk if you can't even be charitable to an unfortunate mute girl. Remember, everyone knows you're the one who brought me here. It would look odd if you were kind enough to give an orphan food and shelter, then neglected her completely."

"Fine," De'Cadomus grumbled. "I will tell whoever looks after Lagarus to provide some things for you. Make yourself unobtrusive, and don't be surprised if Lagarus asks you ten times who you are."

De'Cadomus left, slamming the door behind him. The sound echoed throughout the library. When it subsided, Crystara noticed the old archivist was still talking.

"...and tell her to mind Dusty. He's shy around strangers."

Lagarus was still tinkering with the lamp. Without thinking, Crystara walked up to the desk and took the lamp from him, turning it over to examine the ensconced crystal. Sure enough, there was a crack forming along its surface. Crystara figured the crystal was pretty old, but so long as it didn't shatter, it could provide light. She whispered a re-alignment to work around the crack, and the crystal ceased its flickering. Crystara handed the lamp back to Lagarus without a word. He looked at it, then set it down and beamed at Crystara.

"Well, well," he said as he laced his fingers. "Orvin was right about you. I'm sure you can work with more than just light crystals, hmm?"

Crystara shrugged. "Hopefully that's bright enough that you can read by it now," she said.

"Eh? What's that?" His hand shook as he groped around on the desk for his horn. He placed it against his ear and looked up at her expectantly.

Crystara chuckled despite herself. There was at least one person who might not believe her to be simple. The knowledge that she could manipulate crystals despite not being able to speak to other people was heartening as well. She resolved to examine her crystal ring in detail later on that evening.

Knowing she wouldn't be able to give Lagarus a proper answer, Crystara waved goodbye to him and went to explore the stacks. She wandered through the halls among the shelves and waited for a title to catch her eye.

The selection was impressive. Many of the tomes had bindings so loose and faded the titles had become illegible. On several shelves she spied metal cases. She pulled one off the shelf to discover it was a lockbox. Whatever ancient book lay within, it was being guarded from the elements. Crystara saw no title on the box, merely a number etched upon a brass plaque.

As she placed the metal box back upon the shelf, a quick dash of movement out of the corner of her eye startled her and she gasped. Crystara pressed her back to the shelf and reached out with her mind, but she could sense no other people nearby. She wondered if De'Cadomus was spying on her, making sure she wasn't trying to escape. Cautiously, she rounded the corner of the shelf and looked about.

It was staring at her with huge yellow eyes, black fur wild and matted, tail straight like a sword.

"Hello, kitten," she said. She knelt down and made a kissing sound. She didn't know if she would still sound the same to animals, but she figured it couldn't hurt to try. Crystara couldn't read the minds of animals, but she didn't need to in order to sense that the cat was simply afraid. She wondered if it was the 'Dusty' that Lagarus had mentioned.

"Come here, Dusty," she cooed. The cat hissed loudly and dashed off behind a bookshelf. Crystara doubted she'd seen the last of the cat. It was likely kept around to stop rodents from chewing on leather-bound books.

"What the shard was that?" said a male voice from nearby. Crystara froze.

"Relax," another voice said. "It's just the archivist's old cat. Keeps the rats out."

Crystara couldn't quite hear their thoughts, so she crept closer. It sounded as though they were a few stacks away, but in the big underground space, even whispers echoed well.

"Fine, fine. So what do you want to know?"

"The viper brought someone else with him, other than you four snakes. Who is she and what's her purpose?"

"No idea."

"I'm not paying you to have no idea. If you don't want to talk, then we're done here."

"That secret is worth a lot more than the dinari you paid me."

Crystara found herself on the other side of the shelf from the two men, close enough to hear their thoughts. The crystal speaker was named Aureon. Although his thoughts seemed well-guarded, Crystara did glean that he was just as afraid of De'Cadomus as anyone else.

The other man was August, which didn't surprise Crystara in the least. He had been actively hoping to undermine De'Cadomus's authority.

"Then I'll get you more money," August continued. "Tell me. Who is she? One of his agents?"

"Look, keep your voice down," Aureon whispered urgently. "The viper has eyes and ears everywhere. She's a spy and a speaker in his employ, disguised as an idiot. Be careful what you say around her."

"I already know that." August sounded impatient. "But who *is* she?"

There was a moment of silence. Crystara grimaced. Aureon knew exactly who she was. He'd been there when De'Cadomus had forced the ring onto her finger.

"I don't know."

"That's a cartload of dirt. Who is she?"

"Keep your voice down, I said. The viper doesn't tell me everything, okay? She's not one of us. That's all I can tell you. She doesn't work with us or speak to us. She works for him alone, and she's probably dangerous. If you mess with her, the viper will know, and he'll take swift action."

"Great. So I just paid you for information I already have."

"Not my problem."

"I could easily tell him I've been bribing you, you know."

Crystara felt the shelf shake. A few books fell to the floor.

"Who do you think you're messing with, old man? I'm not some wimpy priest you can push around. Try it, and I'll have you excommunicated before you can say 'shatters.' You temple geezers don't run the church, *we* do. You want information, fine...but when I say I don't know something, don't push it."

"Fine," August gasped. "Let me down."

There were some shuffling noises and Crystara heard August coughing.

"Was there anything else, priest?"

"I paid you. Give me something I can work with." He coughed again. "You know he's going to destroy this temple from the inside out before long."

"You're a dully. You want to know something useful? The viper was picked by the council because he doesn't give a shard about any Old Temple dirt. He's here to make sure the Great Crystal and the church survive a revolution, if it happens."

"Then what does that have to do with the girl?"

"I told you I don't know. Whatever she's doing here, it probably has nothing to do with you. The viper isn't afraid of you. You're beneath him."

"We'll see." Crystara heard retreating footsteps. "The next time I want to know something, you'd better deliver."

"Or what?" Aureon was still just on the other side of the bookshelf.

"Or I'll find someone who understands how bribery works." August's stiff, stilted steps receded. Crystara heard Aureon let out a heavy sigh.

"What a dully." He stalked off, heading in the other direction.

Crystara remained motionless until she was certain both of the men were gone. She did a slow circuit of the library, but it was deserted. She assumed Lagarus had gone down for an afternoon nap. The very thought of rest made Crystara yawn. She figured it was as good a time as any to find her room.

The door to the spare library room was innocuously placed between two bookshelves. Crystara found the area within surprisingly spacious, although several stacks of books were encroaching toward the straw mattress on the one side. The remainder of the room was barren save for a washbasin and a chamber pot, both empty.

Crystara walked over to the haphazard stacks of books, looking for an interesting title. Most appeared to be newer than many of the books in the library – recently published works of note rather than old illustrated manuscripts and dry histories. Crystara quickly scanned the stacks for anything to do with crystals. She didn't have to look long before she discovered *Modern Speaking Techniques*. She carefully removed it and walked over to the lumpy but clean-looking straw mattress and burlap blanket. Lying down, she positioned herself so she faced the door, and began to read.

She was asleep in minutes.

Chapter 22

Leo was certain it was nothing more than foolish sentimentality that made him keep the old tin soldier in his drawer, buried underneath his only spare set of clothes. Sometimes, after a hard night of digging, when nobody else was in the room, he would take it out and hold it for a while. He didn't make believe or anything childish like that, but it was comforting to just stare at the moulded piece of tin and remember a time when his biggest worry was whether or not Renalda was going to hit him with a spoon for misbehaving.

Once, Bernardo had come into the room and caught him staring at the toy. When he made a comment about Leo being a baby, Leo suggested perhaps Bernardo had forgotten what it was like to have his face smashed in by a piece of tin. Bernardo never brought it up again.

Bernardo was all bluster by then. He was still missing a tooth, and there were other reminders that Leo was the toughest boy in the orphanage. He was the only one who could take a hit from Nerus's cudgel without crying out in pain. He could look Nerus in the eye while he was receiving a beating. He knew Nerus would never hit him any harder because he was the best worker.

The year after Teddori's death, Leo had begun to grow, and he never seemed to stop. Somewhere between twelve and thirteen, he was already taller than Nerus. His muscles looked small, but they were wiry and tireless. He could dig in the tunnel for hours after the other boys were dragging their heels.

"You're worthless, casteless dirt," he would say to them as they dug in the tunnel. "You ain't fit for nothin' but diggin'. Real miners would have found more crystals by now."

That's what it was all about, Leo knew. The crystals. He'd thought the whole thing was some abyssal nightmare until they actually started to find them underneath the house. The boys didn't get to look at them for long, though – as soon as they discovered one, Nerus came in and dug it out and then went upstairs with it, taking it away to the world of fields and skies that was beginning to seem like a memory to the rest of the boys.

Not Leo, though. He didn't see the sun anymore but he knew when Nerus slept, and Sofia would unlock the trap door in the old root cellar for him so they could slip past Lutias, who guarded the stairs. Sometimes Sofia came, and sometimes she didn't. Usually it was on the nights when Nerus and Natalya had too much to drink. Through the old vents Leo could hear them scream at each other for a long time, and then things would get really quiet.

Leo would wait underneath the trap door most nights, stretching his aching muscles to keep them loose, or just lying on his back thinking about Teddori and Renalda, and that fateful day months after Teddori's heart failure when Renalda had sold the orphanage to a big woman who wore lots of makeup and claimed to have experience running a house with lots of children.

Leo believed that last part, but he didn't think Natalya meant orphanages. It had taken him a while to understand why the boys had been segregated and what kind of 'education' Natalya was giving the girls, but he figured it out from Sofia's tales eventually.

"They're going to sell me soon, I think," she whispered to Leo one night as they sat on the far side of the old wall, locked in each other's embrace and stealing kisses whenever they could. "I can feel it. Natalya is always talking about my hair, and Nerus says I get more and more beautiful every day." There was more than a hint of disgust in her voice.

"No, they won't," Leo replied. "We'll be gone by then. Shards, we could go right now if we wanted."

"Yet here we are," Sofia sighed.

Leo stared out at the dark fields. He could escape from Nerus, he was certain of it, but a casteless boy in the great wide world was worth nothing. He needed money first, or he and Sofia would starve, or be thrown in jail.

"You know we can't yet."

Another sigh. "Isn't freedom better than this?"

Leo said nothing. The other orphans didn't understand the world the way he did. He read everything he could get his hands on, including encyclopedias, history books, and even Teddori's ledgers.

He didn't know what a crystal was worth, but he knew it was a lot, or Nerus wouldn't have let the farm go to waste while the boys dug tunnels underneath the fields.

"Leo. We should go back."

"Hmm?"

"I said we should go back."

"Don't you want to...?"

"No."

Leo squeezed Sofia's hand. "Don't worry. I have a plan."

Their tryst over, they returned stealthily to the house. They'd never been caught, but they both knew the consequences – the last girl to try and escape was apprehended. After that, the orphans had never seen or heard from her again. Stories floated around the basement that her body was buried under the darkoak tree and that her ghost haunted the tunnel, but Leo knew that was just a fabrication to get the younger kids to shut up and do as they were told. She'd probably been sold to one of Natalya's business contacts before she could make another attempt.

As Paulo crept back into the cellar, easing the door back down as slowly as was humanly possible, he supposed it was possible Nerus was bribing the officials. Funding had to come from somewhere. The farm was no longer producing for the market, and Nerus did nothing other than beat children with a cudgel all day long.

Leo crept, one footstep at a time, up the abyss-black tunnel back to the boys' rooms. Nobody would dare tell on him. They all knew what he was doing, but if there was one person the boys feared as much as Nerus, it was Leo. Even the older ones left him alone.

He knew how to push the door open so it wouldn't creak. In the complete darkness, he couldn't see his three roommates, but he knew where everyone slept. Bernardo would be asleep. Antonio would be mouthing a silent prayer to Jova for deliverance. Arnaldo, the eldest of the four, no longer cried in his sleep, but he made strange noises in the night sometimes. Leo almost felt bad for him. Arnaldo hadn't seen a girl's face in over a year.

Leo slid under his burlap bedsheet and closed his eyes.

Soon, he thought. *We will find the mother lode soon or Nerus will give up. Either way, it will be over.*

Sometimes as he was falling asleep, he would hear Teddori's rumbling voice in his head, and he would wake up and be sitting beside Teddori as the man turned the page of a book with those big, pale sausage fingers of his. Sofia would be picking cherries in the field in a blue summer dress, looking over at him and smiling. Arnaldo would be hitching up the old nag to the cart for the summer festival, and Leo would finally get to see the city. It was exactly like he'd pictured.

Leo was startled back awake by the sound of Lutias barking. The other boys were stirring, too. He hoped Sofia hadn't been caught. They wouldn't hurt Sofia in ways that would show, but Leo didn't think she would suffer long before cracking.

There were footsteps coming down the stairs, and Leo knew them immediately to be Nerus's. Uncertainty began to grip him. Nobody knew what happened to a boy who tried to escape, or one who was caught with one of the girls, but Leo could bet a beating would not suffice. Nerus would make an example of him. Leo was the strongest and the bravest, and if Nerus broke him then nobody would ever cross the man again.

Without thinking, Leo pulled the tin soldier out of his drawer and held it close. As the footsteps approached the door, he heard the other boys roll over to face their respective walls, pretending to be asleep.

The door opened. Leo heard three sharp intakes of breath. He clutched the toy tightly. Nerus had left the lamp on the stone floor of the hallway, and he cast a long shadow into the room. When he walked in, Leo heard Antonio choke back a sob.

Leo had expected to see the cudgel in that bony, gnarled hand, but instead there was a wand. Leo had only seen them in pictures, but he knew exactly what he was looking at. To wonder if Nerus had the courage to pull the trigger, Leo needed only to look into those sunken, cruel eyes.

Leo's face betrayed nothing. He knew he could not run, and Nerus would have to get close enough for him to try and grab the wand. He reminded himself that if he showed the merest shard of fear, Nerus would win whether the trigger was pulled or not.

Arm outstretched, Nerus approached Leo's bed. The hard wooden tip of the wand pressed into Leo's dark curls of hair. Leo held himself steady, imagining he was made of stone.

"Boy." Nerus spat at Leo after he said it, and the gob of phlegm landed upon his clenched lips. Nobody had called him

'Boy' since Bruno. His grip on the toy tightened beneath the burlap blanket.

"If you were any other boy, I would kill you now, but you're my best digger. So you leave me with a difficult choice. Guess I'll have to kill Sofia instead."

Leo narrowed his eyes. "I doubt you'd do that to one of Natalya's investments."

The back of Nerus's fist met Leo's face. Having expected the wand, he gasped. Still alive. *Shut up and you might survive this,* he told himself.

"One more word, boy, and you'll be nothing but a stain on the wall!" Nerus shouted. Leo was amazed when Nerus took a step backward. *He doesn't know how I will react. He's afraid.*

Leo wiped the mucus off his face and looked into Nerus's eyes. He said nothing.

"If I ever catch you upstairs again, boy...I will kill you." He backed out of the room and slammed the door. Antonio started crying. Leo remained like stone, clutching his toy, staring into the darkness. He couldn't stop picturing his brains exploding onto the wall.

Don't cry, Leo. If you do, he wins.

"Nerus, you dully," he said to the room. "You should have pulled that trigger. Instead, now we all know you're afraid to use it."

Chapter 23

Crystara stood on the ledge of a hill, looking down upon a broad plain. Flat, grey stones dotted the landscape below. She jumped from the ledge and floated down to the valley.

A cold wind whistled through the yellow grass. The valley was barren, other than the tiny brook. When Crystara looked closer, she noticed the water was still and red. Little crimson crystals grew out of the earth by the banks of the river. Crystara knelt down and plucked one the size of her thumb from the mucky soil. When she pressed it between her fingers it became liquid and stained her skin.

"You and I are both treading the red," a low voice said. When Crystara looked up from her darkened hands, she saw a pair of expensive shoes sinking into the mud. A clean hand was offered to her and she took it. The nails were neatly trimmed and the fingers were slender. She was helped to her feet.

He tossed a dark lock of hair out of his eyes, lazily, and cast a sideways glance at Crystara. His smile was crooked, suggestive.

"You need me if you want to live," she heard herself say. The red was spreading from her fingertips to his.

"Then speak to them for me," Paulo replied. His words were almost lost on the wind, but he gestured to the masses of stones spread across the field.

Crystara left the mucky bank, hand in hand with Paulo. He was always tall to Crystara, but the shadow he cast across the dusty field seemed grotesquely long.

Her feet brought her to a raised spot just below the bluff, and the throng of stones seemed to hearken as she lifted her arms and splayed her fingers. The red upon her fingertips began to glow. Across the field, into a distance that stretched to the horizon, red markings appeared upon the stones, glowing as brightly as her hands.

There were words written upon the rocks, but she couldn't read them. It was an unfamiliar language, made up of strange glyphs. With chilling clarity, Crystara realized she couldn't *read* the symbols, but she knew the meaning of them, somewhere deep within.

"Awaken," she said. The ground shook and thrummed. The sky opened. Rain tumbled down, and the field was flooded in red. Deep trenches of thick scarlet crisscrossed among the stones. The deluge continued. Soon Crystara was drenched, the viscous rain soaking her hair, staining her white gown.

"Awaken," Paulo echoed, "Awaken and obey me."

A chill rode up Crystara's spine, and with a flash of lightning and momentary lucidity she realized she was dreaming. Then it was gone, and the red streams were flooding over and drowning the stones. Soon the valley had become a lake, and she and Paulo were stranded upon a tiny island of mud, surrounded by a crimson sea.

"Will it be enough?" she asked.

Paulo bowed his head and smiled. His hair covered his eyes and his grin was sinister.

The rains ceased and the sun began to climb up the horizon. The sky had gone from black to a bruised purple-blue. As the lake drained back into the soil, Crystara saw branches sprouting from the earth. Upon them, instead of leaves, crystals of every hue shimmered and dangled in the breeze.

"Are they ready?" Paulo asked. Crystara was swaying from side to side, and the crystals swayed with her.

"Ask me again," she said, "when I wake up."

Something clutched at her arm from beneath her. She screamed. The surroundings changed and she saw walls of stone and piles of books. After a moment of disorientation, the fog cleared and she knew where she was.

In her paltry, windowless room she couldn't tell if it was day or night, but she felt as though she'd been sleeping for a while. A plate of food had been set for her some distance away, and Dusty was gnawing on a leg of chicken.

"Ungh." Crystara rubbed her eyes. She remembered every detail of her dream with perfect clarity. Sitting up, she watched Dusty eat. Her stomach growled and Dusty tensed.

"Dusty," she cooed. "It's okay. I won't take your food." Dusty continued to stare, unmoving. "Can we share?" Crystara didn't care so much for chicken – meat tended to upset her stomach on occasion – but the slices of bread looked fresh.

Slowly, she crept toward the plate. Dusty growled at her but didn't dash off. She took a piece of bread as carefully as she could manage. She began to salivate. Butter had melted into the bread and she could smell it.

"Crystara..." She heard the voice echoing in her mind just as she brought the bread up to her mouth. She froze there, mouth ajar, as butter melted through the slice and onto her fingers. She couldn't quite place it, but she knew that voice.

"What do you want?" she whispered. The butter was trickling down her hand.

"Crystara. Come to me."

She snorted. "So you can shatter my life some more?" She devoured the bread in two bites, forcing the whole thing into her mouth.

"I can help you."

Crystara grabbed another piece of bread. "Just like how you helped me into this dirty mess?" she shouted with her mouth full.

"I can help you...with the ring..."

Crystara raised an eyebrow. She took another bite of bread and waited to see if the Great Crystal would say anything more. The silence was broken only by the sound of Dusty chewing on the chicken wing.

"How?" she asked. Her question was met with only silence. She chewed on her slice of bread and pondered. An opportunity to escape was not something she could pass up easily, even if the Great Crystal was being duplicitous. The real difficulty was sneaking into the Crystal Chamber without being caught. The main floor of the temple was always patrolled by guards, and Crystara didn't have access to any crystals. She didn't think she'd be able to sneak by the guards without a silence crystal, and thus far her ring had not responded to any of her whispers.

She frowned and grabbed the last piece of bread. Dusty had dragged off the rest of the chicken wing to a corner of the room and was happily gnawing away. Crystara bit her lip. There had to be crystals somewhere in the Old Temple. The church contained the greatest concentration of crystal speakers in all of Novem.

Like a crystal light being switched on, the idea came to her in a flash. The old blue crystal in the lamp was already cracked, but if she was very careful, she could re-align it to grey and use it to obfuscate her movements and keep her footsteps quiet.

Crystara shoved the last piece of bread into her mouth and tiptoed out of the room, heading for the archivist's desk. The big lamps that hung from the ceiling had been switched off, and the room was black as the abyss. Crystara had to feel her way along the wall.

She reached the corner of the room and followed the wall until she passed by the library entrance, then slowed down and felt ahead for the desk. Her hand brushed against it and she groped for the lamp, nearly knocking it over.

"Shatters," Crystara whispered. She carefully pried the blue crystal loose from the lamp socket. Breathing out slowly, she felt the shape of the crystal in her hand. Blue to grey wasn't a difficult realignment for her under ordinary circumstances, but the crystal already had a crack growing along its length. If she didn't focus carefully, she could shatter it completely.

"Cannus," she whispered to the crystal. *"Scurio, tassus."*

The crystal didn't shatter, but she had no way to be certain her whisper had worked until she could examine it under some light. She gripped the small stone in a sweaty fist and ascended the steps to the rectory.

The hallway was silent. A lighted candle had been left on the foyer table, next to the idol of Cami. The statue cast eerie shadows across the hallway – the fruit in Cami's bowl of plenty looked like smoky snakes along the floor. She could hear soft snoring coming from nearby. Crystara crept her way across the floorboards, hoping to avoid the creaky ones.

She reached the foyer table and examined the crystal she carried by the light of the candle. Sure enough, it had gone grey, though the crack along its length appeared to have deepened. Crystara was sure one more alteration of the crystal would spell its end.

She opened the rectory door as quietly as she could manage, peering out into the night. It was dark and cloudy. The moon was nowhere to be found, and the courtyard appeared vacant. With grim resolve, Crystara gripped her crystal tightly and sprinted along the courtyard grass, moving from shadow to shadow.

The back door to the Old Temple was not locked. The priests only bothered to secure the outer doors, as well as those that led to restricted places, such as the Crystal Chamber. As Crystara crept along a carpeted hallway, she noticed a shadow coming around the corner. She shoved herself into an alcove, trying to keep her breathing to a minimum. The guard passed her by without even sparing a glance in her direction. It was Rossi, the younger man with the pot belly. Crystara watched him shuffle by, his eyes barely open, dragging the butt of his halberd along the carpet as though it were made out of lead. She waited until he was farther down the hall, then she slipped out of the alcove and around the corner.

Crystara didn't run into any other guards by the time she reached the Crystal Hallway. Skulking up to the keeper's office door, she whispered to the crystal lock and it allowed her passage. She slipped into the office and shut the door behind her quietly.

De'Cadomus hadn't done anything to change Keeper Orvin's office. The same landscape painting was on the wall, and the desk had been kept immaculate. Even the stone nameplate upon the desk still read 'Orvin.' Crystara tried in vain to keep her face passive as she read his name. She didn't have the time to think about regret just then. Crossing the room, she knelt before the door that led to the Crystal Chamber. She whispered to the lock, asking it to open for her.

To her surprise, the crystal didn't change colour. She tried the whisper again. Nothing happened.

"Shatters," she said to herself. De'Cadomus must have altered it, she decided, to keep her out of the Crystal Chamber. Crystara tried the word one last time, just to be certain. Nothing.

The way is open, said a voice in her mind. The crystal lock glowed azure, and Crystara stared with wide eyes. She looked over her shoulder nervously, but nobody was there.

"What in the name of Jova is happening?" she whispered. She pushed the door to the Crystal Chamber open and side-stepped into the room. The door creaked closed behind her and shut itself loudly. She gasped and shut her eyes, telling herself to be calm.

She opened her eyes to the sparse light of the Crystal Chamber. There it was, the Great Crystal, dominating the space. Even half-buried like an iceberg it was awesome to behold. It was the centrepiece of Noven religion, the supposed conduit to the gods. Legends held that the Great Crystal had helped the Novens of the first empire conquer Titania.

Crystara stared at the dark stain on the floor, halfway between the crystal and the wall. Keeper Orvin had felt differently about the Great Crystal. He'd never spoken much of gods or power, only of secrets. He had mentored Crystara in speaking techniques that she'd only dreamed of learning, words and methods that Central School would never have taught to a student. He'd died in that very chamber, shot by a startled Crystara using her father's old wand.

Crystara glanced up. The blood had been wiped clean from the face of the crystal, but a deep set of branching grooves had formed along the surface. Shadows seemed to writhe underneath the cracks of the crystal. Crystara assumed her eyes were playing tricks on her in the dark.

"Can you hear me?" she asked the crystal.

"CRYSTARA." It was a flood of voices in her mind, a dissonant chorus.

"Stop. Run. Don't touch. Beware the Serpent. Remember the vision! Paulo. Your ring, quickly, you must..."

Crystara was driven to her knees, gritting her teeth. There were too many voices, shouting at her, drowning out her own thoughts.

"Bring the...don't let him...must find a way to...your destiny..."

The pressure on her skull became overwhelming. She bit the inside of her cheek to stop herself from screaming and tasted blood. The intensity of the cacophony sent her to the floor, clenching her fists and shutting her eyes tight in an attempt to stop from moaning out in anguish. As she thrashed and kicked, her hand brushed against the Great Crystal. A calm, masculine voice rang out clearly in her mind.

"Box three-five-two. Box one-five-nine-six. Box seven. Go, Crystara. They are coming."

The voices ceased. Crystara opened her eyes. She was staring up at the cracks in the Great Crystal. A deep sense of loss welled up inside of her and she let out a choked sob. She brushed a tear away and shook off the foggy, emotional feeling that was clinging to her.

"Box three-five-two," she whispered. "Box one-five-nine-six. Box seven." As she picked herself up off the floor, she repeated the numbers to herself until she was certain they were memorized.

Crystara heard a muffled voice coming from behind the big whiteoak double doors that led into the room. Glancing about, she discovered the only place to hide was behind the altar up on the dais at the far end of the chamber. Crystara didn't dare risk pressing herself up against the crystal again. As a door creaked open, she dashed over to the dais and crouched down low behind the marble slab.

"...doesn't make any sense. A *voice* just *told* you someone was in here, messing with the crystal? You were dreaming."

Crystara held her breath and sought out the thoughts of the guards as they entered the chamber. It was Aureon and Rossi.

Why would the Great Crystal contact Rossi? she wondered. His thoughts were like cobwebs. He was drowsy, and nervous around Aureon. Aureon's thoughts switched among concerns about De'Cadomus, apprehension about the Great Crystal, and derisive musings about Rossi. Occasionally his mind would wander to lewd thoughts about one of the younger sisters at the temple. Crystara made a disgusted face.

She repeated the box numbers in her mind as Rossi and Aureon shut the door behind them and looked around the chamber.

"I wasn't dreaming, sir. I was on my patrol, and I heard this voice. In my mind, not with my ears. This voice sounded like a girl. She said someone was in here, and that the Great Crystal was in danger. There's someone in here, sir. I'm certain of it."

Aureon snorted. "There's nobody in here. Look. You can see right through the crystal. Nobody. You were dozing off."

Crystara couldn't see either of the men, but she could imagine Rossi shaking his head vehemently, his jowls wobbling.

"Sir. The Great Crystal plays tricks, sir. You can't see all angles from it. I've been a guard here for five betrothals and I know it plays tricks. Makes you see things. The gods, they work in mysterious ways, and..."

"Fine," Aureon growled. "You go that way and I'll go this way. Gods, if it's that dirty cat prowling around, I swear..." As he and Rossi made their way around the Great Crystal, Crystara scanned their thoughts once again. It took a lot out of her, but remaining undiscovered was her greatest priority.

Her heart sped up. Aureon didn't believe Rossi, but he was planning to check behind the altar. Crystara bit into a knuckle and ran through her options. She couldn't make a dash for the keeper's office door without being spotted by Aureon, and she didn't trust her cracked little crystal to keep her hidden from a skilled speaker.

She could run the other way, past Rossi who would never catch her, but she didn't think she could outrun Aureon if she was seen.

As Rossi and Aureon drew closer to the dais, Crystara realised escape without being noticed was not an option. The crystal she held in her sweaty palm afforded her a few options, but most of them would cause it to shatter. She heard Aureon approach the dais steps and whispered a phrase to her crystal. It changed from grey to yellow and the crack upon its surface deepened. Crystara couldn't see clearly through the Great Crystal to the whiteoak double doors, but she could get far enough behind Aureon to make a run for it with a decent head start.

"Yaccobus," she whispered to her crystal. There was a tugging sensation in her midsection and a disorienting feeling. She found herself on the floor next to the shadowy cracks upon the Great Crystal. She could have escaped unnoticed had it not been for the explosive sound of her crystal shattering. Flecks of it dug into her palm and wrist like shrapnel, and Aureon wheeled around sharply. As Crystara pushed herself up off the floor, she noticed a few droplets of her blood had spattered the Great Crystal. She watched with a mixture of fascination and satisfaction as one of the cracks along its surface lengthened.

"Shards and shatters!" Aureon exclaimed. Crystara dashed off toward the exit.

"What in Jova's name was that?" she heard Rossi exclaim.

"It's the little urchin!" Aureon shouted. "Get after her, you slob!"

As Crystara reached the doors, she heard Rossi huffing and Aureon muttering phrases to the crystals inlaid upon his breastplate. She leapt through the opening just before the doors shut themselves behind her.

"Shatters!" she heard Aureon's muffled cry of dismay through the wood.

"You'll have to do better than that, snake," she muttered as she dashed down the hallway. Heavy footsteps followed her. "Those boxes had better be worth it," she puffed. "Three-five-two. One-five-nine-six. Seven."

She threw open the doors and tore through the courtyard, making for the priests' quarters. Behind her, Aureon's footfalls were as rapid as her heartbeat. She was reaching for the rectory door when strong arms wrapped around her shoulders. The ground rushed up to meet her and she found herself spitting up grass and dirt, cursing and howling.

"All right, you dirty little outcaste, let's get you to the keeper."

"No!" she screamed. She struggled against him, but it was no use. He was much bigger and stronger. She wasn't able to use any of the crystals he carried in his armour against him. Each set was attuned to its owner.

Rossi was at the temple doors, panting and sweating.

"You caught her," he breathed. "You'll tell the keeper I helped, right?"

"Sure," Aureon shrugged. Crystara squirmed uselessly upon his shoulder.

"Help me, Rossi," she pleaded. She saw no recognition in his eyes.

Aureon took Crystara up the stairs to the Keeper's tower. She ceased struggling. De'Cadomus would see nothing except her cold dignity.

"What in Jova's name were you doing in there?" Aureon asked.

Crystara didn't deign to reply.

"Whatever his plans with you, I wouldn't mess with that crystal no more. It got you into this mess. You know, my mother used to say, 'the gods work in mysterious ways'...and when she said it, she didn't mean that Jova makes weird miracles happen. She meant that we can't understand their ways, or the Great Crystal. The gods made us like them, kid. Violent and cracked. Whatever they got in mind through that crystal, it ain't good."

Crystara raised an eyebrow and sifted through Aureon's thoughts, wondering exactly what his angle was. She wasn't surprised to learn Aureon was just as scared of the wizened old keeper as she was. She tried to delve further, but his mind was remarkably guarded. Crystara wondered if he had learned to steel his thoughts from working around De'Cadomus for so long.

"I know you're working for him, remember. But I know the viper, and there's no way he would have wanted you to be in that room. Don't be a dully. He can hurt you bad if he wants."

As they reached the top of the stairs, Crystara heard muffled voices through the door. Aureon rapped loudly upon the old, carved wood with his free arm.

"Not now." There was an edge to De'Cadomus's rasp.

"But, Your Clarity..." Aureon protested.

"I said *not now*."

"Guess we have to wait," Aureon muttered. He shuffled from foot to foot as the muted conversation went on. After a minute or so, the voices grew loud enough that Crystara could hear what was being shouted from the other side of the door.

"...one of the other snakes to do it. This is a flagrant attempt to undermine my authority as keeper!"

The other voice was somewhat calmer, but still clearly excited. "...smooth transition. This is not about..." There was another part Crystara didn't catch. She strained again to hear thoughts, but nothing came through. "...that you are the only one who can extract him. Surely the viper isn't afraid of the Nilonnese."

"Don't patronize me. They called me viper before you were even sucking on your mother's tit. Fine. If Aligratta is too much of a pansy, then I will handle this. But you will tell the council I will do it my way, and as keeper there's nothing they can do to stop me. I will need some time to prepare."

He continued to speak, but the rest of his words were muffled. After a moment, the door opened. De'Cadomus didn't seem surprised to see Aureon standing there with Crystara under his arm, but the other man in the room appeared somewhat confused. He was a man growing soft in the middle and grey on top, and he wore the white and grey robes given to members of the Church of Novem's Crystal Council – the appointed high priests who governed church policy and doctrine.

De'Cadomus was leaning over his desk, looking predatory.

Aureon cleared his throat. "Your Clarity. If I may report?"

"No. Show High Priest Di'Montigana to a room and make sure he's comfortable. Leave her with me."

"But Your Clarity, there's..."

"*Aureon.* Are you a Knight of the Crystal, sir?"

"Yes." He shifted from foot to foot.

"Then do as the Keeper of the Great Crystal says. Leave her with me and go."

"Yes, Your Clarity." He let Crystara down to the floor, surprisingly gently, and then motioned for the high priest to follow him.

The door shut behind Crystara. She flinched when De'Cadomus grabbed the half-empty wine glass from his desk, but it shattered against the wall and not her.

"Fuck!" he shouted. "Shards and shatters, fuck!" He paced back and forth for a moment as Crystara prepared herself for flying objects. He was so rattled that Crystara could sense a thought or two leaking through his usually impenetrable mind.

...to go up north. Fools should have elected Di'Maros. At least he can watch the brat. Calm and control. She mustn't...

The trail of thoughts ended and he was right in front of her, peering down.

"What were you doing with the Great Crystal?"

Her ring finger began to itch. "Chasing Dusty."

The pain was immediate. She gritted her teeth and stood her ground as it coursed through her, bringing tears to her eyes. *You can hurt me but you can't break me,* she thought.

"Let's try that again," he said. Some of the bite seemed to have left his voice. "What were you doing in the Crystal Chamber?"

"It called me there."

She didn't expect to see him shocked by the truth, but he raised an eyebrow. "And? What did it say to you? Did you touch it? How did you get past the crystal lock?" He grabbed her shoulders.

"It told me to come and touch it, summoned me from the library. The crystal opened the lock for me. But Aureon and Rossi caught me before I could. I felt like I was in a trance." Years of lying to her father seemed to be paying off. Half-truths worked best. She kept her thoughts well shielded. De'Cadomus stared at her with vivid interest, his fingers digging painfully into her arms.

"Did it say anything else?"

"Free us," she said.

He turned away and paced between his desk and the hearth. "That's all?" he asked, staring into the flames.

"That's all."

"Hmm." De'Cadomus scratched something upon a piece of paper with his quill pen. "We will discuss this when I return. Until then, I am leaving you under the careful watch of Sir Brutah. You will be kept far from the Great Crystal, and anything else that can get you into trouble."

"I can stay in the library," she said quietly.

De'Cadomus looked up and frowned. "No. You will return to the temple dungeon for a time."

"But..." her heart clenched. "I just want to be able to read. The books..."

"I can't have you tampering with the Great Crystal while I'm gone. Or anything else, for that matter. Consider yourself lucky. Any other keeper would have let you hang."

She leapt upon him before he could say 'shatters,' punching wherever she could land a blow and raking her long nails along his face. In the back of her mind, she knew what would inevitably follow, but she was seeing red. A sardonic voice within her wondered if she'd inherited her father's temper.

Startled, De'Cadomus backpedalled and nearly fell into the fireplace. Despite Crystara's fury, De'Cadomus quickly threw her aside, sending her tumbling along the floor. Then the pain began, and the red Crystara was seeing became white-hot. It lasted for quite some time. When her screaming subsided, she could hear De'Cadomus panting roughly.

"That," he hissed, clutching at his bloody cheek, "is why you cannot be trusted."

"Unnh," she sobbed. The tang of blood in her mouth was strong. She spat. "Said...said the viper to the mouse."

Chapter 24

The wands were arranged in the felt-lined chest like museum pieces. Two sleek darkoak shortwands, easily concealable within a pocket or sleeve, were nestled in the bottom corners. Their crystal triggers were crimson in hue.

Jacoby picked one up and examined it, careful not to tug on the trigger as he felt the weight of the wood in his hand. He had never held a wand in his life, but he'd learned quite a bit about crystals from his classes at Central School.

"Easy to hide those ones," Paulo said, "but they're not so great at hitting distant targets. Could get messy with the work we're doing. I recommend we take them as backup weapons."

"I thought the idea was not to use them unless we have to," Jacoby mumbled as he stared down the short length of the wand with one eye open. Timori, who was leaning against the wall nearby, shuffled farther away from the barrel of the weapon.

"That's why we're bringing you," Paulo said. "But we're better off having too many weapons than too few."

Jacoby beckoned Timori over as he examined the remaining contents of the chest. There was another crimson shortwand made of walnut and a beautifully carved whiteoak longwand with a green trigger as bright as an emerald. The centrepiece of the collection was made entirely of steel. About the length of Jacoby's arm, it looked like the pictures he'd seen of firearms used on other continents – weapons that didn't have crystals.

"Careful with that one," Paulo suggested. He lit a cigarette and curled up a corner of his lip as he watched Timori lift the heavy piece out of the chest. "It's a modified scattergun."

"That's a rare crystal," Jacoby interjected as he examined the scattergun's trigger. The bright orange crystal had deep maroon lines that looked like veins of blood. "Where did you get these?"

Paulo smirked and took a drag of his cigarette. "This is my personal collection. I had it shipped here from Chavicci. That scattergun came all the way from the Commonwealth. The added trigger is worth more than everything else in the case."

"Yes, it's all very impressive," Timori said as he carefully laid the scattergun in its resting place. "Can we get on with it?"

"You're right," Paulo agreed. "Some target practice with the wands, and then we come back to test out the pillars."

"I'm guessing you have a better idea than shooting wands in the middle of the city at night," Timori said.

Paulo shot a wolfish smile. "Let's go for a drive."

The boys packed up the trunk and carefully loaded it into the back of Paulo's motorcoach. Pier Street was quiet as they drove alongside the docks and wharfs and the dark night sea. Past the factories and sprawling housing of Southron Hill, they entered the farmlands. Free of city lights and background noise, the eerie, moonless night lent a sense of purpose to their outing.

Jacoby stared out the window at the winking lights of farmsteads, wondering if things were simpler in the country.

"What are you thinking about?" Timori asked him.

"The rescue," Jacoby said.

"Me too," Timori replied. "Can we really do this? Whoever kidnapped Racquela...they're probably professionals."

"They *are* professionals," Paulo said, not taking his eyes off the road. "The NSP's spy network wouldn't be wrong about something like that."

"Then why aren't we going to the police?" Timori demanded.

"I didn't expect you to crack now," Paulo muttered. "I thought you had some balls."

"I have balls, you dully," he spat. "I just have...a healthy sense of caution. Abyss, I'd go in alone if I thought I could rescue her. But her life is at stake...what if we mess this up?"

Paulo let out a theatrical sigh. "I told you. We have no choice. Most of Captus Nove's police force sympathize with the Labour Party. I have it on reliable authority that some of them are in on the kidnapping. It has to be us. If we allow Racquela's father's professional goons to locate her, do you imagine you'll ever be allowed to see her again, Tim?"

Timori made a noise of exasperation and leaned his head against the window. "At least she'll be alive," he muttered.

"Or she won't," Paulo countered, "and you'll get to live the rest of your life with the guilt of knowing you did nothing to try and save her."

The sound of tires on gravel cut through the strained silence. Crystal motors made very little noise, but the country roads were rough, built for stagecoaches and wagons pulled by beasts of burden. Jacoby stared into the darkness, thinking about what was to come. The past was crystal clear but the future was always a mystery...he wondered if it would help him somehow, to have an oracular gift as Lenara did, or if the ability would be more of a burden.

"Where are we going?" Jacoby asked. "Surely we don't need to drive this far out of the city just to shoot wands."

"Is little Jakey worried about curfew again?" Paulo said.

"Fuck you, Paulo," Jacoby spat. "Not all of us are spoiled whitehands with no rules or boundaries."

Paulo chuckled and lit a cigarette, not bothering to roll down a window. "Don't presume to know anything about my life."

He let the silence stretch as he peered into the darkness ahead. "We're almost there."

Paulo turned onto a dark road. Beyond the glare of the headlights, the farmland was a nebulous darkness. The motorcoach began to slow down. Jacoby strained his eyes to see through the moonless night, but all he could make out were the distant farmhouse lights. The coach turned onto another road, even bumpier than the last one. Down the long beam the headlights cast, a building came into view. Paulo reached the end of the driveway and stopped the motor, leaving the headlights on.

Jacoby had never seen such a sad and dilapidated edifice. The wooden beams were sagging, and what was left of the flaking yellow paint was collecting in the overgrown hedges under the rotted windowsills. The windows were all broken. The front door had come off its hinges and obstructed the front steps. Jacoby couldn't see the roof, but he imagined it was in a similar state of disrepair.

"Why'd you bring us to this dirty, abyssal place?" Jacoby asked. "It looks like it's been abandoned for years."

"It has," Paulo said, folding his arms. He smiled from one side of his mouth, as though he was admiring the old structure. "It was a shattered, miserable place, even when people lived in it. Nobody'll bother us here. Orchard got sold, but it's not pickin' season."

Jacoby and Timori hauled the chest out of the back of the motorcoach and set it on the grass.

"You lived in that house, didn't you?" Timori grunted.

"Why would you bring us here?"

"Because we have a nice big target that nobody gives a shard about. And I figured maybe we could practice the infiltration plan."

"We didn't bring the pillars," Jacoby said as he opened the chest.

"*Pretend* we brought them," Paulo suggested. "Anyway, we should do some firing first."

The boys set up on the other side of the house, where they wouldn't risk hitting Paulo's motorcoach with any stray shots. Jacoby's eyes gradually adjusted to the darkness, but the wall didn't offer much of a challenge. Paulo brought out an old oil lamp from the coach and lit it, setting it nearby. With red chalk, he drew a few large circles at intervals along the wall. Standing amidst the tall grass, they started with the red-triggered shortwands that fired metal slugs.

Crystals never ceased to amaze Jacoby. They'd been in use for centuries before the Imperial scientific method was developed, but no matter how much research was done, nobody could explain how they functioned, at least not to the satisfaction of the scientific community at large. Why was the whisper of a speaker sufficient to activate or alter a crystal? Why could some people speak to crystals and not others? How could an orange crystal summon fire without requiring any kind of combustible material? The church maintained that crystals were gifts from the gods, but in an increasingly scholarly, secular, and sceptical world, such an answer was not sufficient for many.

Jacoby's faith in the gods was sparse and wavering, but he couldn't deny what he saw with his own eyes.

The pop of the wands echoed into the night as each boy chose a target and fired. Paulo's eyes darted back and forth as he examined the targets.

"Have you shot wands before, Jake?"

"Never."

"Hmm."

Jacoby glanced at each of the three chalk circles. Timori's shots were all over the place – no consistency.

"I blame the glasses Mom could never afford," Timori murmured.

Paulo's and Jacoby's targets looked distinctly similar. Although there were a couple of slugs that had sunk into the wood near the edges, most had landed somewhere close to the middle. Jacoby decided he was either very lucky or naturally skilled, because Paulo had surely been trained. He had his own private collection of wands, after all.

"Speaker *and* crack shot," Paulo muttered. "I'm glad I recruited you."

It was the closest thing to a compliment Jacoby had ever received from Paulo. He wondered again about the self-assured youth who claimed to be the son of Emperor Longoro. According to history, Paulo Longoro had been gunned down as an infant, along with the Empress, as they fled the crumbling empire at the end of the Great War.

Jake, you need to understand who Paulo is. He could hear her sweet voice in his mind.

Jacoby gazed at the building they were firing upon. Did Paulo grow up in this miserable old shack? If it was all a ruse, was Paulo merely a brilliant, anonymous student of history, seeking to seize upon the opportunity of a name and a reputation, or was he discovered by some old Imperial fanatic, and if so, who was his mysterious benefactor? A noble or wealthy entrepreneur with Imperialist sentimentalities, Jacoby didn't doubt, but it couldn't explain the ease with which Paulo manipulated the other members of the underground National Socialist Party.

He's smart, Jake, and ruthless. I've seen what will happen, and I'm telling you Paulo is going to take over Novem.

"I didn't think I'd be any good," Jacoby said, returning his attention to the targets.

"Let's try the other wands," Timori suggested.

"We're running out of time," Paulo said with a shake of his head. "I want to go through tomorrow's plan one more time, and then we should go back and make sure Jake can work the pillars."

Jacoby and Timori returned to the front of the old house while Paulo remained at the back. The plan was for the three of them to storm the house, forcing the kidnappers to surrender. Paulo's spy had informed him of a secret entrance in the back, which Paulo was going to take on his own. Timori and Jacoby would come in through the front.

The very thought of potential violence made Jacoby's pulse quicken, but he didn't see any other way to rescue Racquela, unless they wanted to leave it to Joven De'Trini and the police.

"Go!" Paulo shouted from the back of the house. Timori rushed ahead. Once Jacoby was through the threshold and within the dark confines of the condemned building, he took a moment to let his eyes adjust.

The foyer was barren, save for the dust Timori had kicked up ahead of him. It made Jacoby sneeze. A hand upon his shoulder caused him to shout in alarm and wheel around.

"It's just me," Timori said. "Where's Paulo?"

"Wherever the back entrance is." Jacoby sneezed again. "This whole practice is kind of pointless if there's nothing to shoot at."

"It's a little strange that he brought us here in the first place," Timori whispered.

Jacoby whispered to his crystal ring and it began to glow a pale blue. Upon the walls, the jaundiced floral-print wallpaper was peeling. Old paint and scratch marks riddled the lower walls.

There were crude stick-figures, illegible names, and indistinguishable figures.

"I have a theory about his reasons," Timori continued in a hushed voice. He said nothing about Jacoby's ring, but Jacoby could feel Timori's unspoken curiosity.

"What's your theory?"

Timori took another step into the room, making his way toward the door at the opposite end. "He's trying to..." The sagging floorboards gave way underneath Timori, and he fell.

"Shatters!" Timori exclaimed. He lost his grip on the wand, trying to scrabble for something to grab. Jacoby's hand shot out a moment too late as Timori plummeted into the darkness below. Jacoby heard a moan of pain as a cloud of dust and debris came up from the pit in the floorboards.

"Holy shards!" Jacoby shouted. He looked down into the crevice to see Timori sitting on a pile of splintered wooden beams. "Tim! Are you okay?"

"Yeah, I think so." Timori sat up amidst the jagged, broken floorboards that had taken the fall with him. "Can you shine that ring down here? I need to find a way out. Try not to fall in."

"Sure thing." Jacoby's hand shot down, illuminating the room about Timori. Against each wall sat a small metal bedframe, rusted from age and the elements. There were no mattresses, pillows or bedsheets to be seen, but there were plenty of rat droppings.

"I think some of the kids used to sleep down here," Timori whispered. "Creepy."

"Why are you whispering?" Jacoby shouted down.

"Because it's creepy."

"Do you see a doorway? If not, I can try and pull you back up."

"Yeah," Timori called back.

"Watch this," Timori said, grinning at Jacoby and backing up to the opposite wall. He let out an energetic shriek and charged at the boards, turning his shoulder to them at the last possible moment. The old boards gave way, plunging Timori again into darkness where Jacoby couldn't see him.

"You dully," Jacoby called out, "what did you do that for?"

"I dunno," Timori coughed. "Don't you ever get the urge to just smash something?"

"Sometimes, I guess. Can you see anything?"

"Not really. It's a hallway. You should come down here and bring that crystal. It's dark as the abyss."

"What if the stairs back up are rotten, too?"

"Don't be such a baby. Paulo is still around somewhere." Timori came back through the entryway he'd made for himself. "Besides, we're about to risk our lives tomorrow to save Racquela. This is nothing but testing the limits of irrational fear."

"Well, gee, when you put it all shiny like that..." Jacoby reluctantly lowered himself into the basement. "I feel like we're wasting time here. I still need to test those pillars."

"Soon enough," Timori said. He lowered his voice to a whisper again. "I was thinking there could be some insight into Paulo."

"What kind of insight?" Jacoby said as he followed Timori into the narrow, stone-masoned hallway. Timori grabbed Jacoby's wrist and pointed the ring like a beam of light, looking for doorways.

"Any kind. There's got to be some reason he brought us here. It's like he wants to tell us about his past, but something is stopping him from saying it directly." Jacoby made a weird face and raised his eyebrow at Timori. "Don't look at me like that. I was just..."

A loud scraping sound came from down the hallway and Timori and Jacoby both let out a yelp. They retreated to the room they knew was safe. Jacoby shone his ring back into the darkness with a shaky hand.

"Paulo?" Jacoby called out. "Was that you?"

There was a shuffling noise. Jacoby tried to swallow his fear but it felt stuck just above his throat.

"This isn't funny, Paulo," Timori said. His voice sounded tight.

Jacoby whispered to his ring and the pale glow became a flaming orange. He entered the hallway, keeping his fist well ahead of him.

"Paulo?" Jacoby called out. Timori followed beside him, his borrowed shortwand at the ready. They reached the end of the hallway. To their right, a set of perilously damaged wooden steps led up to a door, which had been left ajar. To the left, a soft glow could be seen at the end of a long dirt corridor.

"Paulo's lamp," Timori muttered.

"What in Jova's name is he doing?"

"Dunno. Get your wand ready, in case he starts acting cracked."

Side by side, they crept down the cramped hall. Jacoby's imagination and heart raced as they continued toward the pale light. What better way to be rid of two young men of uncertain political leanings than to take them to an abandoned place and shoot them?

They reached the corner. There, the masonry was rough, as though not a part of the original foundation, with dirt spilling through in places. Around the corner, the tunnel sloped down. Paulo's shadow reached up to Jacoby's shoes. He was standing down there in the cellar, staring at something, seemingly lost in thought.

Neither Timori nor Jacoby called out to him, but they continued their approach. If Paulo heard them, he made no indication. He stared out ahead with his fist underneath his chin, the dancing lamplight moving around him as though he was as immutable as the walls themselves.

"Paulo...?" Jacoby ventured.

"Hmm?" It was all the sound the boy deigned to make. Jacoby turned his head to see what Paulo was looking at.

"Gods," Jacoby gasped. There in the root cellar, behind the barren, forgotten shelves and the old clay bricks that had been pulled away, a skull grinned back at the boys. The rest of the bones were still buried behind the wall, leaving Jacoby to speculate as to who the corpse had been and why it was put there...and by whom. He looked back at Paulo, who was still staring at the skull, lost in some silent conversation.

"I forgot you were here," Paulo said. The horror was frozen upon Timori's face as he gaped at the corpse.

Jacoby was more interested in the little tin toy Paulo clutched to his chest.

Chapter 25

Nobody dared speak of what had transpired between Leo and Nerus, but Leo knew it was on all the boys' minds. Where once Nerus would use the cudgel on Leo, instead he focused his spiteful stare as the boys dug in the tunnel, daring any of them to defy him again, letting the silence and tension grow as he displayed the wand holstered upon his hip like a warning.

Leo, working just as hard as he always had, knew it wasn't the warning Nerus wanted to telegraph. It was a warning that the man was losing control. If he killed Leo then he lost his best worker, and the fear of murder would drain any remaining vim from the rest of the boys. If he allowed Leo to show defiance again, his veneer of control would slip away for good.

Leo took care not to smile. He would probably never see Sofia again, after all. He was not free yet. However, events were finally beginning to shift in his favour. He knew it from the moment his pickaxe struck something hard.

"Crystal," he called out. Fearing the cudgel, the other boys rushed over and began digging alongside Leo. Between the distinct sounds of metal striking earth, Leo heard Nerus rubbing his hands together excitedly. Minutes later, a crystal came free and fell to the ground at Leo's feet. It was the size of his fist and black as midnight. He'd never seen a black one before. Leo didn't know much about what the different colours meant, but he recalled reading a rhyme about it somewhere in a children's book. He tried to remember the verse, but the only line he could summon to mind was *Take care not to touch, for your life it will keep.*

"Step back, you dirt-crawling worms," Nerus commanded. He stared at the crystal, scratching at his chin stubble.

Touch it, you rotten bastard, Leo thought. *See what happens.*

"By Jova," Nerus muttered. "Black as onyx." His voice trembled. Leo couldn't tell if it was from fear or excitement. "Keep digging, worms, and for the gods' sake don't touch any of 'em." He ran for the stairs, faster than Leo had ever seen him move. "Natalya!" he hollered. "We just struck it rich!"

Leo heard the basement door slam. When he turned around, the other three boys were already kneeling down, ogling the crystal.

"You heard him," Leo said. "Don't touch it. Keep working or you'll get the cudgel, most like." Leo lifted his pickaxe and continued to dig. He saw other dark shapes gleaming in the soil. Before long, they had gathered a small pile of black crystals at their feet.

"Why can't we touch 'em?" Bernardo huffed.

"You never heard the rhyme?" Leo asked. "They're supposed to be dangerous, the black ones. And anyway they don't belong to us."

Arturo stopped digging. "Since when do you give a shard what Nerus wants?"

Leo shrugged. "I don't. But think about how hard he beat me the last time I picked one up."

"I was thinking, though," Arnaldo said, his voice down to a whisper, "that we could get rich off o'these. Get out of here finally, y'know?"

"And how do you propose to carry them out of here," Leo wondered, "without so much as a burlap sack to your name?"

"I could use my blanket," Arnaldo replied. "Besides, crystals have power. We could use 'em somehow to stop Nerus."

Arturo took another swing at the dirt. "Hey, maybe we should just get back to digging," he suggested. "Nerus wouldn't like us talking about this."

"Somehow?" Leo scoffed. "You gotta be a speaker to use crystals like that." He leaned on his pickaxe. "If you think you're one of the special few, go right ahead and try it. I'll bet you *my* blanket it kills you."

"Don't do it," Bernardo suggested, also returning to his digging. "He's got that tone of voice...the one that means you can't trust him."

"It's just a chunk of rock," Arnaldo insisted. "If I'm a speaker, it'll make me powerful. If not...it'll do nothing." He looked around for confirmation, but Bernardo and Arturo were digging out more crystals and Leo merely shrugged. "Right?"

"Pick it up and find out," Leo suggested.

"Darers go first," Arnaldo said.

Leo made a show of returning to his digging. "We're not kids anymore, Arnie. If you wanna piss around, go ahead. Just don't come crying to us when Nerus beats you bloody or you get your soul sucked out through your nose."

Leo could see Arnaldo in his peripheral vision, standing quietly contemplating the crystals as the other three continued to dig out more of the precious rocks. Arnaldo leaned down and picked one up. Leo waited to hear some kind of exclamation or remark, but Arnaldo made no sound.

"Shards and shatters, he't not moving," Bernardo exclaimed.

Leo turned his head away from his work. Sure enough, Arnaldo was frozen in a stooped position, his eyes open but lifeless. To Leo's amazement, the crystal locked in his grip had gone from jet black to a rich brown.

"Don't touch him," Leo commanded. "Everybody step back."

"Holy shards," Arturo whispered. "Arnie, can you hear me?" He brought his arm forward to shake the boy, but Leo knocked him back roughly.

"Keep your voice down, dully. And for the gods' sake, don't touch him unless you want to suffer the same fate."

Arturo shook off Leo's grip. "What the fuck do you care? You're the one who dared him to grab the godsdamned crystal."

"I didn't think he was stupid enough to do it."

The three diggers stood back and surveyed their paralyzed friend. Leo kept one side of his head tilted, ears perked to listen for footsteps coming back downstairs. Slowly, he brought his pickaxe forward and gave Arnaldo a gentle nudge with it. The boy tipped over so slowly Leo had to suppress a nervous laugh. When the boy hit the ground, his body seemed to relax, and for a moment Leo thought perhaps Arnaldo had been fooling them all along. His eyes, however, remained open and unblinking. Leo dared not touch him, but he waited to see if Arnaldo's chest was rising and falling.

The ominous hammer of footfalls above them brought them out of their shock.

"Nerus is coming," Bernardo gasped. "What do we do? What do we do?"

"Calm down," Leo said. "Just get back to digging, both of you. I'll handle this."

"How?" they both asked.

"Just shut up and dig."

Leo took a deep breath and walked toward the stairs. He could hear Lutias barking, which meant Nerus was at the basement door. Steeling himself, Leo put on an expression of urgent concern.

Nerus opened the door and looked down upon Leo from the top of the stairs. His avaricious grin soured into a spiteful frown. Bony Lutias snarled from beside his sallow master.

"Why the fuck aren't you digging?" Nerus asked as he came down the stairs.

"It's Arnaldo, he's..."

The cudgel hit him across the jaw. He'd been ready for it, but he had to make a show so he gasped out in pain.

"You stop when I tell you to stop." Nerus said. He struck Leo again. "What's Arnaldo up to now? Does he want a beating, too?"

"He just fell over and stopped moving...I think he's worked to exhaustion!"

Nerus snorted. "I know a way to motivate him. I need that whole vein of crystals ready in a week." He stormed off down the basement toward the digging tunnel. Leo followed at his heels, feigning obedience.

Bernardo and Arturo were hard at work when Nerus arrived, likely hoping their buckets of sweat would help them avoid a lashing. More black crystals had come free from the wall and the pile was almost the same size as the immobile figure lying next to it.

Nerus, ashen-faced, stared at Arnaldo. Leo knew it wasn't concern for the boy that he saw on the man's face. It was the distress of losing a working pair of hands.

"Get to digging," Nerus said to Leo without looking at him. "And for the last fucking time, don't touch any of the crystals."

Leo didn't bother moving. Nerus was dumbstruck by the sight of Arnaldo. Whether the boy had become a corpse or just a soul-stripped shell, Leo couldn't say, but he was fairly certain the other two boys were contemplating Arnaldo's choice as an appealing alternative to digging in a basement for all eternity. Leo, however, saw better choices.

As Nerus bent down to examine the boy, Leo's pickaxe struck. Nerus didn't cry out. Instead, a stream of bubbly crimson came out from his parted lips and covered the other stains on his undershirt. His eyes rolled back into his head and he fell over next to Arnaldo.

Bernardo and Arturo, so fearful of Nerus's presence, hadn't even noticed he was on the ground, hand twitching randomly as Leo tried to pull his pickaxe back out. Then Leo remembered the wand and cudgel and relieved them from Nerus's custody.

He could hear Lutias barking again from the stairs and thought perhaps Natalya was coming down to check on progress. Leo examined the wand briefly. It seemed easy enough to use.

"Keep digging, boys," he said as he marched off toward the stairs. "I'll be right back."

Chapter 26

After three days, Racquela's faith in a rescue began to weaken.

Her meals, which seemed to come sporadically, were usually chunks of old bread, uncooked turnips without so much as salt for flavour, or thin strips of unidentifiable meat that made her feel sick to her stomach. To make matters worse, she was growing ill. Racquela suspected the horrible valley water was the cause. She finally summoned the courage to ask Ramus about the water closet on the second day, and he explained that in the valley it was simply referred to as 'the toilet.'

Bartus ranted and roared, but in the end he acquiesced that she could use it, so long as she was escorted to and from the room by an armed guard. They guarded her in shifts, anyway, sitting in a chair right above the cellar door, usually toting the longwand. She really didn't think there was much chance of her being able to escape through their negligence.

When her fever began, Racquela reminded herself over and over again that it was a good thing she'd asked Ramus about the 'toilet.' The horrible, disgusting indignity of it all would have been too shameful for her to bear. She couldn't believe she used to fret over a dirt stain on the hem of her dress.

As the days passed, no whisper of ransom or din of rescue reached her ears through the cracks in the floor. Her captors argued occasionally, but other than that tension by proxy, Racquela was left alone in the dark and quiet, to anxieties that had no resolution.

She knew it was the fourth day since her capture because the men were talking about it above her head, loud enough for her to hear. The man with the nasal voice, whose name was Malak,

212

was suggesting they lower the amount requested, split the money and disappear.

"Have you no honour?" Ramus hissed. "We promised the majority of that money to the party and the poor. What kind of socialist are you?"

"The kind who fears for his life," Malak replied. "I think he's trying to wait us out, Ramus."

"Send him a finger," Bartus suggested. Racquela gasped and covered her mouth. "Or maybe her pretty little nose."

"Look, we can't do anything without taking it to the party," Ramus said.

"The party?" Bartus asked. "Or the boss? Party don't know about this."

"I meant the boss. Obviously." They lowered their voices. Racquela, standing on a lower rung of the ladder and straining to hear, could still make out their words but was no longer certain who was speaking.

"Fine, then let's go."

"Oh, no. You're not leaving me here to guard her by myself while the two of you parlay with the boss. I want my say."

"Well, who's gonna guard her, then?"

"Get the kid to do it."

"You can't trust a Dori with something like that."

"There's still Angelo at the door."

"Fine, let's go, then. Call the kid in."

Racquela climbed back down the rotted ladder and backed into the corner, trying to control her heavy breathing. Above her, the hushed voices continued, and chairs groaned across the floor. A soft, boyish voice entered the conversation. Then she heard clomping sets of boots leaving the room, and all was silent.

Racquela's stomach gurgled. She heard a shuffling sound above her and held herself very still.

"M'lady?" the voice came clear through the floor. "You there?"

"Yes," Racquela said. Dillas didn't scare her the same way Bartus did, but her father had warned her long ago to be wary of the Dori. Every year at Carnival, she had to watch her purse. The Dori were liars, thieves, and wandering scoundrels, and Dillas had already proved they were not to be trusted.

"M'lady, Dillas humbly offers apologies for your treatment, and his involvement. 'sfor the best, y'see. Didn't want it to happen this way, but we're all starving, y'see."

Racquela kept her mouth shut.

"It'll turn out aright. Daddy'll bring the dinari and we give you back, and a balance is struck."

"By sending us to the poorhouse," Racquela blurted.

"A balance, m'lady. Your family, they have lots of dinari. The Dori, they have none."

"And whose fault is that?" Dillas didn't answer, but Racquela could still hear him breathing through the floorboards.

"That's what I thought," Racquela said, wishing Dillas could see her smug smirk.

"The question lies not in fault, m'lady...no fault of yours, that is. All of us, we are held to the successes and failures of our ancestors, and m'lady didn't choose to be De'Trini any more than Dillas chose to be Dori."

"Hmph," Racquela said. "That's a convenient way to absolve yourself of your guilt."

"Not so, m'lady De'Trini. We all make our choices in the span of our seasons, and thus are future generations beholden to *our* errors. Dillas was chosen merely because of his stagecoach, and what else was he to do? Dillas had never met m'lady De'Trini, and though he has now seen her legendary beauty, he knows her ransom will feed thousands."

"So you became a part of this...to help your people? Why would the Dori even remain here, casteless and starving? It seems pretty cracked to me."

Above, Dillas seemed to be holding his breath. Just as Racquela resigned herself to the quiet, he cleared his throat.

"That story, m'lady, it is a long one. And Dillas doesn't tell it well...not in your tongue."

"I have time," Racquela said as she folded her arms.

"So be it. Perhaps m'lady will see things from another facet...but perhaps not. Long ago, long, long before the Novens came to this land, the Dori lived here in peace with all things."

Racquela rolled her eyes. *Everyone knows the Novens were given this land by Jova himself. The Dori really are liars.*

"That's blasphemy," she said before she could stop herself.

"What did m'lady say?"

"I said...I have to pee." As soon as the thought struck her, she knew she would never get another chance. Her hands began to shake, but she told herself to remain calm.

"Ah. Dillas was instructed to not let m'lady out of the cellar."

Racquela tried to make it sound as though she was intensely uncomfortable. Given her nerves, it wasn't much of a stretch.

"But surely they told you they let me use the water...ah, toilet, upstairs. Escorted. You wouldn't want me to get sick, would you? If I die of dysentery, then my father's wrath will be swift and you'll all get nothing."

"Surely if m'lady is merely making water, then..."

"I...it's not...just water I'm making," she stammered, her cheeks flushing red.

Again, Dillas was silent for a moment. Racquela heard him pace the floor a couple of times, from the cellar door to the table and back. Suddenly the trap swung open.

"Come up," he said.

Racquela held her breath. It seemed too easy suddenly, as though perhaps it was a Dori trick. Trembling, she approached the ladder.

"Slowly," Dillas commanded.

Fumbling with the old sagging beams of wood, praying to all the gods she could name that she wouldn't slip and fall or that Dillas wasn't waiting to kill her, Racquela climbed. To her surprise, Dillas offered her a hand up, over the step that had rotted through. He was unusually strong for his size, and then she was up and standing in the lamp-lit room, and as he let her arm go she realized she'd missed her chance – a chance to pull him down into the cellar and slam the door shut, or grab the longwand.

Then the barrel was there in her face. Racquela swallowed the lump in her throat.

"M'lady knows the way."

Her knees were wobbling but she managed to take steady paces toward the hallway door. Dillas followed behind her, making quiet steps. Racquela thought about making a dash for the door, but then she imagined her crumpled and bloody body after a shot from the red-triggered longwand, and her courage left her again.

The water closet was just as dark as Racquela's cellar-prison. She'd forgotten to ask Dillas if she could bring the lamp that usually sat on the table. Not wanting Dillas to overhear any of her gastrointestinal distress, she turned on the rusty faucet and let the cold water run down the sink.

When she was finished, she washed her hands and wished in vain for a simple mirror. Despite her reservations, Racquela also decided to take a long drink of water. It tasted metallic and strange to her, and although she was certain it was making her sick, she had little choice other than dehydration.

When Racquela tightened the tap, she heard voices in the hallway.

"...teach her a lesson fer bein' such an entitled brat, and nobody is gonna stop me, 'specially not some fairy kid who can barely hold a wand."

Racquela pressed her ear to the door.

"Dillas said no. We escort her back to the cellar. She will not be touched, that was the agreement."

"I don't have to honour the agreement of a nobody. Put the wand down afore you hurt yourself, and go watch the back fer the others. I'll bring 'er back in one piece." His chuckle made Racquela's legs feel like water.

"No." Dillas's tone had lost any suggestion of boyishness. "Leave m'lady be."

"Oh, so she's m'lady now, isshe? Yer a fuckin' traitor and a fairy freak. Fuckin' Dori nobody. I'm gonna teach you a lesson first."

Racquela winced, expecting to hear wandshot. Instead there were scuffles and grunts.

"This might be your only chance, you dully," she whispered to herself. She took a deep breath and summoned what remained of her courage, then threw the door open.

She had found her courage a moment too late. Bartus had wrested the longwand from Dillas, who was falling to the floor clutching the side of his face.

"Take a good long look, De'Trini," Bartus said. "Yer gonna be seein' a lot more of this, the longer you whitehands chip away at us n' conspire with anyone who'll take a shiny dinari."

He lowered the wand, aiming for Dillas. Frozen with fear, Racquela could do nothing but watch as Dillas whispered something, perhaps a Dori prayer of some kind.

When Bartus pulled the trigger, Racquela screamed.

Chapter 27

Excerpt from the radio drama 'Crystal
Captain'
Episode 10 - 'Rescue from Stormspeaker
Station'

Narrator: Welcome back for another
thrilling episode of 'Crystal Captain,' the
adventures of sky-speaker Captain Corvelius
and his daring crew of skyship fliers. I'm
your host with the most, Marius Ghost, here
to bring you the next hair-raising, mind-
shattering chapter.

Narrator: Episode Ten - 'Rescue from
Sky Station Alpha.' Tension condenses in the
skies above the downtrodden nation of
Neonovus. An uneasy ceasefire has been
called between Neonovus and the Alliance of
Kingdoms, but as the prime minister of
Neonovus negotiates with the power-hungry
kings for a lasting peace, many mercenary
fliers have turned pirate and joined with
the most nefarious pirate of them all -
Captain Belzegor!

Narrator: Captain Corvelius, eager to
keep his brigade's skills shiny and protect
the innocent from piracy, led a daring raid
against Captain Belzegor's hideout, the
infamous Stormspeaker Station. However, a
trap had been set for the First Sky Brigade,

and Alliance fliers, disguised as pirates, assisted the roguish Belzegor. Outnumbered and overwhelmed, our hero and his friends fought bravely, but just as the good captain radioed to retreat and regroup, his skycraft was hit by scattershot. The last his brigade saw of him, he and his wrecked ship were hurtling toward the dock of Belzegor's nimbus-fortress.

Narrator: Our scene opens in a stone jail cell with no windows. The bars are cold skyiron, harder than any steel we know of today. When we last left our hero, the dashing, handsome, and capable Captain Caius Corvelius of the First Sky Brigade, he had been taken prisoner by the nefarious leader of the Storm Pirates, Captain Belzegor.

Corvelius: Urgh...these bars...stuck tight. No way out. Curse you, Belzegor! You'll pay for this. All I can do now is trust that my men will come. But wait...the lock. It appears to be supercrystal. I'll just get my amulet, and...

(Cue dramatic music)

Corvelius: Shards! My father's amulet! It's gone!

(Cue Belzegor's theme. Sound of marching feet.)

Corvelius: Belzegor. You fiend!

Belzegor: Fiend? My dear Captain, you were defeated, true as Tybal. There is no cause to throw insults, though I can certainly understand your shame, ha-ha-ha! How it must shatter you, to know that your proud airship was scattershot down by the very man who slayed your father.

(Cue dramatic music)

Corvelius: Spare me your lies, pirate. Commander Cassius, my father, is on a mission of secrecy for the Republic. And speaking of my father, what have you done with his crystal amulet, you dirty thief?

(Sound of a heavy metal chain)

Belzegor: Oh, you mean this amulet? I think it is becoming on me, don't you, Captain? You poor wretch. It seems as though there is nothing I cannot take away from you. Your skycraft, your father, your family heirloom which is the secret to your power...

Corvelius: I tell you my father is alive!

Belzegor: Oh, but I just love being the bearer of bad news. I know all about the commander's secret rendezvous with the king of Moonpeak Mountain. But I'm afraid he may have been...waylaid. Ah-ha! Ha-ha-ha-haaaa...

Corvelius: You lie!

Belzegor: Do I, Captain? Then tell me, why would I have...this?

(Cue dramatic music)

Corvelius: But...it cannot be! My mother's ring, companion to the amulet. Where did you get that?

Belzegor: Where else but from your father's cold finger. Mua-ha-ha-haaaa...

(Cue dramatic music)

Corvelius: Nooooooo! It cannot be!

Belzegor: Well, I have gloated enough. There is plenty enough for me to do...hunt down your sky brigade to the last man, use the power of the amulet and the ring together to control the kingdoms and destroy your petty republic once and for all, that kind of thing. After that perhaps I'll conquer the stars, who knows? Goodbye, Captain. I'd let you join your mother and father in the abyss, but it's so much better to watch you suffer. Ah-ha! Ha-ha-ha-haaaa...

(Sound of footsteps)

Corvelius: Jova curse you! Father...can it be true? I cannot believe Belzegor would ever best you in a sky-tilt, but sure enough, there was the ring. I have failed you, Father. The sky-amulet and earth-ring were bequeathed to Mother and Father so that lesser hearts would not be tempted by their power...and now they have both fallen into the hands of the worst kind of power-monger. But how did he ever discover Father's mission?

A woman's voice: Are you going to talk to yourself all day? Some of us are trying to rot away in peace and quiet.

Corvelius: Who said that?

A woman's voice: You're brave, Captain, but not too bright and clear, are you? I'm in the next cell over. My name's Marquela.

Corvelius: Well, my lady Marquela, at least I'll have some company while I wait for a rescue from the First Sky Brigade.

Marquela: You're going to wait for a rescue? But Belzegor is surely setting a trap for any fliers who approach the station.

Corvelius: We already fell into a trap. They will not hesitate to rescue their captain.

Marquela: Well some of us can't wait that long. Don't you have a hidden crystal somewhere that can open the lock?

Corvelius: I did. It shattered when I used it to replace the seventh sky seal of Samalus.

Marquela: I heard once you have a crystal button on your coat.

Corvelius: Ah, yes. I used it to defeat a moon-beast last year.

Marquela: And?

Corvelius: The beast swallowed it.

Marquela: I see. Well, I suppose I'll have to do everything, then. If I toss something in front of your cell, can you reach through the bars and get it?

Corvelius: Yes, I believe so. What is it?

(Sound of a crystal falling on the ground)

Marquela: This.

Corvelius: A crystal earring? Why didn't you say so?

Marquela: I just did, Captain. Try not to shatter it. It was a gift.

Corvelius: Such a gift! Who are you, my lady, to receive such adornment?

Marquela: Can we just worry about escaping first? Gods, Captain, less talking and more speaking.

Corvelius: Just a moment, my lady. And...there!

(Sound of rusty hinges)

Corvelius: And now, your cell.

(Sound of rusty hinges)

Corvelius: You are free!

Marquela: Please, announce it to the entire station.

Corvelius: My lady, some gratitude may be in order.

Marquela: Yes, you are very brave, Captain. Those crystal locks didn't stand a chance.

Corvelius: They were supercrystal, I'll have you know.

Marquela: Ah, a mighty foe, then, for the captain of the First Sky Brigade. My earring, if you please.

Corvelius: My lady, I still have need of it. Otherwise we are defenceless.

Marquela: (Sigh) Lead on, then, Captain.

Corvelius: I was unconscious when I was brought here. Do you know the way out?

Marquela: I suppose I must do everything. Follow me.

Narrator: And so, our hero and the saucy but beautiful prisoner Marquela traversed the cold, damp dungeon of Belzegor's sky fortress. Dear listeners, let us pray the captain's wits hold out longer than his luck, for he is armed with only a tiny crystal from an earring...

Marquela: Look out! Guards!

Corvelius: Ignatio!

(Crystal sound effect. Sound of fire. Guards screaming.)

Corvelius: Quickly, now. I think they may be alerted to our presence.

Marquela: Unless screaming in agony is commonplace here. Take this wand and I'll take the other. I think this is the dock. Where is your ship, Captain?

Corvelius: Grievously damaged, my lady.

Marquela: We must take one of their ships, then.

Corvelius: What? Steal a ship? Why, I'd be no better than they are!

Marquela: You fliers and your honour. We don't have much choice, Captain.

Corvelius: But I...look out!

(Sound of explosions)

Marquela: Look! Fliers! They're firing at the dock!

Corvelius: My lady! Take cover here!

(Sound of explosions)

Corvelius: It is my brigade. Come, we must join the fight. The pirates are taking to the skies.

Marquela: But if you take one of their ships, your brigade will fire upon you, thinking you to be a pirate.

Corvelius: We cannot remain here, the dock is ablaze!

(Cue Belzegor's theme)

Belzegor: Not so fast, Captain!

Corvelius: Quickly, Marquela. Into the flier, go! I shall hold him off.

Marquela: But...

Corvelius: Go!

Narrator: As Marquela climbs into a ship, Captain Corvelius holds a tiny crystal in his hand, preparing to face off with his nemesis, who now wields the greatest power on earth and in the sky! Can Marquela survive against the First Sky Brigade? Will Corvelius avenge his father's murder? Tune in next Joveday, same time, for the next

thrilling chapter of Crystal Captain! I'm
your host with the most, Marius Ghost,
bidding you a pleasant evening, listeners...
        (Cue Crystal Captain theme)

***

The smoke curled up from Paulo's mouth in the hazy autumn sunset. Timori had to wave it away from his face. The three boys were sitting upon a roof, looking down at a particularly grubby street in Avati Valley. Once the sun had sunk behind the crest of Cateli Hill, Paulo signalled them with a nod. They hopped from rooftop to rooftop to reach the fire escape, beneath which was parked Paulo's motorcoach.

"Are we all clear?" Paulo asked as he started the engine.

Timori sighed. They'd gone over the plan too many times to count.

"I escort Jake as he aligns the four pillars in hidden locations surrounding the house. You play lookout and make sure we aren't spotted. Once the pillars are aligned, we charge the front door and you take the tunnel your informant told you about. We do our best to subdue them without bloodshed."

"Well, don't get too excited about it, Tim," Paulo said with a chuckle.

"This isn't a radio play," he replied. They drove down the street to park in an empty spot.

The pillars and wands were hidden in a sports bag that Timori hauled out of the back of the coach. The boys stole away to a nearby alley as soon as they could. Under the cover of garbage bins, they pulled out the dark trench coats Paulo had bought, put them on and turned up the collars. They each donned a fedora, pulled the brims down and hid their wands in the pockets that had been specially sewn to the inside of each coat. Then Jacoby took out a bundle of cloth and unwrapped the first crystal.

"I'm headed to the lookout spot," Paulo whispered. "Remember the signal if you're discovered by the 'liza and we have to abandon the plan. Do not forget they're on the Labour Party's side...they will not hesitate to shoot first. If one of the kidnappers discovers you before the alignment is done, we go in crystals aglow. For Novem." He slunk off down the alleyway.

"For Racquela," Timori said.

"For Lenara," Jacoby whispered.

Timori and Jacoby waited for Paulo to get into position upon his pre-selected rooftop, then they crept through the alley until they found the small 'x' marked in chalk upon the base of a brick wall.

"So his informant came through after all," Timori remarked. "I thought we would have to do this blind."

"As long as the whole house is within the area of the pillars, it should work," Jacoby whispered back. He carefully leaned the deep violet crystal against the wall and whispered a phrase in the Old Noven tongue. "No sign of guards?"

Timori shook his head. "It would seem too conspicuous...but they might be paying people to watch from windows. Let's just be quick. Every second we waste, Racquela is still in danger. Are you sure our wands will still function?"

Jacoby stood and adjusted his flipped collar. "I aligned them all and tested them twice." He picked up the sports bag and continued down the alleyway, searching for the next chalk mark.

Suddenly Jacoby yelped in shock, dropping the bag of crystals. As Timori drew his wand, he saw a cat darting out from behind a garbage can.

"Jova's sake!" Jacoby cried as the cat leapt onto a nearby windowsill.

"Shatters," Timori whispered. He rushed up to the dropped bag and unclasped it to check the crystals within.

"Godsdamned cat," Jacoby said as he knelt down.

"Shh."

"Let me see the crystals."

Of the three remaining pillars, two had come through fine, but the third had a deep crack along its middle.

"Fuck," Jacoby breathed. "Shards and shatters, fuck."

"Can you fix it?" Timori asked.

Jacoby shook his head. "No, a crack is a crack. However, the alignment will remain unchanged. If the pillar works, it works. If not..."

Timori wiped his brow. "Can't you tell if it works or not?"

"Godsdamnit, Tim, I'm not that advanced. I'm barely skilled enough to align these abyssal things."

"I'm not abandoning Racquela now."

"Neither am I."

"So do we give the signal and rush in?" Timori was still tightly gripping his wand.

"We might have to."

Timori stood up and looked around. There was no sign of anyone in the alley, not even the cat. "Okay, let's go."

"Wait."

"What?"

"We can do this with three crystals."

Timori knelt down again. His hands were beginning to shake. "Then why do we need four? I thought we needed four."

"The pillars create an area within which crystals do not function, unless they are specially aligned to the pillars themselves. Four pillars make a nice square area, but we can still make a triangle. We'll just have to set the other two crystals farther out to cover the area of the house. The pillars have a limited range, but we should we well within it, given how big they are."

"Are you sure that will work?"

"Yes. We just have to move farther out from the markers. Cover me while I find good spots for these."

They found the next chalk mark farther down the alley, but Timori and Jacoby continued on until they found a suitable hiding spot for the second crystal, behind a gutted radio. In order to find a good place for the third crystal, they had to walk along a wider valley street. Timori and Jacoby flipped their collars back down, hid their wands and pushed their hats up, chatting about how much hotter it had been last year in Septembra.

Timori had often complained he lived in the poorest corner of Captus Nove, but he knew that was far from the truth. He lived just off of Corti Street, which boasted the busiest row of storefronts in the Avati Valley. Closer to the river and the factories, these houses were crammed together like grown-up teeth in a child's mouth. There was fading paint and crumbling mortar, piles of refuse and hovels where beggars once camped, vacant now as the casteless and growing destitute left to seek more lucrative streets and plazas.

There were no leisurely walks upon those impoverished streets. A pall of desperation hung in the air as eyes watched from behind blinds and shutters. Timori could feel the collective unrest like an accusation. Though he was a dissident and a miner's boy, he spent his time with the upper castes, attending one of their exclusive schools. Sure, he had earned the right to be there, but it did not change the fact that the crystal he carried in the bag could have paid rent for a whole row of those dilapidated houses.

It was easy for Timori to see why Racquela had been kidnapped. Some small, shameful part of him admitted that, had it been some other noble's daughter, he may have felt differently about a rescue.

As he and Jacoby crossed the street, Timori noticed a trio of men exiting their target house. Timori pushed himself and Jacoby against the wall and peered around the corner. The three men walked down the street, urgently, and in the opposite direction.

"Holy shards," Timori muttered. "This is our chance."

"What's happening?" Jacoby asked.

"They're leaving. Three of them." He looked again. The men had rounded another corner and were out of sight. "Quickly, let's find a place for that last crystal." They dashed across the road and peered about for somewhere to hide the final pillar.

"There," Timori pointed, "in that empty stagecoach." The boys ducked behind it.

"What if it moves?" Jacoby asked as he withdrew the crystal.

"Without a horse hitched up to it? Anyway, there's no time. Whisper, godsdamnit."

Jacoby whispered to the pillar, then slowly opened the door of the stagecoach and slid it inside. Timori peered around the stagecoach to discover that one of the three men was returning to the house, looking about himself anxiously. Jacoby was standing up, but Timori pulled him back behind the coach before he was spotted.

"Shh." Timori said.

"Was I seen?"

"I don't think so. If we move now, we can surprise him and force him to surrender."

"Shatters," Jacoby whispered. "I don't know if I'm ready for this."

"It's now or never, Jake."

"You're right, Racquela needs us. Let's go."

He brought his fist up to his chin and whispered a phrase to the crystal ring upon his finger. The pillar in the stagecoach began to glow brightly. It was the signal that would alert Paulo the rescue was commencing. Before he could hesitate any further, Timori dashed out from behind the coach and made a sprint for the door of the house.

Time seemed to slow down for Timori even though he was running. He could feel his pulse quicken as beads of sweat broke out across his body. Dashing up the steps, he kicked the front door, just like they did in the radio show 'Speaker for Hire.' The ratty, rotting plank splintered and gave way easily, hinges popping out as the door cracked the wrong way like a broken bone.

Within the house, a lanky young man was caught in a startled expression, raising his wand at Timori.

"Surrender!" Timori commanded, bringing his own wand to bear. He could hear Jacoby rushing up behind him. A candle sputtered on the floor nearby, lending a grim intensity to the door guard's shocked expression.

The young man pulled the trigger. Timori's heart clenched so hard he thought it would cease to beat forever. When nothing followed, Timori heard Jacoby's breath of relief. Their adversary pulled desperately upon the trigger several more times, an anxious noise rising in his throat.

"I'm a speaker," Jacoby said as he pointed the tip of his wand up at the man's face. "Surrender and we won't hurt you."

He dropped his wand and whimpered, slumping against the wall. Jacoby picked up the spare weapon with a shaky hand.

"The authorities will deal with you," Timori said. He looked at Jacoby, whose eyes were darting between the man they had subdued and the shadowy hallway beyond the foyer. "Let's go."

As he turned to go, Timori heard a shout echoing from beyond the door at the end of the hallway. He thought about waiting and ambushing whoever came through the door.

Then he heard wandshot.

"Fuck," he said. If Paulo had fired his wand, then something had gone wrong. They had agreed to subdue the kidnappers, take them alive, and force them to face justice. Timori looked to Jacoby, who nodded back to him. They raced for the door at the end of the hall. Once more, Timori kicked it down.

Beyond was a small room with a table and chairs and two doors that had been left ajar, one to Timori's right and one in the floor. Timori motioned for Jacoby to check the trap door. As he peered around the other door, his heart leapt into his throat. A dishevelled Racquela was standing beside a slender blonde man, who pointed a longwand at a gruesome pile of carnage upon the floor.

Gods, Timori thought. He felt bile rising in his throat. *Paulo...*

"Run, Racquela!" he shouted, knowing it might be the last thing she ever heard him say. He didn't know why the kidnapper's longwand was still functioning, but he didn't have the time to think about it. He lifted his own sleek grey wand up, beckoning, begging Racquela to move out of the way with his other hand.

"Wait!" Racquela shouted, but it was too late. Timori had already drawn his finger back, but instead of feeling the crystal trigger move, he felt tiny shards fall upon his hand. They almost tickled. The shards tinkled to the floor and the blonde man lifted his longwand. Timori's impulse was to run and tackle the man, but he found himself unable to move.

Shatters, he thought, *another speaker.* Images flashed before his mind's eye: his father's face, a football game in the rain, the first time he and Racquela made love. *The old saying is that you see your whole life right before you die. Maybe it's just shards and pieces. How would anybody know, who wasn't already dead? Jacoby, save me, godsdamnit...*

As though a prayer had been answered, Timori saw Jacoby rush up beside him and hold his wand ready.

"Don't shoot, anybody!" Racquela pleaded. The blonde man leaned toward Racquela but didn't take his eyes off of Jacoby and Timori.

"Does m'lady know these boys?"

"I'm a speaker," Jacoby warned. "Step away from her."

Damnit, Jake, he's a speaker too. Timori wanted to scream for both of them to lay down their wands, but he was still paralyzed by whatever the blonde crystal speaker had done. *Don't threaten him right now. Racquela's life is still in danger.*

"Wait, Jake," Racquela pleaded. As she spoke, Timori saw a tall figure burst up from another trap door behind Racquela. At first he thought it was the guard from the entrance, but when he noticed dark curls and cold eyes, he realized it was Paulo. *Then who's that body lying there?*

"He's helping..."

Racquela's words were swallowed by a burst of wandshot. There was a look of shock on the kidnapper's face. He was staring at his own blood and gray matter on the wall in front of him. Then he fell to the floor beside the other corpse, his eyes open and vacant.

Racquela made a choked sob as Paulo grabbed her hand. Timori felt the paralysis ebb away, and then it was Jacoby who appeared to be frozen still. There were spatters of blood upon his cheeks, and he was still holding his wand up, aiming it at nothing.

"Come on," Paulo said. "Someone will telegram the police about the wandshot eventually. Let's go."

"You killed him," Racquela said as she stared at the body. Timori was looking at Paulo's hand, clasped in Racquela's. *Just to urge her to come away from the body, surely,* Timori told himself.

"I didn't know what he would do," Paulo said. "We came here to rescue you. Come on." He gestured toward the secret entrance he had taken to get in. "It'll be for nothing if we all get jailed."

"Right," Jacoby said. He peeled his gaze away from the corpses. "Let's get out of here."

Timori and Jacoby followed Paulo and Racquela through the back entrance Paulo had taken. It was a rough-hewn tunnel that had been dug under the house. It ended in a small basement room filled with cobwebs, barrels, and empty glass jars. Paulo hoisted himself out of the basement window first, then offered a lift to Racquela.

The sun had set and the clouds were blood-red as the sky darkened. In the distance, a police siren wailed.

"I have to get home," Racquela said, wiping a tear from her eye. "I owe you my life. All of you."

"Let me take you," Timori offered, standing in between her and Paulo. He grabbed her hand before she could pull away.

"No," Paulo said. "I have the motorcoach. That is the quickest way, and her safety is of the highest concern. We should split up so we are not followed. Besides, you and Jake need to get the pillars."

"Racquela," Timori said, "I just want you to know that..."

"Later," she said, cutting him off. "We'll talk later, Tim." She gave him a quick hug and left with Paulo. He grabbed her hand again as they disappeared into the evening's shadows.

Jacoby dashed down the alley to grab one of the pillars. Timori tried to remember where they'd hidden the first crystal. As the blare of the siren drew near, a deep pit of disappointment settled in Timori's stomach. Was it folly to have believed rescuing Racquela could have changed her feelings toward him?

They were holding hands. Surely just out of excitement and fear. He was the closest one to her when we rescued her.

There was a rustling sound. Timori knew it was probably just the cat again, but he lifted his wand, regardless. He heard a wheezing cough. Taking a step closer, he found a man with shattered glasses lying behind a pile of garbage, clutching his stomach. His shirt and hands glistened red as his blood trailed down into the alley's gutter.

"Help," he said weakly. "Please help me, young man. Are you...Labour Party?"

Timori stared at him.

"We should telegram an ambulance," Jacoby said in a thin voice.

"It wasn't..." He was pale as a sheet of paper, and his lips looked blue. Frothy red spittle dribbled from his lower lip as he shivered and coughed. "It wasn't supposed to happen like this."

Jacoby knelt down and moved the man's hand from the wound in his gut. Timori felt faint as he watched a spurt of blood come out of it like a lazy waterfall. His legs buckled and he knocked over some metal garbage cans. Somewhere a cat howled. The siren was getting closer.

"We have to go," he protested as he found his footing. "Jake."

"We need to get him to a hospital," Jacoby insisted.

Timori looked back at the man. His eyes were still open but he wasn't moving.

"He's dead, Jake. We have to go."

"Shatters." Jacoby's voice cracked as he said it. "What have we done?"

"Paulo did this," Timori insisted. "Come on." He grabbed Jacoby's wrist, which was slick with blood. Jacoby followed him out of the alley.

"It's on my hands, Tim," Jacoby whispered. Timori could feel eyes watching from windows as they crept through the dark and quiet streets, away from the valley. He realized they'd left things behind, evidence it was too late to go back for: a longwand, the pillar in the stagecoach. Surely if they returned they'd be hanged for murder.

Jacoby repeated himself all the way back to the river where they went to wash.

"His blood is on my hands."

Chapter 28

It was the same windowless cell they'd put her in when she had cracked the Great Crystal. The same deepstone walls surrounded her, the same mouldy mattress sat in the corner, and the same mute and misshapen gaoler stood guard on the other side of the bars. With nothing to read and no way to tell the time, Crystara spent minutes that became hours whispering to the ring on her finger, hoping some lucky phrase would allow her to remove it. Each time she pulled, a shock of pain went through her, but she began to grow accustomed to it.

It became a test for her – the longer she could pull on the ring, the stronger she was becoming. She went over the steps in her mind: stand straight while pulling on the ring. Then walk while pulling on the ring. Then dash across the cell while pulling on the ring. If she could get that far, De'Cadomus's hold upon her would weaken.

She thought about biting off her finger, but doing so wouldn't give her power over the ring, and she was still locked in a cell. Without a crystal to control, she was still trapped. However, she was beginning to understand De'Cadomus's machinations. He wanted her alive. He wanted a crystal speaker to train, one who was also a reader. She was unique, and he was hoping to mould her to suit his own purposes.

Crystara had also taken the time to memorize the lockbox numbers.

"Box three five two," she recited. The gaoler always ignored her when she made noise. "Box one five nine six. Box seven."

She heard a door open in the distance and stopped repeating the box numbers. The gaoler paid her no mind as she walked up to the bars and strained an ear to listen.

"...know she shouldn't have been in there, but she couldn't have meant any harm." It took Crystara a moment, but she recognized the voice of Sister Florenza. "The poor little thing must be so frightened."

"Just between you and me, I'm surprised the viper put her down here." Crystara couldn't place the second voice. The footsteps were getting closer. "But that's why I'm here...to keep an eye on things for the Council."

Florenza approached her cell, carrying a plate of steamed vegetables and a bowl of water. Standing next to her was a blonde, broad-shouldered young man wearing the snake emblem of the Whisper Society overtop his breastplate. Florenza's mind was an open book. She knew little of the stranger other than his name. Titus.

His mind, though not as ironclad as De'Cadomus's, was carefully guarded.

"Another one of the viper's cronies," Crystara spat, knowing full well Titus wouldn't understand a word she said.

Florenza's wide, grooved face was all pity. She turned to Titus. "See, look at how she wails and moans. Nobody deserves this, especially not a poor, moon-touched little urchin. Why that snake would bring her here just to lock her away like this I'll never understand."

Titus shrugged. "I'm sure the keeper had his reasons."

"Hrmph." Florenza spat on the floor. "No keeper of mine. No offense, sir, but he isn't half the keeper Orvin was. Once a serpent, always slithering."

"Hah. Don't forget you're talking to a snake," Titus said. "Leave the food and go, Sister."

Florenza didn't budge. "What are you going to do to her?"

"The Council might want to know what interest a simpleton holds for the keeper."

Florenza knelt down and slid the plate and bowl in the gap underneath the bars. "You be good, now," she added. "No more wandering around in places you shouldn't be." She reached a hand through the bars and touched Crystara on the cheek. Crystara found herself reaching for the hand as it was withdrawn. "Such a shame, the way she's treated," Florenza muttered as she shuffled off down the dungeon hall.

Crystara and Titus stared at each other for a long while. Neither one spoke. She tried to creep into his thoughts, but all she could gather was that he was curious.

"I know who you are," he said finally. "Or at least, I have a suspicion. The viper will be watching us both, and I'm sure he's cursed you...but I may have a way we can communicate. Sit tight, Crystara Mita." He walked away.

Crystara lay back upon the cold floor and stared up at the rough-cut deepstone ceiling, sighing. Whatever alignment Titus was playing at, she certainly couldn't trust him any more than De'Cadomus, but at least he was easy on the eyes.

When she took her gaze from the ceiling, yellow eyes were staring at her. Dusty was sniffing at her plate of food, but seemed largely disinterested in it. Crystara kept perfectly still, hoping she wouldn't frighten him away again with a sudden movement.

He approached her, and pushed his head against her hand. Crystara ran her hand along his back as he purred, feeling the mats in his filthy fur. She scooped him up into her arms and cried. He made no attempt to flee.

"See," she sniffled, "maybe all you needed was someone to love."

Crystal Secrets

***

Crystara's nightmares returned. Sometimes De'Cadomus chased her instead of her father or Lenara. He pursued her down a dark hall filled with portraits of keepers whose eyes followed her as she went. The closer the viper got, the slower Crystara became. When he finally grabbed her shoulder, her body began turning into crystal. It started at her toes until she couldn't move at all. It spread up her legs, and when it got to her chest she could no longer breathe. By the time the skin of her neck was crystallized, she stopped screaming and awoke.

Sometimes she had the vision of Paulo. That dream was always the same, down to the exact detail. She could recite the entire thing from memory. Crystara wanted to stop sleeping, but there was little else to do except practice pulling on the ring or count the stones in the wall. She even prayed to the gods for deliverance, asking for escape or even a book to read.

They were either deaf or pitiless.

Her only visitors were Dusty and Florenza. Crystara shared her food with Dusty and he would sit with her for a time, purring and rubbing against her leg or cheek. Florenza came and babbled at her. Most of what she said was blithe chatter, but occasionally the gossip was interesting: Sir Titus, whose promise to come and speak to Crystara had clearly been a lie, had been seen several times with Sister Sofia, speaking to her in a hushed voice. August and Sir Brutah had a yelling match one evening during supper concerning the presence of the Crystal Knights at the Old Temple. Sir Brutah had challenged August to a crystal duel but the priest declined, and rightly so -- it was a childish way to solve a conflict and against the rules, besides. A group of anti-crystal protesters had begun chanting heretical slogans at the Joveday mass, and blood was nearly shed when the guards forced them out of the temple. Crystara Mita, the traitor who had murdered Keeper Orvin, was about to be publicly executed for her crimes.

"What?" Crystara ran up to the bars so quickly Sister Florenza stumbled backward in shock. The gaoler said nothing, but kept a careful eye on Crystara. "It was supposed to be a private execution!"

"I...I..." Sister Florenza fanned her face with a hand and looked at Crystara as though she was seeing her for the first time. "Are you...did you understand what I said, child?"

Crystara nodded, slowly so she would not be mistaken. Florenza made a sharp intake of breath.

"Are...are you Crystara?"

There were loud footsteps in the hallway and a shadow passed over Sister Florenza. Crystara stepped away from the bars.

"Sister." It was Sir Brutah, the older one with the scowl. "Leave us. *Now.*"

Sister Florenza shot Crystara an apologetic look before she fled. Despite the calamity of her own thoughts, Crystara touched Florenza's mind one last time. The sister was trying to decide if Crystara Mita was a victim or a monster.

Crystara wondered the same thing about herself.

Sir Brutah stood there staring at her, arms folded. "Crystara," he said. His face was expressionless, his eyes unreadable. "It is time for your execution."

His smile was cold.

Chapter 29

Racquela's tears streamed down her cheeks as Paulo drove through the streets of Novem, heading for the De'Trini estate. Dillas's face wouldn't leave her thoughts. Racquela replayed the moment of his death over and over again in her mind. There must have been something she could have done differently to save him.

Paulo, always cool and collected, seemed completely unfazed by the murder he had just committed. He was smiling, in fact.

"How can you be so calm?" she said as she sniffled.

"You're safe. That's what matters."

"*He* was trying to save me. I tried to tell you."

Paulo didn't look at her. His eyes were on the road. "I couldn't hesitate. It could have meant your death. He was a Dori. Most of them are speakers. There'll be a lot more bloodshed before the year is done."

Racquela fought back more tears. "And you're just...comfortable with that? Sometimes I feel like I don't even know you at all."

"That's some gratitude you have," he growled. "I just saved your life and all you can do is criticize how I did it? Your father will feel differently, I imagine. One dead casteless will mean nothing to him."

She turned in her seat to face him. "And what about you? What about equality for all castes, and the casteless? Like you always go on about."

Paulo's face could have been made of stone. "It wasn't about caste." He raised his voice. "It was about the longwand he had aimed at your friends. They risked their lives for you, too." He stopped the coach. It was a quiet street of middle-caste brick houses. "We could have lost you."

She let go then, let the tears fall freely. All she wanted then was to bathe, sleep, and be held. The rest of it fell away.

"Shh," he said as he embraced her, stroking her hair. She knew she was hideously unkempt and unwashed, but she refused to pull away. He kissed her dirty forehead. "You're safe now."

He kissed her lips next, then her neck.

"Stop," she protested weakly "I'm filthy."

"I don't care," he said. His kisses trailed down her shoulder. She acquiesced, kissing him back fiercely. Suddenly she had never felt so alive. Her clothes were coming off, then his. Home could wait, the world could wait. She was with Paulo, her rescuer, her love.

She remembered their first time then, parked in the same motorcoach on a dark street at night. This time their lovemaking was even more intense. There was no uncertainty, only whispered affirmations in her ear and an intimacy that could only come from the shared rhythm of two people who loved each other intensely.

She called out his name when he climaxed. Then she cried again as they held each other, dirty and naked upon the sweaty leather seat.

"I'll never let you go again," he whispered as he played with her hair.

"It wasn't your fault," she replied. Her leg was beginning to cramp so she sat up and began to dress. Paulo lit a cigarette, perfectly content to remain naked for the moment.

He looked away from her, out the window at the rows of boxy houses. "Still, I should have known something like this would happen. You were an easy target. Your father probably won't let you out of his sight again until you're married."

She put her head on his shoulder. "Do you still want to marry me?"

"As soon as you're ready."

She sighed. "It's not just up to me."

He took a pull of his cigarette and rolled down the window. "It is. I'll ask your father for your hand tonight, even."

"I mean Timori..."

Paulo flicked his cigarette away and began putting on his clothes. "Fuck Timori. Do you love me, or him?"

"Paulo, I...I love you. But I still care about Timori. Don't you think we should wait a bit longer?"

"You already made your choice, so what does it matter?" He didn't bother to fasten his shirt buttons before starting the motorcoach.

"It matters to me," she said quietly.

Paulo drove, saying nothing. They made their way to the De'Trini estate in silence.

Racquela had expected the mansion to be nearly empty, as usual, but it was a bustle of activity as they approached the long, gated driveway. Several stagecoaches and motorcoaches formed a long row leading up to the front doors, and a cluster of police officers, arms folded, were chatting on the front lawn. Hired guards were posted on either side of the gate, looking bored until they noticed Paulo's motorcoach. Racquela didn't recognize either of them. She guessed they were new hires. One of them approached the motorcoach. Paulo rolled down his window.

"Are you two here for the search party?" the guard asked. He glanced at Racquela but said nothing.

"No," Paulo replied, "I'm here to start the rescue party."

***

Racquela thought she would feel nothing but relief, only to find the remainder of the evening emotionally draining. Her mother and father both cried openly in front of all the people who had gathered to help the police look for her. Even Jacoby's parents were in attendance. When they asked her worriedly if Jacoby had been involved in the rescue, Racquela burst into tears and found she could not speak about the event. Her mother had taken her upstairs to her room then, telling everyone Racquela would surely explain what had happened when she was emotionally ready. The last thing she had seen of Paulo before shakily climbing the stairs was a terse glance between him and Joven De'Trini.

Her mother called for Maria to draw a bath. Racquela, feeling weak as a newborn, allowed her mother to undress her and help her bathe. Of the broken blood vessels on Racquela's neck, shoulders, and breasts, Jessica De'Trini made no comment. Oddly, Racquela hoped she would think they were marks from her abuse suffered as a prisoner. She wasn't supposed to have sex until she was married. It was a sacred vow she had taken as a child in the temple. She had broken it after her betrothal to Timori.

For a while as Racquela scrubbed the stubborn dirt from her hands and feet, watching her skin wrinkle and the bathwater turn black, she and her mother said nothing to each other. She knew her mother wouldn't ask about the kidnapping, not yet, but imagined that both of them were afraid a single word would become more crying. Racquela didn't think she had any more tears that night.

"So that's Paulo," Jessica De'Trini said as she pulled a brush painfully through Racquela's matted hair. After finally beginning to relax, Racquela could feel her shoulders tensing up. It was not how she'd wanted her parents to meet him.

"Yes," she said.

"He's handsome."

"Yes."

"Drives his own motorcoach. Did you find out his family name?"

"I've been a little preoccupied this week, Mother."

Jessica stopped brushing. Racquela was facing away from her, but she could hear her mother's voice quavering.

"I'm sorry. I just didn't know what else to talk about. I'm just so relieved to have you home." She continued brushing.

"Well, I'm sure Father is asking him all about his family history. Paulo doesn't like to talk about it."

"He's going to have to, dear. Your father will not let him see you unless he is certain the young man is polite, comes from a respected caste, and is safe. Especially after what happened with Timori."

Racquela was having trouble keeping her eyes open. She stood up from the dirty bathwater and her mother handed her a towel, which she wrapped around herself. She twisted a second one around her hair and stepped out of the tub.

"Pickers can't afford motorcoaches, Mother. His uncle owns mines and factories up in Chavicci."

"What about his parents?"

"He doesn't talk about them. I think they might have died in the war."

Chapter 30

Hundreds had come for the hanging. In the moody autumn fog, they packed the tiny courtyard and spilled out into the street beyond, surrounding the walls around the Old Temple. They chanted religious slogans: 'Jova save the keeper' and 'death to the heretic.' Others had taken the public assembly as an opportunity to spread their own message. Banners from various political groups could be seen. The blood-red pickaxe of the Labour Party was prevalent amongst them. A small group could be heard, just barely, shouting for Crystara's release. Old Temple guards and city police were distributed about the plaza and within the courtyard. Parliament was a stone's throw away, after all.

Crystara could hear the chanting as it floated up over the walls, adding to the cacophony within the courtyard known gruesomely as 'Hangman's Square.'

"It used to be called 'Traitor's Square'," De'Cadomus muttered to her, possibly reading her thoughts. The pockmarked old keeper stood off to the side with her, flanked by Sir Aureon. Sir Titus watched the crowd warily from against a wall. Sir Brutah was preparing the noose upon the platform.

"Before it was a hanging platform, there was an old whiteoak stump used for beheadings," De'Cadomus continued. "The stump was stained as red as a whiteoak's blossoms. It is said so much blood has been spilled upon this hill that when miners sought crystals here, hoping to discover a wealth of clear ones beneath the Great Crystal, each and every one they found was red."

"Why did you bring me out here if you're not going to kill me?" Crystara asked.

"Because you need to see what would have happened if I hadn't intervened on your behalf."

A girl in a hooded brown robe was brought up to the platform, bound and gagged and struggling against Sir Brutah and another crystal knight. Beneath her heavy hood, her features were barely discernible, but she was unmistakeably blonde.

"Sir Aureon," De'Cadomus said, "Crystara Mita is a dangerous criminal and powerful speaker. Please assist your brothers."

Aureon glanced at De'Cadomus, then to Crystara. Upon the platform, the blonde girl shrieked wordlessly and struggled against the knights. The crowd began to press forward, held back only by temple guard halberds.

"This isn't justice," Aureon insisted.

"The gods decide our justice," De'Cadomus rasped, so loudly that several nearby onlookers turned their heads. "That justice is handed down to the Great Crystal and meted out by the keeper. I am currently the Keeper of the Great Crystal, and you, Sir Aureon, are a crystal knight, bound by oath to serve the church. Go and do your duty. We are hanging a murderer and heretic, not an innocent child."

Aureon glanced once more at Crystara before he left hurriedly for the platform. The restless throng shouted insults and hurled rotten tomatoes at the prisoner. Most of the fruit hit Sir Brutah, which made Crystara smirk.

"Who is she?" Crystara asked.

"Crystara Mita." They had the noose around her neck. Even from where Crystara stood against the back wall of the square she could see the girl's cheeks glistening. Her gagged pleas were drowned out by demands for her death or release, and the continuous Labour Party chant.

"*I'm* Crystara," she insisted, "and you can't take that away, even if you kill me or fake my death."

"You are an urchin and the church's property. Crystara Mita is about to meet her destiny at the end of a length of rope. A mercy considering her crimes. She sealed her fate the day she ended Keeper Orvin."

The noose was around the girl's neck. Sir Aureon had stepped back and Sir Brutah was standing by the lever to release the trap beneath her feet. Her sobs sounded all the more pitiful because of the gag around her mouth. Crystara was sure the poor girl was pleading for release, trying to tell the crowd they had the wrong person. It was one more death she was responsible for. She shivered and wondered if the bound and gagged girl would haunt her dreams in nights to come.

Cutting through the din, a young man called out. "Free her!"

The voice was hauntingly familiar. Others began to take up the cry until they were chanting at a fever pitch. 'Free her' competed with 'down with the republic' and 'Jova save the keeper.' The crystal knights and temple guards shuffled nervously from foot to foot.

"Free her!" the voice cried out again. The guards were holding the throng away from the hangman's platform with halberds outstretched, but some of them were growing panicked and fumbling for their wands. Crystara tried to pick out thoughts, but the crowd was a jumbled mess and any attempt at mind-reading made her head throb.

Sir Brutah put his hand upon the trap-door lever and the crowd surged, swallowing the temple guards as they rushed the platform. Bloody screams erupted and the crowd became a confusion of panicked cries, trampling feet, and wandshot. Crystara winced and prepared for the mob to attack her and

De'Cadomus, but there in the shadow of the wall they seemed forgotten.

Having lost its direction entirely, the mob dissembled into skirmishes between Labour Party supporters and temple guards, a frenzied mass trying to escape the square, and a small faction still trying to rush the platform. De'Cadomus remained still as stone, even as Sir Brutah fended off the rioters with a wand that shot slivers of metal.

The soil of Hangman's Square drank in the spilled blood.

A young man clambered atop the platform and Crystara's mouth suddenly felt dry. Dwarfed by Sir Brutah, the weaponless rioter stood his ground. Even at that distance, Crystara knew it was unmistakeably Jacoby. His had been the voice demanding her freedom. She would have given anything just then to be able to hear his thoughts from across the square.

"Jake, you fool, get out of here," Crystara whispered. She hadn't yet forgiven him for leaving her, but his presence there was a balm upon her wounded soul. She hadn't been forgotten, not entirely. Racquela had sent her a letter and Jacoby was there, rescuing someone he thought was his former betrothed. Had she been wrong to despise them? The doubt gnawed at her.

Sir Brutah levelled his wand at Jacoby's head.

"No!" Crystara screamed. Her cries were lost in the chaos. She saw a hand reach up from the teeming swarm and grab Sir Brutah's ankle, dragging him off his feet. The sound of his head striking the wooden platform was audible, even at the back wall.

"Shatters," De'Cadomus muttered. He plunged into the crowd, leaving Crystara alone. She could no longer see Brutah, but a gauntleted hand reached up from the sea of heads to grasp the lever. Whether the knight was fulfilling his duty or merely seeking to clamber to safety, Crystara couldn't tell. As the trap door fell out of the platform, Crystara saw the girl's body drop and Jacoby make a running leap.

Then someone crashed into Crystara and she fell to the ground. Stunned, her world became a confusion of feet and muffled sounds. Pain shot through her as numerous people stomped across her body in their panic. Then she was lifted up, thrown across a strong metal-clad shoulder.

"Jake," she cried. "Is he okay?"

"I can't understand you." It sounded like Titus. She could only see his backside, but he seemed to be clearing a path through the crowd. "Let's get the abyss out of here and then see if we can figure out a way to talk."

Crystara looked back at the platform. It was vacant. Jacoby, the girl, and Sir Brutah were nowhere to be seen. The mob, unchecked, continued to demolish the square.

Chapter 31

Roberto's office always smelled of pipe tobacco, even when the man himself wasn't within. As Julio passed by, he didn't see a silhouette through the etched window in the office door, but he detected a lingering note of sweet smoke. He rapped his cane on the glass.

"I know that knock anywhere," said a voice. "Come in, Jules."

Julio held his cane under the crook of his arm in order to turn the knob with his good hand. Roberto was staring at his bookshelf with his hands in the pockets of his slacks. His pipe was between his teeth.

"Shouldn't you be grading papers?" Julio asked, easing himself into a seat to avoid grunting.

"That's what assistants are for," he muttered. "Did I lend you my copy of De'Barus's *Alignments*?"

"No." Julio lit up a cigarette. "If I want to put myself to sleep I use whiskey."

Roberto chuckled and turned away from the bookshelf. "He doesn't write like a scientist. You should give it a read, Jules. If I can ever find the damn thing."

"I've been too busy reading the papers these days. Did you hear about the riot on the hill?"

Roberto re-lit his pipe and sat down. "Which hill? We have six of 'em."

Julio rolled his eyes. "Yes, but we've only had one riot. This week, at any rate. I guess the execution was the whisper that cracked the crystal."

"Yes, I did hear." Roberto stared at his desk. "Damn shame. I almost feel bad for ol' Largo."

"I feel worse for the girl. Did you have her in any of your classes?"

"No. Did you?"

"No."

They sat in silence for a minute, smoking.

"She sure was hotheaded, though," Roberto remarked. "From what I hear. Just like her old man. Must be something in miner blood."

"He's in jail, last I heard. Tried to start something alongside a bunch of Labour protesters at the doors of the Old Temple."

"Damn dullard joined the wrong riot."

Julio rubbed the scarred side of his face. "What would you do if you lost a daughter?"

Roberto laughed. "Nothing. I've never had children and, gods willing, I never will." He stood up and went over to a cabinet, withdrawing a bottle of brandy and two glass tumblers. "Fancy a drink?"

"It's not even noon yet, Rob." Julio said. Roberto smirked and gave the bottle a suggestive shake. Julio sighed. "Sure, why the abyss not?"

"What's your next class?" Roberto asked as he gave both tumblers a generous pour.

"History one."

Roberto and Julio clinked glasses. "You could teach that zozzled. Speaking of, was I completely cracked last night, or did I hear on the radio the De'Trini girl was returned safely to her family? 'Nappings and riots, I tell you. If those dullards in Parliament don't figure things out soon, it could get ugly on the streets."

Julio took a long sip and contemplated the ochre liquid in his glass. "They're doing the best they can, Rob. It's not as though they can fix the global economy."

"Well, just between you and me, a riot or two could be just what this city needs. Shake things up, force an election, get some forward-thinking minds on the hill. Some socialists and imperialists."

"Imperialists. Because that went so well for us last time."

"That was a coup dressed up as an election. And Longoro fixed our economy, remember."

"I feel like we should be playing cards right now," Julio chuckled.

"Sure, all that's missing is the scattershot, the frozen fingertips, and Largo bullying Pip into folding. And the sheer terror of combat, let's not forget that."

"How could I?" Julio scratched his right wrist, just above the hook.

"Ever wonder what Pip would be doing now if he'd survived?"

"He was a career officer. Probably would've made colonel by this point."

"How's his kid doing?"

There was a knock at the door. Roberto raised an eyebrow.

"Password is the first verse of *Nova Glorifica*," Roberto shouted at the door.

"You could get lynched for singing that," Julio muttered.

"Yeah, but it sorts out faculty from students."

"You could just ask who it is, Rob."

"It's Timori, sir," said the muffled voice from beyond the door. "I don't know the words to Novem Glorificus."

"You also don't know how to conjugate Old Noven, apparently. Come in, Stravida."

Timori entered the room and shut the door behind him. He glanced at the brandy bottle on the table but said nothing. Julio, leaning back and lighting up another cigarette, silently cursed the boy's proud posture and full-fleshed dignity. Julio would have traded his caste in a heartbeat if it would have brought his hand and face back. Plus, the lad had brains – like Julio, he could use that to improve his station. The melancholy of nostalgia and old failures itched at Julio like his scars. He turned to look out the window, away from the virile reminder of what he had once been.

"Doctor. You said you wanted to see me?"

Roberto gestured to the only empty seat remaining. "Come in, boy, sit down. Would you like a drink?"

Julio gave Roberto a sideways glance. The academy had very strict policies about students and alcohol.

"Uh..." Timori stuttered.

"Don't be shy. Sit. Have a drink, I insist. The schoolmaster won't hear of it. You're in my office. And you can trust Master Vellize here."

"You don't have to twist his arm if he doesn't want a drink, Rob."

Timori shrugged. "Why not? I could use one after the week I've had."

"That's the spirit!" Roberto clapped his hands and withdrew another tumbler from the hutch, filling it halfway with brandy. Julio suppressed a knowing smile. It was enough to give almost anyone a lightheaded feeling, let alone a teenaged boy.

"Would you like a smoke, boy?" Roberto offered as Timori carefully examined the liquid in his glass.

"Really, Rob," Julio remarked.

Timori shook his head. "No. Thank you, Doctor, but I don't smoke. It affects your performance on the football field, from what I've heard."

"There's a prudent lad," Julio said.

"Good thing I never liked sports," Roberto said. "So! What brings you in here, Stravida?"

Timori took a sip of brandy. Julio smiled when he noticed the boy trying in vain not to make a sour face.

"Um. Well, you told me to come by your office today."

"Right! I did. Well, I was looking for a book I think you should read, but I can't find my copy anywhere. But it doesn't matter. De'Barus will probably be using his copies as paperweights all over his office and laboratory. He wants you to start this week. He fired his secretary and his last assistant left."

Timori had another careful sip of brandy and furrowed his brow. "I'll see if I can fit it in, Doctor. I have a lot going on right now."

Roberto exchanged a glance with Julio.

"This is the opportunity of a lifetime, boy. Last time we spoke about this you said it wouldn't be a problem."

"That was before..." Timori glanced out the window and rubbed his forehead. "No. You're right. I will make it fit. Sir."

"That's *Doctor* Sir," Roberto said with a wink in Julio's direction. Timori managed a weak smile.

"Something on your mind, Timori?" Julio asked.

Timori shook his head. "Nothing I can share. When should I introduce myself to Doctor De'Barus?"

"He has requested you tomorrow evening," Roberto said. He handed Timori a slip of paper with the doctor's address written upon it.

Timori nodded and downed the last of his brandy, which brought a quick flush to his cheeks. "I'll be there. Thank you for this. Doctor. *Sir.*" He flashed a smile, dispelling the pall of preoccupation from his features for a moment. "And for the drink.

If I may take my leave, I have a study period that I need very badly."

"Mmm," Roberto said mid-sip. He waved Timori away with his free hand. "Don't let Aravelli smell your breath."

Timori chuckled nervously before shutting the office door behind himself.

"Now there was a lovelorn look if ever I've seen one," Julio remarked. "Reminds me of me with Ramona before all that awful poetry somehow worked in my favour."

"Speaking of the old harpy, how is her kid? I think I was asking you when Stravida came in."

"Don't call her that, please. Drago is...good. We've been spending time together." Julio had another swallow of liquor and sighed. "I've been hoping to change his mind about some things, despite the fact that officers have good job security. He...thinks I'm his father, Rob."

Roberto pursed his lips. "I wonder where he got an idea like that. Did you correct him?"

Julio stared out the window, watching the boys kicking the football around the field. "No."

Roberto shook his head. "You always were a sentimental fool. What do you think the harpy...er, Ramona will do when she finds out?"

Julio shrugged. "Drago and I have an agreement. And anyway, you're one to talk."

"I don't follow."

"Please. You've never showed favoritism to a student like that before."

"He's brilliant. Best student I've had in years."

"But it's more than that, isn't it?"

"What can I say?" Roberto winked. "I'm a sucker for underdogs."

Chapter 32

Tales of the Crystal Speakers: Maker, Seer, Reader, Feeler,
Speaker
Written by Ammar bin Tammuram
Translated by Doctor Giorgio Perglioni

Last of all the heroes was Muda, the Dortian warlock, and he rode a lithe and ill-tempered stallion as black as the night. Muda wore a heavy, dark cloak and his hair was white as bone. Upon his hands were many rings, all of which held crystals, for Muda had the ability to speak to a crystal and bind it to his will. Although there were many speakers in Novem at that time, Muda was the greatest of all of them, for he could command many crystals at once, and make them do most anything that he desired. And no matter where he was in the world, he could speak through the Great Crystal, and thus he was always in contact with the Keeper and the Emperor.

It is well-known that the Dortians are thieves and liars and whores and demon-worshippers and infidels, and although Muda served the Emperor, he was also still a Dortian, and in his heart there was much darkness, for he was not in the sight of Almighty God, or even any of the lesser gods of Novem.

***

As the din of the riot receded behind Jacoby, he craned his head to make sure Crystara was keeping up. Hands still bound, she picked her way carefully through the rocky ruins on the steep north side of Crystus Hill. As she made her way down the slope, the deep hood she wore receded from her face and fell.

"You're not Crystara." Jacoby blinked.

259

"Rich boy is perceptive," she said. Although her hair had been bleached somehow, the curls were the same, as was her freckled, pixie-like face with the mushroom nose. The black eye and puffy cheek hadn't been there before, but she was unmistakeably the same young woman Jacoby had met on the hill the other day, a day that felt like a lifetime ago after two close brushes with death.

"Come," she said, "we must away from that hill before the snakes come lookin' for us. Rich boy would do wise to cut these bonds."

Jacoby whispered to his ring, which briefly flashed orange, and he carefully incinerated a line through the rope about the girl's wrists. The knot fell away, leaving a lingering burning smell. The mystery girl rubbed her wrists and winced.

"I don't understand," Jacoby said. "Why were you there? Where is Crystara?"

The girl began nimbly clambering down the cliffside, completely confident in her footing. "Snakes must have her." Jacoby noticed she seemed to be missing a tooth. "Only one reason why they would fake her hanging."

"And what's that?"

"Think, rich boy. Use that education of yours."

"Because she's a reader."

The girl sat resting for a moment upon an overturned, moss-ridden pillar. "She isn't."

Jacoby folded his arms and sat beside her. "Yes, she is. Without a word, she discovered that I'd cheated on her." Jacoby twisted the ring upon his finger absentmindedly.

The girl shook her head. "Any good feeler can see what guilty boys hide. Dori blood runs strong in her, sure, but we haven't seen a reader since the last Dori queen."

"Crystara isn't Dori," Jacoby insisted. "Neither was Queen Celesta."

"So much you know, smart boy," the girl said. She stood, then continued down the hill, gazing upon the Avati Valley. "Spoonfed in meals and lies."

"She's miner caste. Unless her mother was Dori."

"Dori isn't in a caste or a name, rich boy. It's in the blood."

Jacoby stopped in his tracks. "I should go back for her."

The girl shook her head. "So brave, you young boys, and foolish. Your little girlfriend is in the coil of the snakes. Going back for her would send you through the orange."

"She's not my girlfriend. Not anymore...but that doesn't mean I should leave her to that kind of fate. Regardless of what she did."

"Don't be stupid," she called over her shoulder. "You're no match for the snakes, young speaker."

"Where are you going?" Jacoby asked.

"Home."

Jacoby sprinted to catch up to her. "Oh. Uh...can I walk you there? To make sure you're safe."

She snorted. "Rich boy plays at chivalry. Only one thing on boys' minds. Rescue has a reason."

"I thought you were Crystara," Jacoby said.

"Right. Nobodies don't deserve a rescue."

"That's not what I said," Jacoby insisted. "You automatically act like I'm looking down on you."

She stopped again and pointed at the clustered houses of Avati Valley. "Tell me something, rich boy. Standing on the hill, which way do you look to see the valley?"

Jacoby rolled his eyes. "Down. Just because it sounds clever to say, doesn't give it meaning."

She prodded him in the chest. "Why do the rich build on the hill? To *look down*. There they survey their domain. It is about ownership."

"Look, I agree there's an unfortunate disparity between the rich and the poor, but..."

"There are poor, *Padrona*, and then there are the Dori. Your miners complain they are the lowest of the low, but they often forget there are those beneath them, not even given the dignity of a caste. We cannot work, cannot earn respect."

Jacoby watched the girl as she stared down at the valley. He could sense her hesitance then. Despite her pride she had revealed something to a stranger.

"Why do you stay?"

She stared back at him. In the afternoon sunlight, her eyes were more intense than they'd seemed before – almost cinnabar.

"And where would I go, rich boy?"

Jacoby shrugged. "Anywhere?"

She shook her head and sighed. "You understand nothing. Here are family and ancestors. Out there is nothing but more who hate the Dori. More nations where we are seen as dirt beneath a bootheel."

"I didn't realize it was so bad for you."

"How could you know?" She plodded down the hill at a determined pace. "Two thousand years of written word barely spare a thought for the Dori."

Although a sullen silence fell, she allowed him to follow her through the streets of Crystus Hill. The girl had an agitated way about her, constantly looking over her shoulder and avoiding the wide, empty avenues of the hill's estates. Occasionally she flicked her tongue across her teeth. Jacoby could sense more than a little anxiety wafting from her when she did so.

"Did you used to have a crystal tooth?" he asked her.

"Be quiet," she whispered.

"Sorry, I didn't mean to ask something personal, I just..."

"Be quiet," she hissed again. "If I am caught up here I will be sent back to the snakes, or worse. Ask me again when we are in the Casteless Quarter."

Jacoby shivered. He hadn't even considered the hard truth of the matter – he had rescued a Dori, a casteless nobody. It stood to reason she lived in the forbidden zone of squalor known in Avati Valley as the 'fifth quarter.' There were slums, and then there was the fifth quarter, it was said.

Jacoby followed the girl, darting from the cover of walls and fences, descending from the estates of the hill to the valley of brick and mortar and cobblestone he used to call home. He felt like a trespasser somehow, a man of means and influence who no longer belonged amongst the denim-clad, the soot-covered. He felt like he was being watched. The events of Racquela's rescue played themselves out in his mind, and he became nervous as the girl he followed grew more relaxed.

Jacoby began to notice the darker side of Corti Street, the aspects he'd never noticed when he'd lived there. Dockhands eyed his new corduroy jacket enviously. Unemployed miners loitered outside of shops, smoking. He saw the graffiti scrawled in the alleyways, overtop old graffiti never washed clean or painted over, some dating back centuries. Painted slogans of ill sentiment against the powers that be had been a part of Captus Nove for as long as there had been a Captus Nove – Jacoby recalled Master Vellize's story of the old condemned building in the valley close to where the educator had grown up. When they had finally torn it down, they'd discovered not only a mosaic floor dating back to the First Empire, but a chalk-scrawl of slander about a particular senator, who up until that point had been known by historians as a man of popularity and honour.

Human history, Master Vellize had said, was a series of half-truths, omissions, and outright lies built upon each other. Historians were just guessers, sifting through works of opinion and political motivation.

Jacoby gazed up at the rusty iron gate that led to the Casteless Quarter and wondered where the Dori fit into it all.

The city guards paid Jacoby no mind as he passed by them into the most feared and mysterious section of the city – they were only there to keep an eye on people *leaving* the quarter. Jacoby had been told once by his father there was a law forbidding Dori from congregating outside of their quarter.

Jacoby had been expecting desolate streets. Instead he discovered the quarter was full of life. Children chased each other, playing some tag game and whooping loudly. A cluster of women sat underneath a tree, knitting and gabbing. Another thing that surprised Jacoby was the language. For some reason, he had expected the Dori to communicate in some special tongue of theirs, but instead they all spoke in valley-accented Noven. The alarming difference was in their appearance. Their clothing was much the same as any other modern Noven, but where most Novens had dark hair and eyes, the Dori were pale, with fair features, big foreheads, wide-set blue or green eyes, and red or blonde hair.

Yet more shocking were the buildings. Where Jacoby had anticipated shanties and run-down buildings of brick, he found tall structures of stone, many with telltale Mosind domes and classical-era pillars. There was a carved marble communal fountain filled with water, and several women washed clothes as they sat on its precipice.

Some of the older structures were run down, cracked or broken, but Jacoby could see the resemblance to famous places in the hills of Novem: Parliament, the Avati Hill Library, Cateli

Temple. He pondered why he'd never noticed such things before, especially from a good view of the valley from a hill, until he remembered it was considered bad luck to look at the "Fifth Quarter." *Why is it bad luck?* he wondered.

Most alarming of all, however, was the lack of adult males.

Jacoby turned to the mystery Dori girl he was following, hoping she knew he had so many burning questions. Instead she stalked off down the street as though he was a burden to her. Jacoby pretended he couldn't sense the intense curiosity honing down upon him from dozens of pairs of eyes and followed her hurriedly.

Although well-hidden, Jacoby could see the signs of abject poverty as he traversed the small quarter. Most Dori had clothing that, at first glance, appeared clean and pressed, but Jacoby noticed patches and stitches on nearly every outfit. The great stone and marble buildings still stood, but many were missing doors.

The girl led Jacoby under a stone archway and into a vacant courtyard. An orange tree had been planted in the middle, about which hung laundry that billowed in the wind. Above, clouds threatened to open and soak the bedsheets and shirts. Somewhere a windchime jingled in a minor key.

"Shachari," the girl called out to the wind. The chimes continued to tinkle. Jacoby shivered again. Suddenly there was somebody leaning over the railing of a second floor balcony, gazing down upon Jacoby and the girl. Though she could barely see over the railing, the tiny woman seemed to command Jacoby's attention from the moment he noticed her. Her hair was a white blazon setting forth from her scalp and going in every direction. Even the gusts seemed to have no command over it. Her eyes were a hawk's, darting between Jacoby and the girl he had rescued.

"Fultas," the old woman replied. "Who's there with you, girl? I can't find my spectacles."

So much for the hawk's eyes, Jacoby thought.

"I am gone for three days and that is all you ask?"

"You have been gone longer before." The old woman left the balcony and disappeared into the abode. The girl turned to Jacoby. He could sense her tension. She didn't show it outwardly, but something about the old woman seemed to make her nervous. Jacoby supposed it could have something to do with the outsider standing awkwardly in the courtyard.

"Who is she?" Jacoby asked.

"She is *Shachari*. The closest Noven word would be 'elder'...or perhaps 'priestess'."

"And what about you? I still don't know your name."

"Tanni," Shachari said. Jacoby nearly yelped in surprise. How the tiny, fragile-seeming old woman had appeared so suddenly in front of the orange tree, he had no idea.

"Yes, Shachari." The girl named Tanni seemed far less surprised by Shachari's re-appearing trick.

"Who is this boy?" Her hand was wrapped about a wooden cane as gnarled as her knuckles. She approached Jacoby and walked in a circle around him, inspecting him. "Look at these clothes," she remarked, rubbing Jacoby's corduroy vest between a finger and thumb. "He is tall and wealthy, and frightened, besides. He is no Dori. He is *shoshia*. Why have you brought him?"

"He followed me here," Tanni replied.

"Braver than he looks, then."

"He is *aisu*, Shachari," Tanni said.

Shachari craned her head up to look at Tanni. "So are many *shoshia*. It means nothing." Her piercing gaze fell upon Jacoby. "Why are you here, boy?"

"I wanted to make sure Tanni got home safely."

Shachari raised an eyebrow. "What aren't you telling me, girl?" She squinted. "And what in the name of all the ancestors have you done to your hair?"

Tanni's defiant curl of lip began to tremble. "It wasn't my fault, Shachari. They came without warning, and I was no match for them."

Jacoby could feel her trying to rein it in, but the dam burst and she blubbered the rest of her tale. "They dressed me up like the girl, the one who murdered the keeper, and they hit me and took my *closhi* and asked me questions and called me terrible things. Then they tried to hang me..."

"The *nethi* are busy, it seems," Shachari remarked. "You are lucky, girl, to have a young friend obsessed with saving others. I know who you are now, boy. Padrona...the *shoshia* raised up from miner to alchemist. One of the six to touch the *Naf'closhi* last year. What would compel you to brave the *nethi* for the sake of one of us?"

"I thought it was Crystara they were hanging," Jacoby said. "But I don't regret my choice. Tanni is innocent." He furrowed his brow. "How do you know who I am?"

"Because I watch and I listen, boy. So you have brought our wayward *clotan* back to us. We don't ordinarily deal with *shoshia*, other than to trade. What do you want?"

Jacoby glanced about, looking first at the freckled girl with the fiery eyes, then at the quiet courtyard with the orange tree. His eyes finally rested upon the marble buildings of the quarter.

"I want to learn more about you," he admitted. "The Dori."

"Hmm," Shachari said. She removed her fist from the top of her cane to reveal a clear crystal the size of a goose egg. She gazed at Jacoby and without a whisper her crystal briefly flashed a rosy colour. She nodded, somehow satisfied. "Very well, Tanni, you may teach him. But he is not to wander where he does not belong."

Tanni looked sidelong at Jacoby. "Come along, rich boy. I guess I'm stuck with you, for now."

Chapter 33

The Journal of the Prophetess Celesta

13 Yuna, 1611

The Great Crystal is still speaking to me, but most of it is half-truths, riddles, or conflicting information. I have taken to sleeping when Lucianus is not around. My proximity to the crystal allows me many more prophetic dreams than I am accustomed to. Although some of these are unpleasant, they are also useful. I believe that I have witnessed my own death, even. For several nights in a row I have been sent a vision of being dragged into Traitor's Square by the snakes. Lucianus is being beheaded before me, and I must watch him die. I know part of the vision is a message from the crystal, because when his head is severed from his body, it rolls so that he is looking at me and then he starts speaking in tongues. I've written the gibberish down, but it will take some time before I can decipher it all. Some of the languages I recognize, and some of them I do not.

I have come to terms with the thought of dying. Lucianus is much more emotional about it. He believes the Great Crystal is trying to save us both, that the message is a warning, but he is sentimental where I am fatalistic. I have been prepared to die ever since I left the throne behind. The gods did not mean for me to have an easy life, or a long one. I believe I have always done my best to serve the people of Novem, though they do not see it that way. It is only a matter of time before the snakes decide I am a threat to their plans. I only hope I can decipher the Great Crystal's message before I am gone.

***

Titus set down a coiled pad of paper for Crystara and a quill pen with a bottle of ink. He anxiously glanced back at the door. The pandemonium in Hangman's Square wouldn't last forever.

"That's not going to work, dully," Crystara said as she folded her arms and shook her head.

"Just try it," Titus insisted. "Hurry."

Crystara glared at him pointedly as she tried to write "YOU ARE A DULLY" on the pad of paper. Instead, her hand would only make scribbles and her ring finger began to itch.

"Hmm," he muttered, tapping his lips with his forefinger. "Godsdamn but that's a good whisper, whatever it is."

Crystara nodded, sighing.

"Wait," Titus said. "That's it. I'll ask you a question, and you nod your head for yes or shake it for no. Got it?"

Crystara made a noise of agreement.

Titus began pacing the small prayer room. "So you *are* Crystara Mita, aren't you?"

She nodded. Titus grinned.

"I knew it. I knew that's what the old viper was hiding." He clapped his hands. "He wants your power, I'll bet. He knows you've been close to the crystal. All right, that gets us somewhere," he exclaimed. His expression grew grave. "Are you loyal to him?"

Crystara gave Titus her best 'you are a dully' expression and pointed to the ring on her finger. Titus smacked his own forehead.

"Of course. He's got you by the balls...so to speak. So what's your plan, then? Escape?"

Crystara mimed removing the ring from her finger. Then she motioned a finger across her throat.

"You want to be free so you can kill yourself?"

Crystara threw her hands up in frustration. She shook her head and made the killing motion again, then tried to narrow her eyes and purse her lips like De'Cadomus.

"Oh," he said. He glanced at the door again. "That might be a bit more challenging."

Crystara nodded. *No kidding, you dully. Now get to the part where you're going to help me.*

"Look, he's a reader. I know that sounds cracked but it's true. If I start actively plotting against him like that I'm a dead man."

"Then what in the abyss are you helping me for, you big dully?" she demanded. She tried again to read his thoughts, but his mental barrier proved to be quite strong. *No wonder De'Cadomus wants to train me. He was right. I could be a lot better at this. Maybe I could learn what he knows before I kill him.*

"What are you yelling for?" Titus asked, folding his arms. "What do you want, if you don't want to leave?"

Crystara considered for a moment. *Secrets,* she thought. *All the secrets of this place. Answers about Mother and Father and crystals and Paulo and why the Great Crystal is so obsessed with me. That's what I want. The godsdamned truth.*

She pointed to her pad of paper, then mimed opening a book. Then she made numbers for him with her hands. Three, five, two. A pause. One, five, nine, six. A pause. Seven.

Titus scratched his head. "You want to read books? What do the numbers mean?

Crystara mimed a key turning in a lock.

"The lockboxes?"

She nodded and grinned. Perhaps she'd judged Titus too harshly at first. It could have been the Northern accent.

"I could probably get those for you," he said. "What do the numbers mean?"

The door to the small prayer room flew open. De'Cadomus was in the threshold, huffing and sweaty, flanked by a crystal knight on either side. Sir Brutah and Sir Aureon were nowhere to be seen.

"There you are," he rasped. "Good. Titus, escort the urchin to her chambers and see that she remains there, then meet me in my study."

"Your Clarity?" Titus said. "What about the hanging? Should we not find...Crystara? And return her to the dungeon?"

De'Cadomus scowled, his face becoming a myriad of wrinkles. "Do not say that name ever again. Crysara is dead. I have seen to it. Do not question my orders further."

"Yes, Your Clarity."

De'Cadomus and the other knights left as abruptly as they'd appeared. Titus winked at Crystara. "Jova, but that was close. I'd better take you there. Looks like I'm treading the red with the viper as it is."

"Aren't we all?" Crystara asked.

"I have no idea what you just said," Titus admitted. He escorted her back to her room in the library, only pausing to speak once they were back in her book-filled underground chamber.

"I'd better get those lockboxes for you," Titus said. "If you try and get them from the archivist, De'Cadomus will grow suspicious. This...might take me some time. I'm sure the viper has one of the other knights watching me closely. In the meantime, don't do anything crazy."

"Like kill another keeper?" Crystara mumbled as Titus took his leave. She was left alone with her thoughts, which turned, against her will, to Jacoby.

"What in Jova's name were you doing there?" she asked the empty air. "I killed Lenara. You hated every minute of being with me, so why would you bother to try and save me? Just to absolve your sense of guilt?"

Crystara jumped slightly when something brushed against her leg, only to discover it was Dusty. She knelt down and stroked him behind a notched ear.

"What's the point of guilt?" she asked him. "It doesn't change what you've already done."

Dusty's reply was a low purr.

***

Two days passed and Titus hadn't returned. The other two knights, Sir Hugo and Sir Donati, guarded Crystara in shifts. She was allowed freedom of the temple, provided she had an escort and didn't go anywhere near the Great Crystal. From the knights' thoughts, she discovered Sir Aureon had quit the knights entirely. Sir Hugo had witnessed Aureon throwing his tabard at the viper's feet, proclaiming the faked hanging went against every vow he had ever taken.

The riot had also claimed the life of Sir Brutah, Crystara discovered. With one knight dead and another one discharged, that left only Donati and Hugo to keep an eye on her. She was certain the viper didn't trust Titus.

Titus, however, was nowhere to be seen. Crystara began to suspect the young man had been discovered as her accomplice and was rotting in the dungeon awaiting a grim fate: torture or death, or possibly both. Further adding to her unease was the fact that De'Cadomus was also conspicuously absent. Rumours about the keeper circulated freely amongst the priests and sisters as mutterings and thoughts of dissent continued to grow.

Crystara spent her time reading. The Old Temple had been closed to the public for several days because of the riot, and nobody was allowed in or out except for priests and knights on official church business. Crystara was perfectly content to remain in the basement and while away the time delving into church secrets. She considered getting the lockbox keys from Lagarus, but she knew beyond a shadow of a doubt De'Cadomus would plunder the old man's mind for any interactions with Crystara. Though the doddering old archivist would likely forget, Crystara wanted the information in the lockboxes badly enough that she couldn't afford the viper's interference.

Meals were sent to her regularly, and they were decent enough that Crystara suspected she was getting the same food as everyone else in the temple. Although being a prisoner wasn't ideal, she had to admit things weren't so bad. A year ago she'd told Keeper Orvin she would never work for the church. Her safety and comfort looked after, though, she had to admit there was a certain appeal. She had access to more knowledge than she could ever absorb in a lifetime, and training with speaking and reading, besides. Crystara was beginning to understand Keeper Orvin's choice to become a priest. The church allowed a pursuit of one's interests, sheltered from society.

Her only true obstacle was De'Cadomus.

On the third evening after the riot, he came to visit her.

"Crystara." His voice was like a knife scraping across a whetstone. "Your friend's stupidity cost Sir Brutah his life. You are fortunate I was there to finish the task of making you disappear."

"He's not my friend." She paused. "Did you kill him?" She tried in vain to search his thoughts, but his mind was as ironclad as ever.

"No. But I managed to whisper an illusion of ending your life before the mob of pickers and lowlives demolished the square. You are dead in the eyes of all except the Great Crystal and me. Now the real work can begin."

"You seem really shattered about Sir Brutah's death," she noted. "What's the real work?"

"Sir Brutah died doing his duty, which is the best any crystal knight can hope for. The real work is training you properly, provided you've finally realized that compliance is your only option. Come with me."

Crystara thought about resisting, but the ring upon her finger was a constant reminder of how futile such a thing would be. She stood, closed the book she was reading, and followed De'Cadomus out of the library and into the temple proper. He led her to the Keeper's Tower and shut the door behind himself. Within, a cheery fire crackled in the hearth, and a hearty dinner for two had been laid out upon a low wooden table: a lamb roast with baby potatoes and stewed tomatoes, along with a bottle of wine.

"There are advantages to acquiescence," he said as he sat. He motioned for her to take the seat opposite him. "Your room is a bit uncomfortable, is it not?"

Crystara remained standing, her arms folded. "I like being close to the books."

"Surely it wouldn't be such a long walk for a spry girl like you." He poured a glass of wine for himself, then one for Crystara.

"Take the ring off and you can put me wherever you like," she suggested.

De'Cadomus took in the bouquet of the wine and tested it with a careful sip. "Eventually I might, if you prove yourself. For now it's insurance."

"Afraid you might lose me?" The viper's sudden generosity was circumspect, but Crystara opted to take advantage of it while she could. She sat.

His milky eyes glared at her. "You are the only other known reader in existence. It's why the Great Crystal chose you, I have no doubt." He began carving a generous slice from the roast. "Your betrothal to Jacoby Padrona was likely a move to produce another like yourself. Our talent is disappearing as the bloodlines thin out and disappear."

Except that I was meant to be with Paulo, Crystara thought. She carefully noted De'Cadomus's ignorance regarding the Great Crystal's true choices for the betrothals.

"Bloodlines?" She downed a swallow of wine.

"Keeper Orvin kept you in the dark." He laid his serving of roast upon his plate and then carved one for Crystara. "Readers were far more common before The First Empire allowed the people of their vassal states to become citizens. The Mosind Occupation further diluted the talent. Now, when one is discovered, we take care to ensure they are looked after and trained. That is the true reason Keeper Orvin joined the church, which I'm guessing he didn't tell you, either. He didn't care much for the Great Crystal, and had little understanding of its true power."

"You're lying," Crystara said calmly as she cut into the tender flesh of the lamb and savoured a bite. "He wanted to know everything about it."

She felt a telltale itch on her ring finger, but De'Cadomus maintained his composure and sipped his wine, watching her over the rim of the glass.

"Half a lie," he admitted. "Nobody alive knows more about it than I do."

"But it doesn't talk to you, does it?" Crystara said. It was an assumption, but she could see in his eyes that she'd struck upon something close to the truth. "That's the other reason you want me around."

"Now why would I put you anywhere near it? You cracked it. As I told you when I first arrived, I am here to train you as a reader and a speaker so you can help me quell this abyssal lower-caste unrest. The Crystal Knights have long been the stewards of..."

"You said quell a revolution *and* fix the Great Crystal," Crystara interrupted. She was treading the red with him again, but she didn't care. If he was finally playing nice because he wanted something from her, she would take every advantage she could get. "Have you changed your hue, or are you trying to figure out how to get the Great Crystal to speak to me without me influencing it in return?" She popped a satisfying tomato into her mouth.

"You presume, girl."

Crystara smirked. "You didn't say that I presume incorrectly."

Even De'Cadomus's sigh had a rasp to it. "You will speak to it when I say so and not a moment before. Do not assume I will hesitate to punish you just because you are ready for training."

"So where do we start, then?" Crystara asked. She tried not to sound too eager, but decided she may as well learn what the old viper knew before she found a way to get rid of him.

"You will return to your cleaning duties." Crystara mentally restrained her urge to throw a potato at the keeper's head. "High Priest August is plotting against me, and I need to know who is being swayed to his side."

Everyone, Crystara thought.

"Surely you don't think this task is beneath me, at this point?"

He slammed his fork down. "Nothing is beneath you. You are a tool to be used, a snake's fang." He stood, and a twinge of pain ran up Crystara's arm. "Are you going to listen and obey, or would you rather I paralyze you and return you to the dungeon for a time?"

Crystara clenched her teeth and swallowed her pride and her fury. *Patience,* she told herself. *Let him think he's beaten you.* She steeled her mind so he wouldn't read into her true intentions.

"Fine," she said, staring into her lap. "Don't you already know what they're all thinking, though?"

De'Cadomus resumed his seat and picked up his wine glass. "I cannot be everywhere at once, and the shrewd amongst them avoid me. You, however, are inconspicuous."

Crystara prodded the meat with her fork, her appetite gone. "Some of them know I'm your stooge."

"So they watch what they say. However, no one is aware that you're a reader. Your first lesson is to learn not to telegraph."

"What do you mean? People can tell I'm reading their thoughts?"

"I can tell when you're trying to read mine." De'Cadomus placed his fork and napkin upon the plate. He had eaten very little. "But no, ordinarily only the very mentally acute can tell. However, you have a habit of staring at someone when you are reading them."

"So? If they can't tell the difference..."

"It makes them more guarded. They become ill at ease and they cease to wander into their deeper thoughts. Try reading them without directing your attention to them."

"I have a hard time focusing on someone's thoughts if I'm not looking directly at them," Crystara admitted.

"Because you are *untrained*."

"Fine," she said as she stood. The wine had made her feel bolder. She allowed her voice to ooze with mock deference. "I'll start tomorrow. For now, if you'll excuse me, I have a book I'd like to finish."

De'Cadomus merely leaned back in his chair, a satisfied look upon his face. He waved her away and she left, returning through the vacant hallways of the temple to her home in the library.

When she arrived, Titus was waiting for her. In his arms were three items. On the bottom of the stack was a thick, leatherbound tome. Crystara could almost smell the old, yellowed paper from where she was standing. Atop the tome was a more recent cloth-bound book with a title inked upon the spine: The Whisper Society 1196-1874. Above that sat an embossed metal case, embellished with silver filigree in a pattern Crystara felt she recognized, but couldn't place.

Titus glanced over his shoulder, then placed the items carefully on the floor in front of Crystara. "There you go," he whispered. "Box three five six, box seven, and box one five nine six."

Crystara glanced at the items, shaking her head. Three five two, she corrected with one hand. She wondered which item he'd wrongfully chosen. *The Whisper Society* seemed pertinent, and the metal box continued to draw the eye. Upon the surface of the iron case, which had a seam but no discernible lock, crystals no bigger than beads were arranged in a circular pattern, one of each colour except for white and black. Crystara made her eyes go out of focus and realized the embossed pattern was actually an old, worn image of cloaked figures, each holding one of the coloured crystals. They were surrounding a great sphere, whose crystal setting was empty.

Behind each carved person, words were engraved in a strange, looping script.

Crystara pointed at the case. "Box seven?" She made seven fingers for Titus.

He nodded. "I've never seen anything like it," he admitted. "But I can't figure out how to open it. I think you have to whisper to the crystals, but it's in a pattern or combination lock. Maybe you can puzzle it out. I have to go before the viper figures out where I am. You'd better hide those books."

"Wait," she said as her eyes rested upon the leather tome. Titus understood her tone clear enough. He paused in the doorway as she examined the final book. Leatherworked upon the front cover was a depiction of a mantle and hearth, and upon the first page she discovered the title: *Il Gastronomica*.

"A cookbook," she said. "Three five *two*, Titus." She showed him the numbers again.

Titus glanced over his shoulder for the second time. "I can get it for you later. For now, I have to meet with the viper before he sends someone looking for me. You saw how he dealt with Brutah's death. We're all expendable to him."

He has them all on edge, Crystara thought as Titus left the room. Deciding she didn't want to wait another three days for him to return, Crystara hid the metal case and the book about the Whisper Society amongst the many stacks in her room, then picked up the cookbook and strode across the library to Lagarus' desk. She slammed it down in front of him, loud enough to get his attention.

"Oh," the old man remarked, no more surprised than if she had merely said his name. "Crystara, was it? Haven't seen you for a few days. Orvin keeping you busy is he?" He chuckled warmly. "Keeping, get it?"

Crystara managed a smile despite the mention of Orvin's name. "I need lockbox three hundred and fifty-two," she said, forgetting once again that De'Cadomus was the only one who could understand her words.

"Eh?" Lagarus brought his crystal hearing horn up to his ear and leaned in. "What book is that you have there? Looks like the old cookbook Cecelia used to borrow on occasion. I know, the meals have gone downhill since she passed through the orange, haven't they?"

"No, I need lockbox three hundred and fifty-two," Crystara repeated, showing Lagarus the numbers with her fingers.

"Eh?" He leaned in so close the horn was touching her nose. "What's that, girl? My hearing isn't what it used to be, you know."

"Lock. Boxes." She said, miming a key turning in a lock.

"You want a locked book? Well, some young knight was in here just a while ago fetching some things, so I can't promise it'll be there." He leaned back in his chair and put down his horn. "Seeing as how you're helping me now, you might as well fetch it yourself." He opened a desk drawer and removed a massive ring of keys, handing it to Crystara.

Crystara quickly checked the library index for the box's location. She found it tucked away in a faraway bottom corner behind a loose stack. It took her quite a while to pick through the keys, some of which were bent, or worn so smooth the engraved numbers were illegible.

Opening the box, she discovered a small book with a cracked spine and no title, held together by tied strings. The pages were roughly cut, yellow as an old pipe-smoker's teeth. Crystara untied the strings, careful not to let the pages come loose. She opened it to a random page. It appeared to be a journal, written in a practiced script, the language Rebirth-era Noven. As her eyes scanned the page, a couple of interesting words caught her attention: 'Great Crystal' and 'Reader.' She flipped to the first page to find lettering in a more modern script. It read:

Herein, the journal of the prophetess Celesta, former queen of Novem, consort to Keeper Lucianus, known empath, speaker and reader. 1588-1614

Holding the journal carefully, Crystara retreated to her room and began to read.

Chapter 34

Timori read the slip of paper in his hand again before looking up at the brass numbers on the old wrought-iron gate. Beyond was a front yard overgrown with vines and weeds, tall enough that he could barely see the estate in the distance. He glanced about the street. Other houses were newer brick structures, well-maintained, with bright flowerbeds underneath windowsills. Though Southron Hill, which was home to the bulk of the merchant class, had been hit hard by the depression, there appeared to be no forclosures up at the top.

Doctor De'Barus had wealth. What he lacked, it seemed, was a gardener.

Beside the gate a wooden box with a button, a speaker, and a crystal microphone was   riveted to the fence. Timori inspected it carefully. Crystal microphones had only been recently patented. Timori was shocked to see such an expensive piece of technology sitting innocuously where anyone could abscond with it. He pressed the button and waited.

Nothing happened. He pressed the button again.

"Hello?" he spoke into the microphone. There was no answer.

"Hmm," he said, nudging the gate. It swung inward with a rusty groan.

"No lock," Timori muttered. He glanced about, then sidled through the opening and followed the path through the overgrown lawn.

There was evidence here and there of a former garden. Flowering shrubs and brambles fought for space, and bright red whiteoak blossoms littered the ground. There appeared to be foot traffic, however. A rough-beaten path through the growth led up to the house.

The manse boasted a plethora of windows but all the curtains were drawn tight. At Timori's feet a stack of newspapers sat in a soggy heap, rotting from the bottom. The top bundle was still fresh, boasting the current date. Timori stepped up to the door and used the knocker.

A dog began to bark. It sounded like a small breed, yipping just on the other side of the door. Timori knocked again, calling out, "Hello? Doctor De'Barus?"

Only the dog replied. Timori tried to peer in a window, but the curtains were heavy.

"Hmm," he said again.

Around the back, Timori discovered a different kind of garden. Rust-riddled machinery and lab equipment of dubious function littered the yard. An onion-shaped chamber of glass as tall as Timori was collecting rain, and some kind of moss or mould was colonizing its shady side. Timori stubbed his toe over an anvil and fell into the weeds. He came face-to-face with a metal box. Upon its surface was an engraved serial number and the words PRESSURE CHAMBER – DO NOT ACTIVATE WITH DOOR OPEN. A fuzzy red spider crawled across its surface and Timori yelped, scrambling to his feet and leaping over debris to escape the creature.

The dog must have heard Timori's cry of fear, because it had begun to bark at the back door. Timori straightened his vest and pulled out his comb, thankful nobody had seen his fearful outburst. He fixed his hair back into place and tried the back door. It was unlocked. As he opened it a crack the dog's barking grew more frantic.

It was a little curly-haired white thing, still barking incessantly as Timori tried to peer into the abode.

"Hello?" he tried to shout over the dog to be heard. "Doctor De'Barus, are you home?" Timori looked down at the noisy canine, noticing for the first time its tail was wagging rapidly.

"Starved for food or attention?" he asked quietly. Timori allowed the door to open and the dog immediately put its paws on his knee, looking up at him expectantly. He gave it a tentative pat on the head, then it dashed past him and into the yard.

"Ah, shatters," he said. Fortunately, the pup hadn't gone far. It was a boy, Timori discovered, and it was peeing against a nearby tree. After the dog had done his business, he sauntered about the yard, smelling rusty items and adding a bit of extra pee here or there.

"Come on, pooch," Timori beckoned as he stood in the doorway. To his surprise, the dog returned to him immediately. Timori knelt down to pet the animal, glancing casually into the house as he did so.

The back door was attached to the kitchen, it seemed, and not a cramped and littered little sink-and-stove affair like Timori was accustomed to. It reminded him of the De'Trini kitchen: a great open stark-white space with an island in the middle, long rows of countertops and all the latest culinary gadgets hanging from racks, marble floors and cabinet embellishments, and modern colours. It was a kitchen built for servants. Despite the exterior appearance of the house, the area was spotless. There was not a speck of dust or a crumb to be seen.

"Doctor De'Barus?" Timori called out again. His voice echoed throughout the space, but received no reply. The little dog, having had its fill of attention, skittered off down the adjacent hallway. Timori, determined to resolve for certain whether or not the professor was at home, followed the dog.

Down the hallway and on the left was a parlour, just as tidily maintained as the kitchen. It boasted all the accoutrements afforded to the wealthy: a phonograph, a marble fireplace and mantle, a radio, a fully-stocked serving cart, mahogany bookshelves, and enough couches and lounge chairs to host a party. Above the mantelpiece, a portrait of a plain and stern-faced older woman stared out at the parlour, hair done up tightly, looking like she'd rather be wearing pants than a frilly dress. Against the far wall between two tall bookshelves, a series of newspaper clippings had been pinned to a cork board. Compelled by curiosity, Timori approached the board.

"Who are you?" said a voice from behind him. Timori yelped and wheeled around, his hand clutching the arm of a couch.

The man was short and dishevelled, his suspenders askew, his hair a mass of silver and black, as wild and untamed as the estate's lawn. He adjusted his spectacles and withdrew a wand from his shirt. Instead of a crystal trigger, atop the wand was a bulbous piece of blue rock. Timori blinked. He was caught so off-guard he didn't even consider drawing the wand in his own jacket.

"I said, who are you?" The dog had reappeared and accentuated the man's question with a fierce growl in Timori's direction. The tail, however, still wagged.

Timori held up his hands in a peaceful gesture.

"Wuah! I'm Timori Stravida, sir! Professor. Doctor."

"Well, which is it?" The man inched forward. "Sir, professor, or doctor?"

"Uh, student." Timori found that his back was against the phonograph. "Doctor Ruveldi sent me."

"Ruveldi, hmm?" A furry eyebrow was lifted. "All right, boy. Name Vespici's *Laws of Science*."

Timori winced. "All thirty of them?"

"The first three."

Timori ticked them off on his fingers. "Created energy must equal disintegrated matter, and created matter must equal spent energy. The power of an object increases by its mass and speed. Matter, over time, tends toward the spherical."

"What is Gehren's Constant?"

"The median of the width of possible resonance of a crystal."

"Which is?" The barrel was just about poking Timori's stomach. The dog barked again, expecting a pat on the head from Timori. He didn't dare move his hands.

"Uhh...seven point six three superloccis."

"Explain 'Harmonic Theory'."

Timori's breath caught in his throat. *Harmonic Theory?* It was De'Barus's work. He could recall Doctor Ruveldi making an off-hand comment about it in class one time. However, the theory itself had never been discussed. All Timori could remember was:

"It's a revision to Vespici's first law, isn't it?"

"In a phrase. If I were to walk away from you at a metre per second, assuming no obstacles, how long would it take before we could no longer see each other due to the curvature of the earth?"

Timori scrunched up his face. "I...I can't calculate Mikosian Curve in my head. I would need an adding machine."

De'Barus raised a tufty eyebrow. "One day we'll be using crystal logic machines, small enough to fit in a pocket. Still, not bad," he said, tucking the wand into his suspenders. "Roberto said you were smart and gutsy, but I've never met an assistant yet who can factor with a wand pointed at them. It's harmless anyway. Just sends intruders back to the gate." He paused. "Did Roberto mention anything else about the theory?"

"Not that I can recall," Timori replied, relaxing his shoulders somewhat.

"Good, because it isn't published yet. I'd have had his degree revoked otherwise. Come on, I'll show you where we'll be working."

Timori felt a knot of excitement form in his stomach. His other concerns, Racquela and Paulo, the NSP, looking after his sisters, it all faded to the background as he considered the exciting possibilities that would come from working with the greatest scientific mind in Novem.

Moving at a slouched, legs-first gait, De'Barus led Timori down a set of stairs to the basement, which was just a barren concrete hallway lighted by a naked crystal ensconced in the ceiling. At the end of the hallway was a thick metal door with a turncrank handle. De'Barus casually spun a combination lock, seeming to know the numbers by feel rather than by looking at them. Timori heard a faint metal sliding sound, then the doctor turned the crank and pulled open the massive door.

"Welcome to the lab," De'Barus said as he motioned for Timori to follow him in. "Don't touch anything unless I tell you to."

Timori stepped into the large underground space, marvelling at how much of the estate it must have taken up. He had expected a dimly-lit, creepy basement, but found instead a great room illuminated by massive crystal lamps that hung from the ceiling, casting a cool blue glow on every corner of the room, and every corner of a disastrous mess.

Timori could see signs of laboratory equipment half-buried: a blackboard here, a work table there, everything within eyesight littered with dirty dishes, mechanical odds and ends, and piles of notebooks. The floor was even worse, as Timori discovered in his attempt to follow De'Barus's pathway through the maze of cardboard boxes, nails, screws, crumpled pieces of paper, and dried-up old dog feces.

Timori wondered if he was cursed always to be surrounded by messy people.

"Before you touch anything," De'Barus said as he reached a relatively empty workspace against a far wall, "I have a system. I know where everything is. One of the benefits of an eidetic memory."

De'Barus began sifting through a box of fingernail-sized crystals with one hand. The other hand had withdrawn a bronze pocketwatch, which De'Barus rubbed with his thumb. The etching had long ago been worn smooth.

"So where do we start?" Timori asked, clapping his hands together.

"We?" De'Barus lifted his head out of the box. "Didn't Ruveldi tell you? 'We' won't be working on anything. You are going to clean up the lab and look after the mail. And Pippo."

Timori folded his arms. "I thought you needed a lab assistant."

"Yes." He selected a tiny white crystal and dropped it into an empty metal half-sphere. "You are in the lab, and you will be assisting me by handling the day-to-day tasks I can't be bothered with. I'm close to a breakthrough. The last assistant quit, but surely you can handle the monumental stress of a few cleaning duties and some nice dog walks, hmm?"

He picked up the other half of the sphere, which served as a lid. Sealing the container, he placed it in a receptacle that sat atop a metal device covered in dials.

"What about your maid? Someone cleans upstairs, from what I can tell."

De'Barus wheeled around and grabbed Timori by the shoulders. "My dear boy. Surely you can imagine the dangers and distractions of allowing a woman into your place of work."

"In that case, you can forget it. With all due respect, Doctor, I was under the impression I was given this opportunity because of my aptitude. Not because you need someone to clean up after you and your dog."

De'Barus turned back to his machine and turned a dial. "By all means, go. There are other bright young finishing school lads eager for a wage and a scholarship to the Alchemists' Academy."

Timori paused, unmoving. Though he couldn't see the old professor's face, he could almost swear the man was smiling. Who was Timori kidding? De'Barus represented a job and an easy in to the best scientific academy in Novem.

"Fine," Timori grumbled. "Where do I begin?"

"With the dog shit."

Chapter 35

Racquela brought her harp out to the garden, hoping to feel a little less trapped. Since her rescue, she only saw the world outside her home and school through windows. She was constantly under guard, even in class. Worst of all, her only visits with Paulo were at the estate, chaperoned. Her father insisted on 'getting to know him better this time.'

Racquela considered trying to steal away with Paulo at Central so they could find an intimate moment together, but the only place where the guards wouldn't follow her was the lavatory. Paulo had chuckled and said that wouldn't stop him, but Racquela's guards waited right outside the door for her.

She was becoming stir-crazy. The garden, at least, gave her a taste of freedom and a place where leering guards didn't watch her every move. They respected her privacy and secured the perimeter.

The fountain offered a watery babble as the larks chirruped a melody. Nearby, Lucius pruned the rose bushes. Racquela took a deep breath and started tuning. Moments of isolation made her think of the kidnapping, but her harp took her mind off of it.

Out of the corner of her eye, Racquela saw her father approaching. She stopped tuning.

"Play me a military march," Joven said. It was one of his favourite jokes. He used to ask her all the time when she was a little girl, and she would giggle and tell him the harp was for love songs only.

"Versiccio or Vellini?" she asked. It was another part of the joke. Versiccio was a Noven painter and Vellini was an architect.

"Actually, play me whatever you like," he suggested as he sat beside her on the marble bench.

"I'm still tuning," Racquela said. She turned another peg and plucked a string. "You got home too early."

Joven made a derisive laugh. "The meeting devolved into petty political bickering fairly early this time."

He sat quietly as Racquela continued to tune the harp, string by string. She could hear him drumming his fingers on his knees. It was the same awkward-father-daughter-attempted-conversation routine they'd been going through ever since she had become too old to sit on his knee. She just had to wait until he found the words to say. Asking him what was on his mind would merely fluster the man.

Between Joven's long sighs, Racquela could hear the snips of Lucius' pruning shears.

"What's your favourite song right now?" he asked.

"Across the Sea," she answered without hesitation. "I could play it for you. The words are sad, but the melody is beautiful."

"Oh. I thought you liked swing music now."

"I do, but love ballads are still my favourite."

"Good to know you haven't really changed."

The silence hung between them. To Racquela it was a reminder of a dank cellar and long hours of stillness and fear. When the silence stretched out too long, she could see Dillas's face, the casual smirk, and the big, serious eyes. Racquela fumbled for another peg and tuned the next string.

"Listen, sweetheart, I know being under guard isn't easy, but after what happened..." he trailed off for a moment.

"I just wish I could see Paulo more," she admitted. The other restrictions she could handle.

"I know. Now that I've met him, I'm more comfortable with him courting you, but this isn't a crystal betrothal...there are rules to follow. I still need to meet his guardian. Last time, well...your mother and I were eager to impress the church, and to be more progressive about things, but after you didn't come home that night..." His voice trembled and he looked away.

When she was younger, Racquela had asked her parents why she didn't have any siblings. Joven and Jessica told Racquela they'd tried for years to even have one child. It was easy for Racquela to forget sometimes that with the vastness of all the De'Trinis owned, they had built their lives around *her*.

Joven looked away, pretending to watch Lucius prune. Racquela hadn't finished tuning the top strings, but she wouldn't need them. Plucking a chord here and there, she sang:

> *Across the sea and far away*
> *My love has sailed, she's gone to stay*
> *In the chilly fog of Biscayne Bay*
> *To live with a Commonwealth man.*
>
> *They say that he's handsome,*
> *They say that he's rich,*
> *They say that he lives like a king*
>
> *They say that she met him in old Alloise-town*
> *He charmed her with songs and a ring*
>
> *Me, I've got holes in my pockets and shoes*
> *Paid my last centime to those union dues*
> *Now I've got nothing at all left to lose*
> *When even my heart is not mine*
>
> *They tell me forget her,*
> *They tell me don't fret her,*

Plenty of crystals are clear
But they'll never know all the love that I feel
And so I must sail far from here

Across the sea and far away,
That's where I'll go, I'm going to stay
In the chilly fog of Biscayne Bay
And become a Commonwealth man.

"Huh," Joven muttered. "Interesting music you kids listen to these days."

Racquela feigned a reproachful look. "You're supposed to say, 'that was beautiful, dear'."

"Well sure, it was nice to listen to. I just don't know why the words have to be so moody."

"That's what makes it a ballad, Father."

"Oh. Well. Anyway, I just wanted to say I'm sorry for the way things have to be."

"I understand, Father." She stared off at the faraway towers of Crystus Hill.

"Jacoby is under curfew now, too. I was thinking of inviting him over for dinner. You know...to thank him."

Racquela took note of the fact that her father didn't want to thank Timori as well, for his help in her rescue.

"That would be nice." Anything to alleviate her feelings of isolation, she thought. She wondered if Jacoby would be able to think of a way to use his speaking to help her see Paulo.

Joven stood and breathed in the crisp autumn air.

"Oh! And I nearly forgot. Ignatius and Isabella will be back early from boarding school. They'll be transferring to Central in the spring. I managed to convince the dean to accept them. Isn't that great?"

Racquela smiled a duplicitous smile. "Fantastic," she said, as the wheels in her mind began to turn in a new direction.

***

Although it was a frigid and grey noon hour, Bella and Phebe watched the football practice from the vantage of the spectator stands, dressed warmly in designer shawls, gloves and hats. Racquela approached them, flanked on either side by her burly bodyguards. A year ago, being tailed everywhere by a couple of goons hired by her father would have been enough to make her die of embarrassment. Now she had far greater concerns than the opinions of Bella and Phebe.

Except that she'd been asked by her mother to ensure Isabella's social acceptance at Central.

"I thought you didn't like football boys anymore," Bella quipped.

"I'm not here to watch the practice," Racquela said. One of the guards laid his coat on the bench so she could sit. "How are you, Bella? Phebe?"

"I am well, thank you," Bella replied, not taking her eyes off of the boys. "It's so pleasant here at Central now that your Dori-lookalike charity case is no longer around."

The words stung more than Racquela cared to admit. She hadn't summoned the courage to attend the hanging. Crystara, once her best friend, was dead.

"It's bad luck to speak ill of the dead like that," Phebe remarked.

"Everyone knows the Dori don't have souls," Bella countered.

Racquela could see his big, apologetic eyes in her mind, as well as that innocent boy's face. She had to quell her rage before she lashed out and struck Bella.

"Could I ask a favour of you two?"

Bella rolled her eyes. "If it's making nice with another dirty lower-caste miner's daughter, you can forget it."

Racquela stood. "You know what, Bella? You're nothing but a daisy-chasing, hateful bitch. Forget I asked." She looked at Phebe. "See you around, Phebe."

Racquela didn't give Bella the satisfaction of looking back to see her expression. She stormed off in the other direction, her guards at her heels.

"That was impressive," said a deeply melodious voice.

Her fury melted away. Paulo was leaning against a whiteoak tree with a cigarette in one hand and a book in the other. She sauntered over to him and planted a dainty kiss on his lips.

"Is that all I get?" he whispered in her ear. Instantly her skin tingled, all the way down to her toes. She gave him a deeper kiss. Then the goons were there, her impromptu chaperones, unwanted observers to her love.

"I'm not thrilled with the audience," he continued. "What do you say we dodge them and find a secluded place?"

She giggled. "Stop. You know Father is watching me carefully." She thought about telling him her plan, but with the guards right there it was too chancy.

Paulo pulled away and folded his arms. With the book and cigarette in either hand, she couldn't decide if it made him look dignified or comical. "I barely see you as it is."

Racquela was startled to hear Paulo use such a petulant tone.

"It's not ideal," Racquela agreed. She glanced at the guards, trying to silently indicate to Paulo that she was working on a way around the issue. "But it's for my own safety." She refrained from winking, which would have been too obvious.

"Nobody would be foolish enough to kidnap you twice," Paulo insisted.

"Come for dinner tomorrow night?" She swished her hips, trying to entice him to kiss her one last time.

Paulo shook his head and flicked away the last of his cigarette. "I can't. Business."

"What business could you possibly be conducting at night?" she teased.

"The kind that's none of yours."

The words were so unexpected, Racquela felt as though she had been physically struck.

"I told you, I'm running things for my uncle down here and I can't talk about it with you...at least not yet. Maybe the night after that." He flipped his book open.

Racquela sighed. "Yeah. Maybe." The school bell rang, calling a summons to afternoon classes. Paulo barely even turned his head when she kissed him goodbye.

Racquela dragged her feet across the field, walking under the old Mosind arch and past the bell tower into the courtyard. She tried to puzzle out what had made Paulo so distant. It wasn't her fault she was under a careful watch. Surely he had to understand it was all temporary until the tensions in the city died down, and that she was doing everything she could to think of a way around the problem.

A horrifying possibility struck her. What if Paulo was losing interest? What if 'business' was just him gallivanting with other girls? He never lacked for admirers. Doubts and worst-case scenarios played themselves out in Racquela's mind.

"Hey, Racquela," a voice said. Racquela wheeled around to find Jacoby standing next to one of her goons, dressed in his school uniform but still sweating from the football practice. As he ran a hand through his damp hair, Racquela noticed he was still wearing Lenara's ring.

"Jake!" she exclaimed. "I've been looking for you."

"Same here. Only..." He glanced at her guards. "This might not be the best time."

"I agree," she said. "Your family is formally invited to the De'Trini estate tomorrow night for dinner. Maybe we can talk then? I have to get to class."

"Me, too," Jacoby said. He flashed a grin and dashed off into the school.

He came tearing back through the doors a moment later.

"Sorry, I forgot to accept your invitation. So yes. See you then."

Chapter 36

Roberto's attic was one of Julio's sanctuaries, a musty chamber of lost Noven secrets, a cluttered maze of stacked heirlooms and books, tucked away from the rest of the stately, lonely manse that was the Ruveldi estate. Roberto and Julio would often steal away up there during visits, despite having the whole house to themselves other than the rooms occupied by Ruveldi's sparse serving staff. Up the shoddy ladder they would climb, pipe tobacco and whiskey in tow, and while away the hours delving through Roberto's dishevelled museum and talking of whatever they pleased. If they had known each other as children the attic would have been their playplace, their secret imaginative clubhouse where there were no rules other than the ones they set.

It was like a second home to Julio, and one of the only places where he felt as though he was at peace with life.

That evening, Roberto had brought Julio up to show him 'something new.'

"It amazes me." Julio remarked as he carefully shuffled his way between the two narrow stacks of engineering textbooks he referred to as 'the sentinels.' "You still uncover things up here that we haven't seen before."

"Jules, I could spend my whole life up here and not go through it all. My family have been hoarders since before the reunification. I think there's a crystal portal back there somewhere."

"But it's such a small space," Julio argued. He caught his hook on the broken old mantle clock, like he often did, and nearly fell over. "Damn," he muttered. "Every godsdamned time. You know, I don't care how often they mentioned them in the legends, but I still don't think that kind of long-distance teleportation was possible."

"It was a joke, Jules. I keep finding things because every time I get to the bottom of a pile of shit, I bury something else I haven't looked at yet. If I wasn't teaching at Central *and* the academy, as well as attending regular guild meetings..."

Julio lit his pipe, holding it aloft with his hook. "Yes, the sad song of the successful upper-caste doctor. I weep for you."

Roberto laughed. "Fuck off. Maybe I just stagger the discoveries so we always have an excuse to come up here."

"We don't need an excuse."

They reached a far corner of the attic, a space Julio had never before seen cleared. In the centre of the vacated space sat a rusty machine the size of a stand-up radio, its front panel covered in levers, dials, and gauges, topped by crystals of various colours encased in glass.

Julio swallowed his pipe smoke, coughing until his eyes watered.

"Is that," he coughed again, "what I think it is?"

Roberto leaned on the machine nonchalantly and took a swig from his wine bottle. "What do you think it is?"

Wincing at the stabbing pain in his bad leg, Julio knelt down, using his cane as support. The functions of the levers and dials were lost upon him, but the nature of the device itself was all too clear.

"I think it's an old resonance calibrator. But I'm not an engineer."

"It is," Roberto replied, tapping the device lovingly as though it were an old family dog. "This model was the first kind available for general sale, based on my great-grandfather's old prototype. He donated the patent *and* prototype to the fourth republic for nothing but a handshake, the dullard."

"Well, your family have never been great capitalists," Julio mused. "Can you imagine if you found the prototype up here?"

Roberto chuckled. "De'Barus would shit crystals. Nobody knows what happened to the original. Probably collecting dust in the Old Temple basement or some dirt."

Julio grimaced as he stood. "So what are you going to do with this one? Give it to a museum?"

Roberto shook his head. "Nah, the National already has one. Working model, too. I think my dad scrapped this one for parts. It's gutted. Trust an engineer to scavenge coils and bolts and leave a bunch of crystals behind. I was thinking about bringing Timori over to see if he could get it working again, as a side project."

"Hmm," said Julio. "I think the administration frowns on fraternizing with students like that."

"Fuck 'em," Roberto said. "I don't need the job. The kid needs the challenge, though. He skips my class for three weeks, comes back, and gets top marks on a test."

"I thought he was De'Barus's new assistant. Isn't that challenge enough?"

Roberto sighed and leaned against the calibrator again. "Challenge to withstand the old bastard's presence for more than a minute, yes. But De'Barus wants a second maid, not a lab assistant. The boy is cleaning up dog shit and opening mail, he's not learning a godsdamned thing."

"It's an opportunity," Julio countered. "I'm sure De'Barus will teach him once he trusts him. It just takes him a while to warm up to people because he's so socially inept. Look at how long it was before he would even acknowledge my presence."

"That's because he doesn't understand how a genius would choose to study the humanities instead of the sciences. You're a spooky anomaly to him."

Julio chuckled and puffed on his pipe. "I don't know about genius, Rob. Anyway, doesn't the boy have enough going on, between assisting De'Barus, Central, and slave-driver Coach Lagheri? He's a poor kid going to the rich kid school. I'm not sure you see how overwhelmed he probably is."

"There you go, bringing caste into it," Roberto said. "You think I don't understand his pain because I'm nobility? I know what it's like to be spurned by someone you love, Jules, and I know how it feels to have to support a family that suffocates you. Mom was a useless wreck after Dad left for the Commonwealth. I know what Timori is going through."

Julio sighed and stared off toward the heaps of old books and chests and mannequins. "Sorry, Rob. I'm not saying you can't empathize with the kid, but it seems to me like you might be projecting your own feelings a little..."

Roberto folded his arms. "Right. You get to have your nice father-son bonding with Pip's kid, pretending he's yours. Which, by the way, is the dullest idea you have ever had. What are you going to do when Ramona finds out? But I'm not allowed to foster the best in this kid, who doesn't have a father but has every opportunity in the world to turn his brilliance into a better life, for himself *and his family*."

"And there's no other reason you want to be around him?" Julio asked.

"Fuck you," Roberto snapped. "How dare you? It's not like that. Is that what you think of me? Creepy Rob, the lonely old pederast?"

Julio took a step toward his best friend. "No, I didn't mean it like that. Rob, I'm sorry. I was being defensive. I finally made progress with Drago, and I've been jealous of how easily you forged trust with the Stravida kid."

Roberto shrugged. He seemed hurt but willing to let it slide. It wasn't the first time they'd had a heated argument. Usually their fights were about Ramona and Julio's reliance on her for his own sense of well-being. They'd forgiven each other for worse things said, after all.

"It's fine," Roberto said. "He's just a lot like I was at his age. The bond isn't hard to find."

"Mine was," Julio admitted. "Drago is nothing like me."

"No, he's like Ramona and Pip. His actual father."

It was Julio's turn to shrug off a barbed comment. "Better him than Andari."

Roberto sighed and took another swig from his bottle of wine, then rested his head on the old calibrator. It was a rather gentle pose for a gruff man.

"You still think this is a good idea?" Roberto asked. "This little sojourn with Drago?"

Julio nodded. "Yes. He thinks war is all glory."

"And how is a trip through historic northern Novem and Southern Nilonne, swapping war stories among old buddies, supposed to change his mind?"

"I don't know, Rob, but I have to try. That war took nearly everything from me, and I won't let another one take him, too."

Chapter 37

The Padrona family was more than happy to accept an invitation to the De'Trini estate for dinner. Ever since Gilliermo's appointment to the alchemists' guild, he and Joven appeared to have become easy colleagues. Jacoby seemed less thrilled with the idea of his younger brother Marco being present, but grudgingly accepted his presence.

Returning to the table after years of absence were the servants' children, Ignatius, and Isabella. It wasn't often the De'Trinis invited their serving staff to the dinner table, but Joven strove to maintain a better relationship with his servants than most nobles. After all, he had offered to send the children to school so they could one day improve their station.

The change could already be seen in Ignatius. Once the shy son of a gardener, he had grown into a handsome and confident young man. If Racquela hadn't been courting Paulo, she would have considered flirting with him (her first kiss, after all), but her father would never allow such a thing to continue beyond words.

Isabella, who had been sent to an all-girls' boarding school run by the Sisters of Solitude, had a quiet demeanour, but Racquela could see a fire in the young woman's eyes – eyes that wouldn't stop staring at Jacoby.

Racquela was moderately put out by Paulo's refusal to attend, but she reminded herself if she could get what she needed from Jacoby, she'd be able to see Paulo again soon.

The trouble was finding a moment to speak with him alone. Everyone sat in the parlour before dinner. The adults were drinking wine and chatting about politics, books, and the accomplishments of their children. A scratchy old phonograph record warbled a mellow tune in the background. Marco seemed perfectly content to listen to Ignatius talk about his time living in the mysterious, backwards culture of Novem's north, but Isabella stuck to Racquela like a binding crystal, wanting to hear every word about Racquela's tumultuous first year at Central School, and hanging off of every syllable that came from Jacoby's mouth. Racquela supposed she forgave Isabella somewhat. Although not as interesting or as handsome as Paulo, Jacoby must have seemed like a dream come true to someone who had been stuck in an all-girls' boarding school for three years straight.

Racquela didn't think Jacoby would want to have much to do with girls after leaving Crystara and losing Lenara, but his body language toward Isabella said otherwise. Still, Racquela couldn't help but notice a second time that he still wore Lenara's ring. The rest of the crystal betrothed had been asked to return theirs to the church.

Jacoby took a sip of wine and glanced over at his parents, then back to Racquela.

"So what did you want to ask me about?"

"Crystals," she whispered back.

Jacoby raised an eyebrow and Isabella inched forward in her chair.

"It's been established that I'm not an expert," Jacoby said. Isabella giggled. She seemed to think anything Jacoby said deserved a giggle. "But I'll do what I can."

"I need to know if there is a way for me to disguise myself." She exchanged a look with Isabella. "Actually, two disguises. Those exist, right? They use them in the old stories all the time."

Jacoby furrowed his brow. "Hmm. Just because they use them in the stories, doesn't mean it's true."

Racquela slumped back in her chair.

"However," Jacoby continued, "I have heard some stories of my own...Master Vellize told us once that Emperor Longoro issued disguise rings to his spies during the Great War, and that it was an ancient secret previously only known by the church. However, that was all hearsay...and it's nothing they'd dare teach us at Central." He swirled his wine thoughtfully, which Racquela thought made him look silly, but Isabella seemed impressed.

"What do we need disguises for?" Isabella asked, wide-eyed.

Racquela shook her head. "Not yet," she said, keeping an eye on her parents.

"What indeed?" echoed Jacoby.

"Can you do it or not?" Racquela demanded, forcing Jacoby to break eye contact with Isabella.

"I don't know know the first thing about such a complicated alignment," Jacoby admitted. Deflated, Racquela downed the last of her wine.

"Crystara would have known how." She said it without thinking, and felt the tight pang of regret just as the words left her lips. To her surprise, Jacoby didn't appear upset. He leaned forward with a conspiratorial look in his eyes.

"Racquela, you deserve to know," he whispered.

She glanced at the adults. They were already into a second bottle, and Jessica was inviting the Padronas to visit their summer home. Again Racquela thought of Crystara and the wonderful summer they'd shared in Los Maros. It seemed a lifetime ago.

She steeled herself for whatever horrible news Jacoby had. She knew he had been brave enough to attend the hanging, but he hadn't yet spoken a word about it.

"I think Crystara's still alive."

"What?" Her lip was trembling.

"At the hanging. Please don't say a word to anyone because I never told my parents I was there. I've been under curfew since they found out I helped rescue you. If they find out I was at the scene of a riot, they'll lock me up until I'm thirty."

"Jake, what happened up there? And how do you know she's alive? The radio said she died." Her voice cracked.

"It was someone else. Up on the platform. I didn't know it at first. I just...well, it's hard to explain, but I could *feel* how upset everyone was. As though a lot of them weren't there because they wanted to see her hang...they were there because they were mad at the church, or at the government. This whole city is uneasy. I never noticed it before, really, but I do now, and it's not just what I'm learning in empathy class. It's like the pot is finally boiling over."

"Jake, you're rambling," Racquela said. "What happened?"

Jacoby took a deep breath, then a sip of wine. "Okay. So I thought it was Crystara up there because I couldn't really see her face. And in spite of everything that happened, I couldn't just stand there and watch her die. I don't know if I believe she killed Lenara or the keeper, either. She loved Orvin."

"I don't know if I believe it either," Racquela said. "So what did you do?"

Nearly forgotten but completely engrossed in the discussion, Isabella nibbled on a caviar-coated cracker.

"I started shouting for them to free her. I didn't know what else to do. People started chanting with me and I could feel the tension rising. Then it looked like the church knights were going to speed it along because of the unrest, so I...I rushed the platform. I don't know what came over me, but then suddenly there were a whole bunch of us pushing forward. So I jumped up and grabbed who I thought was Crystara and we got the abyss out of there.

"Anyway, the girl is named Tanni and she's a Dori the church kidnapped. They were trying to pretend she was Crystara, and they have everyone duped except for me. Tanni thinks they're keeping Crystara because she's a reader, and I'm inclined to agree. She took me to the Casteless Quarter, Racquela. They're...not quite what I expected. They aren't what people think they are."

"I know," Racquela replied. "Jake, the boy who was there when you rescued me...he was Dori. He was the one who kidnapped me, actually, but then he..." She choked up and looked away. Maria came in and rang the little silver dinner bell. Her parents were getting up off the divan.

"I thought I felt some..." Jacoby began, but Racquela put a finger to her lips.

"After dinner," she suggested. She had to find a way to discuss the rest without Isabella around.

Although the De'Trini servants were invited to sup with the guests, they were still expected to prepare and serve the meal. As the De'Trini and Padrona families sat themselves down, Maria, Mario, and Sarai entered the dining hall and began placing covered silver trays about the table. Marco's eyes seemed as wide as his dinner plate, but Jacoby had been a guest at the De'Trinis for dinner before and wasn't as flabbergasted. As Racquela recalled, Jacoby's mother, Catarina, had come from a noble family before marrying down in station, so the Padronas weren't necessarily strangers to opulence either.

Once all the trays had been laid out upon the table, the servants brought in the first course: a light tomato salad dressed with capers and fresh Nilonnese cheese. Then they sat and conversation was permitted to commence.

Racquela prodded Jacoby in the ribs when nobody else was looking.

"Oof," he muttered, his mouth full of tomato. "Hmm?" He glanced at her in a casual, sideways fashion. Nobody seemed to notice. The parents were continuing their conversation from earlier, and Isabella was seated with the servants at the other end of the table.

"So can your Dori friend do it?" she whispered.

Jacoby swallowed his mouthful before answering.

"I don't know," he said. "Probably. She's never been to school, but she seems to know more about speaking than anyone. But the question is, will she? She acts like she owes me for saving her life, but somehow I'm a burden to her at the same time."

"Well, can't I just bribe her?"

"Because that worked so well last time."

Racquela cast a defensive glare at Jacoby. "I wasn't the one who fiddled around with the betrothals."

"Which means you and Timori were meant to be together," Jacoby suggested.

"No. Keeper Orvin accepted my bribe and convinced the Great Crystal to choose me instead of Timori's original intended."

Jacoby had that furrowed brow he often got, which meant he was heavily contemplating something.

"What did you say you needed the disguises for?"

Racquela couldn't meet his eyes. Jacoby was not allowed to know about Paulo. He would take that information to Timori and ruin everything. She had to be careful to guard her expressions around him. The word around school was that he was no slouch as an empath.

"I can't be under this kind of lock and key anymore, Jake," she said. It was a partial truth. "I feel like I'm becoming cracked."

"I can understand that," Jacoby said. "What about the kidnapping, though? Surely you know it's not safe to show your face around many parts of the city."

"Hence the disguises, dully."

"Well, why do you need two, then?"

There was a pause in the conversation as Sarai came by clearing plates. Racquela held her tongue for a moment.

"Isabella is going to pretend to be me when I'm not here."

"Ahh," Jacoby said. "So what are you going to do, going out disguised? Just...get away from here?" he gestured with his eyes about the room. "I can think of worse prisons."

She contemplated the finely embroidered serviette in her lap. *So can I. Far worse ones. But Paulo is worth any bribe, and any risk.*

"You can't tell me you're enjoying your curfew," she said.

Sarai returned and placed steaming bowls of rabbit soup in front of Racquela and Jacoby. Racquela waited until conversation resumed.

"I have a way around curfew," Jacoby uttered between sips of soup.

"So why can't I have the same thing?"

Jacoby rolled his eyes. "I didn't get kidnapped. I'm not as big a target for starving miners, and I'm not a girl."

"Will you do it or not?" Racquela demanded, loudly enough that all conversation at the table suddenly ceased. Jacoby and Racquela glanced at each other, then at their parents.

"Um, Bella isn't really my type, thanks," Jacoby said.

Racquela breathed a sigh of relief. *Sharp thinking,* she thought. She waited for the other conversations at the table to resume.

"I'll do it," Jacoby acquiesced, "but you can't bribe the Dori with money. They're not allowed to use it."

"Then what do they want?"

Jacoby shrugged. "They certainly don't seem to lack for crystals. I might have to ask."

Racquela beamed a smile. "But you'll do it?"

He had another silent, contemplative moment. "I'll do it, but you know Timori's going to find out eventually."

Her heart seized in her chest. *He knows,* she thought. *How does he know? Lenara? Did Paulo tell him?*

"Find out what?" she asked, delicately adding nonchalance to her voice.

The servants were taking the lids off of the dishes in the centre of the table. The main courses were being served.

In the din and clatter, she heard Jacoby say, "About you and Paulo. That would be the whisper that cracks the crystal."

Chapter 38

The Nine Sons of Novem: A Parable

Once upon a time there was a wealthy duke with nine sons.
One day, the duke took his sons to the top of his tower and showed
them the virgin, untamed land around the estate. He told them that
when they became men, they would each earn an inheritance: one
ninth of the duke's wealth.

When the first son became a man, he used his inheritance
to buy up vast parcels of land, and so he and his wife and children
became farmers. 'Thus will I feed my younger brothers,' said he,
for as the eldest, he was a responsible provider.

The duke warned him, however, that his brothers would
take advantage of his generous nature.

When the second son came of age, he spent his wealth on
tools of iron and went into the mountains, for as the second-born
he naturally sought to become more successful than his older
brother. 'Here shall I find the riches of the earth,' said he, 'and
my older brother shall feed me so I may work uninterrupted.'

And the duke warned him that a nugget and a coin are not
the same thing.

When the third son was old enough, he used his money to
buy tools of crafting, for he looked up to his elder brothers who
worked with their hands, but he had the heart of a creator. When
the second brother complained that his hard work was going to
rust, the third brother said, 'I will pay you to work, brother, and I
will pay the eldest to feed you, if I may take what you have and
build to my heart's content.' And with the riches of the mountains
he bought from his brother, he built a great city, and many people

paid him for his houses, and so he became wealthier than his older brothers.

But the duke warned him that city walls do not protect against greed.

When the fourth son earned his inheritance, bandits came from the forest and besieged the city the third son had built. The fourth son asked the third son to build him weapons and armour, and then he went out and slayed the bandits, and his brothers were thankful. 'You must pay me,' said he to his brothers. 'I am risking my life to protect your fields, mines, and city.'

His brothers paid him to keep them safe, and he became wealthier than they, so wealthy he had the third brother build him a fine fortress in the centre of the city.

Then the duke warned him that his brothers would not need him during a time of peace and would become wealthier than he.

When the fifth son was given his gold, he saw how busy his older brothers were, and how they did not have time to enjoy the fruits of their labours. So he bought a horse and cart and offered to take their goods to the next city to sell.

By selling his brothers' goods, he became wealthier than they, and he brought back exotic things to sell in return. His house was larger than the fortress in the centre of town.

The duke warned him, however, that his younger brothers would find a way to outdo his wealth.

Now the sixth son was not hard-working or brave or cunning, but he had spent his childhood observing the world and he knew many things, and there came a time when his elder brothers' goods no longer fetched a fair price, and all the brothers were in danger of losing their wealth. So they all went to the sixth brother and said, 'You understand the world. How do we save our wealth?' The sixth said, 'Why, we must create something new that people need.' And he used his understanding of the world to make new things that were useful, and from his share of the profits he built a place where others could learn what he knew. For a time, he was the wealthiest of all his brothers.

The duke warned him, though, that not everyone understood the value of truth.

When the seventh son achieved independence, it was discovered that he was a crystal speaker. He took the knowledge of all his elder brothers and bound that wisdom into crystals. He went forth and conquered neighbouring nations with his power, and he had the wealth of an emperor, and he ruled over all his brothers.

But the duke told him his fortune was forever fated to rise and fall along with his empire.

The eighth son, unlike his brothers, had no concern for material wealth. His share of the duke's legacy was spent building a place of worship atop the Great Crystal, which spoke for the gods. The eighth son's church became influential even beyond the borders of the empire, and thus became wealthier than the empire alone could ever be.

But the duke told the eighth son that the gods did not concern themselves with the folly of man.

Then came a time when the empire was beset by rival nations and fell to their might, and the brothers and all they had built were reduced to poverty and ruins. Then the ninth and final son was given the ninth and final share of the duke's estate. The ninth son looked to his elder brethren and said, 'Brothers, I shall use my wealth so we may rebuild, provided each of you pays me a regular share of your wealth hereafter, and name me ruler. If you refuse, I shall take my wealth and leave you to ruin.'

And so the ninth son became the wealthiest and most powerful of all, without ever lifting a finger.

But the duke warned the ninth son that his brothers would forever resent him for what he had done.

***

Tanni had shaved her head.

It surprised Jacoby – her hair had been so long before, with a wonderful curl to the tresses – but somehow the look seemed to suit her fiery nature. He could feel an odd sense of satisfaction from her as he appraised the orange fuzz upon her scalp.

"Rich boy is late," she said. She was seated in a rickety chair in front of an equally rickety table, upon which rested an array of multicoloured crystals. Where the Dori found so many expensive pieces of rock when they could barely afford to feed themselves, Jacoby couldn't even begin to surmise, but he knew it was just another mystery surrounding them that he had yet to unravel.

"Rich boy had football practice," Jacoby replied as he unshouldered his satchel. "Coach Lagheri let me rejoin the team."

He sat across from Tanni in the other chair and examined her. The haircut made her head look large, her nose even larger, her eyes enormous. Jacoby didn't find her beautiful by any stretch of the imagination, but she certainly was striking.

"Well, what does he need the Dori for, when he has football? Go on, then." She gestured for him to leave. "Back to your highborn glory."

"I'm not highborn," Jacoby insisted as he brought a notebook, pen, and ink bottle out from his satchel. "And I'm here to learn from you."

"High*raised*, then," Tanni said. "Here to steal Dori secrets."

Jacoby rolled a crystal back and forth on the table. He had discovered that Tanni liked to test his patience.

"Are you willing to teach me or not? I came here to learn about your people, not steal your speaking secrets."

Tanni folded her arms and leaned back in her chair. "What interest could we hold for you, rich boy? We are the nobodies."

"But you know so much about speaking," Jacoby replied. "And you've been here for as long as Captus Nove, maybe longer. All the old histories talk about the Dortians and how they helped unite Novem, but they don't really mention them much after that, other than to say they can't be trusted and that they're different. Everyone says you don't belong in the caste system, but nobody seems to know *why*."

She seemed to study Jacoby for a moment, chewing upon her lip.

"Whitehands don't care much for curiosity. They care for profit and power."

"And I told you, I don't care for those things either. I may not be Dori, but I understand what it's like to be at the bottom. Maybe not casteless, but downtrodden. I won't let myself forget where I came from. Okay?" He leaned forward. "We are no different, you and I."

Tanni allowed herself a smirk.

"Foolish highraised boy. We *are* different, whether you see it or not. Not because of caste or appearance."

"So what makes us different, then?"

Jacoby could feel hesitation from her then, as though she wanted to reveal something to him, but could not. Whether it was the rules laid down to Tanni by Shachari when dealing with outsiders, or something else, Jacoby could not tell.

"What do they teach you about crystals in your fancy school?" she asked.

"Plenty," Jacoby said. "But the Dori seem to know more." He twisted the ring on his finger and thought of Lenara. Most of his speaking techniques he had learned from Crystara, but everything he had ever known about empathy had come from the girl whose ring he still wore. If he hadn't been so practiced at reading the emotions behind façades, he never would have succeeded in making friends with Tanni.

"We do, perhaps," Tanni agreed. "But what do they teach you about the *origins* of the crystals?"

Jacoby tried to suppress a smile. *Precious little*, he thought.

"There's conjecture, but it's not really talked about," he said as he twirled an uncut azure crystal between his fingers. "Most people revert to their religious beliefs and say the crystals were put there by the gods. A lot of scientists just think it's another mystery to be solved, and that one day we'll know exactly why crystals can do things that go against natural laws everything else in the observable universe seems to follow."

"And what do *you* believe?" she asked.

Jacoby furrowed his brow. He had never taken much stock in the power of the gods. Sure, his parents had taken him and Marco to church, just like every other conscientious Noven family, but until the day he'd touched the Great Crystal, he'd had no experience of any kind that could have been considered religious or spiritual. As Timori and Paulo had pointed out, the ability of the Great Crystal to grant visions did not prove the existence of the gods. It merely demonstrated the power of the crystal itself.

"I believe you know something," he said, leaning in a little bit more.

"Tanni knows many things," she admitted.

"About crystals," Jacoby said, urging her to continue. "Their origins. You seem to have an abundance of them here, and the republic doesn't appear to care, despite the fact that they're the nation's most precious commodity. I haven't seen you or Shachari whisper, even once, to activate a crystal. You even have your own name for the Great Crystal. Rich boy is not a dully, Tanni...I know there's more going on here than meets the eye, and there must be a reason those with a caste to their name don't enter the fifth quarter."

He was inches from her face then and he could tell her emotions had intensified. Whether Jacoby was acting upon attraction or merely trying to fluster her into giving more information, he couldn't tell. His impulses often got the better of him, but this time they were leading him to knowledge that perhaps even Master Vellize didn't possess.

She glanced at his lips, more than once, before standing abruptly and walking to the door.

"Boy is clever," she said as she pulled the tarnished old latch, "but Tanni is not the one who decides what secrets the Dori keep. Come."

Jacoby gathered his ink bottle, pen, and notebook.

"Are you kicking me out of the quarter?" he asked.

Tanni shook her head.

"No. But this crystal lesson must be shown, not told."

Jacoby followed her out of the abode and into the afternoon sunshine. It was a warm day for autumn and the Dori were out in multitudes, drying their clothes on laundry lines, weaving baskets, tending to the boxed vegetable gardens in the square, and whiling away the time with chatter. The children chased each other about the streets, free from the bonds of school and responsibility the rest of the boys and girls of Captus Nove suffered. As usual, there were no grown men in sight. Jacoby had asked Tanni several times why he only saw women and children, but his Dori friend was as tight-lipped about that secret as she was about practically anything else that didn't strictly concern crystals and their functions.

The Dori were accustomed to Jacoby's presence by then, but they didn't tend to wave or say hello, except for some of the children. They all referred to him as 'Rich Boy.' Jacoby blamed Tanni for his moniker.

Tanni walked briskly down the lane, not appearing to care whether or not Jacoby followed. The pack of children trailed behind Jacoby at a distance, some teasing him, some asking if he had brought any sweets. A few took to chanting their favourite suggestion whenever Jacoby and Tanni were seen together:

"Kiss! Kiss! Kiss!"

A few paces later, Tanni wheeled around, her cheeks as red as her hair.

"*Fal-kay!*" she yelled, and the children scattered into the alleyways, screaming and giggling. Jacoby imagined that 'fal-kay' was some kind of Dori term for 'piss off.' Tanni's shriek only worked insofar as the children ceased to be visible. Jacoby could still hear their footsteps and excited whispers as they followed from the side-streets.

"So what's the lesson?" Jacoby asked. "Or are we just sightseeing in the quarter?"

Tanni's glare could have started a fire.

"You *shoshia* have no patience. Everything must happen now."

"What a sweeping generalization," Jacoby countered. They both stopped in their tracks and faced each other. "You Dori are all so judgmental, assuming every non-Dori is the same. As though caste and upbringing don't alter your experiences or opinions. Gods, you act like I'm to blame for every problem you face."

A pall of quiet fell over the children. They eavesdropped from the shadows.

"You were a poor boy from the valley," she said. "Even then, you had more than the Dori. More than Tanni. And you were given a new caste and education for nothing."

"My father worked hard to earn that for us," Jacoby said, folding his arms. "And you can't hold me personally responsible for your situation. I'm at least trying to understand your people."

"Rich boy is trying to understand our secrets, more like. How it would damage his pride to learn that..." She clammed her lips shut, mid-sentence.

"To learn what?" Jacoby could feel her usual reticence, along with embarrassment for revealing more than she meant to, once again. "What secrets do the Dori know about speaking? Why do you have so many crystals here and nobody seems to care? Why did Novens put you here and why do you stay? Why do you keep me around and teach me things, but resent me and berate me with every breath? Is it just because I saved your life? How can you activate crystals without whispering?"

Jacoby was running out of breath. "Where are all the men? This quarter is a mystery nobody else seems to give a shard about." He almost shouted the last part. "What is the godsdamned connection between you and the crystals?"

Tanni grabbed his wrist and roughly pulled him into an alleyway. They were standing nose-to-nose, so close he could see the flecks of gold in her eyes.

"Rich boy is so close," she said, "but he doesn't see what's right in front of him."

"Yes, he does," Jacoby said as he planted his lips upon hers. They lingered there for a long moment before she pushed him away.

"Not what I meant," she said. Despite her words, the emotions she projected were riddled with contradiction, repulsion

320

and desire, affection, and resentment. She pointed to Jacoby's hand. "Whose ring is it you still wear?"

"How dare you? You don't know a thing about her."

"I know she was one of the six. I know she was promised to someone else, and..."

"She was promised to *me*, except she switched places with Crystara. Instead she was put with someone cold and careless, who treated her like dirt. And just because we never had the time..." Jacoby choked up and felt a tear fall. "Godsdamnit." He wiped it away. "It doesn't mean we weren't in love. This ring is all I have left of her."

Tanni's face softened somewhat, but Jacoby could still feel her indignance at having been kissed. "Why kiss someone new, then, when your heart is still in shatters?"

"I lost my true love," Jacoby said. "It doesn't mean I don't find you attractive."

"Just what all girls want to be, second choice. Rich boy doesn't fancy me. Nobody does. He was confused by his underdeveloped *mota* skills and thought one feeling was another. What do you want here, Jacoby Padrona? You are curious about our culture, yes, but do not think Tanni is so dumb as to believe that is the only thing you want from us. You are not so altruistic. You play with crystals and hearts, rich boy. Which use does Tanni hold for you?"

Jacoby paused to consider. Tanni had surprised him by using his real name for once. He was not trying to replace Lenara, but he considered the possibility he was trying to forget her. Forgetting was easier.

"I do want to learn about you," he admitted, "and your culture. And if I'm not overstepping myself, I'd say we've become friends." He waited for her reaction, which was a simple roll of the eyes. "But I need to know about crystals, too. This whole thing with the...naf-clow-shee or whatever you called the Great Crystal, it isn't over yet. And I need help. My friends need help. You have the crystals and the knowledge."

"Your friends need help with what? What can the crystals do that upper caste money and power cannot?"

Jacoby clenched his jaw. Tanni was still tight-lipped about her own secrets, but he had to tell her if he wanted to earn her trust. He owed it to Lenara to see things through. He owed it to Racquela, to rescue her from what she thought she wanted. He owed it to Timori, for the secrets that had already been kept from him. A series of images flashed through his mind: the skeleton in the basement, the dying man in the alleyway, the young Dori's face just before he had been shot.

"I have to stop Paulo Longoro."

Chapter 39

After the last of the black crystal vein had been unearthed, there was enough room to bury the body, behind a hastily-mortared wall of clay bricks from the old farm boundary wall.

It wasn't Arnaldo's bones behind that wall. At the other boys' insistence, his corpse had been sent through the orange, burned on a small pyre by the cherry tree in the fallow field out back. Leo had argued against it, saying that nearby farmers were going to come around and wonder why they were lighting a fire in the dry heat of mid-summer. If it was discovered a boy was running the orphanage, they'd surely all be sent to some other miserable place for casteless children.

But burn him they did, and Leo allowed it only because he needed to establish control rather than incite a mutiny. They needed to believe Arnaldo had been sent to live in the land of the gods. Leo didn't know what he believed, but he had more cause to think Arnaldo's soul, if such a thing existed, was trapped in that brown crystal somehow.

Arnaldo was given his funeral pyre as a member of the respected dead. Nerus, on the other hand, had been buried. It was a fate reserved for those undeserving of peace, doomed to wander the abyss for eternity. Leo hoped that if such a place existed, Nerus was there.

If he was, his wraith was haunting Leo still. Leo's sleep was often disturbed by nightmares of the man. In the dreams Nerus's spirit had melded with Lutias, the mangy dog. Together they had become a monstrous, slavering dog-man. In one hand was Nerus's old cudgel, and in the other was the net the god Lutias used to capture and devour lost souls.

In the dreams Leo was dressed like his little tin soldier and his arms were glued to his sides. His knees wouldn't bend, so he could only hop forward awkwardly as the man-beast lumbered after him and caught him in the net of souls.

During his waking hours, however, Leo made himself appear invincible. Nerus was dead and couldn't hurt him anymore. Lutias had become dinner, the boys' first taste of meat in over a year. None of them was certain if you were supposed to eat dog meat, but as soon as the flesh started to cook, their mouths had salivated as much as the nasty old mutt's used to.

Natalya had cried from the moment the boys had started discussing the fate of the dog's carcass, but one flash of Nerus's old wand had been enough to keep her from voicing any manner of protest. Leo had to keep a careful eye on her. She was the last of the old regime, and would kill him if she was given half the chance. So Leo kept her chained up at night, and she was forced to dig with the boys during the day.

He knew he should have killed her right away, back when he'd offed Nerus and the dog. That would have been the practical thing to do. No loose ends or waking in the middle of the night to see if she'd slipped her rope bonds. Something had held him back, though, something he couldn't name or even begin to understand.

He wanted to call it mercy, but mercy was weak and foolish. Leo couldn't afford to be either. He had to protect those who were, the boys and girls of the orphanage. Natalya was neither, but she was a link to the outside world, and the only remaining adult.

I need her, Leo told himself. *That's why I spared her.*

In a strange way, things continued as they had before the 'change in management,' with Sofia and Leo taking the roles of masters of the house. Sofia's plan was to whip the girls into shape and start farming again, even though it was already well beyond planting season, and Leo carried on with the mining operation, hoping they would find enough crystals to buy better lives for every child in the orphanage. Leo, of course, would take the lion's share as the instigator of their freedom, enough to at least buy his way to the city and a school. He deserved it, after all, for risking his life facing Nerus.

Leo spared the cudgel, however. The cold glare of his eyes and the sight of the wand tucked into his belt were enough to convince the boys to keep digging. He would not become the man he most loathed, he promised himself.

The new hierarchy lasted a week, until the fateful knock at the door. Leo didn't know it at the time, but it was the knock that would change the course of Noven history.

***

Leo used to hear the voices of visitors through the cracks in the floorboards, accompanied by Lutias's frenzied barking and growling. The dog, however, was nothing more than a memory. When the ponderous, heavy knock came, it was followed only by Leo's sharp intake of breath.

He drew his wand and pressed his back against the wall by the window, peering outside.

His worst fear was a contingent of Noven soldiers, but the man at the door looked more like a government inspector. Leo decided the latter was worse. He examined the short, squat man further from his hidden vantage point, trying to espy some kind of official badge or symbol. All he could garner was that the man was very rich. Even the buttons on his suit seemed to be made from fine, clear crystal.

His face looked odd, as though it was misshapen. Leo realized he was looking at a mask. The closer half of the waiting gentleman's face was prosthetic. Lacquered wood was painted in the approximation of a pale skin tone, complete with an unblinking eye and a mouth left in a neutral, straight line. From what Leo knew, it meant the man had probably been involved in the Great War.

Leo had no choice but to answer the door. The girls were out working the field and it was unlikely the man hadn't seen them already. It was best that Leo was the first point of contact, rather than someone who would be foolish enough to tell a government inspector *the truth* or something equally devastating, like the fact that they were holding the only remaining adult prisoner and forcing her to mine for crystals in the basement.

Leo ignored his churning guts, patted his belt to ensure he was carrying his wand and cudgel, and opened the door.

The man on the porch barely deigned to acknowledge Leo, brusquely moving past him and looking around the house.

"Where's Nerus?" he asked. "And why the fuck are you upstairs, boy?"

Leo had the wand out, pointing it at the fleshed side of the man's head.

"Who the abyss are you?" Leo demanded.

The man blinked with his one good eye, staring down the length of the wand's short barrel to its wielder. Unlike Nerus, whose eyes held naught but disdain for the world, this man had a different gleam to his. It was an old look Leo hadn't seen since Teddori, the gaze of a man with measured, crafty patience.

"I am Gordo Bellacolla," he said, "and I own this orphanage. Who are you?"

"Leo. And I run this place now. I've taken it from Nerus."

"I can see that," Gordo said. "You've got that ridiculous club of his. Did you kill him?"

"Yes, and I'll kill you, too, if you ask any more questions."

"You're the one with the wand, Leo. You call the shots...as the kids say."

"Good." Leo relaxed his shoulders somewhat, but his wand arm didn't budge. "Why are you here?"

"I told you. I own this place. I've come to collect on an investment. Two investments, actually, unless you've killed Natalya, too."

"She's a picker now."

"And the crystals you've found?"

"They're mine."

"Is that so?" Gordo asked. He began pacing about the room. It had once been the old play area for the smaller boys and girls, where Leo had beaten Bernardo bloody with his tin soldier. Leo could still see his own name scrawled in chalk on a lower section of the wall.

"Are you gonna try and take them from me?" Leo demanded. "I don't see a wand on you."

"By all rights, they're yours, then. But tell me this, Leo, and please forgive me breaking the 'no-questions' rule we've established. How are you going to sell them? Do you know their value? Would anyone in their right mind buy unregistered black crystals from a casteless boy, risking swift retribution from the authorities of the republic as well as the guilds and church who control such trade? And even if you were to stumble upon a black market buyer, what's to stop them from killing you and taking the lot of them? Because they are valuable. More so than you might believe, and you are just one boy with one wand. They are a powerful criminal element with cartloads of illegal weapons and no compunctions about murdering a child."

Uncertainty gripped Leo, but he dared not show it. "I'll find a way."

To his surprise, Gordo Bellacolla smirked. "I'm certain that you would. Try, at any rate."

He was staring at the wall, at the very spot where Leo had written his name. Leo was amazed the man would turn his back to him. He could shoot Gordo at any moment. He contemplated it, but he was stopped by that little voice in the back of his head, the one telling him that Gordo *knew* things. Splattering his heart against the wall would end the font of freely given information.

"Do you remember when you first came here, Leo?" Gordo asked. Leo was so surprised by the question he nearly dropped the wand.

"I said no questions!" he shouted. From the side of his vision, he saw Sofia peek around the corner. Footsteps were coming up to the front door as other girls peered inside. Leo was certain the boys downstairs had heard him, too.

"You're outnumbered, pally," he told Gordo.

"Am I?" the man turned around to face Leo. "These children have no more or less than they did before you killed Nerus. You just said, they're *your* crystals. You lot are casteless castaways, unwanted and..."

Leo fired.

The trigger pulled back to the barrel of the wand, but nothing happened. He tried again, with the same result. The girls watched from the doorway, expressions of horror locked upon their faces. Gordo's smirk grew upon the living side of his face, giving the whole of his mouth the shape of a cruel hook.

"Shatters," Leo breathed. He withdrew Nerus's cudgel with a sweaty palm.

Gordo calmly slid a hand into his jacket and brandished a glinting, golden wand. Upon it was a deep crimson crystal, much larger than the pitiful thumbnail-sized stone of Leo's. Leo screamed when Gordo raised it.

The shot hit the ceiling, scattering a cloud of wooden splinters and debris. The girls screamed as well. Leo opened his eyes from his wince to see that Gordo's smirk had become a crooked, satisfied half-smile.

"You've got rocks, kid," Gordo said. "But there's a lot about crystals, and the world, you don't understand."

Leo suppressed his urge to run. "Are you going to kill me?" he asked.

Sofia came around the corner then, tears in her eyes. "No," she pleaded, standing beside Leo.

Gordo laughed. "No. I'm going to make you an offer. You can keep all of this, the farm, the house, the girls, the crystals, all of it, your own little casteless kingdom. Or you can come with me."

"Why the fuck would I do that?"

"Because you impress me, and I can teach you everything you want to know about the world, and how to get anything you ever wanted. And because I know who you really are, before the orphanage and before Bruno's farm."

Leo's mouth was dry, his feet leaden. He couldn't have moved or spoken just then to save his life.

"I know the very name of the soldier who brought you to Bruno's farm. So come with me and I will tell you everything you ever wanted to know. Or remain here and chance the world of nobodies and uncertainty."

The witnesses who hadn't fled the wandshot held their collective breaths. Even Bernardo and Arturo had come upstairs to witness the commotion.

"One condition," Leo said, finding his voice. "Sofia comes with me."

Gordo Bellacolla shook his head. "This offer is for you alone."

Leo studied Gordo for a moment, his confident expression and fine-tailored clothing, his mystery and success that surrounded him like an aura. Then he looked to Sofia, his casteless, weary companion, his erstwhile bit of solace under sight of the stars, the girl who couldn't even kiss him anymore without bursting into tears.

He forced himself to look her in the eyes.

"Goodbye, Sofia," he said. He wouldn't tell her he was sorry, because that would have been a lie. With no possessions to gather, he allowed Gordo to lead him toward the front door. Leo heard Sofia fall to the floor behind him and sob piteously. He told himself not to look back, and followed Gordo out into the summer sunlight.

Chapter 40

Lecture Transcript
Doctor Quintus Di'Mare – Faculty of History
Noven History 2-3: 1196-1736
Lecture #31: Maya 02, 1895

"The Noven advantage in warfare has always been flexibility. Conventional ammunition is heavy, but crystals don't need to be reloaded every few shots. A speaker can change the function of a crystal in the middle of combat. The Mosind Empire, happy to take advantage of our crystal knights, put those speakers to heavy use fighting their foreign conquests. The glory of Noven tactical superiority stretches back almost two thousand years. Our pride, the reason we lost our last war, has been Novem's hubris for even longer."

***

Julio and Drago met Roberto at the approach to the Ruveldi estate. Roberto appeared to have spared no expense for his travelling outfit: a tailored, cream-coloured trenchcoat lined wth fox fur about the collar, sleek leather driving gloves, bold black boots in the new 'motorbiker' style, and brass racing goggles. He had a cigar between his teeth and was leaning an arm over his brand-new Spirelli Tybal 350 with attached sidecar.

"Morning, boys," he exclaimed as he tapped the ashes from the end of his cigar. "Ready for adventure?"

Julio examined the sidecar, which was low to the ground but surprisingly spacious. "I'm going to have fun climbing in and out of *that*," he remarked. "Where on Titania did you find those goggles? Nobody sells those anymore."

"Mail order, dully," he replied. "Trust me, the trend is coming back. All the kids will be wearing them in a year. Keeps the bugs out of your eyes."

"Apparently you've picked up the kids' vernacular, too," Julio muttered.

"You'd better ditch the uniform, son," Roberto said as he examined Drago. "They'll never let you cross the border in that."

"Why not?" Drago lit a cigarette and took a good look at Roberto's bike. "It's not like we're at war."

"No," Julio agreed, "but we were, and the Nilonnese have long memories."

Drago sat down on Roberto's bike and tapped the handle switch to start the crystal motor. Despite the engine being exposed, it had a remarkably quiet hum.

"So?" Drago said. "We lost, didn't we? So what are they all misaligned about?"

Roberto and Julio exchanged a glance.

"Maybe you'll get a chance to find out," Roberto said. "But you'll have to leave your patriotism here in Novem. And your sense of entitlement. That is *my* bike, kid."

"I'm not a kid," Drago said sullenly as he dismounted the motorcycle. "And isn't this supposed to be a father-son trip? I thought me and Julio could take the bike with the sidecar."

Roberto folded his arms and glared.

"Fine, I'll go fucking change," Drago said. "Seems like I'm the only one with any pride in my nation." He stormed off toward the estate, hefting his travel bag.

Roberto made a face. "I don't know about this, Jules. I think the harpy spoiled him too much...he doesn't show any respect."

"That would be Andari's doing," Julio said defensively.

"Whoever is at fault, I don't relish the idea of treading the red in every Nilonnese town we pass through."

Julio ran his hand along the leather seat of the sidecar, remembering darker times. Perhaps the trip wasn't a good idea.

"I don't think he's as impulsive as Pietro was."

"You see him through a crystal lens," Roberto said. "He's like Pip in every way."

"He's not that soft."

"True. His hardness he got from his mother."

Drago returned, putting an end to their discussion. He had changed into canvas slacks, an airship-style leather jacket and a bright red scarf. He looked to Julio like Captain Corvelius from the radio play *Crystal Captain*. To Julio's dismay, the boy had refused to remove his officer's cap, adding to his heroic (and defiant) appearance. His stubbornness, it seemed, had also been inherited from Ramona.

"Better?" Drago asked as he began lashing his pack to the rear of his motorcycle.

"So long as you doff the cap at the border," Roberto replied, starting the Tybal's engine.

"We'll see."

Roberto laughed and offered Julio a helpful arm to lower him into the sidecar. As he did so, he took the opportunity to whisper into Julio's ear.

"Kid's got some orange in his aura, at least. I like him more than Pip already."

***

Julio had forgotten how fresh the air could be outside of the city. Away from the smokestacks and grit and the smell of collective metropolitan sweat, he could feel life infusing his lungs. On the open road, the wind burnt his cheeks, and his lips curled up into a misshapen but honest smile. He couldn't recall the last time he'd smiled like that. It was worth the occasional swallowed bug.

Roberto had never driven a motorcycle before, but he took to it like he did every other skill he tried his hand at, making the tight turns and switchbacks of the mountain roads look effortless. Drago drove much more recklessly, spinning his tires to spit up dirt and gravel, dragging his knees along the turns, showing off by lifting the front tire on occasion, and whipping by Joveday drivers in their family 'coaches by hugging the shoulder of the road. Julio would occasionally yell at Drago to be more careful, but if the young man heard him, he didn't listen.

They set out north from Captus Nove, avoiding the wide main road known as Sundus Motorway. At Julio's suggestion they took the winding inner-country route known colloquially as the 'Old Mine Road,' passing through small villages and alongside scenic upper-caste farmland estates. The day was brisk but they had lucked out. The clouds were fleeting and there was little threat of rain.

Along the way, Julio would shout out historic anecdotes to Drago about the townships they passed, or the landscape. Here at this bluff the barbarian tribes of Denlandia were held off by a meagre force of well-trained First Empire soldiers led by General Abritus, there the greatest crystal mine ever discovered gave up its last shard during the Fourth Republic, putting thousands of miners out of work. Whether Drago was truly listening, Julio couldn't tell, but Roberto would occasionally add asides or ask questions.

They stopped on a pastoral hillside for lunch, snacking on cheese, sausage, and a healthy few swigs of wine. Below, sheep grazed. A weather balloon floated lazily overhead. Roberto brought out his loccimetre to check the resonance of both engines' crystals.

"Bet you I could hit one of those sheep from here," Drago boasted.

Roberto looked up from his device and shook his head. "What, by pissing off the cliff?"

Drago rolled his eyes. "No." He rummaged in his pack and brought out a small wand. "With this." He twirled it in his fingers.

Julio frowned. "We're not shooting a farmer's sheep."

"Jova's sake, Dad." Drago shut an eye and levelled his wand at a grazing ewe in the valley below. "What's the point of this trip, if not to have fun?"

Julio and Roberto looked at each other. Roberto raised an eyebrow, as if to suggest it was Julio's task to mete out discipline.

Julio placed a hand on Drago's wand and forced the barrel to point at the ground.

"The plan *is* to have fun, Drago, but that farmer relies on those sheep for his livelihood. Why don't we make some stationary targets?"

Drago shrugged. "Sure...gotta use something you old guys can still hit."

Roberto put his loccimetre away and lit a cigarette.

"Fuck you, kid. I was dropping soldiers before you were a twinkle in P...er, your pop's eye. Worst shot has to buy the wine when we stop for the night."

"A completely fair wager to the man with *one* eye," Julio interjected. "The man who hasn't shot a wand since he had to switch to his left."

Roberto pointed to a set of old fenceposts down the hill.

"There. We can set up some stones and wager for best shot. Spook the sheep while we're at it so you can get your kicks," he suggested, looking at Drago. "And I know for a fact you didn't lose your balls in the war, Jules, so quit whining. You were far from the worst wandman in the company."

Julio grabbed a fist-sized stone and pretended he was aiming to throw it at Roberto's head.

"Says he who was second best."

"Who was the best?" Drago inquired as he lit a cigarette of his own.

"Corporal Bocco," Julio and Roberto said at the same time. Rocks in hand, they began clambering down the hill to the fenceposts.

"One of only four from our company to survive the war," Roberto remarked. "Along with us and Largo Mita." He reached the base of the hill and began placing the rocks upon the fenceposts. Then he backed away until he stood thirty paces from the rocks and held up a thumb. "What do you think, kid?"

"Too close," Drago said. "Unless we're blindfolded."

Roberto chuckled and stepped back another twenty paces.

"There you go. The enemy is no longer in spitting range. What kind of crystal have you got on that wand, anyway?"

"Brown," Drago said as he twirled the wand again. "Heavy grade precision stone, Noven officer's issue. Same kind of crystal they use for the telescoped longwands."

Roberto whistled.

"Shatters, we sure coulda used some of those in the war. They gave all the browns to us engineers for trenches and fortifications, but I would've been sent through the orange on the spot if I'd tried to re-appropriate crystals without a commanding officer's express say-so. 'Course, that didn't stop us from getting Pip to re-align all the damn time." He looked at Drago. "Well, highest ranking soldier gets the first shot."

Drago smirked, levelled the wand, and took careful aim. Julio could tell even by the young man's stance that he was a practiced wandman.

"Trench warfare is a thing of the past," Drago muttered as he pulled the trigger. With a deafening crack, the first rock went whizzing off the post. Shooting Roberto a satisfied grin, Drago handed the wand to him.

Roberto glanced at Drago, then examined the wand. He seemed to be admiring its craftsmanship. Julio leaned in to note that *Officer Drago Andari* had been carved into the barrel, and that the grip was custom carved to fit Drago's hand. *The republic certainly seems to favour its officers,* Julio thought.

"Some of us were hoping warfare in general was a thing of the past," Roberto replied as he lifted the wand. He seemed to take a while to steady his hand. When he shot, however, his aim was true, and Julio heard shards of the rock scatter into the grass. The nearby sheep made a few noises of alarm and sought out a more placid section of pasture.

"Nice shot, old man," Drago said. He turned to him. "If warfare is all in the past, then why is the republic still hiring soldiers?"

"Because without a military we're asking for trouble," Julio replied as Roberto handed him the wand. "I'm sure an opportunistic nation wouldn't hesitate to get payback for the Great War, not to mention access to our crystal mines."

Julio took aim with a shaky hand. The feel of the wand in his palm brought back old memories. He could see them up ahead, brutish Parsish soldiers in their winter furs storming the trench, screaming the abyssal screams of those who knew they were about to die.

Julio opened his eyes and lowered the wand. There were no fur-clad soldiers, only woolly sheep grazing in the distance.

"What makes you say trench warfare is in the past?" He asked Drago.

"Come on, *Master* Vellize, you're the historian," Drago replied. "You always said wars were a series of trials and errors when it came to tactics, and the brilliant generals were the ones who challenged the status quo of what no longer worked. Well, what did we learn from the Great War? We had all the best crystal technology, but we dug ourselves into the dirt and played back-and-forth until one side broke. It was all about numbers. Then the Dennish got clever and borrowed non-crystal weapons from the Eastern Empire, which required an ammunition supply but fired rapidly. It was incredibly effective in entrenched positions, and especially against massed charges. So when Denlund was freed and we lost the Parsish front, we broke *hard*."

"That was Longoro's fault for fighting on two fronts in the first place," Roberto argued.

"Sure," Drago agreed. "He should have taken out Faxon or arranged some kind of treaty with them. But any general worth his rocks these days knows the future of warfare is in multi-layered assault."

Julio gazed at Drago, the boy he wished was his son. He'd given the lad too little credit. Behind Drago's braggadocio was a keen mind. He must have inherited that from Ramona, Julio told himself.

Roberto raised an eyebrow.

"Explain what you mean by multi-layered assault." Julio could hear the interest in Roberto's voice.

"I will," Drago said, "if you explain to me why we have more crystals than any other nation but we're still dirt-fucking-poor. Economics was never my colour."

"Rundia Accord," Julio offered. "Our currency is undervalued because we have to make reparations for the Great

War. Granted, we still need to trade, so we still sell, and the other nations are reaping the profits from cheap crystals. So the republic limits trade, which isn't helping given the depression, and the Noctra sell illegally and make millions of dinari."

"You know they're in bed with the republic," Roberto added. "On the clear side, it means the Noctra are probably stockpiling crystals somewhere for when this godsdamned depression ends." He popped a cigarette in his mouth and prodded Drago. "Your turn. Multi-layered assault."

Drago gave his usual half-cocked grin.

"Uh-uh. Jules hasn't shot yet. No military secrets until I know I'm talking to *soldiers*."

Julio tried to suppress his sigh. Only the draft had made him a soldier. Only a lifetime of duskblossom and whiskey and work had separated him from the war, and even then, when he closed his eyes at night, sometimes he returned to those trenches. He had spent his whole life trying to escape that uniform, but Drago wore it with pride. He wondered what Pietro would think of it.

Julio raised the wand half-heartedly and glanced at the stone upon the post. His depth perception had never been the same since losing his eye. It was difficult to tell if the barrel was lined up with the target. Julio hated to admit it, but somewhere deep down he wanted to impress the boy. He shut out the distant sound of booming scattershot from his ears and pulled the trigger.

The rock didn't move, but somehow there was still an explosive noise.

"Oh, fuck," Drago said. "Nice shot, Jules."

"So much for not hitting the sheep," Roberto said with a snicker. Sure enough, one of the beasts had fallen over in the pasture, and a bright red stain spread out from its head in a circular pattern – or what was left of its head. Cautiously, the three men approached the corpse. All that remained of its skull was a bottom jaw and some bits of bone and brain tissue. Julio began to feel ill. An image flashed in his mind: Pietro's body twirling, thrown into the air by scattershot, blood spraying in a spiral.

"Hey!" The rancher had appeared at the other end of the clearing, brandishing a woodsman's axe. "What in Jova's name are you doing to my sheep?"

"Shit," Drago said. "Run!"

If it hadn't been for his lame leg, Julio would have felt nineteen again. They scrambled up the hill to the bikes like they were storming the next trench – full of fear, full of life.

Chapter 41

Leo stood before the matte-black, boxy motorcoach and ran a hand along its frame. He had never seen a motorcoach before. The idea of riding inside of one nearly made his jaw go slack. However, he kept his composure as he examined the machine, circling it and nodding as though he knew exactly what to look for in a well-made 'coach. It would not do to show any kind of weakness in front of Gordo Bellacolla, or the orphans who were watching from the windows as the greatest amongst them left for clearer skies.

Clearer skies, Leo thought. *Wealth, knowledge, and power.* He told himself again not to look back.

"No need to admire it," Gordo said as he opened the passenger door for Leo. "Plenty more of these in your future."

Leo hopped in excitedly, marvelling at the sound of the leather seat giving way to his weight. The interior was just as slightly. A lacquered wooden dashboard held gauges and buttons. The model of the vehicle was engraved upon a brass plate: 'Larsin II Personal Motorcoach.' Gordo hefted himself onto the driver's side and pressed a large red button to start the crystal engine. The motorcoach hummed to life like a horse chomping at the bit, ready to dash off toward a brighter future.

They drove away without ceremony, through the dusty farm roads that led to the Sundus Highway. Leo saw few motorcoaches, but quite a few stagecoaches and horses with wagons. He imagined how jealous the farmers and merchants felt, watching the motorvehicle zip by them at a good four or five times their speed.

Questions burned upon Leo's tongue but he held them there, waiting, watching the scenery roll by. Everything was new.

He hadn't seen anything outside of the orphanage since Bruno had brought him to that ill-fated farm cottage, and those memories were nothing more than an unhappy haze.

He told himself to appear calm and confident. That was the way to get information from a man like Gordo, he was certain of it.

"You've never seen the countryside, have you?" Gordo asked finally.

Leo shrugged and pretended it didn't interest him.

"It's your heritage. Your ancestors have ruled these lands for millennia, minus a certain foreign occupation. You've got a lot to learn about. Good thing we have a lengthy drive ahead. In hindsight, perhaps it was foolish to keep you in ignorance so long, but it certainly made you tough."

"You had a plan for me all along?"

Gordo laughed.

"You are shrewd. Not right away, no. That orphanage has been in my possession ever since I bought it from the state. Just another piece of land and a potential investment...one that turned out to be quite lucrative when we discovered the crystal deposits in the basement. However, there's a reason I buy and look after orphanages."

Leo cocked an eyebrow. He could only see the false side of Gordo's face.

"Other than for cheap labour?"

Gordo laughed a deep belly laugh, filled with dark mirth.

"Yes. You see, orphans have been in plentiful supply since the war. However, there is a mystery surrounding the Great War that has always piqued my interest. Tell me, how much do you know about the Second Empire?"

"I used to read about it before Nerus took away our books," he replied acidly.

"Do you know how it ended?"

"Novem lost."

"Do you know who ruled Novem during the Second Empire?"

"Emperor Longoro."

"And what happened to him?"

"He was shot by wand squad."

"And his family?"

"The same."

"All of them?"

Leo shrugged.

"I only read about it once. I liked to learn about the armies and battles more."

They had come to a long, straight stretch of road. A hillside bordered the highway on the right, dotted with duskblossom. Leo had read in the same book that the duskblossoms grew wherever soldiers had fallen. Novens didn't dig graves like the heathen nations of Titania who worshipped false gods, but where the bodies were burnt, duskblossoms grew. It was said if you saw a field of them, it meant a great battle had taken place there.

"Do you know why the duskblossoms grow like that?" Gordo asked. Leo's eyes widened. Could the man read thoughts, as well? He shifted uncomfortably in his seat but tried to appear at ease.

"Because that's where the bodies of Noven soldiers were sent through the orange."

Gordo nodded.

"Yes, but why do the duskblossoms grow? Because the men were given duskblossom seeds to chew on as a painkiller. When the armies of Titania marched on Captus Nove, they didn't stop to honour the dead of Novem. They just killed them and moved on. The bodies weren't burnt, they decomposed, which fertilized the duskblossom seeds they carried in their jacket pockets. That field of purple you see is the restless dead, waiting to be avenged."

Leo thought of nightmare-Nerus and shuddered. Restless dead, indeed. He hoped nobody would come to avenge *that* tortured soul.

"What does that have to do with the emperor?"

"He's the most restless of all, given what they did to his corpse...and considering his legacy."

Leo tried to piece together what Gordo was saying. He pondered the hints about Emperor Longoro, Gordo asking about the fate of the family, the failure of the war, and Leo's own murky origins.

"Is that why you wear a mask?" Leo asked. "Because you're a member of the family who survived?"

"I wear a mask because my face got fucked up in the war," Gordo replied. "I was merely a friend of the family, a supporter. You've got a clear mind, boy, but you're missing something. You're too young to remember, but I did tell you earlier. A soldier brought you to Bruno's farm."

"So? Bruno told me about it. Said I was the soldier's bastard and he didn't want me."

"You're no soldier's son. He took you there because he was supposed to kill you, and he couldn't do it. None of them could. Now, a true Imperialist would have raised you, but those soldiers were just as cowardly as the ones who defected to the alliance. They didn't shoot you because you were an infant...it had nothing to do with the fact that you are Emperor Longoro's last living heir."

Chapter 42

The Five Hills: A Dortian Legend
Pithicus
As translated by Lorenz Di'Mattinia

Once upon a time the Dortians lived in a beautiful, fertile river valley surrounded by five hills. They farmed the land of the valley and lived in peace.

One day a King named Cateli the Wealthy came with his people and settled upon one of the five hills.

"But that is our sacred forest," said the Dortians.

"You have four other hills," said King Cateli. "I ask for only one."

Yet the King gave recompense to the Dortians, for he was very wealthy.

"We cannot grow a forest with gold," complained the Dortians.

"You can trade your gold for other things," King Cateli suggested. "Fine clothes and tools and jewels."

"We have no need of such things," said the Dortians.

King Cateli was insulted and took back his gift. And so the Dortians knew the meaning of human greed.

Then came a Queen named Aestala the Wise, and she settled with her people upon another hill.

"But that is our lookout hill," said the Dortians.

"I shall keep watch for you," said Queen Aestala.

Then she came down to the valley to see how the Dortians lived.

"I could help you get more food from this land," she suggested.

"We do not need more," the Dortians said.

"You could trade the excess to King Cateli and me," said Queen Aestala.

"But the land will suffer," said the Dortians.

"Then my hungry people will suffer," complained Queen Aestala. "You control the fertile valley. If you do not trade what you have, I will not watch the horizon for danger."

And so Queen Aestala returned to her hill in her anger, and the Dortians knew the meaning of human pride.

Then came King Patinus the Bold, who settled on one of the hills with his people.

"I want your bountiful valley," King Patinus told the Dortians.

"But it is ours," said the Dortians.

"Give it to me or I will have it anyway," said King Patinus.

And so the Dortians knew the meaning of human bloodlust.

As King Patinus entered the valley with his soldiers, King Avati the Cunning came and settled upon the fourth hill.

"Give me but a small share of your valley," he said to the Dortians, "and I will help you defeat Patinus. Otherwise you will be defenceless and killed, for you know nothing of war."

The Dortians agreed, for they saw little other choice. With the help of King Avati, they drove back King Patinus and his soldiers. When the battle was over, the Dortians offered King Avati the agreed-upon piece of land.

"You will give me all of it," said King Avati. "Now my soldiers are here and you are just farmers. You will work for me or you will be exiled."

And so the Dortians knew the meaning of human cunning.

Then came King Crystus the Pious, who settled upon the fifth hill. He wanted to learn the secrets of the crystals beneath the hill.

"Teach me your mystic ways," he asked of the Dortians, "and I will save you from slavery."

"But that hill is our sacred burial ground," said the Dortians.

"The hill and all beneath it are mine now," said King Crystus. "Join me or suffer to live in squalor forever."

And so the Dortians knew the meaning of human evil.

***

Based on the old fairy tales of the Dori that Jacoby used to read, he expected Shachari's dwelling to be a ramshackle mess of books and baubles, complete with hazy-sweet incense smoke and oracular crystal ball.

Instead he stood in the afternoon sunshine next to Tanni, gazing about at a courtyard framed by mostly-tumbled marble pillars. Within, rows of garden vegetables were planted, bordered on one side by olive trees. At the centre of the garden were two huts. One, built mostly of glass, was filled with potted flowers and herbs. Jacoby recalled his mother's "box greenhouse" that she had built for herself when they'd lived off Corti Street.

The other hut was fashioned from brick, boasting a tin roof and a windchime beside the only door. Jacoby blinked. The interior had to be smaller than his bedroom.

"Do I...knock?" he asked.

Tanni shook her head.

"She will know we are here. She might even know *why*. There are times I believe she is a reader herself."

Shachari's voice came not from the hut, but from somewhere in the olive grove.

"The *shoshia* wishes to know more of our secrets."

Yet she did not emerge from amongst the trees. Instead, the door to her hut opened. At the same time, a tiny, wizened figure stood from behind rows of grapevines. *My gods,* Jacoby thought, *I guess you're never too old to enjoy showing off.*

"Enter then, *shoshia,* and learn." Shachari motioned toward the beckoning threshold of the hut. "But know this. We exact a price for sharing our home, the fruits of our labour, and our knowledge with outsiders."

Jacoby nodded respectfully and entered the tiny abode. The room within was cool and dark. Simple wooden shelves held crystals of all sizes and colours, haphazardly placed as though they held little value or interest. A hammock was strung up by the far wall.

The only other feature to the room was the ladder poking up from the great hole in the floor.

Tanni and Shachari entered behind Jacoby. Before Jacoby could ask any questions, Tanni brushed past him and slid deftly down the ladder. Shachari gestured for Jacoby to climb down after Tanni.

Expecting the remainder of Shachari's house, Jacoby was surprised to find himself in a stone-masoned tunnel crossroads, lit by crystals that had been mortared into the walls at intervals. Shachari came down the ladder after Jacoby, managing the steps remarkably nimbly for her age. Without a word, she chose a passageway and beckoned for Jacoby and Tanni to follow.

Tanni appeared to know where she was going, but Jacoby had to keep in step or risk getting lost in the labyrinth of winding turns and side passages. Shachari wasn't exceptionally speedy, but some of the stretches of passageway were dim, and the echoes did strange things to Jacoby's sense of his surroundings. From other tunnels he could hear distant susurrations, low voices and footsteps, and metallic clanging. Jacoby wanted to ask about the noises, but he was more than certain he would be 'shushed' by Tanni, who seemed anxious enough about his presence. Shachari was, unsurprisingly, impossible for Jacoby to feel out with empathy.

The tunnel opened up into a vast natural cavern. Stalagmites taller than Jacoby stood like lances, lining the natural pathway to an underground river. Here and there, crystals poked out of the rocks, some bigger than Jacoby's open palm. At the banks of the shallow waters, he finally saw his first glimpse of the elusive Dori men. A pale, slender fellow not much taller than Tanni was washing his dirt-soaked hands in the water. His slate-grey eyes watched Jacoby warily, but he remained where he was.

Jacoby had trouble keeping his jaw from dropping, and even more trouble remembering he was still within the city. The Dori were worlds apart from everything he had ever known.

"They don't often see outsiders here," Shachari explained. "You are the first in years, actually. But outsiders don't often see *shoshia*, either."

"Why are they always down here?" Jacoby asked. "I've never seen them in the quarter."

Shachari exchanged a glance with Tanni.

"Follow, *shoshia*," Shachari beckoned. They crossed the shallow river and left the cavern behind for another passageway, this one rough-hewn and supported only by wooden beams. The tunnel ended abruptly in a chamber that looked quite a bit more like what Jacoby had imagined for Shachari's abode. Shelves of baubles and tinctures were riveted into the marble walls, and an ornate white pedestal carved into the shape of hands held a football-sized crystal in its clutches. A crude mattress seemed to be the interloper amongst the artifacts and potions, shoved into a corner like an ugly lamp – necessary but embarrassing.

Shachari walked over to the pedestal and her hand brushed the crystal, changing its hue from clear to purple. She looked not at Jacoby, but at Tanni.

"For what have you brought him, girl?"

Tanni stepped forward.

"He is still close to the others chosen by the *naf'closhi*, Shachari. Its plans for them are not yet complete...and he would like our help to stop Paulo Longoro."

Jacoby saw an expression he did not expect to witness upon Shachari's face: surprise. Shachari spat upon the ground and scowled.

"The *amshi'kada* and his kin were all killed," she said, turning her attention upon Jacoby. "What makes you certain he is of Longoro's blood?"

"He said so himself."

"Well, I say I'm a young thing of sixteen, ready to give my heart away to every boy I see," Shachari replied, her gaze darting to Tanni for a moment. Tanni didn't appear impressed by the comment. "Spoken words are not the same as true words, boy. What else has he said or done?"

Jacoby took a deep breath. *He's smart,* Lenara had told him*, and ruthless.* Without thinking, Jacoby was playing with the ring. *I've seen what will happen, and I'm telling you Paulo is going to take over Novem.* Lenara's words, however, were no longer the only evidence Jacoby had.

Jacoby opened his mouth to speak and it all came tumbling out. The betrothals. Lenara and Crystara switching places. Paulo convincing Timori to 'work' for him, and later Jacoby, too. The secret NSP meetings. Racquela seeing Paulo behind Timori's back. The abandoned orphanage. Racquela's rescue. The look on the Dori boy's face right after Paulo shot him...

"Dillas," Tanni breathed. Her cheeks were glistening. "Oh, poor Dillas."

"I'm sorry," Jacoby said. He bit his lip and took another deep breath to prevent himself from choking up as well. "I didn't know you knew him. I think...I think he was trying to save her, not hurt her."

"You should have saved *him*," Tanni wailed, shoving Jacoby. "Dillas should never have been there! Sucked in by some doe-eyed daisy-chaser playing helpless."

"I was trying to diffuse the situation!" Jacoby shouted back. "And it was Paulo who shot him, not me. He's the cold bastard who doesn't care who or what gets shattered as long as he gets what he wants!"

"Children!" Shachari's voice seemed to boom with an unearthly energy. Though her face remained as passive as stone, Shachari's eyes softened somewhat. "Dillas knew the risks, Tanni."

"And he was involved in my friend's kidnapping," Jacoby countered. "Can we stop pretending anyone here is innocent?"

"You..." Tanni lunged as though she would throttle Jacoby, but Shachari's crystal glowed yellow and the two teens found themselves staggering away from each other.

"Stop!" she commanded. Jacoby pressed a hand to his forehead.

"Ow."

"It is clear the boy needs to be stopped," Shachari said decisively. "Whether or not he is the son of the emperor, we will not suffer under the yoke of fascists again." She glanced at Tanni once more. "Fetch Osti."

"But..."

"*Now*, Tanni."

Tanni stormed off down the tunnel, clenching her fists and muttering. Shachari shuffled over to her shelves and began going through tiny stoppered bottles, squinting to read the labels.

"I'm sorry about Dillas," Jacoby said. "Really I am." He contemplated his shoes, trying his best not to see that lifeless body in his mind's eye.

"Do you believe he is evil?" She brought a tiny blue vial up to her eyes, wrinkled her nose, then set it back down.

"Dillas? I barely..."

"No, the boy. Paulo."

Jacoby frowned.

"Self-serving, certainly. But 'evil'? I'm not sure if I believe in 'evil' as a concept. "

She turned so sharply Jacoby thought one of her bones would snap. She approached him with an intense gleam to her eyes.

"You have a good heart, boy...you believe in ideals of equality. It is written in your story, and your treatment of the Dori. Your curiosity and openness. But you are dishonest."

"I..."

"Don't interrupt. It is written on your face. You feel the feelings of others, so you keep your own feelings hidden. You hide truths because you fear hurting others. But lies dig deeper at the heart, boy. I know what it is to be *mota*, to be a sponge full of others' shed tears. But your lies are motivated by the fear of harming others. Has he ever shown this? The boy Paulo?"

Jacoby tried to think back. Even when he was helping Timori, Paulo's motivations were clearly self-serving. He seemed to be romantically interested in Racquela, but there could have been any number of ulterior motives, her family's money being foremost on Jacoby's mind, not to mention her obvious beauty.

Paulo had shown absolutely no remorse about Dillas, or the man Jacoby and Timori had found dying in the alley. Even the skeleton in the basement, whoever it was, seemed connected to Paulo somehow. Paulo had brushed its presence aside, even avoided the hollow-eyed gaze of the skull as though a glaring, silent accusation was being slung.

He is a murderer, Jacoby realized. *Not a killer out of necessity or because of war, but because he believes it is the best course of action.*

"I believe he would stop at nothing to achieve his goals," Jacoby replied finally. "And that he would try to destroy anybody who gets in his way."

"That," Shachari said, "is what it means to be evil. So you told Tanni he must be stopped. What can the Dori provide that you do not already possess?"

"Crystals," Jacoby replied. "Racquela needs to know what kind of man...er, boy, Paulo really is. She plans to disguise herself and follow him because she thinks she's in love with him. Seeing how he behaves when he thinks she's not around should open her eyes to his true nature. But she needs a second disguise so her friend can fill in for her. A lot of the old stories mention crystal disguises. I don't know if such a thing really exists, but...if anybody knows a whisper like that, it's you."

Tanni returned then with a Dori man. He was exceptionally tall by their standards, almost Jacoby's height, but whip-slender with tough, sinewy cords of muscle on his bare arms. His dark locks had an almost gentle curl to them despite being mussed and sooty. His eyes, however, were anything but gentle. They were ice-blue and as piercing as a pickaxe.

"Osti," Shachari said. "Our guest requires two crystal rings and a shortwand."

Jacoby's eyes widened. *Shortwand?* He'd had enough of wands after Racquela's rescue, and had been glad to return Paulo's to the 'collection.'

Osti folded his arms.

"So we're just giving them away for free to *shoshia* now?" He spat upon the ground by Jacoby's feet. Jaocby noted that he had an odd accent – not quite Northern-sounding.

"Who in the name of *Gai* does Osti think he's speaking to?" Shachari demanded. "You are speaking to *Shachari*, not this *Shoshia* boy. Do I not act in the best interests of all?"

Osti challenged her gaze for a moment before his eyes fell. "Yes, Shachari." He left at a stiff gait, head held high.

"He doesn't trust you," Tanni remarked.

"Yeah, doesn't take an empath to notice it," Jacoby muttered. He glanced at Shachari. "Is a wand really necessary? I can protect myself. The church never made me relinquish my crystal ring."

Shachari had returned to her shelves, fumbling with bottles, searching for some unknown formula.

"This is not about protection, young man." Her eyes lit up as she found what she was looking for, a vial of deep ochre with a peeling yellow label. She uncorked it and held it under her nose for a moment.

Osti returned with a plain-looking cedar shortwand that appeared to be lacking a crystal. He raised it and pointed it at Jacoby's face.

"I could kill you right now, *nak'shoshia*," he said. Tanni and Shachari didn't so much as bat an eyelash. Jacoby stared down the barrel.

"You think it's the first time I've had a wand pointed at me? Pretty sure they don't work without a crystal."

Osti smirked.

"*Nak'shoshia* believes he's sharp. What does he know about Dori whispers? Nothing. He knows nothing about us."

"Not for lack of trying," Jacoby said.

Osti lowered the weapon and strode up so that he was nose-to-nose with Jacoby.

"Why are you after our secrets?" he said in a low voice. Jacoby forced himself to stare into those intense eyes.

"Because I think you're misunderstood."

Osti stepped back a pace. Jacoby could feel he was genuinely surprised by the answer.

"Stop your whisper-shouting, children," Shachari demanded. "Hand me the wand and crystals, Osti."

Osti did so, reluctantly. As Shachari held the rings in her hand, Jacoby saw them glow pink briefly, then shift back to clear, all without a single whisper from the old matriarch. Then she returned to her shelves, fetching a small canvas sack. From it she withdrew a green crystal and popped open a latched chamber in the wand Jacoby hadn't noticed before.

Out into Shachari's open palm tumbled a red crystal, which she deftly exchanged for the green one. Then she unstoppered the vial and let a couple of inky drops fall into the chamber of the wand with the green crystal. This time she did whisper, but Jacoby didn't catch the words, and suspected they may have been from the Dori language.

"What did you do to the crystal?" Jacoby asked. "I've never seen someone do that before."

Shachari pressed the rings into Jacoby's palm, then offered him the wand after closing the small latched chamber under the trigger.

"If you wish to learn our ways, *shoshia,* you must earn your keep, and our trust. It is clear the *naf'closhi's* agenda is not yet complete, but whatever was meant to be was disrupted by the corruption of the betrothals and the death of your young love. As always, we Dori must stumble along blind, hearing only the whispers of lesser crystals, so long as the snakes are on the hill."

"So...you're connected to the Great Crystal somehow? Your...naf-clo-shee?" He asked the questions, knowing Shachari wouldn't answer them until he proved himself to the Dori. "What do you need me to do?"

"You must speak to the rings, with a clear image in your mind of who the wearer should appear to be."

"And the wand?" he asked.

"The wand is for Paulo Longoro, dull boy," Tanni said.

"For him?" Jacoby turned it over in his hand, feeling his stomach turn along with it. Lenara's words returned to him: *Short of somebody killing him, nothing will stop it now.*

"Yes," said Osti. "One shot should be enough."

Chapter 43

Timori didn't *like* small dogs, but he and Pippo had come to a degree of understanding. Pippo had been trained out of peeing on Timori's shoes, and Timori silently agreed not to punt the creature off the Memorial Bridge during dog walks.

Timori had to admit to himself the walks weren't so bad. He was getting paid to do it, and pretty girls often came up to him so they could pet Pippo.

The rest of his chores weren't unbearable, either. Timori was glad he had decided not to brave the picket lines for the dismal pay of the crystal mines. Although Dr. De'Barus shared very little information about his work, the tasks he set out for Timori were easy to accomplish. Cleaning and organizing the laboratory had been the most gruelling, but even that had only taken Timori a few dedicated hours of stacking, sweeping and mopping. Timori's jaw had dropped when De'Barus admitted that it was only a month's worth of mess. He didn't think a tiny dog could poop so much.

Timori also brought De'Barus his mail and the newspaper. Because the old physicist was constantly working, he usually asked Timori to read him his mail. It provided some fascinating insights into the life of the crotchety recluse. For every fascinating and brilliant colleague he corresponded with, he had an equal number of intense rivalries. Timori wrote all of the replies, many of which were filled with enough verbal venom to cause even a soldier or sailor to blush.

Since his mother was no longer working and could look after Nicola and Carlotta, Timori spent an increasing amount of time at De'Barus's estate. On an average evening after football practice, he would bike from school to the lab, walk Pippo, fetch the mail, read it and the paper to De'Barus, write any letters that needed writing, then spend the remainder of the night finishing homework and trying to observe the physicist at work without distracting him with questions.

When Timori entered the lab with Pippo that evening, De'Barus was engrossed in a complex equation on his mural-sized blackboard. Timori always hoped that it was De'Barus's *Unified Theory*, but most of the previous formulae had been for what De'Barus referred to as 'his soon to be brilliant contribution to crystal theory.'

Pippo placed his paws on De'Barus's leg to demand attention, bringing the doctor out of his trance-like focus.

"What are the headlines today?" he asked without turning around. He gave his dog a half-hearted pat on the head.

Timori unrolled the newspaper and laid it out on a spare section of lab table.

"Tunnel collapse kills five," Timori said. "Picketers blame lack of experience for cave-in."

"Hmph," said De'Barus. "Not that it will compel them to get back to work, though."

"Probably not," agreed Timori. "They want fair compensation, which the guild won't offer right now."

"They can't," said De'Barus. He scratched his beard and stared at the board. "Not enough dinari to go around. Longoro really fucked us hard on that one."

Timori grabbed the broom and started sweeping. At some point, he knew De'Barus would tell him to 'get back to pickin' work' even though they were having a conversation.

"Don't you mean the Rundia Accord did?"

"Pff." De'Barus started hunting for his pipe, occasionally glancing back at the blackboard. "And whose fault was that? Longoro's the one who decided Novem was better than the rest of

Titania. Proved himself wrong on that one...here we are, just as dirt poor as we were before the war. Shattered on two sides from the accord and the recession, and all the best minds come from Denlund, the Eye, and the Commonwealth now. Except for me. Don't they teach you history in that damn academy anymore?"

"Yes, Master Vellize is actually..."

De'Barus located his pipe behind a crate full of miscellaneous gears and shook it out to empty the ashes.

"Things were probably better before the reunification. Small-scale local government. Patronage for the arts and sciences. Just take away the castes from the equation and you have utopia."

The word 'equation' drew Timori's eye back to the blackboard. He wondered if there was anything De'Barus could remove from his own equation to make it work.

"Do you really think city-states would function in the modern world?" Timori asked. "Or would they be too susceptible to the pressures of big, powerful nations? Unable to compete or exert control over their own populace?"

"That's just it, kid," De'Barus said as he tamped some fresh tobacco from his shirt pocket into the pipe bowl. "Governments seek control. There's no altruism. Capitalists, socialists, fascists, they all want to manage the population in one way or another. Even the caste system is a leftover of an old means of power division, designed to keep one group wealthy and influential. It's all about control..." His eyes darted back and forth across the blackboard.

Timori tried not to trip over Pippo, who always chased the broom.

"Even the parties who want to abolish the caste system?"

"They would re-structure to suit their own needs," De'Barus said as he puffed. "If you look at the Labour Party and the NSP, they both advocate socialism but neither group talks about anarchy. No, it's all about control over others." He began mumbling as he studied the board. "Hmm...control, re-structure...if I change..."

De'Barus picked up his eraser and clambered up his ladder, replacing a section of the formula near the top.

"Nope, wouldn't work then," Timori said before he could stop himself. "That is, if *'e'* represents energy."

"Why not?" De'Barus was still muttering and pouring over other sections of the board.

"Stenegger's Law. As energy increases..."

"Fuck Stenegger. He's a crackpot. Modern crystal theory clearly shatters any law stating that energy cannot be created."

Timori chuckled. De'Barus and Stenegger had a rivalry that was a modern legend in the making. Although De'Barus refused to acknowledge Stenegger's law, most scientists accepted it as a part of the current working model of the universe, and it was causing a big problem for De'Barus's *unified theory*.

"Try it," Timori suggested, feeling bold.

De'Barus growled in his throat and scrawled a new equation in the upper right-hand corner, then looked over the rest of the board again.

"*X* is changed now," he said. "So what happens to the matter over here, Mr. Shiny?" He pointed to another spot on the blackboard.

Timori scratched his head.

"Not sure. But if Stenegger's Law holds true, it would imply the energy comes from the matter. Converted."

De'Barus shook his head.

"Some crystals last for centuries, kid. Or millennia, like that giant one people still worship. And they continually produce. One alignment produces energy: kinetic, chemical, combustion, whatever. Another could make matter *out of nothing*...metal and stone and so on. So you can't tell me that Stenegger's Law fits in here, because crystals break every law. And every time I try to harmonize crystal theory with *this*..." he gestured to the blackboard, "I get stuck as a pickaxe in clay."

He glanced back at Timori and sucked on his pipe. "You...can actually make sense of this, hmm? Half of my junior students can't."

"Some of it," Timori said. "I can guess what most of your letters mean, but it would help if you just told me."

De'Barus snorted. "Not if you're going to keep telling me Stenegger's Law can harmonize with crystal theory. Shut up and let me think. If you're bored, fix my crystal resonator."

"Resonator? Don't you mean resonance calibrator?"

"I know what I said." De'Barus' eyes didn't leave his blackboard. "Resonance calibrators were designed to replace crystal speakers, but they're not quite as mobile. A resonator acts as a purple quelling crystal within a localized area, only it uses cheap-as-dirt white crystals. At least, that's the idea. My prototype doesn't work."

Timori glanced at the corner workbench. He had placed the handheld device there during his massive cleanup of the lab and promptly forgotten about it. He wondered if the old scientist was testing him somehow.

"Sure, I'll have a look," he said.

"In silence," De'Barus reminded him.

Timori glared at the back of De'Barus's head, then walked over to the workbench and sat to examine the device. It was little more than a loccimetre display with a dial, a trigger button, and a sliding glass panel, behind which was a spent white crystal. Judging by the exterior, Timori couldn't see anything wrong with the gadget. He grabbed a screwdriver and began taking the machine apart.

The loccimetre appeared functional. Timori put the device back together and pulled the trigger. Nothing happened. He tried the dial, to no effect.

"So it's supposed to cancel the resonation of another crystal?" Timori asked. "Infinitely useful, especially if you can figure out a way for the loccimetre to automatically attune itself to..."

"What part of 'in silence' did you fail to comprehend?" De'Barus asked. "Pretend you have a grey crystal in your hand and I can't hear a word you say. A 'field' of silence, if you will."

"Wait, that's it," Timori muttered to himself. He turned to look at De'Barus. "The white crystal can't project without a power source...so you will need either a purple crystal in there instead of white, or a secondary crystal to provide a field of projection for the white one."

"Thought of that," De'Barus replied. "The two crystals are too close...the white one cancels out the other."

"So use a purple crystal."

"That would completely negate the idea of the device, which is supposed to be a *cheap alternative* to purchasing a very expensive purple crystal. You know what? Maybe you should just focus on your finishing school homework...this might be a bit beyond you."

"Well, it's certainly beyond you, too, if it doesn't work yet." Timori shot back. The doctor ignored him. Timori turned back to the bench and scratched his chin, trying to think about the problem from a different angle.

"Angle..." he mumbled. "If the *white* crystal could be made to project only in an arc, say a ninety-degree radius...you would just need a *tiny* power crystal for the projection...still more expensive, but it would work."

"There, that project should keep you busy," De'Barus said. "I'll order you some crystals so you can finish the device for me. Now shut up and let me work on this."

Timori folded his arms, leaning against the workbench and examining De'Barus's equation. "Maybe there's something you're missing still. About crystals. Doesn't the church keep a lot of those secrets?"

"They pretend to, but I think they're just trying to cover up the fact that their Great Crystal is a sham. It's a masterpiece of engineering, that's all. And at the rate we're going, we won't even be able to study them in fifty years."

Timori raised an eyebrow.

"I didn't realize the church was hoarding them."

"They're not," De'Barus said, laughing. He grabbed his blackboard and painstakingly wheeled it around to the other side, then began to erase a spot near the bottom. "They don't grow on trees, you know. Or even in the ground."

He picked up a piece of chalk and began to scrawl a new equation on the board.

"They're limited, and we're sitting on the biggest supply in the world. A supply that is quickly running out. We sell some, we use some, but based on density of mines, number of mines, plus any potential mines we haven't discovered yet...not too likely considering modern crystal dowsing techniques, then factor in the rate at which industries and new technologies integrate crystals...factor in lifespan of your average crystal...we are looking at a shortage and energy crisis within the next..." He finished the calculation. "Thirty to forty years. Within your lifetime...possibly mine, if I'm unlucky enough to live that long."

Timori blinked.

"Wait, are you serious? Why doesn't anybody know about this?"

"Oh, the scientific community has known for years, kid...but mentioning things like this to the press causes widespread panic. For now everyone who knows is keeping quiet, including the church and the guilds."

"So where will everyone get their power when crystals run out?"

"Well, that's just one more reason why I'm trying to figure out this theory." He folded his arms and looked back at the blackboard.

"Do you want any help?" Timori asked.

"Fuck you," De'Barus said with a laugh. He glanced at Timori and, after a pause, said "Maybe."

Chapter 44

Despite her incarceration, life for Crystara had finally settled into a comfortable rhythm.

Her days were spent cleaning and spying, reading the thoughts of those around her, and observing the various carryings-on of the Old Temple as though she were nothing more than a fly on the wall. It was incredible the kinds of details that were shared in her presence, and what the priests, sisters, and guards didn't say out loud that Crystara fetched from their minds.

All of this she reported to De'Cadomus, who seemed to be predominantly concerned with August's fumbling attempts to move against him. August didn't have to try hard – De'Cadomus was not especially popular – but nobody was willing to stage a coup without the sanction of the church council, who had voted De'Cadomus in as keeper and seemed unlikely to oust him.

Every evening over dinner, Crystara and De'Cadomus would train in speaking and reading techniques. He was not a patient man, but Crystara was a fast enough learner that it didn't matter. Crystara was confident that eventually she would be able to penetrate even De'Cadomus's steadfast and iron-clad mind.

He had not used her ring to hurt her in a while. Crystara was perfectly willing to bide her time because she was delving into the true secrets of the Church of the Great Crystal.

She had read the journal of the prophetess Celesta several times over, which offered some valuable insights into the nature of the Great Crystal. The most intriguing discovery was Celesta's theory that the Great Crystal was not a singular entity. Its personality had facets, which Celesta thought of as the voices of separate deities, each with their own agenda. The Great Crystal would contradict itself, offering conflicting bits of information or instructions. It liked to pit people against each other, and spoke to some but not others.

The patterned iron lockbox remained a mystery. For all of Crystara's speaking talent, she could not discern how to solve the crystal puzzle upon its surface. She tried all manner of whispers in various sequences and combinations, keeping a mental record of each attempt because the ring would not allow her to write anything down.

The history regarding the Whisper Society was also quite useful, offering a wealth of information regarding the church's most secretive organization. Originally developed as a group dedicated to safeguarding the secrets of crystal speaking, it eventually became a powerful faction able to wield a great deal of political clout, within not just the church but Parliament as well. Many of Novem's most prominent keepers came from its ranks, and the crystal knights were regarded as the most dangerous speakers known to humanity, colloquially referred to as 'the snakes' and led by a high knight who was known as 'the viper.' They were the watchdogs of the church, willing to do whatever was necessary to maintain the power of the high priests. In darker times, they were used to quell support for other religions, most notably during the Mosind Occupation when they had to go underground.

Thus far, the most interesting bits of information she had discovered from the book were the lists of the men and women who had served as members of the society. Although women were not allowed to serve as priests for the Great Crystal, they could earn distinction as speakers instead, and more than once in Noven history a woman had been named Viper.

The lists included their names and ranks, as well as which caste they had been born to. Crystara was fascinated to discover that a great many snakes had originally been 'casteless.' It made her pause and wonder. There had been a few times in her life when, because of her blonde hair, she'd been accused of being Dori. Her father looked nothing like one, but her mother...

She had made her way through most of the book, reaching another list of society members that followed a fascinating section detailing the Whisper Society's involvement in Emperor Longoro's rise to power. Upon the page, a familiar name caught her eye:

Sir Allegro De'Cadomus, noble caste. Inducted 1850.

"Haha, 'Allegro,'" she chuckled. She imagined De'Cadomus had tried to lose *that* name as soon as he was able.

"Eighteen-fifty," Crystara mumbled. But De'Cadomus was so *old*, he'd probably been born before the Fourth Republic, which would have meant he was well into his adulthood by the time he'd been inducted into the ranks of the snakes. Even more curious was that he'd come from the noble caste. It wasn't often that nobles became priests. It was considered a slight step down in terms of privilege and a priest had to abandon all claim to inheritance.

"Crystara..." said a breathy voice. Crystara slammed the book shut and froze. For a moment she thought she'd been caught by De'Cadomus, but the voice had been wispy, not raspy. She glanced about her surroundings. Not a soul in sight, other than Dusty, who was sleeping on the tallest stack of books in Crystara's room.

Her chest began to pound as she realized exactly who was speaking to her.

"Not now," she said. The timing was all wrong. She was making *progress*. She just needed to finish the book, figure out the lockbox, find a whisper that would help her remove her ring, and *then*...

"Crystara!" The voice was urgent. *"There isn't much time. The chest in the keeper's room. You will need what's inside."*

Crystara threw up her hands in frustration.

"You told me to get the lockboxes," she said, "so I'm reading what's inside. Just tell me how to get inside the one with the crystals or fuck off."

"THE CHEST!" It was multiple voices, hammering upon her mind. Her eyes began to water.

"What's in it?" she demanded, unsure if the Great Crystal could reply or merely issue commands.

A singular voice replied, in a pleasant and clear tone. Its familiarity haunted her, but still she could not place it. If only the pounding in her head would *stop*...

"A solution to your ring problem."

Crystara was off like wandshot, up from the floor and sprinting past the library stacks.

"Well, hello there, Cryst..."

She was dashing up the stairs before Lagarus could even finish saying her name. When she reached the table altar in the foyer, she paused. It would take stealth to reach De'Cadomus's chambers without being caught. The viper liked to rotate his knights with the guards and she never knew where one would turn up.

Crystara nudged the door open. It was getting colder at night and a light rain was falling. Most of the priests and sisters of the Old Temple were in their senior years, apt to spend the late autumn evenings close to a hearth. The courtyard was blessedly empty as Crystara crossed to the main building.

Rossi was on patrol, dragging his halberd around the halls like a burden, but he was easily avoided. Crystara took the long way around to the tower, all the way up to the entrance and back down through the 'gallery of keepers past,' as Orvin used to call it. Other than Rossi's bumbling presence, the temple was eerily quiet.

Luck seemed to be on her side that night. Titus had been chosen to guard the Keeper's Tower. Crystara dispensed with any pretence and walked right past him.

He dogged her heels up the stairs.

"Where in Jova's name do you think you're going?"

"Where does it look like?" she asked.

"Are you cracked? You can't go up there. If the viper catches you, we'll both get sent through the orange."

"I don't care. This is my chance to be rid of him and this godsdamned ring."

Titus shoved his way past her and blocked the doorway ahead.

"No. I can't let you do this. Whatever you're plotting, this isn't the way to stop him. He'll know you were in there. Turn around and go back to the library."

Crystara smirked. De'Cadomus's lessons would prove to be his undoing. She called out to the crystal lock upon the door latch, commanding it to release. To change a crystal's hue at a distance was a greater challenge, but she managed a re-alignment to yellow without cracking it. Then she asked the crystal to *push*. Behind Titus, the door creaked open. At the sound, his eyes widened.

"How did you...? I've never seen someone..."

While he was stunned and stammering she slid under his guard and into the room, bolting straight for the chest near the windowsill.

"Crystara," he said in a loud whisper, knowing a shout would be heard from the window, "stop." By the time he reached her she'd opened the trunk's crystal lock and was prying up the heavy lid. Titus scooped her up in his well-muscled arms and held her tight, but the trunk's contents were already there for both of them to see.

It appeared to be mostly clerical: stacks of letters, papers and scrolls, a few books. Crystara could see the gleam of something shiny buried near the bottom.

"Huh," Titus muttered. He glanced back at the door. "I wonder what he's hiding in there."

"Then let me go, dully, and let's find out."

To Crystara's surprise, Titus let her down. They began rummaging through the chest together, both periodically stopping to listen for footsteps coming up the stairs.

Most of the letters were correspondence between De'Cadomus and other members of the church. Crystara was certain there was a wealth of secrets to be found within the letters, but she didn't have time to read through anything and didn't want to risk stealing more than she had to from the chest. The books were varied, most dealing with speaking techniques, but one in particular caught her eye: an untitled volume with a crystal lock, wrapped in a red ribbon. She set it aside.

The shiny object turned out to be a crystal sword. Titus gasped as soon as he saw it.

"Shards and shatters, where did he get this?" Titus exclaimed. "They stopped making these centuries ago." It seemed he couldn't resist picking up the blade. Cut from pure, clear crystal, it was as long as Titus's arm. It had a hilt forged of steel, embellished with smaller crystals, including the pommel. Titus began swishing it around in the air.

"He'd kill me if he caught me with this," Titus whispered.

"Or you could just kill him with it," Crystara suggested. She went back to rummaging. There didn't appear to be much else of interest in the chest, until her hand brushed against something other than paper. She withdrew it.

It was a crystal necklace.

Her heart felt stuck in her throat. The memory came rushing back to her: her mother lying on the bed, the necklace hanging between them like a promise. Then the true gravity of the discovery hit her. *There was a connection between her mother and De'Cadomus.* Crystara couldn't breathe. She gripped the chest tightly and tried to focus on not fainting.

She had been toying with the idea of convincing Titus to kill De'Cadomus, but it would have to wait. She had to know the truth. On a hunch, she held the crystal next to the ribbon-bound book. The lock unlatched itself.

"Gods, Mother, it's your journal." She held it to her chest and tried to force back the tears.

"What did you say?" Titus asked.

Crystara snapped out of it. She had to get out before De'Cadomus returned, and she wasn't safe until she found a way to remove the ring. An answer had to be in her mother's journal, she was certain of it.

"Quick, put the sword back, dully," she commanded. "We've been here long enough."

Titus stared at her as though he was seeing her for the first time.

"Gods," Titus breathed. "You're beautiful." He knelt down next to her and gently eased the sword back into the chest, stacking papers on top of it and trying to arrange them the way they had seen when they first opened the top. Then he shut the chest.

"Huh?" Crystara asked.

"That crystal you're holding...it must have done something. I can understand you. I can *see* you." His gauntleted hand touched her cheek and he pressed his lips to hers. His were surprisingly soft.

Crystara pushed him away.

"Not *now*, you dully. We have to get out of here."

The sound of distant footfalls echoed up the stone stairs to their ears.

"Fuck," Titus whispered. "We're trapped."

Crystara glanced at her mother's necklace, then at the window. She'd managed it before, she told herself. The distance wasn't *that* much greater...

"No, we're not," she said. "Shut the door. Quietly."

Titus did so, meeting her at the windowsill. She glanced down to the courtyard below, trying to estimate the distance.

"You *are* cracked," Titus muttered under his breath. "We can't jump that far without breaking something."

"We're not going to jump," she said. "It's a teleportation whisper."

"From this height?"

"Some brave crystal knight you are. Just hold my hand and make sure none of your own crystals go off," she said, tapping his armour. "It's that or face him now." The footsteps were close enough that she could hear them through the door.

Titus grasped Crystara's hand. She breathed in deeply and whispered to her mother's crystal, focusing on the hedges below the tower.

There was a sickening, heart-lurching moment of weightlessness, then she and Titus crashed into the bushes.

Off by a couple of metres, Crystara thought as she stood up and shook twigs out of her hair. *Not bad.*

Titus, still entwined in the shrubbery, stared at her.

"You're incredible," he huffed. Crystara put a finger to her lips and offered him a hand up. Forgetting how heavy he was with the armour, the effort of dragging him to his feet pulled her back to the bushes on top of him.

"Oof," he said. "Hello."

"Shh." Crystara put a hand over Titus's mouth. De'Cadomus had incredible hearing for his age, and she couldn't risk being caught. Not when she was so close.

Being that close to Titus was a distraction all its own. He was strong and warm, and dared to kiss her hand while she held it over his lips. He was so excited that his guard was down, and she could clearly hear his thoughts...none of which was anywhere close to pure. It made her blush and she cursed her rotten luck. It was the first time since Jacoby that anyone had shown an interest in her, and she couldn't do a damn thing about it just then.

"Circle around and tell the viper you heard something in the hallway and followed it to the courtyard," Crystara whispered. She licked his ear, just to tell him his advances weren't completely undesired. "You thought it might be me sneaking around, but it was just Rossi's halberd. Or Dusty. Whatever he'll believe. I'll find my way back to my room. Come and find me later. We have a lot to...talk about."

She gazed into his eyes for a moment, kissed him, then aligned her mother's crystal to grey and slunk along the shadows of the temple wall.

Her heart raced as she snuck her way back to the library, clutching the book in one hand and the necklace in the other, constantly looking over her shoulder. Fear, excitement, and hope waged war within her chest.

The library was dark and silent. Lagarus had gone to bed. Crystara's every careful footfall echoed among the stacks. Knowing the way by heart, she returned to her room, not bothering to flick on the crystal light. She knew where her bed was, even in the dark. Crystara had to pretend to be asleep, at least until enough time had passed to let her know De'Cadomus would not descend upon her in a fury.

And if he does? she wondered. There was only one way to know if she could defend herself. Crystara donned the necklace. She found the crystal's weight upon her chest comforting.

A cold sweat broke out upon her brow as her right hand reached for the ring. Despite the darkness, she shut her eyes, grimacing. She felt the cool crystal upon the pads of her fingers and pulled.

It came off. She exhaled heavily, nearly panting with relief.

In the pressing, silent dark she worked, whispering to the ring, re-aligning by slight increments. To De'Cadomus, it would appear to function. Her disguise would remain. The rest – the crippling pain and the viper's control whisper – were gone.

She slid the ring back onto her finger. It would have to be her speaker's tool. The necklace, powerful and personal as it was, gave her away. It held the most advanced protection alignment she had ever seen, and could completely negate the effects of the ring.

"Thank you, Mother," she whispered as she took off the necklace. She hid it behind a loose stone in the wall. It was as safe a place as she was likely to find.

As she slid the stone back into place, a slew of dark thoughts crossed her mind: revenges upon De'Cadomus that she could swiftly enact, death by wand or sword or free-fall from a tower window. Deaths that could be made to look accidental (not that many would mourn his passing). Quick deaths and torturous ones...

Crystara took a deep breath and told her mind to slow down. It was not yet time. De'Cadomus was still a canny speaker and reader, in fact the cagiest opponent Crystara could imagine. She had to catch him off-guard, and she had to know her mother's secrets. The diary would contain some. The rest she would get from *him*, right before she killed him.

Chapter 45

Timori had begun asking Miss Tricchio for more advanced physics work. She seemed more than happy to oblige him. On evenings when he didn't have football practice, Timori would visit her in her office and ask her innumerable questions, challenging himself to learn all he could so he could help De'Barus with his unified theory. Miss Tricchio appeared content to remain at Central and while away the time with Timori. He wondered occasionally why she would choose to spend her evenings with a student, but he told himself firmly that her interest in him was purely pedagogical.

Besides which, Timori's heart was still Racquela's. That didn't stop him from blushing anytime Miss Tricchio was physically close to him, however.

"I brought you some of my books from my academy days," she said as she entered her office that evening. Timori had been waiting for her in the tiny but immaculate room. Once it had been a prison cell. Doctor Ruveldi often joked that the teachers of Central were still prisoners in a way. As she struggled with the books, Timori leapt out of his chair and helped her get the massive stack onto her desk without it toppling over. Their hands brushed, which made Timori's neck feel warm.

"Uh...uh, thanks, Miss Tricchio." It used to be so easy with her, so casual. Timori couldn't figure out what had changed.

"Oh, please, Tim." She leaned against the desk to catch her breath. "By now you should know you can call me Michaela."

"Yes, sorry. Michaela."

She laughed and tossed her hair aside. Timori tried not to stare, but their eyes met and then he was blushing all over again.

"And you don't need to apologize. Just take what you think you can use there. Hopefully they help you and De'Barus."

Timori's hand paused over the stack.

"How do you know about that?"

"Because I talk to Rob. Er, Doctor Ruveldi, that is, and De'Barus was one of my professors at the academy. He's a surly old bastard, but brilliant. It's exciting that you get to work with him. You need a challenge."

"Hardly," Timori admitted. "I barely even see my sisters anymore because I'm so busy. I'm doing this for the money and the recommendation to the academy that I'll get from him, and I think I've cleaned up enough dog shit to earn it."

Michaela put a hand on his shoulder.

"I'm sorry, Tim...I'm sure it'll be worth it in the long run. I could tell you some horrific stories of the jobs I had to do to put myself through school."

A deep voice came from the doorway.

"Am I interrupting something here, Tim?"

Startled, Timori almost fell out of his chair. Paulo was leaning on a folded umbrella. His school uniform was soaked, but he was smirking as though he had caught them in the act of something more intimate.

"I'd prefer it if you knocked, Mister...?" Paulo was not in any of Miss Tricchio's classes, as far as Timori could remember.

"Bellacolla," he said. "Paulo Bellacolla. The door was wide open. I just need to speak to Timori for a moment, and then you can resume your...tryst. And may I say, that is a fetching ribbon in your hair, Miss Tricchio."

Michaela frowned, seemingly unimpressed by Paulo's attempt at charm.

"It's okay, Tim, we can cut this short for today," she said. "Take what books you want to start with and I'll leave the rest here for you. And make sure De'Barus credits you for your assistance the next time he publishes. It'll make a difference in a few years, trust me." She sat at her desk and placed a fresh sheet of paper in her typewriter. "Go on then, boys."

Feeling rushed, Timori grabbed the top two books from the stack.

"Thanks for all your help, Michaela," Timori said. "Miss Tricchio," he added, recalling that Paulo was standing right there.

"Anytime, Tim," she replied. Her smile was genuine.

"What is it?" Timori asked Paulo. He shut Miss Tricchio's office door behind him.

"More than just a teacher's pet, aren't you?" Paulo remarked. "Nice work. I hear older women are..."

"Jova and Titania's sake, Paulo, what do you want?"

"A little misaligned today? I didn't mean to interrupt your little love scene. I'm just here to tell you there's a meeting tonight."

"I can't tonight...I'm helping Dr. De'Barus with his work."

"You're not going to lose out on a scholarship if you miss one day with some old scientist." Paulo began leading Timori down the hallway, away from the science faculty offices. "He won't even notice you're gone. Haven't you been reading the papers or listening to the radio? The time to act is drawing closer."

"Because of the cave-in at the mines? The Labour Party is waiting for elections, so..."

"Of course the cave-in." Paulo and Timori left the school, trudging through the empty football field in the dismal autumn rain. Paulo shook out his damp curls and opened his umbrella, then lit a cigarette. He offered one to Timori, who refused, as usual.

"What does that have to do with it?" Timori asked as he tucked the books into his jacket to keep them dry. "It was an accident. Sure, it's making tensions rise, but..."

"Don't be a naïve dully." Paulo sucked on his cigarette and stared off at Crystus Hill in the distance. "The news is owned by the Republic. That cave-in was sabotage. I heard it from a reliable spy within the Labour Party. They're trying to manufacture discontent and ensure that *only* the miner caste can control the flow of crystal. Remember that the whole caste is picketing, other than a few who are considered to be traitors. The party is pretending they want to wait for elections, but really they're trying to sow enough anger amongst the lower castes to incite a revolution and march on the hill."

He lowered his umbrella and let the raindrops fall upon his face. "Feel that? The famine will end now that we're getting rain again. The republic will try to use that to restore their idea of 'balance'...we have to act while the fires of discord are still stoked. The farmers and the miners, the bread and coal of our society, they're the weapon. Poor, unhappy, and ignored...but necessary."

Timori scratched his jaw. He was beginning to grow stubble on some parts of his chin. It was an odd sensation but made him feel like more of a man.

"You might have to specify what separates the NSP from the Labour Party, Paulo. It seems like you both want the same thing."

Paulo turned and grabbed Timori by his blazer, not angrily, but excitedly.

"That's just it," Paulo said, blowing smoke into Timori's face. "We do, but the leaders of Labour are complete dullies. They'll misalign everything if they get into power and we'll have anarchy on our hands within months. But they have the numbers. Come to the meeting tonight, Tim. Things are happening quickly now and I need people I can trust."

"You don't trust the rest of the party?"

Paulo shrugged and began walking again. "I do...most of them. The General is a mystery, but we need his clout. If anyone will betray us to Labour or the republic, it's Dante. But you're my friend, Tim. You know things about me I haven't told anyone. I need your help...and someday I'll have you running a guild."

"With you at the head of it all? *Emperor* Longoro the Second? Not exactly socialism, is it?"

They had reached the edge of the field where the hill sloped sharply downward toward the middle-caste houses. Paulo gestured to the city below.

"Look at all that Novem has built and accomplished. This was done by individuals, working collectively. At this distance, think of it like an anthill. Somewhere out there is a monarch, making the decisions that coordinate the entire society. These great monuments and public works, these wide and clean streets, these houses of learning and proud castles, all of this..." he gestured again, "was done with direction. Left to their own devices, those 'ants' would be lost and wandering, prone to give in to selfishness and trivial engagements. Humanity needs a hand to *guide* it, Timori. To help it fulfill a destiny of prosperity and progress. Novem needs that, more than ever right now."

Timori glanced at Paulo. There was a burning look in the young man's eyes.

"And...you think you're the best hand to guide it?"

"Yes," he answered without hesitation. "But I could use some help from other men of brilliance. We could change the world, Tim."

Timori suppressed his sigh.

"What time is the meeting?"

***

The tensions were high and the stares long as the men of the National Socialist Party entered one by one. They sat about the low, dimly-lit table in the old wharf warehouse, covered by the usual pall of cigarette smoke. Timori gave Jacoby a grave nod as he saw his friend enter, and Jacoby returned the gesture, along with a look that suggested Jacoby had a number of things weighing on his mind.

Paulo had not yet arrived and it seemed that, true to Timori's suspicions about the Longoro legacy, the meeting would not start without the young 'heir.'

What is it? Timori mouthed to Jacoby from across the table. Jacoby merely returned a slight shake of the head, a *not right now* gesture Timori had seen innumerable times.

"The fucking kid is late again," Dante muttered. "When you call the godsdamned meeting, you show up on time."

"Relax, Dante," Faustus said, pushing his glasses up his nose. "He'll be..."

"Here," called a deep voice from the entrance. Paulo approached the table, looking uncharacteristically dishevelled. The boy always had a careless attitude about his appearance and somehow still came off as poised and deliberate, but there was a distinct air of panic about Paulo. His underarms were sweaty, his gaze rapidly shifting, his knuckles white. Paulo's jaw appeared swollen on the one side.

"Well, look what the cat dragged in," Dante said. "What the fuck happened to you?"

Paulo didn't bother sitting. He slammed his fists upon the table, eyes aglow, scowling.

"They're moving against us," he said as he rearranged his suspenders, which had gone askew.

"The Republic?" The General asked.

"The Labour Party," Paulo said with a shake of his head. "I barely got out of there. Didn't have my wand or they would've learned a thing or two about fucking with a Bellacolla."

"Out of where?" Faustus asked. "Paulo. Sit down and explain yourself. How did you get tangled with Labour? They've never even considered us a threat."

"They do now," Paulo replied. He refused to sit, pacing around the table instead, channelling his nervous energy into the others. "I was trying to recruit. The leaders are complete dullards, but a few of them...show potential. At least, they did...their misplaced loyalty is unquestionable."

"What the fuck were you doing talking to Labour?" Dante demanded as he stood. "Do you want to shatter our entire fucking plan?"

"No." Paulo shook his head, approaching Dante. They were standing face to face. Dante seemed like a freakish goblin next to the handsome, confident young man. "But we can't hide in the shadows any longer. Labour is bloated and fragmented...If we act now, especially playing on their upset with this situation in the mines, we could win the entire party over...provided we take care of a few problem elements." He looked to the others for support. "What do you all say?"

"I'm all for putting it to a vote..." Faustus said.

"Vote?" Paulo had lit a cigarette and was waving it about dramatically, making trails of smoke in the air. "Now is the time to act. The Labour Party votes on everything and look where it gets them. They're stagnant, waiting for the republic to have an election...as though the upper castes would ever allow a socialist party to be *voted* in. They'd do everything in their power to curtail that from happening, using wealth and influence to keep things the same, as always. Do I need to remind everyone who is *funding* everything this party does? Who set up our connections with the

Noctra? Who secured us the influence and support of house De'Trini?"

Timori and Jacoby exchanged a glance.

"Who do you think is the fucking brains of this operation?" he continued.

"Careful, Paulo," Faustus warned.

"No." He spun on his heels and pointed a finger at the bespectacled man, who remained seated, shuffling papers. "The NSP has a reputation and we can only garner the true support of the people with the help of the Labour Party. We are men of action, are we not? We are the change that Novem needs. Before a true political coup, we'll need to have another, different one."

The General cleared his throat.

"And how do you propose we win over Labour, boy?"

Paulo seemed irked by the 'boy' comment, but shrugged it off.

"Consider it...strategic elimination of the opposition, combined with a few well-placed agents and a properly timed merger."

The General smirked, but Faustus's eyes widened.

"You mean...assassination?"

Paulo rolled his eyes.

"Don't be naive. We'll have to get our hands dirty eventually."

A picture flashed in Timori's mind of the Dori boy lying dead on the floor, eyes open, and the skeleton behind the wall. He frowned.

"The filthier they are now, the more time we have to wash them clean later," Paulo said. "All we need are a few well-placed daggers and the party will fall apart, anxious for strong leadership. Our leadership. And relax, Faustus." He blew smoke into the older man's face. "I'll do most of the dirty work. You can keep pushing our paper."

"I still say we need to vote on this," Faustus insisted.

"Fine," Paulo acquiesced, blowing more smoke out of his nostrils. He faced the table and opened his arms. "We're all equals here. All in favour of a coup against the Labour Party, raise a hand."

Paulo and several at the table lifted an arm. Timori, considering the gravity of being implicit to murder, kept his down.

"Seven for and eight against," Faustus noted.

Paulo shot Timori a glance of incredulity.

"What the fuck, Tim?"

"We didn't sign up to be murderers," Jacoby said.

"Didn't I just say I would do the dirty work?" he demanded. "How the fuck else are we supposed to depose the most popular socialist movement in Novem, hmm? Ask them nicely? They tried to *kill* me tonight. It's us or them at this point. Come on, you daisy-chasing pansies. Show some godsdamned backbone, or you might as well just join Labour." The entire table was staring at him. "This might be our one chance to change the course of Noven history."

A long-suffering sigh came from the middle of the table.

"Fine, Paulo," Dante said. "I change my vote. But this had better fucking work, and you'd better fucking kill who you say you're gonna kill. Maybe everyone else is ignoring the fact that a kid is trying to give us orders, but I haven't forgotten. At least if you fail you'll finally quit whining."

Jacoby, whose eyes were darting between Paulo and Dante, raised an eyebrow quizzically and looked at Timori again.

What? Timori mouthed.

"I won't fail," Paulo insisted. "And you won't regret this. I have a plan."

Chapter 46

Jacoby puffed on a cigarette outside the wharf warehouse, shivering, his eyes darting from Timori to the warehouse door and back again.

"Shoulda brought a jacket tonight," he declared. Thunder rolled in the distance, though the sky had not yet opened up and rained upon them. It threatened to. When Jacoby glanced up there were no stars, no moon. Timori's face under the bald crystal light by the back door was half-shadow.

"Well, make it quick then," Timori suggested. By his posture and Jacoby's empathic estimation, Timori was equally nervous. "What did you want to talk to me about?"

"We have to stop him," Jacoby said under his breath.

Paulo? Timori mouthed. Jacoby nodded.

"We're finally getting somewhere, Jake. I agree that...methods have seemed unorthodox or extreme, but if we're ever going to get anywhere...like he said, we might just have to get our hands a bit dirty. No offense meant, but maybe it's harder for you to see that now. Now that you're up on the hill."

"I haven't forgotten. Have *you* forgotten all we've seen so far? The orphanage? Racquela's rescue?"

"It could just as easily have been one of us pulling that trigger," Timori admitted.

"And we would have felt remorse, Tim. I feel nothing from him. He's just cold. I don't think he's afraid of stepping on anyone to get what he wants, and that includes me, you, and Racquela."

Timori stared at Jacoby for a long, drawn-out moment.

"Do you...do you know for certain if anything else is going on between her and Paulo? Other than his manoeuvre to get Joven in his pocket? Other than just a suspicion?"

Jacoby stared back, scrambling to think of an evasive statement.

"Well?" Timori's face flushed.

"Look," Jacoby began, lowering his voice, "I might know something. But now is not the time to crack over it...we're deep in his world right now."

"Jake." Timori gripped Jacoby by the arms. "I'm not a complete fucking dully. But I need to know if you know something. Please."

"Ow, Jova's sake." Jacoby squirmed out of Timori's grip. "You don't have to crush my godsdamned arms, calm down. Yes, I might know something. The emotions I read from both of them are...well..."

"I thought you said Paulo was cold."

"Usually. Except when she was kidnapped. Then...there was something else."

Timori stared at the pitch-dark sky.

"How long have you known?"

"Racquela sort of...let it slip the other night."

"Fuck," Timori said. He punched the warehouse wall and his fist came back bloody, full of splinters.

"Fuck!" he screamed up to the sky.

"Shards, keep your voice down," Jacoby said.

The door opened and Paulo peered out, cigarette hanging from his lips. Jacoby could feel nothing but barely suppressed rage from Timori. Paulo was as cool and inscrutable as ever.

"What the abyss are you two doing out here?" Paulo asked. He didn't seem to notice Timori's bloodied hand or baleful expression. "You can smoke inside, Jake. Tim, we decided you should be with us when we march...solidarity of the lower castes and all that."

"Won't I be marching, too?" Jacoby asked, despite having no intention of marching with the NSP anymore.

"No," Paulo said. "I have a much more important job for you."

"What's that?"

"I need you to spy on Labour for us."

***

The motorcoach trip back to Timori's house was uncomfortably silent. Jacoby sat in the rear and let the tensions wafting off of Paulo and Timori compound his own feelings of anxiety. Jacoby felt cornered by the NSP, forced due to his skills as a speaker and empath to play the spy.

When they reached Corti Street, Paulo flipped the switch to kill the engine and looked over at Timori. "I can't do this without you, Tim," he said, placing a hand upon Timori's shoulder. Timori's face betrayed nothing, but Jacoby felt his friend's ire swell.

"You have plenty of lackeys," Timori replied. Paulo laughed heartily, appearing to miss the venom in Timori's tone.

"That's true. But what I don't have a lot of are friends. So few understand, Tim. Stick with me and we'll change the world."

The evening's silence stretched. Jacoby was dimly aware of a battle going on within Timori between his rage and his rationality.

"For the people," Timori said finally, returning the gesture by placing a hand on Paulo's shoulder. Paulo's smile was uncommonly warm. Without another word, Timori left the motorcoach. Paulo looked to the backseat and gave Jacoby a wolfish glare.

"Don't forget the plan. Moonday at the Labour meeting."

"I'll be sure to leave my NSP membership at home," Jacoby said drily as he, too, left the vehicle. He gave the door a satisfying slam only to have Paulo spin the tires and drench him in muddy water as he pulled out.

"Fucker of a dully," Jacoby said, wringing his shirt. He stalked off toward Timori's house. Timori walked beside him, staring at the cobblestones, full to the brim with silent anguish.

"I can't believe you didn't punch him," Jacoby said.

"I would have done worse," Timori replied, "if it wouldn't have gotten me killed. Jake, you have no idea how close I am to shattering right now."

"Trust me, I can feel it. We could have taken him back in the 'coach."

"No. I have to know first. I have to hear her say it." They were at Timori's front step.

"Tim, don't..."

"I'm not going to hurt her, Jake." Timori's voice cracked. "I just need to know why. Why him? Why am I not good enough? Is it caste? Is it looks? Did I come on too strong? Does she..." His tears went unnoticed in the uncaring drizzle. "...does she *love* him? And how long...how long has this been going on? I need to know if she cheated on me."

"Why? It doesn't change any..."

"Because I need to fucking know, all right?" Timori shouted. A dog started barking nearby.

"Tim, I..."

"Let's get out of here," Timori suggested, grabbing Jacoby's bike from its spot by the porch. "I don't really want to be home right now. I need to...clear my head."

They rode double. The night's drizzle seemed to calm Timori somewhat. In unspoken agreement, they stopped when they reached Memorial Bridge. Other than the rain and the occasional motorcoach, the world was silent.

"Some weird memories associated with this place now," Timori remarked as he looked over the railing.

"It's still our spot," Jacoby said. "Wish we had some sunflower seeds though."

"I've got something better." Timori dug into his ratty old book bag and produced an unlabelled bottle of something brown.

"What is it?"

"Dunno." Timori shrugged. "We can find out, if your parents won't send you through the orange for missing curfew." He offered Jacoby the bottle.

"Fuck curfew," Jacoby said as he pulled the cork. "There's more important stuff going on." He took a swig, swished it around in his mouth, made a face, and spat. "Gods, that's awful."

"Don't waste it, dully." Timori grabbed the bottle and drank. He shut his eyes, clenched his jaw, and forced himself to swallow. "Jova's shattered sword, how does Mom drink this dirt?"

"Maybe it's for cleaning spoons."

"Probably." Timori laughed and handed the foul drink back to Jacoby. Jacoby managed to keep it down this time, even though it made him feel like he had to vomit. For a while they were silent, listening to the drizzle and the 'coaches underneath the bridge. They passed the bottle back and forth. Jacoby began to feel lightheaded after a few minutes.

"So what are you gonna do?" Jacoby asked.

"I just need to know why and when. From her own lips."

"Just don't do anything crazy. We need to stick together."

"If I go crazy, it won't be on her. I could never hurt her. Paulo, however...if I find out he's betrayed me..."

Jacoby thought of all he knew of Paulo, and all they'd already seen. How could Timori even imagine the boy had a shard of remorse or humanity? The crystals and wand weighed heavy in Jacoby's jacket pocket and even heavier upon his conscience.

"What will you do to him?" Jacoby lit up his last cigarette with his lighter.

"I don't know." Timori drank deeply.

"Do you need a wand?"

Timori turned around and looked down at the street below. "No."

Jacoby regarded Timori. It was tough to tell if there were tears falling or if it was just the rain on his face.

"Do you think Lenara was right?" He twisted the ring on his finger. "That he's the son of Emperor Longoro and that he'll start another war? That he has to be stopped?"

"He believes he is, or he's pretending. Doesn't matter."

"Is he...your friend?"

"If this whole thing with Racquela proves false? Yes. If he's a two-faceted liar, then he's dead to me. If he's willing to lie about that, he's willing to lie to anyone and shouldn't be trusted to run Novem."

Jacoby sighed. "Do you think we can really change things for the better? For the Dori and the lower castes?"

"If we don't believe in change we might as well give up now, Jake." Timori took another generous swig.

Jacoby, feeling a churning in his gut from the alcohol, cigarettes or nerves, refused the bottle. He looked out at the hazy blue lights beyond the misty rain, a glimmering dark ocean of city souls, the heartbeat of their society. *Do we owe it to them,* he mused, *because of what we know?* He thought of Master Vellize suddenly, and the tale of Emperor Longoro.

"How do you think history'll remember us, if we kill him?" His valley accent was becoming more pronounced the drunker he got. "Will we be heroes? Or villains because nobody'll ever know th'crisis we averted?"

"Doesn't matter," Timori replied, turning around to survey the city with Jacoby. "Heroes'n villains, they're just concepts in stories, imaginary perceptions of good and bad. We're just people makin' choices, Jake. Doing a mix of what we think's right and what we want, motivated by fear and desire."

"What's the consequence gonna be, if we do what's right?"

"Shatter a crystal'n pick up a shard, Jake. You don't know what colour it'll be."

Chapter 47

"So we're expecting this big huge Nilonnese brute with a bushy moustache and arms like scatterguns, and he opens up the door and the guy is tiny, I mean like no taller'n a metre stick, and he's as big around as he is tall…or short, rather, and…"

"He was taller'n that," Julio interrupted Roberto. As he quaffed the last of his ale he looked around for the innkeeper, who had been ignoring them all morning.

"Fine, so I'm exaggerating." Roberto began stuffing his pipe. A sizeable pile of ash was collecting in the tray next to him. "Anyway, he would'a made Pip look like a Parsu giant, 'cept Pip wasn't there. But this little guy's voice is still like a foghorn, so the three of us'r hiding our mouths'n laughing, an' he's already giving us the stinkface 'cause'o'the uniforms. Kinda like the bartender here," he said, too loudly.

In fact, the whole room had been eyeing them with suspicion since they'd entered the cheery neighbourhood inn to find breakfast. It seemed to be a place the locals frequented rather than tourists, despite its convenient location and aesthetic appeal. Julio suspected the stone building was one of few to survive the brutal fighting during Novem's retreat at the end of the Great War.

After breakfast the men had counted the hours in beers and soldiers' tales, chatting away nonchalantly in slurred Noven, rapidly moving their way toward a liquid lunch.

Drago put his index fingers to his lips and whistled, loudly enough that the whole room turned to look at them.

"Another round, barkeep," he said in hill-accented Noven. Julio sighed.

"Please," Julio added in Nilonnese. It didn't appear to brighten the innkeeper's mood any.

"Anyway," Roberto said, lighting his pipe, "where was I? Oh, yeah. So he eyes us up and shouts with this really thick Nilonnese accent: 'zet's nine Nils fer de tree of you.' O'course we don't have the Nils but Bocco's been holdin' onta some ol' dinari an' he pays fer the 'tree' of us since this was all his idea. Guy opens the door an' takes us down these stairs to a basement with this hanging sign that just says 'fems' on it and a painting of a naked lady, 'cept it looks more like a peach-coloured cow with tits…"

"Maybe we shouldn't tell this story, Rob," Julio interrupted again.

Roberto took a thoughtful puff of his pipe.

"Come on, Jules, Drago's a grown man fer Jova's sake. I'm sure he's seen a pair'o tits before."

"No, not that. I'm just thinkin' there are more…culturally appropriate war stories we could swap. About Parsu, perhaps?"

Roberto made a face.

"Parsu was more miserable'n the abyss. An' this story is great. So we go in an' sure enough there's girls, an' none of 'em look like cows. They've got this stage set up fer a burlesque show, doin' this nearly-nude, all-ladies version of some opera…"

"It was *Di Banasi*," Julio added.

"How in the abyss d'you remember stuff like that?" Roberto wondered. "Anyway, this little tart comes up in this getup that's a cross between a Noven officer's uniform and lingerie, an' Bocco says something 'bout how it's a good thing the Colonel wasn't around to see such an affront to the Empire. We all have a chuckle an' she says there's room fer us at the officers' table…an' sure enough, there's the Colonel, smokin' his pipe, with a girl in his lap wearin' the exact same outfit. I ask him if he's gonna spank 'er fer insubordination or not wearin' a regulation uniform, an' he tells me to sit down, shut up an' get drunk, or else 'e'll court-martial me."

"And did you?" Drago asked, leaning forward. Julio glanced at the innkeeper. He was chatting with another table, completely ignoring them other than the occasional sideways, disapproving glance.

"Everything 'cept for the shut up part. So anyway, we spend most of the night tryin' to get one of the girls over for Bocco, 'cause it's his birthday, an' they send this little thing, can't be more'n sixteen, but she keeps payin' attention to Jules here, an' Bocco is gettin' jealous an' Jules keeps tryin' to get rid of her, but the more he ignores her, the crazier it makes her. Daddy issues or somethin'."

"Rob," Julio said. Everyone in the room was staring again.

"Hang on, this is the best part. So Bocco gets fed up an' finally asks the girl what Jules has got that he hasn't, an' the girl just says ''ee's polite an' 'ee's got a pretty face.'"

"Roberto."

"Will you let me finish? So then Jules tries to leave but the girl is hangin' all over him, and then finally she asks *him*, 'What's your girlfriend back een Novem 'ave zet I don' 'ave'? And Julio just looks her in the eyes and says, 'Self-respect'!" Roberto pounded his fist on the table, pushing back tears of laughter. "So Jules gets a drink in the face and *then*..."

"*Rob.*" Roberto hadn't noticed the crowd of Nilonnese men surrounding their table, but Julio and Drago had. Drago puffed out his chest and looked about for the easiest head to smash his stein against, but Julio merely offered an apologetic look to the posse.

"My apologies," he said in fluent Nilonnese, "My friends and I will..."

"Leave," said the innkeeper, folding his arms. "*Now.*"

Drago seemed ready to do something heroic, but Roberto grabbed his arm and hauled him out the door. Julio hobbled after them.

"Come on, we could've taken 'em," Drago complained as they walked, semi-inebriated, down the wide lane in the brisk autumn sunshine.

"Oh, sure," Roberto agreed. "Two and a half of us against a dozen. Plus they wouldn't hit a cripple, I'm sure."

"Wrong story to tell, Rob," Julio said.

They strode sullenly through the streets. Julio ignored his melancholy by admiring the provincial architecture and breathing in the fresh, small city air. He was amazed at how quickly and efficiently the city had rebuilt itself, until he remembered that Novem had paid reparations to most of Titania for the war. The quiet survival of the town of Cheberre was just another reminder of how dire things were becoming in Captus Nove.

"What's wrong with telling old war stories?" Drago asked. "I'm sure the Nillies do."

"Don't say that word out loud here, please," Julio said. "The Nilonnese do. But like I said before, for many the memory of the war is still fresh. It certainly is for me." He struggled to keep up with the other two, occasionally tripping or getting his cane caught in cobblestones. "Imagine how you would feel if a bunch of Commonwealth soldiers were sitting in your favourite cabaret, telling tales of how they obliterated Imperial soldiers at the end of the war."

"It's different," Drago said. "They won."

"That doesn't matter," Julio insisted. "Both sides suffered heavy losses. It may not look like it here, but Nilonne was damaged terribly by the war. It is a price Novem is still paying. But Novem's people are just that, people. We didn't order the wands to fire, we just got drafted and had to survive. Same as the enemy. I certainly don't blame whoever fired the scattershot. Longoro, on the other hand..."

Drago rolled his eyes.

"You can't pin *everything* on Emperor Longoro, Dad."

"Yes, I can. But he paid the price for his crimes. Sometimes, Drago, you just have to accept that life is just a series of events that happen to you, and neither you nor anybody else has any control over them whatsoever."

Roberto scoffed.

"As though the gods have nothing to do with it at all. Where are we going, anyway?"

"The memorial."

The memorial was just outside of town at the centre of one of the largest military graveyards in Titania. The bodies of soldiers from eleven different nations were buried there, including Noven ones. Some considered it an honour that their enemies had been noble enough to do so. Others considered it a subtle insult, a way to keep the souls of the Noven dead from rejoining their gods.

The gods. It was easy for Julio to see their invisible hands in the great works of humanity and nature: the sky-touching towers and temples, the beautiful young maidens of Nilonne, the placid rolling pastures of sheep and cows.

When he looked upon the fields surrounding the town, however, he could also see what the land had once been: charred clumps of earth littered by corpses. His hand began to tremble and he could hear the scattershot booming again, the rumble of collapsing buildings, the men shouting and firing, the screams of the dying. They said there were no atheists in trenches, but once you looked back, it was hard to see the reason of a god who would allow such horror, even a god of war. The Great War had changed it all, down to the concept of nobility during combat.

Perhaps there were gods, Julio reasoned, but they weren't beings of benevolence.

The memorial was a circle of headstones, large enough around to fit an army, standing or lying down. In each section, dedicated to a different nation, the grave markers were carved of a distinct type of stone. Noven and Nilonnese, easily the largest groups, were carved from deepstone and marble, respectively. Pathways dividing each of the nations led to a statue in the centre of the memorial, boasting plaques with the names of the dead. Atop the plaque was a stone angel, a decidedly Nilonnese symbol. Although a religious representation, it watched over the massive graveyard like a guardian, a testament to peace.

If the tens of thousands of graves and the families visiting them weren't enough of a deterrent to war, Julio didn't know if anything ever would be. Julio glanced over at Drago occasionally, hoping for some kind of reaction to the rows of headstones, but if the boy equated his profession to an early grave, he made no indication.

The resting place they sought was still there, kept polished by the attendants. A beautiful, simple headstone read CPT. SPKR. PIETRO GARUS, NOVEN 103rd INFANTRY COMPANY C

The men removed their hats and offered Pietro a moment of silence. Julio stared at Drago, seeking a sign, but the young man believed his father was alive and standing next to him. Julio sighed and wondered again if the lie was worth it.

"Shame he was buried," Roberto said to break the silence. "Even if he was a dullard at times. No Noven deserves that."

"We could dig him up and burn the bones," Drago said.

"Sure," Roberto replied. "Let's rob a grave in the middle of the day. We did crazier things during the war, right, Jules?"

Their voices sounded fuzzy and far away, overpowered by the din of scattershot. Julio stared at the name on the tombstone and he could see Pietro in his mind's eye, that easy smile, the boyish good looks. He looked at Drago, Pietro's spitting image, staring at the grave as though the man interred beneath his feet was nothing more than a fellow soldier, a friend of his father's.

As his eyes grew misty, Julio looked away, out toward the rolling hills. It had been a mere few kilometres away that the 103rd battalion had made its last stand in the ruins of Cheberre. There they had fought and lost, those hapless and powerless tools of the empire, flesh against flesh fighting for someone else's ideology, someone else's glory. The right side of his body felt hot then, and his scars were itching.

He shut his eyes, but it only made the images stronger. In his mind, suddenly it wasn't Pietro but Drago flipping through the air end over end, his body blown into pieces by scattershot. Julio lost his footing and fell, before Roberto or Drago could catch him, and wept over the grave. He wept for Pietro, who died too young. He wept for Drago, whose uniform was little more than a death sentence.

Most of all, Julio wept for the part of himself that had never returned from the war.

Chapter 48

There was a stranger seated in the parlour when Jacoby arrived home.

He'd been hoping his parents wouldn't notice his breach of curfew, but their expressions were loaded with disappointment as Katarina called Jacoby into the room. Underneath the betrayal of trust a nervousness emanated from both of them, presumably to do with the stranger in their midst.

The stranger made no pretence to hide his badge of office. The 'Inspector' badge was clearly visible upon the breast pocket of his shirt. He had doffed his grey trench coat and fedora in favour of the warmth of the fireplace and, presumably, the warmth of the wine in his cup. Equally visible was the casually-holstered wand at his hip. Underneath creased eyebrows, the inspector's glance was calculating.

"Jacoby Padrona," the inspector said.

Jacoby could read nothing of the man's emotions. He glanced at his parents. Concern crossed their faces, but they offered Jacoby no indication as to how he should respond.

"Y-yes?" Jacoby stammered.

The man downed the remainder of his wine and stood, proving to be much taller than Jacoby expected.

"I'm Inspector Martinus. I'd like you to answer a few questions for me."

Jacoby glanced at his parents again. They looked away from him, saying nothing. Concern and tension radiated about the room.

"And if I don't?"

"Then you can answer them at the nearest station, instead. It's all the same to me, but your folks were kind enough to offer me their hospitality, so I thought I'd extend you the offer to remain here. What do you say, Jake? You can tread the red or we can keep this discussion clear and easy."

"Do as he says, Jake," Gilliermo said. "Please."

Jacoby resisted the urge to check for the wand and rings in his pocket. He stared at the inspector.

"Ask away," he said, feeling like a caged animal.

"I'm glad you've decided to be reasonable." He grabbed his hat and motioned for Jacoby to follow him out of the room. Martinus led him out of the house and onto the back porch that overlooked their small yard. Although it was little more than a patch of grass and some flowerbeds, it was more outdoor space than most Novens could claim as their own. Martinus lit up a cigarette, and offered one to Jacoby.

"My parents don't know I smoke," Jacoby whispered. He accepted the offer anyway. Anything to calm his nerves. He used his own lighter, careful not to let the wand in his pocket show.

"There's a lot your parents don't know about your activities," Martinus said. "Nice ring, by the way. Where'd you get it?"

"Betrothal ring," Jacoby said. "The church never asked for it back."

"Hiding any other crystals?"

"No," he replied quickly. His pocket felt heavy just then.

"Really?" Martinus dug into an inner pocket of his coat and withdrew some photographs, handing them to Jacoby.

Somebody had been following him.

A distant part of his mind wondered at the cleverness of a camera that could operate at night without a noisy flash crystal, but the better part of him was concerned that nobody had noticed a spy of any kind. There were pictures of him with Paulo going in and out of the NSP warehouse, pictures of him heading into the

Casteless Quarter to meet with Tanni, and even one of him and Timori fleeing the scene of Racquela's rescue. A chill went up his spine.

"Am I under arrest for something?" he asked.

"Not yet." Martinus took a puff from his cigarette. "I'm digging for larger rocks and I know you're deep enough to have some information that could be very valuable to the Republic. The NSP is moving unregistered crystals, and I need to know how."

"I don't know how," Jacoby admitted. "I know they come in by boat, but I don't know from where, and I don't know where most of them go. They hide some at the warehouse, but most of them are shipped off somewhere else as soon as they come in. I overheard once that they are making weapons with them, but I couldn't tell you where."

"I'm sure you know more of the NSP's plans than that. You've been attending their meetings for months."

"I got roped into this, but I have no loyalty to them, I swear."

"What about the kidnapping of Racquela De'Trini? We know you were involved with that."

"Kidnapping?" Jacoby tried to keep his voice down but it was stretched tight. "I was involved with her *rescue*."

"We suspect the NSP was involved with her kidnapping. A ruse to garner the support of the De'Trini family. There was a reason we couldn't find her easily despite the cooperation of the valley...you kids got her out of there right before we were set to move in. However, two bodies were left behind that night...a casteless and a scholar with Labour affiliations."

"It wasn't us!" Jacoby blubbered. "It was Paulo. I swear. At least, he killed the Dori. I watched him do it. We were trying to talk him down and then Paulo just shot him in the back of the head." The tears were falling, and with them, the rest of his confession tumbled out. "I don't know for sure that the other guy was killed by Paulo, but we found him in the back alley already shot, I swear. Me and Tim, we were just trying to save Racquela. We didn't mean for anyone to die. I didn't...I never wanted anyone to get hurt..." He twisted the ring on his finger, thinking of flowers and flames.

"Relax, kid," Martinus said. "I believe you. They don't make empaths into detectives for nothing." He handed Jacoby a handkerchief.

"You're an empath?" Jacoby wiped his eyes.

"Yeah. Never was much of a speaker, but feelings like your guilt ring pretty clear to me. You're a good kid, but you're involved with a bad crowd. Your parents are pretty concerned. I can't say what they'll do, but I can tell you that the more information you can give me, the easier it will be to stop these guys from killing anyone else. Your friend Timori, he's in pretty deep, isn't he?"

"He'll be getting out soon, I think. He's starting to see Paulo for what he really is."

"Paulo, he's the ringleader? The kid?"

"I think so. He works for someone up north. Uncle Gordo, he calls him. Most of the group listen to Paulo. He's planning to take down the Labour Party soon...I'm supposed to spy on them."

"Listen, kid..." Martinus glanced back at the house and lowered his voice to a whisper. "I want you to see if you still can. Your parents will probably come down hard on you, but I could really use your help. The republic could. Your friend Timori...isn't as cooperative, and the information you gather could help put away these criminals for good. They *are* criminals, you understand? They might act like they're out to make the country a better place, but you don't start that by moving illegal goods that have the potential to hurt people, right? So if you can still make like you're their friend, you'd be doing me a huge favour. Tell you what? I'll even make you a deal. I won't mention anything about your involvement with the casteless."

"Is that illegal?"

"No. Unless you brought any of their crystals out of the quarter."

"How do you know they have crystals?"

"I know a lot, kid. Do you have any?"

"No." He prayed silently the inspector wouldn't search him.

"But you're still feeling guilty."

"I have a lot to feel guilty about," Jacoby said, truthfully. "I might not have shot those people, but I was there. I helped the NSP."

"You can still make it right, Jake." Martinus put out his cigarette and shoved the butt into his pocket. "You're a lucky kid, you know. Nice parents...generous ones. Got brought up to Padrona thanks to the republic. Speaker and empath, big scholarship to Central. You've got a bright future ahead if you stay out of trouble."

"After I finish spying on the NSP, that is," Jacoby muttered.

"Hey, it never hurts to have a police inspector for a friend. If you find out anything else...more information about any of the members of the party, or where those crystals are coming from, ask for me at the station. I've left my telegram number with your parents." He turned to leave.

"He thinks he's the son of Emperor Longoro."

Martinus stopped.

"Who does? Paulo?"

"Yeah."

"Interesting. Thanks for the tip. Sorry if your folks come down hard on you. And be careful making friends with nobodies...never know what they're thinking."

"The Dori."

"Hmm?"

"They're called The Dori."

"Right. Be careful out there, Jake. The Republic appreciates your help." He entered the house, leaving Jacoby alone in the misty night.

Jacoby felt shattered, with every piece scattering in a different direction.

Chapter 49

Up until that moment, Leo had understood the majesty of the Cliffs of Chavicci only through a photograph in one of Teddori's old books. The page-sized image came nowhere close to capturing the defiant splendour of the city.

As they drove alongside the placid, sparkling waters of the bay, the cliffs loomed ahead of them, a city in *bas relief* carved into the rock, dotted with shadowed doorways. Two deep ravines, like scars, divided the cliffs. Across the ravines were two deepstone bridges, massive-looking even at a distance. Smaller outcroppings, stone stairways, and wooden bridges crisscrossed the rock face. On the broad plain atop the cliffs was a shantytown. To Leo it looked like an ugly error added haphazardly to an otherwise flawless, enormous sculpture.

"It's a work of art now," Gordo said, "but it used to be a fortress guarding Novem's richest crystal mine. Of course, all that comes out of the mine these days are gemstones, but Chavicci was notoriously wealthy when it was a city-state...some of its dukes lent other kingdoms enough money to fund entire armies. See down there?" He pointed to the base of the cliffs, where a vast series of docks boasted ships bearing all manner of colourful flags. "There are drawbridges at the end of the docks in case of invasion. The Alliance tried to take it during the war, the fools. They sacrificed thousands of soldiers...most of them drowned, actually. It was a combined attack. They also came down from the lower-caste village up top there."

Leo could picture the little soldiers in Alliance green pouring down the cliffs onto the bridges and catwalks that connected the outer buildings.

"Some fools never learn from history. Chavicci has the most built-in defenses of any fortress in Titania, and has never been seized by an outside force. Unlike the blunder and subsequent ruin that was Saliara, this jewel in Novem's crown held out until Max's murder and the empire's surrender. They even blasted the walls from their battleships, but we retreated into the mines. Technically Chavicci was the last city to surrender, nine days after Captus Nove. That whole relief you see there was rebuilt after the war. Nearly bankrupted the city, but it was a matter of pride, you see."

Leo stared at the man. His threatening façade had faded somehow. As they approached the legendary cliff city of Chavicci, his tongue loosened and his demeanour grew more genial.

"Who's Max?" Leo asked.

"Your father," Gordo replied. "Maximus Longoro. I'm going to have to educate you about your family legacy. In fact...I'm going to have to educate you about a great many things."

The cliffs seemed much larger than they had been a moment ago. They were impossibly tall suddenly, as though the buildings would crack and collapse at any moment, and the entire rock face fall into the sea and onto the shore, crushing Leo to death. He shut his eyes and shook his head. His imagination was getting the better of him, but it was foolish to be afraid of such things. Lions weren't afraid of anything.

He found himself thinking of his little tin soldier, the one he'd left behind. Unbidden, a tear tumbled down his cheek.

"Are you crying?" Gordo asked.

"No," Leo said, turning his head to look out the rolled-down window.

"Tears are weak. You are the son of the last emperor of Novem. Most won't see your weakness, boy, but I do. When I'm done with you, you'll be nearly invincible. So stop your fucking crying already."

"I wasn't crying. And my name is Leo."

"Not anymore it isn't. Leo is a good name, but it's not *your* name. From now on you are Paulo."

"Paulo Longoro?"

"Privately, yes. But if anyone asks, you are Paulo Bellacolla, my adopted son."

"Why?"

"Because the world is not ready for the Third Empire. But it will be. Soon."

They had reached the base of the cliffs, where the city sprawled out from the rock like a growth. Leo was amazed to see so many *people* on the streets: men in white cotton shirts hauling crates or nets of fish, women in colourful dresses haggling prices with market-stall vendors (he had never seen so much bare skin or so much beauty -- it made his head spin), children playing marbles on the sidewalk, wearing finer clothes than Leo had ever worn. Some of them pointed and stared at him as he drove by.

"This is Seaside," Gordo explained as he drove through the wide brick streets. "That mess up above is known as Topside, and what you can see on the cliffs we call Sunnyside. The miners live in Darkside."

He parked next to a mural-painted brick wall. Leo's eyes widened. Every moment was another experience in sensory overload. The mural depicted a scene of proud men and women on a sturdy stone outcropping, overlooking a harbour clogged with gunships. A boy in the painting waved the red and black flag of the Second Empire defiantly.

"Welcome back, Mister Bellacolla, sir," said a man's voice. Leo turned away from the mural to see Gordo handing the crystal key for his motorcoach to a finely-dressed young man with a well-trimmed moustache. "Can I get you anything?"

"Some hay for the horses," he said, and the men shared a chuckle. The man with the moustache glanced at Leo but said nothing to him. "Oh, and the newspaper. I've been driving all godsdamned day. After the 'coach is put away, of course."

"Shall I fetch a litter, sir?"

"No need. Paulo needs to become familiar with the city."

This time the servant seemed to give Leo a much more appraising look. Leo returned a challenging glare.

"Very good, sir. I shall park your 'coach and fetch a paper. Shall I find you here?"

"No, you'll find us at the estate. Come along, Paulo."

Passersby didn't pay Leo much mind but everyone seemed to know Gordo. The minimum courtesy was a friendly handshake, but many vendors offered free fruit or the catch of the day. He was asked about his journey to the capital along with several 'have-you-heard' pieces of gossip, and even a reminder regarding an unmarried daughter. While Leo drank in the sights of idyllic Seaside, he found he spent a lot of time staring at Gordo in wonder.

Teddori had been loved but never feared. Nerus was ruthless but despised. Leo tried to puzzle out how Gordo Bellacolla managed both.

Their walk took them from Seaside up to a raised portcullis, the threshold to a walled canyon. Guards dressed in traditional armour and red-and-green livery, carrying halberds and bored expressions, flanked the entrance to the crevasse. Both of them tipped their helmets to Gordo as he passed by.

Entryways to homes and businesses lined the walkway, built right into the sides of the canyon. Windows dotted the walls above. The most prevalent features of all were the laundry lines, strung across from one side to the other, sheets and unmentionables billowing in the soft sea breeze that whistled through the canyon.

"There's a saying here," Gordo said as they strode down the narrow street. "In Chavicci everyone can see your dirty laundry. The miners, however, have a different saying: When you fart in Chavicci, everyone gets a whiff."

Leo chuckled despite himself.

"Everyone is going to have eyes on you here, especially because you're with me, and everyone is going to have an interest in what you do. This is a tightly-knit community...though perhaps I don't have to impress upon you what that means, given where you came from."

The winding street opened onto a railed precipice overlooking the bay, devoid of other pedestrians. Undaunted by heights, Leo leaned over the railing to see the ships down below that looked like bathtub toys. He spat over the edge and watched the gob sail down, then snickered. Gordo stopped walking and gave Leo a long glare.

"And Paulo. Stop that nonsense. You left childish things behind you when you killed a man, I hope. You are my ward now and will behave accordingly, or I'll send *you* over the edge."

Leo didn't believe Gordo would make good on such a threat, given how invested he seemed in Leo's future.

"Just enjoying a taste of freedom," he said.

"Freedom," Gordo said as he continued walking, "is an illusion. We all carry burdens, Paulo. Chains of responsibility, fetters of love, shackles of caste. The key to power is to choose your chains."

They had come upon an immense carved threshold done in the classical style of the first empire. Two great pillars rose up on either side of the entrance, embellished with depictions of gods and goddesses. Like the portcullis, the entryway was bordered by two guardsmen in livery and armour. Above the darkoak double doors, a slogan in ancient Noven had been carved into the rock. Leo didn't know what it meant, but he vowed to find out as soon as possible.

This time, the guards didn't just nod to Gordo. They bowed.

"And holding the key to the chains of others, Paulo, trumps all."

"Why?"

"Because then you can offer them freedom."

Beyond the threshold, a furnished foyer was lighted by crystals. It was empty save for a lone boy. Judging by his face, the boy looked to be about Paulo's age, but he had the shoulder width and musculature of a grown man. He was seated upon a lounging bench, reading a book and absentmindedly twirling a small blue crystal with one hand. As Gordo and Leo approached, the boy looked up and tossed a mop of blonde hair out of his eyes.

"Who's this kid?" he asked as he assayed Leo.

"This is Paulo," Gordo said before Leo could reply for himself. "He's going to be staying with me now, as my adopted son."

"Adopted son?" the boy looked affronted.

Gordo cuffed the boy upside the head.

"The correct response is 'nice to meet you, Paulo.'"

Paulo could tell the young man was fighting back tears.

"Nice to meet you, Paulo," he said through gritted teeth. "I'm Titus."

Chapter 50

22 Aprila, 1879

Farewell to research, farewell to career, farewell to succeeding De'Cadomus someday. I'm fucking pregnant. One of the snakes sabotaged my green ring, I just know it. Fucking Largo, knocking me up. I should have killed him when I was supposed to. Typical Maria, though, doing the opposite of what's good for her...marry the asshole just because he's the only man with balls in this city who doesn't wear a robe.

And now my research journal is becoming a godsdamned diary of tears. Still, if I don't get this out I'm going to explode. If I don't get rid of this baby I'm going to explode, but every time I bring out the green ring I get all shaky and start crying. I can kill anything without remorse except for a thing that doesn't even draw breath yet.

This would have been easier if I'd known my own mother.

They'll take it all away as soon as they find out about it. The crystals. My knighthood. Gods know what else the old viper will do. Probably try to kill Largo himself. That would be interesting to see.

Sometimes I wonder how my life ended up this way. What if I'd run off with the Dori when I'd had the chance? What if I'd never joined the priests? What if Largo had died in the war?

It's a good thing nobody will read this so long as I live. An insight into the anticlimactic downfall of Novem's greatest modern assassin.

Crystara read the last line over again and again.

Novem's greatest modern assassin.

It cracked everything she had ever believed about her family. She'd had precious little to believe in the first place, given a father who never shared anything and a mother she barely remembered. A mother who killed for the church, killed for the very man who now kept Crystara under his thumb. The man who had, in turn, killed Crystara's mother. That was Crystara's deduction, at any rate.

Crystara's life seemed to be one bitter irony after another. She had unwittingly continued her family's legacy: murder.

The door to her room opened so suddenly that she gasped, tossing the journal into the stacks in her panic. She scrambled for her mother's necklace in its hidden spot, clutching the chain between her fingers and whispering a red alignment as she spun around on her knees, prepared to face off against De'Cadomus at last.

Except it was Titus who stood before her with an odd smirk upon his face.

"Sorry I took so long," he said. He stood in the doorway, staring at her with a hungry expression.

"You cracked dully," Crystara said, releasing her breath. "I just about sent you through the orange."

"I came as soon as I could." He took a step toward her. "I don't have much time." His arm reached around her waist and he pulled her in for a kiss. She allowed it, for a moment, flirting with the notion of letting go completely.

"Wait," she said, holding his jaw in her hand. "What's your hue in all of this? What do you want?"

"You," he said as he planted kisses along her neckline. She shivered and told herself to remain focused. Crystara gently placed her mother's necklace on a stack of books, making herself appear ugly again.

"Yeech," Titus exclaimed as he backed up. "Put the necklace back on."

"What, you don't find me attractive anymore?" she teased, swaying her hips.

"I don't know what you're saying now," Titus said, reminding her of the ring's curse.

"Godsdamnit," she said as she donned the necklace. "I'm not letting you near me until I know you're on my side."

"*Your* side? I'm the one who has no idea how you're aligned." He folded his arms, curiosity winning out over lust. "You crack the Great Crystal, kill the old keeper and one of the betrothed, then get cursed by the viper but take lessons from him. What's your plan?"

"My plan is to kill the viper, then survive a possible reprisal from the Council. Shouldn't be too hard, considering I'm supposed to be dead anyway...besides which, I'm sure they have a vested interest in me beyond De'Cadomus's teachings. What about you, hmm?" She circled him slowly, assessing him. "Who do you work for, really? On paper you're a snake, but I know there's someone else whispering in your ear. Is it *just* the Council?"

He grabbed her arm and pulled her in for another kiss.

"No more talk," he said, balling up his fist in her hair. In his impassioned kiss, he let his guard down slightly, and while he focused on her lips, she concentrated on his mind.

Her training under De'Cadomus hadn't been for nothing. She decided to shelve the knowledge of Titus's true intentions until she needed it. For the moment, it was enough to know he wasn't working for the viper *or* the Council. It was enough to know that he wanted her.

She grabbed his baldric and dragged him backward until she stumbled over a stack of books, falling over with Titus on top of her. He started laughing and so did she, imagining uncomfortable places to have papercuts and the nervous thrill of possibly being caught.

"Fuck me," she whispered into his ear, knowing full well that making love had been his intention since barging in on her. As he excitedly peeled off her roughspun tunic, she whispered a bodily protection alignment to her necklace and it glowed green. Just a little insurance against accidents, she told herself, thinking of her own mother's plight. Then Titus was kissing and nibbling her breasts, almost gently, not appearing to be in any kind of rush.

He looked up and planted a kiss upon her chin.

"You're godsdamned beautiful, Crystara," he said. She looked into his pale blue eyes, her heart soaring with the knowledge that he meant what he had just said.

Though no longer a complete mystery, Crystara found that Titus was still a surprising young man. As his kisses went lower and lower upon her body, she decided she would make an ally out of him yet.

***

Crystara's next visitor was De'Cadomus.

She was glad she'd sent Titus away after their lovemaking. His presence would have been a dead giveaway to the keeper that Crystara had overcome the curse of the ring. When De'Cadomus burst in without so much as a knock, Crystara was also glad she'd maintained the presence of mind to hide her mother's necklace.

A dim blue glow from one of the viper's rings was the only light as he walked up and loomed over her. "Wake up," he rasped.

"I'm awake," she said, rubbing her eyes. "What time is it?"

"No questions. Follow."

Crystara suppressed her urge for defiance. It was unnecessary until she at least knew what the viper wanted. He seemed to alternate between cruel and conniving. For the moment, Crystara was relieved he was in the mood for the latter. She stood and followed him out of the library and into the courtyard. It was dark and foggy. There was no sign of the moon.

"You've said it speaks to you," De'Cadomus said.

"Yes."

"I want you to speak with it now."

"Why?"

"I said no questions." He entered the temple proper alongside her.

"I can't help you if you keep me in the dark."

"Fine." They entered the keeper's office. De'Cadomus shut the door. "I know what books you've been reading and I know about your friendship with Sir Titus. I know that you've learned a bit about me. I came from a noble line, but I'm also half Dori."

Crystara raised an eyebrow. De'Cadomus was still unpredictable at times. She certainly hadn't expected him to be forthright regarding such a secretive subject as *himself.*

"What does that have to do with the Great Crystal?"

"Come now. You don't really believe it speaks for the *Noven* gods, do you?"

Crystara suddenly recalled an old legend Orvin had mentioned to her once: *Many heathen religions believed that it contained the souls of dead gods, hence its power...*

"I don't believe it speaks for *any* gods. Or that it has only one voice."

De'Cadomus's smirk was altogether sinister in the dim light. "Clever," he said, opening the door to the Crystal Chamber. Beyond, the Great Crystal seemed to beckon. "The study of the Great Crystal has been a scholarly pursuit for many keepers...but there are several millennia of secrets hidden within."

"Aren't you concerned with what *it* wants?" She stared up at the brilliant sphere, her hands upon the railing.

"No."

"Maybe that's why it won't talk to you." Crystara winced and prepared for a rebuttal. She reminded herself not to push him too far. Her freedom from the ring's curse had to remain secret, for the moment.

"You cracked it and it still speaks to you."

"Because it has plans for me."

"What plans?" An urgency grew in his voice.

"I don't know," she admitted.

"Touch it."

Crystara bit her lip. Whatever the Great Crystal's plans were, she knew they involved her working against De'Cadomus. A voice had given her the lockbox numbers, another had helped her find her mother's necklace. She didn't imagine the crystal would reveal its intentions to the viper so readily.

After a moment of hesitation, she touched the crystal, hoping to allay De'Cadomus's impatience. The surface was cool to the touch, smooth and unyielding. It felt as any other crystal would. Crystara heard no voices, felt no pulse from within the great rock. It was as silent as ordinary stone.

"Well?" the viper asked. "What is it saying?"

Crystara was aware of a presence behind her, loitering at the keeper's office door. It was Titus. She sensed Rossi's thoughts a moment later. De'Cadomus appeared so focused on the Great Crystal, he hadn't noticed the interlopers.

"Nothing," Crystara said, truthfully. "It's saying nothing."

"What do you mean, nothing? It has spoken to you before, unless you were lying to me."

"Well, it's not speaking to me right now."

He grabbed her by her collar and shoved her toward the crystal's surface. "Make it!" he commanded.

"I don't know how," she said, hoping that he couldn't see her smirking. Titus had clearly orchestrated something. There were other witnesses, priests and sisters, listening in at the main door to the Crystal Chamber. They could hear everything De'Cadomus said, but Crystara's words would still be garbled nonsense. She couldn't have planned it better. The viper was cracking.

"Make it!" he shouted, striking her face with the back of his fist. She fell to the floor, then felt the telltale itch of her cursed ring. Making a show of it, she screamed as she pretended to feel the old pain rippling through her body.

Red-faced, De'Cadomus turned to the Great Crystal.

"Why won't you speak to me?" he demanded. He struck it with a fist. Crystara thought she heard one of his crystal rings pop and shatter. Then he spun and glared at Titus and Rossi, who were still standing in the doorway, mouths agape.

"What the fuck are you two staring at?" he demanded. "This room is restricted to all but me."

Titus ran over to Crystara and lifted her to her feet. She tried not to blush.

"What in the abyss are you doing to the urchin?" Titus asked.

"You know damned well that..." De'Cadomus stopped himself. "Get her out of my sight. All of you. Get the shard out of here. Now!"

Chapter 51

Every poor child in Novem dreams of being discovered as a crystal speaker, and with good reason. In a nation where your identity is shaped so rigidly by your family name and your caste, speaking is a path to a better life. For the noble or wealthy, it means prestige.

Any sufficiently talented and motivated speaker in Novem has a number of opportunities available to them upon completion of their studies. Once they receive certification from the Republic and are licensed to speak to crystals outside of an academic setting, most are approached with offers of employment. Reports from the academies of Novem state that 90% of graduating speakers are employed as speakers within a year of completing their studies. Of the remaining 10%, it is suggested that up to 8% of these speakers spend time abroad or accept positions at companies and academies outside of Novem, although the Noven Republic works diligently to keep its speakers at home. The post-war society learned well the value of propaganda, and entire media campaigns are targeted at crystal speakers, citing the monetary and social benefits of remaining within Novem's borders as a speaker. Three of Novem's most popular radio shows, Speaker for Hire, Crystal Captain, and The Knights of Jova, feature crystal speakers as protagonists.

Speakers gain respect in Novem, but most organizations start at the top of the ladder and work their way down. This perpetuates the institutionalized caste, family, guild, and fraternity system that has been Novem's social model for over two thousand years. Nobles, due to family wealth and social standing, will always have their pick of the best openings available, unless a truly prolific speaker comes along. Over 60% of government speakers are reported to be from the noble caste, although statistically less than 5% of all Noven speakers are nobles. Of the less than 40% from the lower castes, most are employed within municipal police forces. The guilds tend to hire from their own families, and the alchemist caste hires exclusively alchemist speakers as a matter of policy.

For the impoverished speaker, options are fewer. However, a speaking license alone is a symbol of success. The Church of Novem has always been regarded as the least picky when it comes to social standing, and many speakers will opt to join the priesthood as an easy way to gain comfort, security, and a quick leap from the lower to upper castes. The Engineers' Guild will also pluck a few talented individuals from the lower castes, but this is fairly rare.

The bulk of lower-caste speakers choose to climb the ladder by becoming scholars or military officers. Many scholars continue their studies until they achieve Master or Doctor status, going on to choose from the best tenured positions at Noven academies and finishing schools.

While most of Novem's military speakers, and indeed, most of a generation of Noven men were lost during the Great War, the military of the Fifth Republic had little trouble recruiting young speakers to fill their officer positions. Although the conquests of Emperor Longoro are seen as a great source of national shame by the Noven people, an officer's salary is a difficult thing for the son or daughter of a miner or farmer to pass up. Novem was not the only Titanian nation that found itself luring the lower classes into the military after the devastation of the Great War.

Licensed crystal speakers also find positions as private consultants. Occasionally, affluent Noven nobles or entrepreneurs will hire a speaker for a 'residency,' though most of these are glorified bodyguard positions. More common are arranged noble marriages, where a female crystal speaker from a lower caste will marry a male noble. Although nobles often seek to establish speaker legacies in this manner, the unacknowledged statistical truth is that most Noven crystal speakers come from the lower castes, despite centuries of cross-caste marriages.

--Edward Burke: A Study of the Modern Speaker and the Utilization of Crystals in Post-Industrial Novem

***

"Where are you going?" Marco asked.

Jacoby, whose hand was on the knob for the back door, rolled his eyes at his brother.

"None of your business," he said, carefully adjusting his book bag. Marco glanced at him accusingly.

"Except it is my business," Marco insisted, folding his arms. "You're grounded, remember? Mother and Father asked me to tell them if you went anywhere while they are out."

"I'm just going over to Racquela's," Jacoby replied. "I have some homework for her." It was half a lie. He *was* going to see Racquela, but his visit had nothing to do with schoolwork.

"You're lying," Marco said. "I can tell."

Jacoby took his hand off the knob.

"You are so annoying. Why couldn't I have been an only child instead of having a brother who's not only a stupid snitch but a better empath than me?"

Marco smiled at the back-handed compliment.

"Where are you actually going?"

"Racquela's, I told you."

"Why?"

"None of your godsdamned business!"

"I'll telegram Dad right now and tell him," Marco threatened.

"I'll beat the shatters out of you if you do."

"Then I'll double-tell on you for sneaking out *and* for beating me up, and then you'll be in *real* trouble."

Jacoby let out a long-suffering sigh. He could tell from his own empathy that Marco wasn't bluffing. His only option was to reason with his brother, convince him it was in his best interests not to tell a soul.

Try honesty, a part of his mind suggested. Lying always seemed to get him into worse trouble, and Marco was sensitive enough that Jacoby could appeal to his sense of fairness.

"Okay, look. Marco. I *am* going to see Racquela. But it's not about homework." He opened the icebox and withdrew the half-full bottle of milk, pouring out a glass for each of them.

"I knew it," Marco said, pleased at his own deductive reasoning.

"You have to promise not to tell anybody this," Jacoby insisted.

"Except for Mom and Dad."

"*Especially* not Mom and Dad. Do you understand what's at stake here?" Jacoby grabbed two apples from the icebox and tossed one to Marco.

"I like it without the skin."

"Then cut the skin off, you big baby."

"Mom does it better."

"Gods, Marco. How are you ever going to get good at something if you don't do it for yourself?" He huffed and withdrew a knife from the drawer, slamming it down on the counter in front of Marco. Marco stared at it like it was a crystal grenade.

"What if I cut myself?"

"Then you learn to be more careful. Just try it, for Jova's sake. And listen."

Marco grasped the knife, holding it gingerly. With a look of intense concentration he began to peel his apple. Jacoby's own apple was crisp as he bit into it.

"Do you remember that detective who was here the other day?" he asked between bites. Marco stopped mid-peel and stared at Jacoby.

"Of course I do, he sat in the parlour talking to Mom and Dad for over an hour waiting for you to get home. I...listened in on your conversation in the back yard."

Jacoby was about to get angry at his brother for eavesdropping, but it saved him the time of explaining the situation.

"Then you understand what's at stake."

"So this is about spying on your friend Paulo's secret group?" Marco put down the apple and knife. "Why can't Tim do it?"

"Paulo's not my friend. And this isn't about spying. It's about looking out for Racquela. She's in danger, and so is Tim. I just have to deliver something to her."

"What?"

None of your business, he wanted to say again, but he needed Marco on his side.

"Crystals."

Marco raised an eyebrow. "But you told the inspector you didn't have any."

"Marco. Lives hang in the balance. If I told everybody the truth, I would probably get arrested and be powerless to stop anything from happening. Timori and Racquela are both in very real danger and I'm the only one who can help get them out of it.

Do you understand? You heard me talking to Martinus. Paulo isn't my friend. He's a killer and a criminal. And he's..."

"Did you really see him kill someone?" Marco's voice grew quiet.

Jacoby paused. He was about to take another bite of his apple but realized he had no more appetite.

"Yes."

"Don't go, Jake." Marco's eyes were watering. "I have a really bad feeling about this. Please just stay home."

It was enough to give Jacoby pause. The last time Lenara had said something similar the premonition had led to her death. She had claimed her clairvoyance was a unique, unprecedented ability, but Jacoby had seen enough of the world to expect the unexpected. Whether or not Marco's plea was motivated by a sense of the future or out of fear, Jacoby couldn't let it deter him. Racquela had to be able to see Paulo for his true self.

"I have to do this," he insisted, gathering up his book bag.

"Then I have to tell Mom and Dad," Marco insisted, folding his arms.

Jacoby downed his milk in a single gulp, wiped his lips with his sleeve, and regarded his brother carefully.

"You're damned stubborn for someone who can't even cut a piece of fruit."

Marco picked up the knife again, as though determined to prove Jacoby wrong.

"Keep this a secret and I'll teach you speaking," Jacoby offered.

"I'm going to learn it next year anyway." The knife slipped as Marco was cutting and dug deep into his finger. He flinched and shook his hand, spattering blood across the counter. A droplet or two even went into his milk. "Shatters," he exclaimed. "See? This is why Mom does it for me. I'm a dully with a knife. And you gave me the *dull* knife from the drawer."

"Don't be such a baby. Here." Jacoby whispered to his ring and it glowed green. Marco's wound mended itself, leaving no trace of torn flesh.

"I didn't know you could heal people with crystals." Marco examined his hand with disbelief.

"That's something they don't teach you in school. If you keep this a secret I'll teach you everything I know." Tanni had made Jacoby swear not to reveal any of the speaking techniques she'd taught him to another living soul, but it was the only enticement he thought would motivate his brother.

The war of family loyalties played itself out upon Marco's face. He was a skilled empath for his age, but his expressions always betrayed his feelings.

"Okay, deal. I swear by Jova. But you'd better teach me."

"I promise, Marco." Jacoby tossed his apple core in the scraps bin and reached for the back door.

"Jake?"

"Yeah?"

"Can I have your football if you die?" He shot Jacoby an impish grin.

"You little picker," Jacoby chuckled. "No, I'm having it buried with me. If they get home before I do, stall them, okay?"

"For the price of a football."

Chapter 52

Racquela had brought a parasol not because she disliked the rain, but because wet hair and a damp dress would be a clear indication to Maria that she'd been sneaking around outside past curfew.

Not that she was leaving the De'Trini estate grounds, but she wouldn't be able to put anything past Maria if she was caught.

Racquela knew the guards rarely patrolled near the greenhouse, preferring instead to keep to the perimeter of the grounds and the main entrances to the mansion. The servants' entrances, like the servants themselves, were rarely given much attention.

As far as Racquela knew, Lucius was the only other person who used the greenhouse to enter or exit the mansion. Nobody else liked the greenhouse entrance because it was attached to the basement, a damp and dark series of narrow passageways that were once linked to other estates and castles. The passages themselves were a remnant of a time when nobles were the ones scuttling about using side entrances, serving the ruling Mosind merchant-princes.

Racquela tried to keep the cobwebs out of her hair as she navigated the corridors, crystal lamp in hand and parasol tucked under an arm. The basement had given her nightmares as a child. She had refused to play hide-and-seek with Ignatius and Isabella there, even after they called her a coddled baby. Racquela threatened to have her father fire theirs, of course, but such threats turned out to be empty.

Racquela reached the greenhouse, which was separated from the basement only by a rotted wooden door with a bolt-and-ring latch. Even though she pushed the door open as slowly as she could, the hinges still groaned out a loud note of protest. She waited, listening for footsteps from above, behind, or ahead. The only proceeding sound was her breath, heavy in her own ears. Racquela slid past the threshold and the scent of damp soil came over her. Briefly, her mind flashed back to her kidnapping and she shuddered.

Rain was tapping on the glass above Racquela's head. The greenhouse, like everything else Lucius set his hand to, was arranged in a way that was both pragmatic and aesthetically pleasing, with food-bearing plants on the right and flowers on the left of the lane that traversed the length of the room. The pots were artfully decorated, depicting Noven gods in a Classical style on the right, and on the left, eastern-influenced pastoral watercolours.

Racquela crossed the room hastily, gazing through the glass into the garden beyond for any sign of guards' lanterns. Confident that her tryst would go undetected, she opened her parasol, flicked the 'off' switch of her crystal lamp, and entered the garden.

Without the light of the moon it was difficult to see, but Racquela knew her way through Lucius's stone pathways by heart. Her first word, her first harp recital, and even her first kiss had all been within the confines of the De'Trini garden. Her plan was to be wed there, too. She tried not to become distracted as she fantasized about wedding dresses and kissing Paulo under the whiteoaks.

"Racquela," a voice whispered from the bushes. She nearly screamed. Jacoby emerged from a hedge, brushing off twigs and leaves. A part of her wished it was Paulo instead, sneaking into the estate because he couldn't keep himself away from her, but the last time she'd spoken to him at Central, he'd brushed her off. *Busy indeed,* she thought. With the help of Jacoby's crystals, she'd find out just how busy he really was.

"Do you...?" he began, but she shushed him with a finger to his lips. They were still too exposed. She grabbed his hand and led him down the pathway to the hedge maze. The guards never bothered with the maze. Only a handful of the denizens of the estate knew how to successfully navigate it.

Thankfully, Jacoby said nothing as Racquela led him swiftly through the lanes among the ten-foot-tall manicured hedges. She imagined that after the things he'd done he was accustomed to the unspoken rule of a secret rendezvous: say nothing until you are certain there are no witnesses.

At the centre of the maze was a white gazebo covered in ivy that climbed to its peak. They found shelter there, taking a moment to catch their breath as the rain intensified. Suddenly it was pouring so loud Racquela was sure she would have to shout to be heard. Lightning flashed, illuminating the two of them. Jacoby's face was a tableau of amusement.

"Kind of sexy, isn't it?" he said into her ear. She could feel his breath upon her neck and shoulder. "Meeting late at night at a secret gazebo, rain soaked?"

"Sure," she admitted. It did have a romantic appeal, but it wasn't why she had asked him there. "Why couldn't we have done this at Central?"

"I was worried Miss Telmari would sense my crystals," Jacoby said. "This was the only safe way to deliver them to you. They are...unregistered."

From his book bag he produced two clear crystal rings, both of which were completely unmarked and unadorned. They looked nearly identical to the betrothal rings.

Racquela took a ring from Jacoby's outstretched hand and examined it.

"How do they work?" she asked. "I don't know speaking."

"You and I set up the illusion ahead of time," Jacoby explained. He pushed his rain-slick hair out of his eyes. "A disguise. One for you and one for...Isabella? The Isabella one is easy because we tell the crystal to make her look like you. The other one depends on what kind of disguise you want to use. This is...to see Paulo, right?"

"Yes," she said. "But I can't go as myself. Not after what happened at Crystus Hill."

"Some other disguise, then? Maybe a valley girl?"

"No," Racquela said decisively. "Not a girl at all."

"That...will require some careful whispering."

"You can do it, though?" she grabbed his arm. "You're good at speaking."

He shrugged. She couldn't tell due to the darkness, but she guessed he may have been blushing.

"I can give it my best swing. Here." He took the ring she was holding and placed it on her finger.

"Jake, I..."

"Shh. I have to concentrate." He got to his knees, holding her hand in his. His lips were so close to her fingers it made her spine tingle, but he didn't kiss them. He merely whispered a phrase or two, too quietly for Racquela to make out over the rain. The crystal ring glowed pink briefly, then was translucent once more. Racquela twisted and scrutinized it.

"I don't feel any different."

"You won't, even with the disguise. And you won't look any different. That ring is for Isabella."

"What about mine?" She removed the ring and handed it to Jacoby, switching it for the one in Jacoby's palm.

"Well, I have to whisper to it first," he said, grasping her hand and pulling himself to his feet. The pull brought them together, so close that Racquela could smell Jacoby's aftershave.

Inadvertently, she made a puzzled expression. When had her first finishing school crush started shaving?

"Do you ever wonder...?" he began, his fingers touching hers.

"Wonder what?" she asked. She remembered a night she and Jacoby had shared at a school dance. It seemed so long ago, but it had been little more than a year since that kiss. As Jacoby's fingers intertwined with hers, she felt the cold stone of the rings -- hers in her palm, Jacoby's in his, and the betrothal ring, still there upon Jacoby's finger. It was a reminder that brought her back to reality.

It was Paulo's ring she wanted upon her finger.

"I love Paulo," she said simply, pulling away from Jacoby. Where she expected a look of dismay from him, she instead found concern.

"What...is it that you see in him, exactly?"

"I love him."

"Right. But what do you *see* in him? You can feel love for a variety of reasons, but it isn't necessarily rational."

She folded her arms. He was spending far too much time glancing at her damp neckline.

"I shouldn't have to explain it to you of all people, Jake." If he understood that she was referring to Lenara, a name she was tactful enough not to summon, Jacoby gave no indication.

"I just...well, maybe it is something you need to understand for yourself. You won't see it, not if you're blinded to it." He brought the second ring to his lips and muttered another inscrutable phrase. Again, the crystal emitted a pinkish glow, just for a moment. "There...that disguise should be enough. Nobody should bother you."

"Blinded to what, Jake? Do you know something?"

Jacoby looked up from the ring.

"You saw him kill the Dori boy."

Racquela blinked.

"He didn't know. He thought Dillas was going to hurt me. It was a misunderstanding." Her voice faltered.

"Do you...know what he does? At night? Where he goes? Has he told you his...what he thinks is his heritage?"

"He was raised by his uncle up in Chavicci, he told me. Where are you going with this? I have to be back soon or I'll be caught by Maria. Jake, please. What is he up to at night? Is this something serious, or did Tim send you? Or are you trying to break us up for your own...reasons?"

"This isn't about me or Tim. This is about you. Listen, what if..."

Jacoby paused and the din of the rain filled the silence. He stared at her, his eyebrows knit. Not for the first time, Racquela wished she had his empathic ability, to sense what he was feeling. It would certainly help with Paulo.

"What if *what*?"

"What if your kidnapping was staged?"

"What do you mean staged?" Against her own will she raised her voice. "I was practically tortured, Jake, and I'm not interested in reliving those memories anytime soon."

"No, I don't mean staged in that way...I mean, what if it was a ploy? By Paulo. To seek your family's favour."

She laughed.

"That's ridiculous. Why would Paulo do such a thing? He has my love, Jake, and my hand if he wants it, which he has already said he does. He doesn't *need* Father's approval to marry me."

"No, I mean politically. What if it was to secure your father's support politically?"

"Is that what he's...?"

"Lady Racquela!" the voice called out shrilly from somewhere beyond the hedges and Racquela's heart lurched. It was Maria, undoubtedly, and she would set the guards to search, telegramming her parents away from their party if she was not swiftly found. "Are you out here?"

"Shatters," Racquela whispered. She grabbed Jacoby's hand, leading him through the maze once more. There was no time to open her parasol. She kept the rings palmed, knowing Maria would be far less suspicious of jewellery than anything else. Racquela would just have to twist the truth. Her soaking wet hair and dress would give her away, in any case. She'd had a secret meeting with a boy in the garden. Her parents would be scandalized and double the guard. She would probably even lose her garden priviliges, but it soon wouldn't matter.

Isabella would be the one locked up.

Maria and the guards continued to call for her as she led Jacoby out of the maze to a section of wrought-iron fence. She could see his bicycle propped against a tree by the sidewalk.

"Thanks for the disguise," she said. "You'd better scatter."

She pushed him playfully. Jacoby kissed her cheek before she could stop him. Then he deftly scaled the fence despite its slickness, landing in the soft grass on the other side.

"Racquela," he said, clasping the bars that were now between them. That same inscrutable look crossed his face and he passed her something through the fence. When she realized what it was, feeling its weight in her hand, she gave Jacoby a look of puzzled concern.

"What in the abyss would I need this for?"

"Protection," Jacoby replied. "You might need it more than I. Be careful. And trust your instincts."

He hopped onto his bicycle and pedalled away, leaving Racquela to ponder how to hide a crystal wand.

Chapter 53

Madini
The Happy Thief
Act II, Scene III

Scarlo: Now with this disguise
  Shall I woo the bewitching Donatella
  She who is in love with Rolando
  Shall one day love me, instead!
  Ah, what a thrill!
  As the grouse falls to the bloodhound
  The moon to the conquering sun
  She'll fall for me

(Enter Donatella, upon balcony)

  But quiet now!
  Here I shall hide in this bush
  While the song of the nightingale lulls her senses

Donatella: Oh, what an evening.
  The moon, mistress of the night,
  Bathes the garden in the silver glow of enchantment
  As the nightingales trill their lullaby
  If only Rolando were here
  To share with me this treasure

(Scarlo, disguised as Rolando, reveals himself)

Scarlo: But I am here, my darling, my love!

Donatella: Rolando! How can it be?
I thought you were across the sea!

Chorus: But no, it is not he!

Scarlo: My dove, what a tale!
What a tragedy!
Come down to the garden
And I will sing you the song
Of my perilous journey gone wrong

Donatella: But if my father should see...?

Chorus: But no, it is not he!
Rolando is across the sea!
Whom Scarlo pretends to be!
Oh no, it is not he!

***

"It just had to rain," Timori grumbled in the dark as he shook out his soaked jacket. "I hate the fall."

He stared up at the De'Trini estate from his hiding spot in the hedges across the street. A light was on in Racquela's room, like a beacon beckoning him. It would not be easy sneaking in, and the consequences of discovery could be disastrous, but he had to know the truth from her lips.

Though his face was no longer welcome at the estate, he knew his way and he knew the patrols. Racquela had snuck him in and out of her room a few times when they had been betrothed, but some of the servants had turned a blind eye toward the rendezvous given the circumstances. Timori didn't imagine that they would anymore.

Feeling like half a burglar, Timori crept across the street to the spot where the bushes grew tall and he could scale the wrought-iron fence without being spotted.

His jacket tore on a point of the fence, making his landing less than graceful. A distant beam of light shone in his direction and he rushed over to the cover of a whiteoak. The guards were whispering to each other, too far away for Timori to make out what was being said. He heard the tromp of their boots upon the damp grass as they grew closer.

They were shining their lights in patterned arcs, scanning the gardens for any sign of movement. When Timori saw an opening he dashed over to the next tree. He had found his way to the rock garden. Kneeling down, he grabbed a larger stone and tossed it in the direction of the bushes. The noise caught the guards' attention as their beams of light turned away from Timori, and he took the opportunity to sprint his way to the mansion, avoiding the noisy pebbles of the rock garden.

Timori knew of several ways into the building. Most were patrolled by guards, and the less-frequented entrances were used by the servants. He cursed himself silently for a dully and wondered why he hadn't found the patience to wait for classes on Moonday to wrest the truth from Racquela. Sneaking into the estate was merely the last in a long list of foolish things Timori had done in the name of love.

He knew he would have to make a decision before the guards came back his way. Dashing past the rear entrance, he opted for the greenhouse. Lucius used it frequently, he knew, but not at night.

Once inside, he shook out his coat again, slicked his hair back from his eyes, and tried not to knock anything over as he crossed to the steps that led down into the estate.

He'd never been down in the tunnels underneath the mansion, but Racquela had told him all about how they were once used by the Noven resistance during the Mosind Occupation, and how she and the servants' children used to play games away from the stern eyes of the adults. Timori took a deep breath and braved the jet-dark hallway. It wasn't the dark that bothered him. It was the notion that he couldn't see the spiders lurking nearby.

It took several minutes for Timori to cross a space he was certain was no more than half the length of the manse up above. Several times he'd take a step only to get a face full of cobweb. Timori was sure that, had someone been able to espy him there in the dark, the image of him silently flailing and swiping at his face would have been sublimely comical.

Eventually he saw a dim crack of light, illuminating a narrow staircase leading up. He took the steps one at a time, pausing for several moments to listen every time a beam creaked. The house above made its usual night groans and sighs, but Timori heard little in the way of footsteps or voices. With the tensions growing in the valley, the De'Trini household was not the bustle it once had been.

Timori peered under the crack in the door. He saw red carpet on a wide hallway, with no legs to be seen. He pushed the door open a crack, silently thanking whichever servant kept the door hinges well-oiled. Timori slipped through the threshold, creeping swiftly over to the staircase that led up to the second storey.

His imagination wandered as he tiptoed from alcove to alcove, thinking of all the radio plays where the good guys had to sneak into a wealthy villain's estate or an office building. There were always armed guards, and the heroes were usually caught just as they discovered a vital piece of information or the damsel they'd come to rescue.

Just as he was dashing to the next recess, Timori saw Maria coming around the corner up ahead. He froze, pressing himself against the wall as firmly as he could. From her angle she wouldn't be able to see him, but if she came down the hall and turned her head to the side...

Timori heard Maria turn the latch of a door.

"Mistress Racquela, are you awake?"

"Yes, gr- uh...yes, Maria. I was just...doing some homework."

Timori dared to turn his head and look. Maria was at Racquela's bedroom door.

"Have you seen Isabella, by any chance? I can't find her anywhere."

"Um, no. No, I haven't. Sorry. Wasn't she at dinner?"

"Yes, but now I can't find her. She's not in her bedroom."

"Well...it's a big estate. Maybe she isn't used to it after being up north for so long and got lost. She used to spend a lot of time in those tunnels...did you look there?"

"Why would she go to the tunnels?"

"She...told me once she used to go there sometimes when she was upset or stressed. The dark and quiet made her feel better. She did tell me she was having a hard time adjusting at Central, as well."

"I see. Well, I'm sure she'll come out of there eventually. Are you...feeling all right, mistress?"

"Yes, I feel fine, why?"

"You just don't sound like yourself today."

"I think it's the fall weather. I may be getting a cold."

"Would you like some tea with lemon?"

"No...no, that's fine. I took a sweet drop. Thank you, Maria. That...will be all."

Maria shut the door and came down the hallway toward Timori. He shoved himself up against the recessed wall and held his breath, praying in his head to Saccarus for silence. Maria walked by without glancing his way and continued down the stairs. Timori let out a slow breath, cursing himself for a dully for actually resorting to *prayer*. The habits of early childhood died hard, it seemed.

He remained where he was for a few heartbeats to be certain nobody else was approaching from either direction. Once his pulse slowed he made his way to Racquela's door and knocked as quietly as he could.

"What is it now?" Timori heard her voice clearly through the door.

"It's me," Timori whispered. "Tim."

There was a pause.

"Tim?"

"Yes. Please don't yell. I just wanted to talk to you for a moment."

The door opened. As always, the sight of Racquela took Timori's breath away. Her outfit, however, was uncharacteristically casual. She was in a silk evening robe overtop a dressing gown. Timori supposed that he normally didn't see her when she expected to be alone. The slightly suggestive nature of the attire, coupled with Racquela's wide-eyed wonder at Timori's presence at her door, had an intoxicating effect upon him.

She leaned past him to look down the hallway and he caught her scent. Racquela was using a different perfume than she used to. Timori drank it in, further muddling his concentration.

"Come in," she whispered, grabbing his wrist. "Quickly." She shut the door behind him, locked it, and led him farther into

436

the room. When they reached her dressing table, she let go and they stood, tantalizingly close to each other.

"Why didn't you just talk to me at school?" she asked, folding her arms across her chest. Timori told himself to keep his eyes *up*.

"You're...not mad at me? I didn't want to cause a scene."

"Should I be mad?"

"I don't know." Timori began pacing about the toom to occupy his wandering eyes. "We don't talk anymore. We've barely spoken a word to each other since your rescue. I thought maybe that...something was going on between you and Paulo. In secret."

In the silence that followed, Timori wished in vain for the powers of an empath. It certainly felt as though Racquela was hiding something. Coupled with Jacoby's suspicions and Paulo's behaviour, Timori was all but certain there was something going on. The true question was how long it had been going on *for*...

"What...makes you say that?" she asked, finally.

"Something Jacoby said. You were holding his hand during the rescue...and you're acting strange. You don't sound like yourself."

Timori noticed a crystal ring upon her hand he didn't recognize and his eyes widened. By appearance, it definitely wasn't her old betrothal ring. That had been given back to the church.

"And where did you get that ring? Paulo?"

She stared at him, her chest rising and falling with heavy breaths. Timori was amazed she hadn't already summoned the guards. Ordinarily Racquela wouldn't stand for being questioned or accused in such a way. Something was certainly different about her. Timori wondered if it was guilt.

"It's a friendship ring," she said after an agonizingly long moment, approaching him. It was on her right hand, Timori discovered to his relief. "I exchanged one with Isabella after she returned. Isn't it beautiful?" She turned it on her finger to show him the design. The crystal band had been carved into a swirled knot. It reminded Timori of the symbols the casteless Dori wore on their outfits.

She was so close that her stray hairs tickled his nose. Without thinking, he grasped her hand to examine the ring more closely, a gesture that would have been second nature to him a few months ago. To Timori's surprise, she didn't pull her hand away. The question of Paulo suddenly seemed very distant.

"I..." She turned to face him, eyes looking up into his. She seemed taller than he remembered, but those sensual almond-coloured eyes of hers, unmistakeably Racquela's, somehow seemed more vulnerable. "I shouldn't..." Her breathing grew shallower as their fingers entwined.

"Because...of Paulo?" Timori asked. His head felt fuzzy and he couldn't stop looking at her lips.

"Because..." she leaned in.

Don't question it, Timori thought. *You might never get this chance again. If she kisses you, it either means she's not with Paulo or you can win her back.*

His lips found hers. For a while they stood there, hands locked together, lost in the bliss of the moment. Timori found that Racquela was certainly more aggressive than she used to be. When she began to lead him over to her bed, he wondered if it was all some cracked but amazing dream he was experiencing.

When she bit his lip it was as good as a pinch, and he knew it was real. His heart fluttered not just with the tension of the moment but with the knowledge that Racquela would be his again.

A part of his mind began to protest. Something didn't seem quite right. It was all too ideal, but he couldn't bring himself to say anything. When she shrugged out of her robe and pulled him down onto the bed, he lost all sense of trepidation.

She didn't bother taking off her nightgown and he didn't completely shed his clothing. There was too much urgency and passion to worry about it. They were quiet because they had to be, but it made the lovemaking all the more exciting, full of heavy breaths and muffled cries.

Right at the height of their passion, she cried out.

"Gods! Donaldo!" And her nails raked down his back. The shock of pain was completely eclipsed by Timori's surprise at the name she called out.

He stood suddenly and buckled his belt.

"I can't believe I just did that," she admitted, smoothing down her hair.

"Neither can I," Timori fumed as he began fumbling with the buttons on his shirt. "Who the fuck is *Donaldo*?"

"Oh, shatters," she said. "I didn't mean for this to happen, you were just *there* and I..."

"So, what?" Timori was having trouble keeping his voice down. "That was just pity? Godsdamnit, Racquela, you just know exactly how to take my heart and shatter it with one..."

His words stuck in his throat. She was crying. It never failed to hook him. Fury became concern.

"Hey," he said as he sat down beside her. He put his arms around her shaking shoulders. "I didn't mean to yell. I'm just confused. And...admittedly a little upset myself. All this time I thought you were secretly seeing Paulo. Who's Donaldo?"

At the mention of the name she sobbed louder. "I...I...I'm so sorry. You were just there and handsome and I was feeling so alone and I'll never...see him...agaaugh..." The last word trailed off into a fit of sniffles and sobs.

"Well, don't I just feel a little bit used," he exclaimed as he stood. "Timori, the ex-betrothed you decided wasn't good enough for you, just conveniently there when you need a little bit of physical comfort because you miss your secret mystery lover you didn't bother to *tell* anybody about. Did you think I'd be suckered by the Paulo ruse you fed to Jake?"

In her exasperation she was shaking her hands, trying to calm down. The crystal ring, moistened by her tears, slid off her finger to bounce across the floor but Timori barely heard it. The girl he was staring at was no longer Racquela.

"What the shard...?" he whispered.

"Oh!" the mystery girl exclaimed. "The ring! Oh, shards and shatters. This is not how I envisioned my night going."

"Who..." Timori could do little other than stammer and stare at her. She *was* taller than Racquela, not as beautiful by Timori's estimation but still sensual in a doe-eyed, freckled kind of way. "Oh gods. I took advantage of you."

"I wouldn't go that far," the girl replied with a wry smile.

"Who *are* you?"

There was a loud knock at the door.

"Racquela?" It was Lady De'Trini's voice. "Is everything all right? Maria can't find Isabella and the guards thought they saw someone skulking around outside."

Isabella? Timori mouthed to the girl. She nodded, scrambled for the ring and slid it upon her finger. Instantly, she transformed into a perfect likeness of Racquela. A wave of emotions struck Timori: shock, confusion, arousal.

"I'm fine, Mother," Isabella replied in Racquela's voice. "Just doing some homework."

"I didn't hear a man's voice in here, did I?" The doorknob rattled and every muscle in Timori's body tensed up. "Why is your door locked?"

"I..."

Timori grabbed Isabella by the shoulders.

"Where is Racquela?" Timori whispered.

I don't know, Isabella mouthed.

"Racquela. Open the door, please."

"Just a moment!" Isabella called back. She looked back at Timori. "I promised I wouldn't tell," she whispered.

"Is it Paulo?" he whispered back. The guilty look on her face was proof enough. "Listen," he said as the doorknob continued to rattle, "I need to know where she is. She could be in danger."

"I don't know," she replied. Timori heard plodding footsteps beyond the door and male voices. "She didn't tell me, she just said she was going to see Paulo."

"Dammit," Timori muttered as he made his way over to the balcony. "I have to find her. Listen..." He turned back to Isabella and held her hand in his. "I'm sorry that I took advantage of you. I feel really..."

"I think you've got it backwards," Isabella replied. "You're not going to jump off the balcony, are you?"

Timori heard the fumbling of a key in a lock and he swung his legs out over the railing.

"Wouldn't be the first time," he said. To his surprise, she kissed him before he jumped down. It made him tumble on his landing, but he decided it was worth it. He dashed off for the fence, dodging the lamplight, hoping to find a proverbial crystal in a coal mine.

Chapter 54

Leo's face was a study in revulsion. He turned his head away from the pickaxe, nose in the air.

"You've got to be fucking kidding me," he said to Gordo. "I swore I'd never touch one of those again."

Gordo sat himself at his desk and returned to his paperwork. The pickaxe remained leaning against the bookshelf, ignored.

"That's a dull promise to make when you don't know what the future holds. And cut that language out right now. You're my son now, Paulo, so start acting like it."

"I'll speak however you want me to speak, but I'm not spending another moment of my life picking for crystal in the dark."

"Yes, you are. The miners need to see that you share their burdens if you're ever to gain their trust. And if you want the nobles' trust, you need to behave like one."

"I can't be both," Leo protested.

Gordo looked up from his papers and smiled a knowing smile. "Not yet. It's a long road to a casteless utopia, but as a leader of such an empire you'll need to know how to appeal to everyone. Titus will be mining too, you know."

"Titus can lick my stones."

Gordo slammed his hand upon the desk.

"I said that's enough. You'll do as I say or I'll find another son of Maximus Longoro."

"They're all dead."

"You will be, too, if you don't obey. I have no compunctions about tossing you from the cliff."

Leo assumed Gordo was bluffing, about the cliff and about Longoro having any other surviving relatives, but he opted not to test the man. He'd seen the bruises Titus had earned for mouthing off, and while Leo was accustomed to a beating, Gordo's wrath was far more frightening than a cudgel had ever been. The man held Leo's future in an iron grip.

Without a word, Leo sullenly grabbed the pickaxe.

"Very good. Go through the darkside tunnels to the mine and report to the one-armed man. His name is Lorenzo. Do as he says and report back to me when the shift is over."

Leo slung the pickaxe over his shoulder and left Gordo's office for his room, muttering to himself about Gordo being worse than Nerus. It wasn't true, of course, but it made him feel better to say it.

Leo's bedchamber was on the other side of the estate, past the dining hall and the armoury. He always liked looking in on the armoury, admiring the racked longwands and old swords and shields. They were certainly more deadly, not to mention more beautiful, than a rusty old mining tool, and he vowed to one day learn how to use them all.

Then again, he supposed, a pickaxe could still kill in a pinch. One had to be resourceful.

Before Chavicci, Leo had never been able to call a room completely his own. His bedchamber still felt alien. It was too big, too quiet. Even the bedsheets were worth more than anything he'd ever possessed. The books, however, he wouldn't want to do without. Gordo afforded Leo plenty of alone time in the evenings, which he used to read anything he could set his eyes upon – most of it Noven history.

Above the bookshelf was the only other aspect to the room that Leo liked. It was a tasteful portrait of a beautiful, dark-haired woman. Although it was signed by the artist, it gave no clue as to

443

the identity of the mystery woman. Her face stirred in Leo a plethora of teenage feelings. He would find himself stealing glances at her as he sat on the floor of his bedroom most nights, reading. One day, he promised himself, he would marry a woman who looked like her.

Leo brusquely changed out of his fine clothes – another perk of accepting Gordo's guidance – and donned his old mining rags from the orphanage. The sleeves and were too short and had been so for over a year, but they were serviceable as a working outfit. No sense dirtying up something nice.

Leo took the back exit from the estate into Darkside, where the tunnels were narrow and lit by rough-hewn blue crystals in wall sconces. Darkside was impossibly labyrinthine to any non-local, and after a month of living in Chavicci, Leo had only just begun to feel comfortable navigating the oppressive passageways full of strange echoes and travelling whispers.

Fortunately for Leo, the streets of Darkside were marked by carved wooden signs, though Leo had a hard time discerning why. The locals knew them like a fish knew the current, and visitors generally didn't visit Darkside. They weren't welcome as far as the miners were concerned, and Cliffside or Seaside afforded prettier things to look at or buy.

Leo didn't feel welcome either, not yet. He could still hear the susurrations of gossip from doorways, speculations and judgments about Senior Bellacolla's gangly and sullen adopted son. They didn't know his past and they didn't seem to care, preferring instead to let their imaginations dictate to Chavicci who he was. Leo decided it was better that way. Their guesses were likely more romantic and complimentary than the truth.

He knew where the mines were but he'd never been to visit them. There were too many bad memories. He could still see Arnaldo's lifeless body in his mind's eye. Leo shuddered. Arnaldo had been dull enough to deserve such a fate, but it certainly wasn't how Leo wanted to die. Better to perish with a wand in hand or, better yet, with a woman.

The entrance to the mine wasn't merely inconspicuous. One moment Leo was running his hand along the wall looking for the next street sign, the next he was in a long, cold underground chamber with an uncomfortably low ceiling, littered with carts and sacks and tools. A few men were smoking by a cart full of coal, chit-chatting between the racking coughs characteristic only to those of the miner caste.

Leo was certain *someone* would inform Gordo if he dallied. Everyone knew the masked entrepreneur in Chavicci, and if anyone thought ill of him, they were either too polite or too fearful to say so. Leo decided to approach the men at the cart.

"I'm looking for Lorenzo," Leo said, trying to sound older than he was. His voice had deepened considerably in the past year, but it still betrayed him by squeaking at inopportune moments.

"Who's asking?" a man said between cigarette puffs. His teeth were as black as his soot-stained hands.

"Don't recognize him," a second one said. His teeth were more red than black. It was the telltale sign of a tobacco chewer. "Too scrawny to be a miner."

"Dullard, that's the Mask's new kid," a third one said, swatting the second one upside the head. He had his cigarette between his lips and his eyes held a gleam that suggested he was far more discerning than his two compatriots. Leo, having never heard Gordo Bellacolla referred to as 'The Mask,' filed the piece of information away for later.

"Well, what the shard's he doing down here, then?" the tobacco-chewer inquired.

"I was asked to report to Lorenzo," Leo said. Drawing himself up to his full height, he was pleasantly surprised to find he was taller than any of them.

"Hah!" the man with black teeth guffawed. "Dunno why a whitehand would be sent to take orders from Lorenzo."

"He's no whitehand," said the third man. "Look at those calluses. And his clothes."

"I know my way around a mine," Leo asserted. He understood men like this. You had to be bold.

"So why'd the Mask send you down here, kid?" Tobacco-chewer asked.

Leo shrugged, opting to ignore the 'kid' remark. "To help, I guess," he offered. The men laughed.

"Dunno how much help you'll be, scrawny arms like that," Black-teeth snickered.

"I'll bet he's stronger than he looks," the third man observed.

"He'd better be," said a gruff voice behind Leo. He turned to behold a behemoth of a man whose left arm was clipped off just below the elbow. His surviving arm was heavily muscled, thicker around than Leo's leg. He was holding a sledgehammer as though it were a children's toy.

"You Paulo?" the one-armed man asked.

"Yes," answered Leo.

"I'm Lorenzo, and I don't have time to deal with you. Ferris, take him to the crystal mine. And get him some gloves. Last thing I need is the Mask throwing me off the cliff for letting his new brat touch the black on my shift."

"I'm not a complete dully," Leo protested. "I know what black crystals do."

Lorenzo's laugh was so deep Leo thought it would take down the ceiling.

"Well, he's got enough backtalk to be a picker." Lorenzo left as he'd arrived, with surprisingly quiet footfalls for a man so large.

"Looks like smoke break's over," Ferris remarked as he flicked the remainder of his cigarette aside casually. "See you at shift's end, fellas." With a subtle gesture he motioned for Leo to follow him and left the cart for one of the tunnels.

"You've mined before, haven't you?" Ferris asked, grabbing a crystal lantern on his way into the tunnel.

"Senior Bellacolla was my boss's boss."

"So he adopts you because...you're a skilled picker? No shortage of poor kids in these parts, kid."

"I was raised in an orphanage, but I'm not lower caste."

"Then why did he send you to the mines?"

Leo shrugged again.

"Experience?" Leo could tell the man was prying, but he knew half-truths would serve him better than making something up. "He says that burdens in Chavicci are best shared."

Ferris laughed. The mine tunnel had a deeper echo than the basement dig-site Leo had come from.

"He's got lofty ideals, the Mask does. Lorenzo knows it, or he'd never let the Mask's kids come down here to pick. Takes more than a single whisper to shatter a crystal, though. Still, if anyone can change the whitehands' minds, he can."

"You're not worried I'm spying on you?" Leo asked. "That I'll go back and tell him you all call him 'The Mask' behind his back?"

Ferris laughed again and clapped Leo on the back. "He wears that name like a medal of honour, kid. He doesn't have a lot of enemies left here in Chavicci."

"Did he throw them off the cliffs?"

"Just the one. The rest left after that."

"And...everyone loves him even though he threw someone off a cliff?"

"Kid, I'll need at least two bottles of wine before I engage in a history lesson." He sighed. "Let me give you the short version. After the war there were two men vying for control of this city. The Mask was one of them, and at the start he didn't have a lot of support because he was an Imperial sympathizer and not Chaviccian, either. It all changed when we found out Lomassi – that was the other guy – was the one who had secretly sold us out to the Commonwealth during the siege at the end of the war. You follow me?"

"I know my history," Leo said.

"So we threw Lomassi off the cliffs. Bellacolla did the honours but it's an ancient tradition here. It's how we try traitors. If they survive the fall into the sea, they're innocent as proven by Neovus. Lomassi...well, you could probably find his bones if you're a good swimmer. Only two people have ever survived that fall, far as I know. And one of them is probably just an old legend, unless your history books can prove Princess Caliestra was a real person."

They rounded a corner in the tunnel and came upon a brawny, shirtless blonde man who was hacking away at a section of tough rock by lantern-light. Upon hearing the voices, the man turned to reveal a boy's face. It was Titus. Leo stepped back in surprise. He hadn't realized that Titus, who was a mere year older than he, was so big for his age. The two were of an equal height, taller than most grown men, but Titus was built as though he'd been mining his whole life.

"Me and, uh...what was your name again, kid? We're joining you, Titus."

"Leo," said Leo, before he could stop himself. "Er, Paulo." Ferris arched a curious eyebrow but said nothing.

"Don't need any help," Titus said as he wiped the sweat from his brow with a filthy cloth from his back pocket. He turned back to the stone and swung, piercing the rock.

"Need, want, don't matter, those are Lorenzo's orders. First one to find a crystal goes home for the day."

"Really?" Leo asked excitedly, lifting his pickaxe.

"Don't get your hopes up," Ferris chuckled. "Hasn't happened in almost two years."

"So we're just here to keep busy?"

"No. Lorenzo thinks there's another vein down this way. Ah, shatters, I forgot to get you gloves. Be right back." Ferris left.

Titus continued working, silent except for the grunting and picking.

"You can leave if you want," Titus said, right before Leo took his first swing at the rock. "You don't look built for this. I won't tell Gordo."

"Fuck you," Leo said, putting his shoulders into the swing. "I can pick just as well as you can."

Titus's shoulders shook with laughter but he didn't turn away from his work.

"Uh-huh. I've seen broom handles thicker than those arms."

Leo imagined what his pick would look like sticking out of Titus's skull. An improvement to that smug face, he thought.

"Bet I could outpick you, even," Leo continued.

"Oh yeah?" Titus swung at the rock again, not even deigning to look at Leo. Leo found it infuriating. "Put your shovel where your mouth is, why don't you?"

"What the fuck does that mean?"

"It means prove it, dully."

"I will. I bet I find a crystal before you, too."

Titus merely laughed again and swung, chipping away a skull-sized chunk of rock. Leo flushed all the way to his ears. Lifting the pick, he imagined he was back under Nerus's lash, digging furiously for crystal to avoid a beating and to make up for the other boys when they faltered or fell.

The sounds of the tunnel became rhythmic, almost musical, as the two boys huffed and grunted and their tools chipped away at the rock wall, piece by piece. Leo held tight to the image in his mind. The fear, the hatred, fuelled his work. To look away from his efforts would slow him down, but he did allow himself a satisfied grin when, out of the corner of his eye, he saw Titus glance his way. Immediately afterward, Titus's swings sounded as though they were coming down harder, faster. Leo redoubled his efforts and they worked on.

Soon there was a cartload worth of chipped stone scattered about the tracks. Leo swung down and the sound his pickaxe made was different suddenly. He pulled away a chunk of rock wall to reveal a smooth, fist-sized black stone embedded within.

"Careful," Titus warned, "or you'll chip it. And don't touch it, whatever you do."

"I know what I'm doing." Leo swung again, determined to pry out the crystal so he could return to the estate.

"I can't believe you actually found one. Thought this mine was just dirt now." Titus paused as Leo continued digging around his prize. "Maybe we should wait for Ferris to get back."

"Fuck you. I found it and I'm going to get it out of there."

"But you don't have gloves."

"Don't need 'em."

"Then you're a fucking idiot."

Leo glared murder at Titus.

"You think you're so fucking tough just because you're big? I could take you."

450

"Are you cracked? It was a suggestion so you don't accidentally lose your soul. Gods only know what Uncle Gordo sees in you, but hey, if you want to lose a couple teeth, put the pick down and we can settle this like men."

Leo threw down his axe. He knew he couldn't give the beefy lad time to prepare himself, so he rushed Titus and started swinging, taking care to use his slightly longer reach to his advantage.

Years of fighting the other boys of the orphanage showed in his scrappy style. He managed three solid blows to Titus's jaw before the boy deftly caught a wrist in his grip and wrenched Leo around, then slammed him up against the cavern wall.

"Cry mercy, dully," Titus said. Leo knew Titus would be strong, but he had underestimated the boy's speed. He knew he wouldn't be able to worm out of the grip, so he brought a leg back and kicked out Titus's ankle, wheeling around with a right hook when Titus let go to keep his balance.

Titus pulled away from the punch in time and held his fists up in a boxer's stance. As Leo circled to give himself room to manoeuvre, Titus began throwing jabs. Leo had to bring his arms up to protect his head.

The punches hurt a lot more than Nerus's cudgel ever had, but Leo wasn't afraid of a few bruises. He waited for Titus to extend then ducked, stepping into his opponent's guard and delivering an uppercut to the jaw.

Leo didn't know if he actually hurt the boy, but Titus certainly seemed irate as he threw his full weight at Leo, sending them both to the hard-packed ground. Leo tried to roll so that he was on top, but the other boy was just too heavy, landing with a well-placed elbow that knocked the wind out of Leo. It was followed by a series of blows to Leo's head.

"Nobody wants you here, you piece of dirt!" Titus screamed as he punched. Leo managed to buck with his legs and get his shoulders up. He smashed Titus in the nose with his forehead. They both reeled back for a moment, stunned. Then the punches started flying again.

"Hey, hey, hey!" screamed a voice. "Cut it right now, you two! This is the last fucking time I let kids into the mine." Arms were trying to separate Leo and Titus but they were locked in a choking grip. Leo's vision went starry and he tried to pull away, striking something with his elbow. Suddenly Titus let go. Leo was distantly aware of the sound of something falling to the tunnel floor.

"Oh, shatters," Titus wheezed as he caught his breath. He wiped his bloody nose on his shirt. "Shatters, shatters, shatters. Fuck."

"Relax," Leo said between coughs. "You hit like a fucking hammer, so don't be a wimp about a couple of bruises."

Titus ignored Leo, rushing past him, still muttering curses. Leo turned around to see Ferris slumped on the ground, staring lifelessly at his own feet. The partially-unearthed crystal above him had gone from black to grey.

"Ah," Leo said, rather calmly. He thought of Arnaldo suddenly. "Well, he shouldn't have tried to break us up. He's wearing gloves, though, so..."

"Just shut up." Titus knelt down. He seemed to be examining Ferris, peering into the man's eyes. "It must have touched another part of his skin when you knocked him away." He pointed to Ferris's clenched hand, which held a pair of worn leather gloves. "Put those on and dig that crystal out."

Leo shot Titus a bemused look.

"You still give a shard about that crystal now? We'll probably get thrown off the cliffs for this." Somehow he felt

452

Gordo would save him from such a fate, but he could only hope Titus wasn't shown the same forgiveness.

"Not if we act fast," Titus said. "Get the fucking crystal out of there *now*, or run off like a daisy-chasing coward and I'll do it myself."

"Jova's sake, fine," Leo muttered as he donned the gloves. "Don't see what the shard you're gonna do. His soul is sucked out. Or whatever it is black crystals do."

"Just shut your hole and pick," Titus commanded.

Leo rolled his eyes as Titus dragged Ferris's body out of the way. He began picking around the crystal, which had gone almost the same colour as the surrounding stone. It came free surprisingly quickly, though it was still embedded in a big chunk of rock. Leo turned it over in his protected hands, reminding himself it was time he learned more about how crystals worked.

"Quit staring at it and hand it to me," Titus commanded. "Quickly."

Leo thought about bashing Titus's head in with it, but tossed it to the boy instead. Titus caught it in a gloved hand, glaring angrily at Leo. Titus leaned down so that he was almost cheek-to-cheek with Ferris, the crystal between them. He began whispering. Leo desperately wanted to know what Titus was doing, but thought better of interrupting.

Titus's susurrations ceased. He remained motionless, still holding the rock between himself and the body.

"Come on," Titus said. He muttered something else, but whatever came from his lips, it didn't sound like Noven. Leo supposed crystal speakers probably had their own special language.

Just as Titus's shoulders sagged in defeat, Ferris drew a sharp intake of breath and his eyes fluttered open. He seemed dazed. The crystal had gone from grey back to black.

453

"Oh, thank the gods," Titus said. There were tears down his cheeks and he hugged Ferris, who appeared to be confused as to why he was on the floor.

"Would you two ladies like a private room?" Leo asked.

"I should fucking kill you," Titus said, not breaking the embrace. He helped Ferris to his feet, who merely looked at Titus with a puzzled expression, saying nothing.

"I don't think Gordo would like that much," Leo said, folding his arms. "Besides, I'd like to see you try."

"Why are you even here?" Titus steadied Ferris on his feet and began leading him toward the mine's entrance.

"None of your godsdamned business. Gordo will tell you if he wants you to know. What's wrong with him? Didn't you bring him back?"

"He touched the black, you dully. It'll take him a week before he can even remember his own name."

"Is he going to snitch to anyone?"

"He won't remember a thing. If anyone asks, he was struck by a piece of falling rock. The other miners will know better, but they'll be too excited about the crystal mine re-opening to worry about it. We just need to make sure neither of us treads the red with Uncle Gordo. I'm still gonna punch your teeth in one day, just have to wait for the right time."

"Right after I punch yours in," Leo replied as they returned to the staging area. "Hey, if you're a speaker, what are you doing up here picking?"

"That," Titus said, leading the silent Ferris over to where Lorenzo was standing, "is none of *your* godsdamned business."

Chapter 55

32 Decembra, 1876

Sometimes I wonder if there really is a soul. Black crystals suck your life away and then change hue, and supposedly there's a bit of you left inside the rock, but what about the rest? Nobody's ever come back from the abyss, if it exists, despite what a few crackers claim. And what happens to that supposed piece of soul when that crystal shatters? I've definitely shattered a few in my time.

De'Cadomus once theorized that a big enough crystal with the right alignment could bring a person back from the dead, but I'm not so sure. Priests of the dark ages experimented with re-animating corpses, but that's not the same as bringing life back. Bringing a soul back.

The church's official position is that the Great Crystal is one voice, a voice that speaks for the gods. I have heard many voices. Are they the gods themselves...or something else?

Someday, when I am free of the viper, I will find out.

Crystara bit her lip and shifted on her lumpy cot. She'd read over her mother's diary twice already, but she always stopped to think at that part. If her mother had discovered anything further about the Great Crystal, she hadn't written it in the journal. The entries had ended abruptly not long after Maria's lament about her pregnancy with Crystara.

Crystara pondered souls and alignments and shattered crystals. She never used to believe in a soul, but things had been changing so quickly since her exposure to the Great Crystal. She had heard those voices, the same ones her mother had, and they had agendas...conflicting ones, it seemed.

She glanced over at the loose stone in the wall, behind which she'd hidden her mother's necklace and the book with the crystal puzzle. Crystara had a hunch there were some answers in *there*. It was an ancient book, after all. Box *seven*, no less. If only she could find some way to decipher the symbols upon its cover.

An idea struck her and she rose excitedly from her bed, prying the great brick out from the wall and withdrawing the book. She brought it back to her bed and examined the symbols once again. Somewhere in the massive underground library there had to be an answer.

She heard Dusty hissing somewhere nearby and her clutch upon the tome tightened. Crystara hadn't heard any footsteps, but Dusty hissed at anybody in the library except for her and Lagarus. With cat-like steps, Crystara returned to the hidden spot with the book.

Before she could slide the heavy stone back into place she saw a shadow upon the bricks in front of her. She spun, praying silently that it was Titus.

De'Cadomus was there in the doorway.

"Did you honestly think I wouldn't notice?" he asked, laughing hoarsely.

"Notice what?" she said, voice quavering.

His eyes narrowed and he stepped into the room. "I'm feeling benevolent today," he said. "If you give them back, I'll forget this happened."

"Give what back?"

"You took a necklace and a book."

"Fuck you," she said. "Those were my mother's, and now they're mine!"

She felt a twinge upon her finger as De'Cadomus attempted to work his whisper, but nothing else happened.

Crystara couldn't help but smile threateningly. She felt another twinge.

"Some Master of Whispers you are, *Allegro.* I know what you did to her." Behind her back, she grabbed the necklace from the hiding spot and gripped it tightly, knowing it would undo her disguise. "I've learned more without your help than you could possibly..."

The ball of fire that erupted from De'Cadomus's hands was bigger than Crystara's entire body. It engulfed her, setting the nearby books aflame. Although Crystara felt some heat, she was unburnt.

"You have disobeyed me for the last time!"

Another ball of fire burst forth and Crystara winced despite herself. The power of the necklace appeared to be holding. She kicked her locked book from box seven back into the crevice, hoping it would survive the flames. As the stacks began to burn, the room filled with smoke.

"What are you gonna do?" Crystara asked as she circled, dancing away from the licking tongues of flame. "Burn down the whole library and smoke out the priests upstairs? They already hate you. Just give them one more reason to take you down."

"No, dull child, I'm just going to send you through the orange as soon as your crystals crack. Just like I did to your mother, only this time I don't have the patience for..."

Her fury and retaliation were swift as her ring glowed first brown, then yellow. De'Cadomus's own crystals protected him from the volley of fist-sized rocks that appeared, pelting the walls but bouncing harmlessly off of him. However, it left his guard down when the yellow whisper followed, not a push backward but an unexpected shove from behind, sending De'Cadomus through the doorway and into the burning chamber with Crystara. He was off-balance, careening forward, holding his hands out reflexively to break his fall.

Crystara kicked him hard in the face as he fell and heard his nose give in with a sickening yet satisfying sound.

His arm shot out as he landed on his shoulder, surprisingly spryly for a man of his age. He pulled Crystara's ankle out from under her. She fell, smacking her head against the stone floor. Her ears rang and her vision went fuzzy. She could taste the iron tang of blood in her mouth.

He was atop her suddenly, pinning her shoulders down with his knees. An ornate, jewel-hilted dagger was in his hand.

"Shatter," Crystara whispered.

When the viper plunged the blade downward, it came apart in pieces and he hit her chest with the hilt alone, bruising her sternum. Crystara attempted a push again but he was prepared, the many crystals upon his fingers protecting him from her whispers.

"Die, you back-stabbing little bitch!" he screamed, punching at her wildly. Crystara's protection held and his fists bounced back harmlessly, but she was pinned by his weight, unable to think of a way to bypass his own protective whispers. All around her the books were reducing to ash and the smoke made it hard to see or breathe.

Crystara decided to take a chance. Her ring glowed orange and she drew the flames toward her, hoping against hope that none of De'Cadomus's rings were aligned to protect against the flames he had created. De'Cadomus continued swinging, red-faced with rage, oblivious to the fact that his robes and hair had caught fire.

He swung at her again and she felt the necklace in her hand shatter, having protected Crystara for as long as it could against the flames and the viper's onslaught. The punch connected with her jaw and she thought, rather suddenly, of her father. When

De'Cadomus noticed his burning robe sleeve he re-aligned one of his rings to put it out.

It was the opening Crystara needed. Using her ring, she whispered yellow to teleport to the doorway, yellow again to push De'Cadomus into the burning pile of books, and orange to fan the flames.

Yellow to slam the door, blue to bar it. Grey to make her footsteps silent. She ran.

"Did you hear that?" a voice said from somewhere in the stacks. It sounded like one of the snakes. Crystara didn't have time to read their thoughts.

"The viper said he'd handle it," the other one said. Neither voice belonged to Titus. As she sprinted down the library aisle, Crystara wondered if Titus had been caught as well.

She heard the door to her room burst open and her heart pounded. She sped up. Behind her there was a thunderous crashing of wood as stacks began to tip and topple.

"Find her!" she heard De'Cadomus rasp at the snakes. By then Crystara was passing Lagarus's desk, who asked her idly,

"Do you smell something?"

She had no time to reply. She raced up the stone steps to the priests' quarters, feeling sorry for the old archivist and the mess she was leaving behind. As she peeled out of the quarters and into the sunlight, it occurred to her that she didn't have to kill the viper at all. She could just leave, run straight out the front gate and be free.

As far as the world was concerned, Crystara Mita was dead.

The viper appeared in front of Crystara so suddenly that she reeled and fell backward.

No, she thought. Her ring flashed yellow as she switched to a protection whisper. *I owe it to Mother to defeat him.*

"I've had enough of your defiance!" he shouted as another ball of flame erupted from one of his rings. Crystara's ring sheltered her from the impact, but the flames still scorched her ratty dress and made her hair curl and singe.

Crystara noted that one of the viper's rings had shattered. She knew she could defeat him if only she had more crystals to work with. She wiped the blood from her lips and tried to think of a way through his defenses.

The snakes came barrelling out of the priests' quarters and ran across the courtyard lawn, drawing their swords. Meanwhile, priests, sisters, and guards, curious at the commotion, watched nervously at a distance.

"By all the daughters of Jova," someone exclaimed, "it's Crystara." It sounded like Rossi. Crystara smirked. She was treading the red, but she had put the viper in a position he'd never wanted: one with witnesses, and lots of them.

"Go ahead," Crystara goaded, "get your snakes to kill me, right in front of all these people." De'Cadomus seemed paralyzed by fury as the crowd drew in to hear her. "I'm sure the Council would love to hear about that. But wait...didn't you kill me once already? No? Then who *was* that in Hangman's Square, hmm?"

"This won't save you," De'Cadomus warned. The knights, glancing between De'Cadomus and Crystara, kept their swords at the ready.

"I'm not looking for salvation, *Allegro*. At this point I'll settle for your destruction since you killed my..."

"Silence her!" he commanded his knights. A blade swept down and Crystara winced. She heard the sound of metal on metal and opened her eyes. Titus was standing over her, sword in hand, parrying the other blade.

"Sir Titus," the viper intoned. "I should have known she'd seduce one of you. You've just lit your own pyre, *boy*."

"Y-you can't kill her," Rossi said, standing on Crystara's other side. "Not without going through me, too."

"And me," said August, coming forth from the crowd.

"Would you slay me, too, Keeper?" Sister Florenza said. Soon the crowd was pressing in on all sides, daring the knights to try and take another swing at Crystara.

"You are all going to regret this," De'Cadomus hissed, his voice barely above a whisper. "I am your Council and gods-sanctioned keeper. Did you conveniently forget that she *killed* Keeper Orvin?"

"No," said August. "Nor are we ignorant of your own bloody past, viper. But you will not stain hallowed ground, not to mention our home, with any blood. Not while I draw breath. This is not justice. You promised it and deceived us to fulfil your obsessive ambitions. And now you..."

"Fire!" a quavering voice lilted over the crowd. "Fire in the stacks! Help me!" Lagarus was waving his arms over by the priests' quarters.

"My books," Crystara said, trying desperately to hold back her anguish.

"Gods," August breathed, "it could burn the whole residence down. Go! Fetch the water buckets and call the fire brigade! Every available speaker, get down there now!"

"I'm not going anywhere," De'Cadomus said with a smirk.

"You!" August screamed, pointing his finger in the keeper's face. "You did this, didn't you? Do you realize what you've done? I'll have you de-ringed and hanged for..."

Suddenly August's head left his body, bearing a morbidly comical expression of surprise. Crystara saw a telltale flash of green from a ring on De'Cadomus's hand just before the explosion of blood from August's neck forced her to shield her eyes.

"Fuck," she heard Titus say.

"He's gone mad!" a priest screamed. "Run for your lives!"

"Get out of here," Titus urged. He squared off against the viper and his snakes, flanked only by Crystara and Rossi. All around them the sisters and priests panicked, some fleeing in terror, some dashing toward the smoke emanating from the quarters. Upon seeing August's headless body and the great ring of blood, a trio of guards began to close in on De'Cadomus and the knights.

All had weapons drawn save for Crystara and the viper. They stared murderous vengeance at each other from a blade's length. Nobody dared to move.

"You've cracked," Crystara goaded. "All because you couldn't control me or your precious Great Crystal, and now it's all gone to shatters around you."

"You see nothing, you dull young fool," he replied. "I could have made you the greatest speaker the world has ever seen, but you are too shortsighted and unruly. I've waited my whole life to become keeper, and I'll not let anyone get in my way now."

"Oh, I'm sure the government and the Council will just sit back and let you murder the whole temple."

De'Cadomus's smile was so wide he looked truly snake-like.

"Who do you think appointed me to this position? And why do you think they let you live?" he said. "The Council has more important concerns than the lives of a few useless priests."

"That's not what the Council stands for," Titus said. "Or the Whisper Society."

"No?" the viper replied. "They didn't seem too concerned about the death of the last keeper."

"That was an accident," Crystara said, almost to herself.

"Well," said De'Cadomus, "I'll just tell them this was, too." He flexed his fingers and all his rings glowed.

The shockwave hit Crystara before the sound did and she was blasted off her feet. She tumbled backward across the grass. Her protection whisper seemed to have shielded her from the worst of the blast, but the force alone rattled her thoughts. As she got up she could hear nothing save for a ringing in her ears. Titus was shouting in her face, fumbling for his sword, which had flown out of his hand. Rossi was a crumpled heap nearby. Of the other three guards, one was on the ground coughing up blood, and one had a knight's sword straight through his stomach. The third had a broken halberd pole and was holding the top half like an awkward axe.

Crystara's hearing returned just in time for her to hear Titus scream at her to run before he lunged at De'Cadomus. His blade was met by one of the knights' and they circled, slashing, as the viper glanced back to Crystara with a murderous glint in his eye. Chancing her own life, she added another yellow whisper to her ring and took Titus's foe by surprise, knocking him off his feet. Titus wasted no time in slashing the man's throat, and the soil drank in more blood.

Crystara rushed to Titus's side, fully prepared to die alongside him as the remaining crystal knight finished dispatching the unfortunate temple guard. Far away, priests shouted for more water, and Crystara was acutely aware of the fact that she had nothing but a single crystal ring with which to defend herself.

"Now you will witness the consequences of betraying your oath," De'Cadomus said.

Titus brought up his blade to slash at the viper. At the same time, the crystals on his pauldrons changed to green, and the one in his breastplate became brown. Titus dropped his sword and staggered backward, clutching at his throat as though he couldn't breathe.

"As for you," De'Cadomus said, turning his attention back to Crystara, "I have something *far* more painful in mind."

Crystara's crystal, still yellow, only required a slight re-alignment. She put her arms around Titus's waist, shut her eyes, and prayed that her plan would work.

Crystara opened her eyes to darkness. The change from calamity to quiet was so sudden that the sound of Titus choking was deafening as well as sickening. She heard him clatter to the floor heavily, writhing and kicking.

Amazed that she hadn't teleported herself into a wall or blown herself up, Crystara re-aligned her ring to blue and a cool light filled the space. She was in a hallway of marble, choked with cobwebs. It certainly wasn't any part of the old temple that she'd ever seen.

She knelt down to examine Titus. His armour appeared to be tightening and he was clawing so hard at his throat that the scratches were bleeding.

"Okay," she said, searching for clasps. "Shatters. Shatters, shatters. How the abyss do you take this off?" She hastily re-aligned her ring to purple, and as the light subsided she heard a telltale tinkle. The ring was still holding but she knew it had cracked.

"Fuck," she said. She held the ring over the armour, hoping it would be enough to suspend whatever it was the green and brown crystals were doing to Titus. His intake of breath was so sharp it echoed down the hall.

"Buckles," he said. "On the shoulders. And waist. Both sides. Under…tabard. Hurry."

She did as he instructed, searching in the dark for the leather straps that held the breastplate in place. It was tricky working without light. She had to tug a lot harder than expected to release the straps from their buckles. After a minute or so she had the breastplate removed. She tossed it aside triumphantly and it clanged down the corridor, gathering cobwebs along the way.

"That's one way," he coughed, "to quit the snakes."

Chapter 56

"What in the name of all the gods were you two thinking?" Gordo Bellacolla demanded. Hands clasped behind his back, he paced to and fro behind his desk, a look of deep concern written upon the unmasked side of his face. Leo was certain the man was being somewhat theatrical.

"Leo started it," Titus said. Leo snickered.

"Of all the childish things to utter," Gordo continued. "I don't give an outcaste's shard who started it. You two are godsdamned lucky nobody was seriously hurt, and even luckier the crystal mine is re-opening. The miners are too busy to really look into what happened to Ferris." Leo wasn't certain, but he thought he saw a smile inadvertently force its way onto Gordo's lips.

"So why are we here?" Leo asked. "Everything turned out for the best."

Gordo's eye caught his and there was a grave look there, something Leo had not yet witnessed in Gordo. It spoke of a man whose patience had been pushed past its limit.

"Titus," Gordo said, "go to your room and remain there until you are summoned."

"But..."

"Now, and be thankful I don't mete out further discipline." He waited until Titus had withdrawn from the room. "As for you, orthodox punishments clearly aren't sufficient. Come with me."

"And if I don't?"

"Then you'll wish you'd remained at the orphanage, when I'm done with you."

Reluctantly, Leo followed. Gordo led him out of the estate and onto the Cliffside walkway. The sun was dappled upon the waves of the sea, glistening brilliantly, illuminating the carved face of Chavicci. Leo had not yet set his eyes upon the wondrous city of Captus Nove, but Chavicci certainly had its share of beauteous charms.

"Chavicci has a rich history," Gordo said, echoing Leo's thoughts. "It is the most defensible fortress in Novem, some say the world, and has often been ruled by military men." He strolled down the narrow walkway. Leo followed. "From these cliffs you can see ships approaching from any direction long before they arrive in the harbour. An important talent for a general or politician to have is the ability to discern an ally from an enemy at a glance."

He turned around, bearing upon Leo the full weight of his cold eye and crooked expression.

"You do not possess that talent. Yet. Your upbringing has made you tough, but it has also made you needlessly defiant. You see an enemy in anyone who challenges you. You need to know who your allies are."

Gordo withdrew something from his pocket. Before Leo could react, a trigger was pulled. His body fell to the stone of the walkway, paralyzed.

"Even if it is a harsh lesson they must teach," Gordo continued.

Leo could feel his heart racing in his chest but he couldn't move, couldn't react. His mouth and eyes were still functioning. He screamed in horror as Gordo lifted him up and held his body over the cliffs.

"Help!" he screamed. Below his dangling feet was nothing but open air and the sea far below.

"Nobody will come to help you," Gordo said. "These cliffs play tricks on the ears."

"Fuck you!" Leo shouted.

"I could mold you into the greatest leader this nation has ever seen, or I could kill you now. Your life is in your hands, not mine. Are you going to leave the life and habits of Leo behind, or do I drop you?"

Leo stared down. His impulse was to curse at Gordo again, but he didn't believe the man was bluffing. There was a chance he could survive the fall – someone had before, after all – but Leo doubted his paralysis would wear off before he drowned. He asked himself what was more important: surviving, or showing no fear.

He decided he could still do both.

"Fine," Leo said, his voice devoid of emotion. He told himself to hold it all in, just like he'd done with Nerus. Don't cry or Bruno will hit you again. Lions aren't afraid of anything.

"Fine what?" Gordo demanded.

"Fine, I'll listen to you."

Gordo paused for a moment.

"And what is your name?"

He almost said 'Leo,' but stopped himself.

"Paulo. Paulo Longoro."

"Shout it!" Gordo commanded. "Be proud of who you are!"

"I am Paulo Longoro!" he screamed at the sky, the sea. A wild surge of emotion burst forth from him then, unexpectedly. It was a release of all the rage, all the guilt, and all that he'd left behind in the orphanage. Teddori. His tin soldier. Nerus. Sofia. Bruno. It was a release of Leo.

"I am Paulo!" he shouted again. Gordo threw him to the stone, releasing him from death's grasp.

The paralysis wore off. As he stood, he could feel the fury of Leo receding. In its place was something colder and far more dangerous.

"Well, then," said Gordo, seemingly pleased with himself. "How do you feel?"

"Much better," answered Paulo.

Chapter 57

Jacoby pushed his way into the throng that congested the street around the cabaret, hoping to at least be able to *hear* the man who addressed the gathered crowd. He received a number of elbows to the ribs for his attempt to worm his way through the tightly-knit bodies, and nearly decided to give up and run back to school. He didn't relish the idea of Central telegramming his parents when he was already grounded for missing curfew. However, attending the Labour Party's address was the final thing Jacoby needed to do before he was done with Paulo and the National Socialist Party for good.

"Quit pushin', kid," a tall young woman said as the ranks tightened. "You won't get through that crowd at your size. Shouldn't you be in school?" She turned around to look at him. Her hair was cut short and severe, and her pale blue eyes were equally intense. She couldn't have been older than twenty-five.

"The concerns of Labour affect all of us," Jacoby shouted over the din. He still couldn't hear the man making the speech, and could barely hear himself amidst the onlookers gabbing and yelling at each other. "That means students, too."

"Do you fight for those who can't afford to finish?" she asked.

"Of course," Jacoby replied. "My dad was a miner. If it wasn't for Class Action, I wouldn't be finishing, either."

"So you're a Padrona," she said with a smirk. Behind them, the assembly pressed forward, crushing Jacoby against the woman's backside. Once she steadied herself, she grabbed him by the shoulders and placed him in front of her.

"I've got you, little pally," she shouted into his ear. "So caste issues concern you, then. What about gender equality...does that fit into a young man's vision of Novem's future?"

Jacoby creased his brow. It hadn't crossed his mind until that moment. Crystara would have been raised to noble if she had married Jacoby. Jacoby's mother, however, had forsaken all claim to station in her marriage to Jacoby's father. It occurred to Jacoby that not only did marriage coerce women to more frequently marry up in station, it also limited the options for those who wanted to improve their lot on their own. Positions of esteemed rank in the guilds and academies were only available to men, after all. Suffrage had brought women the vote, but the right to vote was not the same thing as true equality.

He thought of Tanni then: woman, casteless. She was a friend to Jacoby, disadvantaged in every way imaginable. Then Jacoby thought of Paulo and how the young revolutionary had treated Lenara and Timori.

"I fight for everyone," Jacoby told the woman behind him, "regardless of gender or caste...or even those who don't have one. But if I don't get into that cabaret to speak with the leaders of Labour, it could precipitate a major disaster for the party. That may sound cracked, but I swear by Jova I have information they need to hear."

The woman didn't reply immediately but braced Jacoby against another press of the crowd. He could almost hear the voice coming from the crystal microphone inside the cabaret, but it was muffled and indistinct.

"Don't we all," she replied. "Their latest manifesto didn't even *address* sexism in the factories."

"You don't understand," Jacoby shouted. "I have information the leaders of Labour need to hear about a rival party.

Information to protect them. Their lives and the success of the party may be in danger."

She wheeled Jacoby around to face her and regarded him coolly.

"You selling me a false whisper, kid?"

He shook his head. The crowd surged again and he was nearly knocked over. The woman steadied him.

"I know the NSP," Jacoby said, "but I support Labour. Please. I need to get up there."

"All right, kid," she said. "If you're just glowing pink at me you're in big trouble. Come on." She tapped on the shoulder of the man in front of Jacoby. "Hey, Mika. I need to get in there."

"You and me both, Yara," he called over his shoulder. "Did you hear what he just said? It's like they've forgotten about masons entirely. Do they know who built this city? What the shard do they think the miners *do* with clay once it's out of the ground?"

"Easy, Mika. This isn't about platform. This is about the NSP."

"Huh?"

"Just help us get through, would you?"

Amidst shouting, shoving, and arm-pulling, Yara and Mika led Jacoby deeper into the gathered supporters. Soon he could hear the leader of Labour, miner spokesman Barto Sappolio, shouting out to the crowd.

"The Republic knows it's failing, my comrades! It has known since the beginning of the depression, when it could not ease the woes of the hungry and the homeless. It has known since its inception at the end of the Great War. The Republic is the brain-child of those who seek to plunder Novem. It was built upon principles of platitude and passivity, and indeed we have been placid. Making reparations for a war that we, the people, never asked for – paying for the crimes of a greedy ruling caste...is this

471

to be our fate? Slaves forever to the nobility and the foreign kings and capitalists who govern the new god of Titania, the almighty gold coin?"

The crowd began chanting in reply:

"Freedom! Equality! Labour!"

Jacoby noted that Mika was chanting along with them, but Yara seemed more intent on moving Jacoby into the cabaret. The sea of people was even thicker at the doors, and it took Mika plenty of coaxing among the fervent cries of 'Freedom! Equality! Labour!' to be allowed entrance to the building.

The cabaret was packed to the doors with sweaty, shuffling bodies, most of them lower-caste men by the look. Their attention was drawn to a stage in the rear, which Jacoby could barely see. Upon the stage, a tall, ruggedly handsome man with salt-and-pepper hair was screaming into the microphone, backed by a cadre of older gentlemen. All of them wore street clothes and bands upon their arms bearing the red Labour symbol of the pickaxe.

"Well, there they are, kid," Yara said, "but Bart's in the middle of a speech."

"I can wait until it's over," Jacoby said. He noticed the 'Liza officers against the far wall, who were shuffling nervously back and forth as the man on stage decried all government officials to the restless mob. Though the policemen's wands were not drawn, many had their hands upon their holsters. After the events at Hangman's Square, Jacoby knew a few men would not be enough.

"We are the many," Bart continued, "the hard-working majority, and we will be silent no more. When the vote comes, we will show the whitehands that we are the voice of Novem!"

"Freedom! Equality! Labour!" cried the crowd.

"No more gazing up in silence, palms open, waiting for handouts and help that will never come. We are the calloused hands that built this nation and we will take it back!"

"Freedom! Equality! Labour!"

A pit formed in Jacoby's stomach. There was a sense of foreboding, a feeling he got from somewhere in the crowd, and it wasn't merely the unrest of the downtrodden lower caste.

"I have a bad feeling," Jacoby said to Yara.

"What?" she asked. They were chanting again. 'Freedom! Equality! Labour!'

"I said, something doesn't feel right!" he shouted in her ear. "When is his speech over?"

"I think right now!" she shouted back. "Then I'll make sure you talk to him. You might have to wait a while, though, kid. Usually a lot of supporters want to..."

There was a scream from the front of the room by the stage and Bart cut a sentence short. Jacoby couldn't see what was going on but he clearly heard a cry.

"Look out, he's got a wand!"

It was immediately followed by a fanatical scream from the stage:

"For the Republic!"

The wandshot drowned out the din, and the screaming began. The pit in Jacoby's stomach became full-blown panic. The crowd in the cabaret began to push away from the stage as the people outside tried to rush in to find out what the commotion was. Jacoby was crushed between them, the wind forced out of his lungs. He was knocked to the ground and people began to trample over him. He thought he heard Yara shouting for him, but he had his arms protecting his head and couldn't see her. He heard more wandshots and screaming.

Jacoby thought about using his ring to teleport off of the floor but it was a tricky whisper. If used incorrectly it could kill the speaker or someone else. Another boot struck his head, and in his fear he decided to act, whispering a *push* to his ring. The ring pulsed yellow for a second and the people atop Jacoby were thrown aside. He got to his feet and gathered his senses.

Yara and Mika were nowhere to be seen but the stage was awash in blood. There were spatters across the wall, leading to the barstools. A few bodies lay there, one holding up a shaky arm in a silent plea for help. Jacoby heard more wandshot and realized the 'Liza were fighting the crowd, right there beside him. He ducked his head and tried to make his way to the stage without being seen, hoping that at least one of the leaders of Labour was still alive and could be healed.

"Not so fast, junior," said a gruff voice. Before Jacoby could react, he was tackled in a crushing grip and carried off his feet. He tried to whisper another *push,* but a hairy arm was shoved into his mouth before he could finish the word.

"No whispers out of you yet, you little daisy-chaser," the voice said. The man's breath reeked of whiskey and stale cigarettes. Jacoby's panic reached a fever-pitch when he realized who it was. "They used to cut out the tongues of speakers who shattered their promises to the gods. You're lucky I still need yours."

Jacoby's screams, muffled, would never be heard over the din of wands and curses. Jacoby felt weightless as he was carried out of the cabaret.

The fighting had spilled out onto the street. Jacoby's captor muscled his way through a cluster of men and ducked into an alley. Jacoby was shoved up against a brick wall, coming face-to-face with Largo Mita. Largo gripped Jacoby's ring finger in one meaty hand and pinned his shoulder with the other.

"Whisper and I'll break it," Largo said.

"What do you want with me? I need to try and save the Labour Party."

"Didn't you fucking see anything that just happened in there? They're dead, and the party is in shatters. You're gonna help me save my daughter, or I'll send you to the abyss along with 'em."

Chapter 58

"You told him you were his father? Why, in Jova's name, would you do a thing like that?"

Julio had never seen Ramona so upset, not in all the years he'd known her. He wished she hadn't chosen an evening boardwalk stroll for such a discussion.

"I didn't tell him anything. He just assumed that I was." Julio tried to resume his walk but Ramona was rooted in place, arms folded.

"And you didn't bother to correct him? What were you thinking?"

"I don't know...maybe that I've been more of a father to him than anybody else over the years."

"You have *not* been more of a father to him than Ralfi." She shook her head.

"Oh, come on. You only married him because you were starving. You hated him. Or do you have a selective view of the past suddenly?"

"People change, Julio."

"Yes. Yes, they do. You went from a woman who loved me to married with a child in a pretty abrupt period of time, Ramona." Julio had thought their argument would inadvertently draw a crowd of onlookers, but the boardwalk was oddly deserted.

"We've been over this. I thought you were dead."

There was no mirth in Julio's laughter.

"No, no, no...you don't get to turn this around on me. I was alive and well, and you knew it, when you slept with Pietro."

"And so pretending that Pietro's son is *yours* makes it better?"

"It's what he wanted, too!" His scars were itching. "He's all I have left...him and Rob...the war took everything else from me. No matter what I do, I can't escape it. It took you, it took my hand and half my godsdamned face, and it took my ability to lead a normal fucking life, Ramona. So don't get all misaligned about..."

"You chose this," she accused, cutting him off. "You like being a lonely martyr. Admit it. Your life isn't that bad...you're a published Master for the gods' sake! Nobody forces you to walk around without a mask and I know plenty of married men who were scarred during the war. So don't you go around pretending everything that's ever happened to you is my fault or the war's, because you've made plenty of your own choices in..."

She stopped, mid-sentence. There were screams and shouts coming from a street over. Julio heard the sound of breaking glass.

"What the shard is happening over there?" she wondered aloud. Amidst the screams, an angry chant floated over the rooftops: *Freedom! Equality! Labour!*

"Gods, it sounds like they're rioting," Julio remarked. "I'll bet that's over at the Pick and Cannon Hall where Labour always meets."

The angry crowd was bursting over into the side streets. A small mob lifted a bench and tossed it into a storefront window. Three men were kicking a downed police officer and one took the officer's wand, running off to join the bulk of the mob. Some were leaving the boardwalk for the epicentre of the riot, taking up the Labour chant as they did so.

"Jova and Titania," Julio whispered. "I think it's really happening this time." He found that he was holding Ramona's hand. Their eyes met. "We have to get out of here."

Chapter 59

The Wandering Trio -- 'The Bridge'

I saw you there, upon the bridge
Gazing down at waters of darkest blue
I leaned over the rail to see what you saw
And my eyes were filled with a reflection of you

You looked at me through the water's sheen
But you saw right into my soul
Captivated and transfixed
Your spell had taken its hold

I met my love upon a bridge
She caught me in her spell
But while I was gazing at her
She gazed at herself as well

She spoke so softly I strained to hear
And bade me to come across
But as I ran to her with open arms
I wasn't prepared for the loss

I ran to you, upon the bridge
But you were gazing down
And I was but a step too short
Within your reflection you drowned

Oh, had I but known upon the bridge
You never were speaking to me

Your sweet reflection caught us both
But you, it has set free

***

Racquela sought shelter from the rain under the drooping awning of a boarded-up brick building. When Paulo turned his head, she ducked behind the wall of an alleyway and turned up the collar of her coat. She couldn't be spotted by him, not yet, and she was quickly discovering that tailing him was more difficult than she'd imagined it to be.

It would have been easier if she'd been able to simply follow Paulo after classes, but her parents and Maria had to firmly believe that both she and Isabella were safe at home.

She'd taken Isabella up to her room to ensure the 'Racquela illusion' was functioning properly. Then she'd donned her own disguise: men's clothes including a brown trench coat and fedora. Once Isabella was settled in, Racquela had jumped down the balcony and set off for the valley. Her only clue as to Paulo's nightly whereabouts was a matchbook she'd found in his motorcoach. It was from a cabaret called 'The Coal Bin.'

Racquela glanced around the corner. Paulo had resumed his stroll down the lane, quickening the pace of his long stride. She waited until he was a fair distance ahead then began to follow him again, walking as nonchalantly as possible. She kept her hands in her pockets and the brim of her hat pulled down.

It was difficult for Racquela to admit to herself, but she knew she should have followed him a long time ago. It wasn't his love that she questioned – the intensity of his passion was impossible to deny – but Jacoby had planted a seed of doubt within her and it had grown into questions she'd been too blind to ask herself earlier.

Where did he go at night? Why had she never seen the place where he lived? When they met, it was always in his motorcoach, to go to a secluded location. For a man who wanted to marry her, he shared very little about himself. Racquela was no dully. She wanted to believe the best of Paulo. She loved him. She refused to be deceived by her feelings, however. They'd already put her through enough.

The question wasn't whether or not Paulo loved her. The question, to Racquela, was what the boy was hiding, and why.

He looked back at her suddenly and darted around the street corner.

"Shatters," she muttered. She was suddenly glad for the men's shoes she was wearing. Heels were useless at pursuit.

When she rounded the corner the street was empty.

"Godsdamnit."

She could hear nothing but the sound of the rain. There were no footsteps, no hushed voices. It was the too-quiet silence made by people who were trying not to be seen or heard. Racquela checked her pocket to ensure that the wand Jacoby had lent her was still there. She didn't think she could actually use it on someone but it made her feel safe.

"Evening, Cap'n," said a hoarse voice behind Racquela. She gasped and wheeled around, wand drawn. The man who had spoken was short, with a crooked back and patchwork clothes. He held up his hands and backed up a step.

"Easy, Cap'n, easy. Vito ain't done nothin' wrong. Not tonight anyway, heh, heh. I kid! Just out for a stroll, same's you."

Racquela let out a heavy breath and lowered the wand. *He thinks I'm someone else*, she realized. *An officer of the police? Way to make a disguise nobody would recognize, Jake. Well, at least nobody should mess with me now.* She decided to put her acting tutelage to some use.

480

"Did you see a young man come by this way?" she asked. Although her voice sounded, to her, the same as always, she was certain the ring would alter it somehow. "Tall, curly dark hair, handsome...er, well-put-together."

"Maybe I did, Cap'n," he said, sidling up to her at an uneven gait. "Maybe I did. I'd be willing to tell you...for the usual fee, o'course."

Racquela pocketed the wand and raised an eyebrow. It was just like in a mystery story...the detectives always had shady informants with connections in the seedy parts of town. Life imitated art, it seemed...or was it the other way around? Racquela couldn't remember how the saying went. She fished in her other pocket, glad she'd brought some coin with her just in case.

Racquela brought out a centima to show the informant. He scrunched up his face.

"C'mon, Cap'n, you must be joking."

"Fine," she replied, pulling out a dinari. "Tell me where he went."

He shot her another look of incredulity.

"How much is it worth to you, hmm?"

Fine, thought Racquela, *if I'm a tough 'Liza detective, I'll play the part.*

"I don't have time to fuck around," she grumbled at him. "Three."

"Six," he insisted.

"Four and I won't turn you in for trying to bribe an officer."

Vito scrunched up his face.

"Come now, Cap'n, we're friends, ain't we? There's no need for threats. Four it is."

Racquela fished into her pocket and withdrew a five-dinari note, pressing it into Vito's greasy palm.

"Keep the change," she said with a smirk. "Now. Where did he go?"

"Same place he always goes, Cap'n. Home."

Racquela's heart sped up. *Home? Here in the slums? But he has a motorcoach. Fine clothes. A wealthy uncle. There's no way he actually lives here.*

"And where's that?"

Vito gestured over his shoulder at an apartment building.

"Three hundred 'n eight."

"How...do you know this?"

"Ah, Cap'n. I'm paid to be in the know. You wouldn't happen to have a cig on you, would you?"

"I'm fresh out," Racquela said, making a show of patting her pockets. "And don't push your luck." She ran off toward the building, hoping to make up for lost time.

The door, though still attached to its rusty hinges, had a broken lock.

Racquela was accustomed to concierges, butlers, and guards. The apartment building employed nobody of the sort. The dark lobby reminded Racquela quite distinctly of where Timori lived. Junk littered the unswept hallway, most of it consisting of broken dishes and furniture, and the only crystal lamp was flickering slowly, leaving the area in darkness occasionally. Racquela could hear shouting between a man and a woman coming from one of the apartments and a baby wailing somewhere else. She saw a set of stairs at the far end of the hall and crept around the debris of the floor.

The shouting receded as she ascended the stairs, replaced by other sounds: the creaking of the steps, a radio blaring out an episode of *Speaker for Hire*, the sound of a mother cooing and hushing the crying baby. By the time Racquela reached the third and final floor, the only discernible noise was another sputtering crystal lamp.

Number three-zero-eight was at the end of the hallway. The floorboards groaned horribly and Racquela was forced to take her time crossing the space. When she reached the door, she heard muffled voices coming through from the other side. She pressed her ear to the wood and listened.

"...was followed." It was Paulo's voice. "It was that godsdamned snoopy detective again."

"Are you sure?" Upon hearing a woman's voice, Racquela felt her temperature rise. "There's more than one person walking around in a trench coat out there."

"It was him," Paulo said. "Same face, same fedora, even. He's been tailing me for months."

Godsdamnit, Jacoby, Racquela thought.

"Well, what's he want?"

"The NSP, no doubt."

Racquela didn't need to rack her brain to understand the significance of the NSP, but she'd been under the impression that they ended along with the Great War. Paulo's secrets were starting to coalesce into a picture of what he was really doing, but it didn't explain the woman, unless she was involved in the same underground politics.

"So what are you gonna do?" the woman asked.

"Nothing, for the moment." There were some muffled noises, as though he was gathering some things off of a desk or other surface. "If he confronts me, we'll see. Soon it won't matter. The 'Liza will be in my pocket along with everyone else. For now...let's forget about all that. We'll need to join the rioters before long."

The room beyond grew quiet, save for the sound of something just beyond the edge of Racquela's hearing. Then she heard Paulo say:

"Mmm...Sofia..."

Racquela didn't realize she was opening the door until it was already happening. In her rage, not knowing her own strength, the deadbolt holding the door shut came out of its screws and Racquela flew into the room, almost losing her balance.

There in the dingy and dim single-room apartment, Paulo was locked in an embrace with a dark-haired girl about Racquela's age.

"You..." Racquela began, but Paulo slammed into her, forcing the breath from her diaphragm with his elbow and slamming her into the wall. His other arm was against her throat, preventing her from drawing breath or crying out.

"Who sent you?" he shouted in her face. Racquela could feel tears forming in her eyes. She tried to reply but Paulo's arm was cutting off her circulation. "Are you with the 'Liza? Who are you? Tell me!"

"Calm down, love" Sofia said. The casual way she referred to him as 'love' hurt Racquela far more than Paulo's betrayal, even more than the fact that he'd *hit* her. She began to see stars as everything she'd ever believed about Paulo came crashing down around her.

Paulo eased his arm away from her throat.

"Who the fuck are you?" he demanded.

Racquela coughed roughly, trying to fight back tears and formulate a reply.

"Paulo," she said. "It's me..."

He struck her hard in the jaw. Her neck snapped sideways and her face hit the wall. She crumpled to the ground and moaned.

"How do you know my name?" Paulo roared. He followed the question with a kick to Racquela's ribs. She doubled over and coughed wretchedly.

"Jova's sake, let him answer!" Sofia pleaded.

Racquela reached in her pocket for the wand, hoping it would at least deter Paulo from hitting her again while she explained herself. When she withdrew it Paulo stomped on her wrist and she cried out, dropping the weapon to the floor. He held his foot there, grinding her arm with his heel. Racquela tried to force the ring off with her thumb, but the pain shooting through her arm was too great.

"Here to kill me, are you?"

She was about to say her own name, hoping in vain that it would give him pause, but he let her arm go and wound his leg back. He kicked her in the face. The sound of her jaw clicking out of its socket was nauseating – she retched and nearly vomited – and she blacked out for a moment. When her vision returned, Paulo was pointing the wand at her head. There was a ringing in her ears, but Sofia had him by the shoulders and seemed to be making a plea, pointing at the window. He said something without looking at Sofia. His eyes were locked with Racquela's. She saw no recognition there, only hatred.

The pull of the trigger was agonizingly slow.

Chapter 60

The din of the rioting reached Timori's ears all the way up on Avati Hill. He dismounted his bike to watch the lights in the distance, thousands of crystal lamps and torches clustered together, moving through the night like a massive glow-worm. Timori couldn't make out the words of the mob, but it seemed to be a chant of some kind. The throng of lights was close to the docks, but Timori could see it was moving toward the hills.

He tried to decide which way to go. His sisters' safety was a primary concern. Racquela was out there somewhere, looking for Paulo, who was probably at the epicentre of the riot. Jacoby could be out there as well.

He thought suddenly of his doctor friends, Ruveldi and De'Barus. The mob seemed likely to march all the way to Crystus Hill and Parliament, but there would be plenty of looting and destruction along the way. The estates of the hills were likely targets.

"Shards and shatters," Timori muttered. He re-mounted his bicycle and sped down the hill.

The streets were deserted. There was not a horse-drawn carriage or motorcoach to be seen. Shutters were drawn and the occasional Labour manifesto pamphlet blew by on the evening breeze. Far away the din of the riot continued, but nearby was the heavy silence of fear.

Timori could see what the mob had left in its wake. Benches were overturned, mailboxes thrown through store windows. There were scorchmarks on brick walls, and even the doors of some private residences had been knocked off their hinges.

As he approached the wharfs, he started to see bodies in the streets.

Some were in uniform, mostly Captus Nove police officers. Many were miners, Timori could tell by their soot-stained hands. Most had been killed by wandshot but it looked as though a few had met worse fates. The only people on the street weren't there to gather up the bodies. The two frightfully thin young men Timori noticed both shot him wary glances as they picked through the jacket and pants pockets of the fallen.

When Timori reached the warehouse he was relieved to find it empty. The NSP was on the move, as he'd expected, spurring the less reactionary Labour Party into a frenzy with the hopes of using their sheer numbers to overwhelm Parliament. Paulo and his cronies would easily take control, thanks to their planning and the strategic murders of several key members of the Labour Party.

He found the chest where he'd expected it to be, concealed in a corner behind stacks of empty crates that had once contained unregistered crystals. Sometimes Paulo kept the chest hidden in the trunk of his motorcoach, but Timori guessed it had been opened recently.

The chest had a crystal lock but Timori was confident he could bypass it. He withdrew a handheld device from his bookbag. The gadget was little more than an encased white crystal, a dial, and a needle behind glass that gave a loccimetre readout. Timori held the device over the lock and watched the needle rise, then turned the dial to match the number the needle gave him. He heard a click as the lock released on the wand-chest.

"Thank you, De'Barus," he whispered. "Bet Jake would be surprised to learn that white crystals aren't *completely* useless."

Timori opened the chest to find that most of the wands had been removed, undoubtedly by Paulo. Remaining, however, were

487

the walnut shortwand and the beautiful whiteoak longwand with the green trigger, complete with telescoping sight atop the barrel. The longwand certainly wasn't concealable but it served Timori's purposes. Gently he withdrew it from the chest and slung it down the back of his shirt so that the handle stuck out behind his neck. He stuffed the shortwand into his pants pocket in case he needed to draw it swiftly.

He left the warehouse and avoided the main streets, heading for home. Timori couldn't stand the thought of Corti Street, the pride of his neighbourhood, destroyed by looters. He decided he simply wouldn't look.

Thankfully the mob appeared to have left the valley neighbourhoods alone. Most of the looters likely came from such homes, hoping to direct their anger at the wealthy rather than their families and friends.

Timori sighed with relief to find his own home untouched. The mess on the street was the same one he saw every morning when he left for classes. He left his bike leaning against the porch railing and ran inside to the apartment.

Carlotta and Nicola were in the common room. Nicola's nose was deep into a book, and Carlotta was doodling with a crayon on the face of one of her dolls as an episode of *Speaker for Hire* blared in the background from the radio. Timori smiled. He was glad he'd fixed the radio, but doubly relieved to see that his sisters were so blissfully unaware of any political goings-on.

"Why do you have a wand sticking out of your back?" Nicola asked as she looked up from her reading.

"Where's Mom?" he asked.

"I dunno," Nicola shrugged. "Working, I think. She got a new job somewhere. Where'd you get the wand?" she asked again. "Whiteoak doesn't carve itself."

Timori was both proud and annoyed that nothing got past his middle sister.

"Do you know *where* Mom is working?" he asked, opting to ignore the wand comments entirely.

"I think..."

Nicola was startled by the sound of a crackling microphone coming through the radio speaker.

"We interrupt your regularly-scheduled episode of *Speaker for Hire* to bring you an emergency report, listeners. Looting and rioting that began at a Labour Party rally in Avati Valley has spread across Captus Nove. The Republic has issued an emergency telegram, requesting that all citizens remain in their homes. I repeat, stay in your homes and lock your doors. We are getting telegrams from listeners detailing property damage, fighting in the streets, and reports of wandshot being fired. The good police officers of Captus Nove are doing everything they can to quell the violence, and we've received a notification that the army is being mobilized, as well. We are told that currently the rioters are moving through..."

From the radio speaker came the sound of chairs moving and an eardrum-splitting squeal of feedback from what Timori imagined was a microphone being knocked over. Timori and Nicola stared at the radio in horror. Carlotta seemed to be trying to discern if it was all a part of the radio play.

"Up against the wall, all of you." The voice sounded farther away from the microphone. "You, too."

"They've taken the radio station, listeners, I repeat, they've..."

There was a loud crack of wandshot and a chorus of screams.

"Turn it off. The rest of you, faces up against the wall or you'll get the same."

Then there was only static. Timori's mouth felt dry.

"Tim," Nicola said in a small voice. "What's happening?"

He looked in her eyes. She was smart enough to understand, and, like him, wouldn't be a kid for very much longer.

"The Labour Party is rioting because their leaders were assassinated by members of the National Socialist Party, whose plan is to blame the republic. Their goal is to let the rioters and supporters of Labour clash with police while they stage a coup and take Parliament, with help from the Noctra and a faction of the military still loyal to the original NSP."

Nicola blinked. "How do you know all this?"

"I was working for the NSP, back before I realized it was the ideals of Labour that I truly believed in. Go up to your room with Lottie and lock the door. Now."

"What are you gonna do?"

"I have to go back out there."

"What? No. Are you cracked? They're killing people out there." There were tears in her eyes.

"Who's killing people?" Carlotta asked.

"Please, Tim," Nicola continued. "I'm scared. Stay here."

He let out a resolute breath.

"Nicky, Mom's still out there somewhere. And Racquela and Jake and gods know who else."

"So, what? You're just going to leave us here defenceless?"

"Of course not. What kind of brother do you think I am?"

He withdrew the shortwand from his pocket and offered it to Nicola. She stared at it for a while, either in apprehension or admiration, Timori couldn't decide which. Finally she took it from him.

"The kind of brother who gives a wand to his little sister, I guess," she said. "You don't have time to give me a lesson?"

"Just point and pull the trigger. Abyss, you're probably a better shot than I am. Just stay in your room and keep the door locked. If anybody breaks in, don't hesitate to shoot. I have to go. I've lost enough time already." He kissed both his sisters on the forehead. "I'll be back. Don't let anybody in."

"What if Mom comes home?" Nicola asked.

"Mom has a key, dully." Timori turned to leave. He heard Carlotta behind him.

"Why are we shooting people who come in? I thought shooting people was bad."

"Ordinarily, yes," Nicola replied. "But if the people coming in are more bad, we have to defend ourselves."

"How will we know?"

Timori shut the front door quietly, locked it with his key, and sighed. His sisters were growing up far too fast for his liking. He mounted his bike and sped off for Crystus Hill, which he was certain was the mob's destination.

The cluster of lights could still be seen from afar, which Timori spotted making its way up the Avenue of the Gods toward Crystus Plaza. The rioting was becoming widespread as the whine of police sirens and the crack of wandshot echoed through the streets from all throughout the city. There was enough random din that Timori almost didn't hear his name being shouted as he turned onto a valley side street, taking a shortcut to the Memorial Bridge.

"Stravida! Kid! Hey, you! Timori!"

Timori pulled on his brakes so hard he almost went over the handlebars. Ready to dash off or whip out the longwand at any moment, he looked around the vacant street. Emerging from an unlit doorway was Inspector Martinus.

Timori didn't have time to wonder whether or not Paulo's prized whiteoak weapon had a registration number, however. Martinus was carrying an injured man in his arms. Blood was caked on the wounded man's face and he seemed to have taken shrapnel wandshot from up close. Although his wounds appeared disfiguring, he bore a chilling resemblance to the inspector. His arm dangled limply and Timori noticed a curiously effeminate clear crystal ring upon the man's finger.

"Officer," Timori said. "I'm not looting or rioting, I swear to Jova."

"I've got bigger rocks to dig for at this point," Martinus said, "though under normal circumstances I'd ask you where you got that wand. Tell you the truth, I'm surprised you're not with the picker who shot this guy."

"What's that supposed to mean?" Timori asked. He kept one foot on a pedal of the bike.

"Well, you work for him, don't you? Or are you just going now to catch up with the rest of the Socialist Party pickers who are shattering my town?"

"Work for...Paulo? He did that? It doesn't surprise me. But no...I quit the NSP. And watch who you call a picker, 'Liza.'"

"Do you know if he's up there with the mob, then? If so, I'll trade you your bike for the chance to save a life. Someone needs to take this poor guy to a doctor...I shattered my last crystal giving him the green treatment, and I need to find that Paulo kid and bring him to justice. He slipped past me since I had to check on this guy."

"You might have bigger problems. They're about to stage a coup and..."

Timori glanced at the crystal ring again and his legs felt like water. It was the exact same design as the one Isabella had been wearing.

"Oh gods," Timori said as he threw down his bike. "Oh gods, gods, no, no, no..."

He ran over and pulled the ring off. Instantly the hand became slender, feminine. The clothing didn't change, but the hair, the features, were Racquela's. The horrific wound upon her face remained.

"Oh, shatters, fuck, shatters." Timori grabbed her hand and fell to his knees on the street. He pressed her fingers to his forehead and moaned as hot tears streamed down his cheeks. "Gods, this is all my fault. All my fault."

"Oh, shatters, kid, I'm sorry. That's one hell of a whisper on that ring. Is this your girlfriend?"

"Racquela..." Timori whispered.

"De'Trini?" Martinus asked. "Shards and shatters..."

Timori shook away the tears and stood, quite suddenly.

"She needs a doctor," Timori said.

"Okay, you get her there and..."

"No. I have to end this. You're a speaker, right? Take the ring and use it to keep her alive, get her to a hospital or a doctor. It's her best chance."

He pressed the ring into Martinus's palm. The detective gently let Racquela down upon the damp street and whispered to the ring. It glowed green.

"Are you going to shoot him?" Martinus asked.

"Are you going to stop me?"

"No," Martinus said. He turned his attention back to Racquela and began waving the ring over her face. "For the Republic."

"For the people," Timori replied. He grabbed Racquela's hand one last time and kissed it. "You're strong," he told her. "You'll make it through this."

He ran over to his bike, nodded to Inspector Martinus, and left.

High above the wandshot and sirens came the deep, resonant tones of the Old Temple bells ringing through the night. It was the traditional, ancient signal for a citywide emergency. Timori pedalled faster.

The mob had reached Crystus Plaza.

Chapter 61

Julio rapped his hook upon the sealed vault door.

"Doctor!" he shouted. "Open up! It's me, Master Vellize! Please."

"What if he doesn't let us in?" Ramona asked. "Or isn't here?"

"Then we try Rob's place. It's not as safe, though, and yours is too far away."

"Not as safe? You had us *following* the mob, for Jova's sake!"

"This is the safest place in the city. It's sealed tighter than..."

The door's turncrank handle spun and then opened with a heavy groan. Behind it, De'Barus glared at Julio with an unimpressed expression. His dog growled at Julio, then approached Ramona, wagging his tail.

"Well, be quick about it, then. You were shouting loud enough I could hear you through the door...which means the entire hill probably did, too."

"Nobody followed us," Julio insisted. He ushered Ramona into the basement laboratory ahead of him. "The mob is going right for Crystus Hill...it's only the selfish opportunists who are looting." He remained in the hallway. Ahead, past De'Barus, he could see others occupying the surprisingly tidy lab: Roberto, as well as fellow teacher Michaela Telmari, who was holding the hand of a tall crying woman.

"Jules!" Roberto exclaimed as he approached the doorway. "Am I glad to see you. Get in here."

"I...have to go back out there," Julio insisted. He was surprised De'Barus hadn't physically dragged him in yet.

"Are you cracked?" asked Michaela from the corner. "Those miners could tear you apart."

"They're out for blood," the mystery woman added with a sniffle. "I was there. When the leaders got shot. Oh gods, Michaela, that poor boy. I couldn't find him." She sighed, shaking back tears.

"What leaders?" Julio asked. "Labour?" Drawn in by curiosity, he approached the woman. De'Barus quickly sealed the door behind him.

"Julio, this is Yara," Michaela said by way of introduction. "My...friend."

"Pleased to meet you, Yara," Julio said. He was nearly too rattled to notice that he was shaking the woman's hand with his hook. "Please, if you don't mind recounting what you saw..."

She told Julio all of it: the rally, Bart's rousing speeches, meeting young Jacoby. She mentioned Jacoby's earnest plea to speak to Labour and pressing through the crowd, arriving in the cabaret just in time to witness the murders. Then, she said, she lost the boy during the panic, though he did not turn up amongst the bodies after the mob had begun to march.

"After that I found Mikey and we came here," Yara said.

"Well, whoever did it," Roberto said as he lit a cigarette, "I don't think they're supporters of the Republic. This was all too well timed."

"Not that it matters," De'Barus said. He was fiddling with the dial of a radio that appeared to be broken. "We'll be safe in here until the violence is over."

"We might be singing a different anthem tomorrow," Julio mused. He glanced at Ramona and remembered why he wanted to return to the streets. "Those of us who make it."

"I built this bunker to protect the neighbourhood in case I cause a crystal to massively explode," De'Barus said. "Should work both ways. Nobody can get in unless I want them to." He fiddled with the dial again. "This damn radio...I replaced the crystal, so why isn't it working?"

"They blacked out the station, I bet." Roberto sat back in the corner rocking chair and put a hand behind his head. "And I don't care what you say, Orfus...theory or not, there's no way you can create an explosion *that* big."

"I don't *want* to, Roberto, but if my theory is correct, it could happen. Gods help us all if the government ever..."

"Orfus," Julio said as he paced, "I need to go."

"Abyss you do." Roberto stood up.

"Drago is out there," Julio said. He glanced at Ramona, who was biting a nail.

"Doing his *job*," Roberto reminded. "A job that he chose. He is defending your precious republic from..."

"He's still my..." Julio almost said 'son'. "Friend. And Ramona's son."

"Please, Rob," Ramona said.

Roberto scowled, glancing between Julio and Ramona.

"You two seem to be forgetting there is a murderously violent pack of pickers out there. If the army has been called in to deal with them, which it probably has because the Republic is scared to shatters by now, they'll be trying to keep the rioters *out* of Crystus Hill, which means that if we try and get *in*, we'll be perceived as one of *them*. We'll get killed, in other words, probably by the very person we're trying to save, because he won't be able to tell us from anyone else in the rainy dark. I know it weighs upon your consciences because the two of you both feel *insufferably* guilty about everything, but the best thing for Drago is if we sit tight and remember that he's a trained fucking officer. And pray. And smoke, for the gods' sake...it'll calm you down."

Julio leaned against a workbench and folded his arms, resigned. He withdrew his pipe and tobacco pouch from his inner jacket pocket and began clumsily to pack the pipe bowl. The pipe slipped from between his hook hand and his body where it had been wedged and clattered to the floor.

"Fuck!" he shouted, kicking the pipe.

"Want me to get that for you, Jules?" Roberto asked.

"No," he sighed. He stared at his hook with his one good eye. Both missing body parts were the legacy of the war, of a draft he'd never wanted, of a friendship he'd fought for despite losing his lover to it. "No," he said again, staring at Roberto. "I'm not giving up on the republic, or on Drago. Are you coming, or not?"

"I never said I was letting *anybody* out of here," De'Barus muttered from the corner.

"You're a fucking fool," Roberto said, cigarette between his lips. "You always were and you always will be. The republic is dirt, Jules." He took off his cap and rubbed his head, sighing. "But that godsdamned kid grew on me, despite my best efforts. So let's go, then, since you've got to fulfill that martyr complex of yours, as always."

"Nobody's leaving," De'Barus repeated.

"Orfus, I swear to Jova I will punch you in your smug face if you don't let us out of here," Roberto threatened.

"Fine, fine, go and get yourselves killed," he growled as he walked back to the metal door. "See you at the conference next year, if you survive." He turned the crank and the door groaned open.

"Be careful," Michaela called from the back of the room. "I'll see you both at Central tomorrow, do you hear?"

Ramona kissed Julio on the cheek.

"I should be going with you," she said.

"Are you kidding? Ralfi would murder me with his bare hands if I let anything happen to you."

"Since when do you care what he thinks?" she asked.

"I don't. I love you, Ramona. I always have and I..."

"Will you just go already?" De'Barus said. He gave Julio a shove.

The door slammed shut.

"Wands at my place," Robeto said. "Do you know how in the abyss we're going to get past the mob?"

Julio nodded.

"Remember the old resistance tunnels they built during the occupation?"

Chapter 62

Although Largo's longwand wasn't trained on Jacoby, he was no less aware of its presence. The thick darkoak weapon was slung over the man's meaty shoulder. In the pandemonium of the night, there was no point in hiding it.

Largo kept to the back streets, picking his way through alleys and avenues that he seemed to know well. Jacoby assumed the man had lived his whole life in Captus Nove, other than when he'd served in the war. It occurred to Jacoby then that he didn't really know much about Largo apart from what Crystara had told him, which was precious little.

All Jacoby really knew was that Largo Mita was unflinchingly hostile at the best of times.

For a while they walked silently, Largo craning an ear occasionally to listen for shouts, wandshots, or police sirens. Jacoby felt a bit like a bird, head darting to and fro nervously at the sound of every deadbolted door or closed shutter. Largo seemed to be trying to stay ahead of the mob.

Jacoby stared at his shoes as he walked. He had been too late to warn the Labour Party. If only he had –

"Keep your head up, boy. No telling what people will do when there's a riot. I need you alive."

Jacoby glanced at him.

"What...is your plan exactly?"

"Get in. Get Crystara. Get out."

"Why didn't you try this earlier?"

"Was in jail."

"And how did you know the hanging was faked?"

"I know how the viper thinks."

He stopped at a street corner and peered around the wall. When Jacoby opened his mouth to speak, Largo clamped a hand over it. Several seconds passed as Jacoby tried not to think of the horrific places Largo's hand may have been.

Then he was on the move again just as suddenly, beckoning for Jacoby to follow. Jacoby didn't dare refuse.

"What do you need me for, then?" Jacoby whispered.

"That church ring still work?"

"Yes."

"That's why. I sure don't need you to break a fuckin' crystal lock. Temple guards, 'Liza, army, no problem. Snakes...not so easy to kill."

"Snakes? You mean...the Whisper Society?"

"Yeah. Snakes. Fucking Viper De'Cadomus and his fucking snakes. Took my wife and now they're trying to take my daughter, too."

He held Jacoby back again and watched as a band of youths cracked open a door with a crowbar. Closer to the hills, the stores often had bars across the windows, but it was clear that dedicated looters would find a way. Largo crossed the street as the young men pried the door open and hacked at the deadbolt chain until it broke. Jacoby followed Largo, feeling both guilty and powerless.

"So you...want to use me as a defence?" Jacoby asked. "Against crystal knights? I'm just a..."

Largo wheeled around and shoved Jacoby up against a brick wall, holding him by the throat.

"Listen, you little daisy-chasing, cheating piece of dirt. You're the reason my daughter is locked up, so you'd damn well better help me get her outta there or I'll take *your* life in exchange for hers." Jacoby tried to reply but his windpipe was completely choked off. He felt dizzy. "I don't wanna hear no godsdamned coward's excuses, you hear? Saw too many good soldiers get killed 'cause of cowards. If I tell you to kill a fucking snake, you kill that fucking snake. They deserve it, the lot of them, so forget about the guilt."

Largo let Jacoby go and he fell to the ground, wheezing.

"Fuck you and fuck Crystara," Jacoby spat. "She killed two people. I didn't *make* her do anything. And she hates you, probably more than she'll ever hate me. What makes you think she would willingly go with you?"

"I'm her father. She has no choice. Now get the fuck up, you weakling. I don't give an abyssal shard that she offed somebody. Do you know how many people I've killed?"

Jacoby stood, rubbing his neck. He looked Largo in the eyes. The expression in them was world-weary, uncaring. Jacoby imagined that Largo had lost count.

"What's that supposed to prove?"

"That it runs in our family. Even before the war. Crystara, her mother, *and* her father. Whether she wants to admit it or not, she's my blood."

He craned his ear for a moment, listening to the chant of the mob: *Freedom! Equality! Labour!*

Then he was on the move again, not quite running, glancing backward occasionally to ensure that Jacoby was following.

"I know what you've done to her," Jacoby accused. "Why, if she's your blood?"

Largo looked up at the cloudy night sky and Jacoby felt out with empathy. Though it didn't show on the man's face, there was certainly a sense of remorse coming from him.

"Life is tough. I made her tough enough to survive it."

"That doesn't excuse a fucking thing."

"Shut your fucking mouth before I smash it. Keep watch. I need to see if this is the right entrance. Haven't gone this way in a while." He knelt down and lifted a sewer cover as though it weighed no more than a pillow.

"Entrance to what?"

"Tunnels." His echoing voice receded down the hole.

Jacoby pressed his back to the wall and watched the street. He remembered Master Vellize saying something in history class about old tunnels built during the Mosind Occupation, linking many parts of the city. Jacoby shivered. Sneaking through tunnels during an upheaval wasn't exactly how he'd wanted to connect with the city's colourful past.

Jacoby heard footsteps. He looked up and fumbled in his pocket for the wand Shachari had given him. His heart clenched. He'd lent it to Racquela.

"Well, well," said a familiar, snivelling voice, "lookie what got tracked in with the dirt. Little Jake the Labour Party snitch, all by his lonesome."

It was Dante, smiling his crooked, yellow smile, flanked by two men about Largo's size. He had a cigarette in one hand and a shortwand in the other.

"What do you mean, snitch?" Jacoby said. He tried to be loud enough for Largo to overhear, down in the sewers. "Paulo asked me to attend the rally, remember?"

"You seemed pretty pally with them," Dante replied. "Saw you there. Right before..." he snickered as though there was some joke going on in his head, "...before the republic took a few shots." He put the cigarette to his lips. The way he sucked on it made Jacoby's skin crawl.

"Didn't think you were so pally with Paulo, either," Jacoby said. He tried to sense what Dante was feeling, but he couldn't get past his own overwhelming panic. Besides, Jacoby didn't think that Dante had any kind of humanity left.

Dante's gurgling laugh was like listening to a rat drowning.

"Yeah, well...we clear duped you. I'm his fucking right hand man. And you're about to find out what happens to dullies who cross Paulo Longoro." He snapped his fingers and his cronies advanced on Jacoby.

"Oh, fuck," Jacoby said. "Largo! Help!"

As the men approached, Jacoby whispered to his ring and it glowed yellow for a moment. He thought about climbing down the ladder, but the men would surely apprehend him, and it was too far down to simply jump. He'd only ever attempted a push whisper, never full teleportation, but Crystara had explained it to him once. The trick was to look *directly* at the place you intended to be or you risked serious bodily harm.

As a pair of burly arms came at him, Jacoby stared ahead at the empty street, made a silent prayer to nobody in particular, and whispered to his ring again.

Jacoby nearly lost his balance as he pitched forward behind the men. He broke into a run. His ring, he noticed, had developed a crack. Jacoby glanced over his shoulder to see Dante raise his wand to shoot. Jacoby re-aligned the ring to purple, wheeled around, and stared intently at the green trigger under Dante's tobacco-stained finger.

"Shatter," he whispered. It wasn't the traditional Old Noven whisper, but it seemed to work. The trigger exploded, releasing whatever alignment the crystal had. A shower of green liquid burst forth, engulfing Dante's arm. He screamed.

"Oh, no! Fuck! Shatters!" He fell to his knees clutching his arm in agony. The green acid-like substance had melted his jacket to his skin and his hand was a livid lobster-red. "Augh, it burns!

Fucking kill him, you godsdamned picker dullies!" Dante's curses devolved into a string of agonized nonsense.

Jacoby bolted, sprinting down the road.

"But Paulo said not to..." he heard one of the men say.

"I don't fucking...augh, just do it! Ohhhh my fucking arm!" The screams echoed in the night.

Jacoby rounded a corner and kept on running. He was glad at that moment that he had kept up with football practice. He reached the store where the teens were surely still looting and sprinted on, thinking of home.

Fuck this, he thought. *Fuck Crystara and Largo, fuck politics, fuck Paulo. I'm going to focus on school again, and stop getting involved in illegal dirt, and Dori who want me to kill people. I'm going to graduate and get recommended to an academy so I can get my speaking license. It's what Lenara would have wanted. Then...*

Heavy footsteps plodded behind Jacoby and his panic returned. He dared to look.

One of Dante's goons was chasing after him, gaining ground. Jacoby cursed his short-legged stride.

"Just leave me alone!" he pleaded. Dante's crony did not reply. He was only a few metres away. Realizing he couldn't outrun the man, Jacoby whispered his ring to yellow and cut to the left, turning to aim.

The whisper hit like a punch, knocking the top-heavy man off his feet. The cobbles of the road were not kind to him. Jacoby quickly whispered again, shifting the alignment to orange. As his opponent got to his feet, Jacoby blasted fire at his face. The man panicked and screamed, swatting at the air in front of him as the jet of flame ignited his hair and singed off his eyebrows.

Jacoby backpedalled, whispering for a red alignment. He didn't want to kill the man but he saw little choice.

His ring glowed red, then the crack spread and the crystal fell apart, tinkling onto the cobblestones.

"Lenara," Jacoby cried out. He had meant to say 'shatters.'

"Sorry, kid," the man said as he drew a wand from inside his jacket, "It's nothing personal." Jacoby had a moment of calm clarity when the man's feelings came to him. He had meant what he said.

When the trigger was pulled, Jacoby's panic returned.

Oh gods, he thought. *Jova save me. Fucking save me. Largo, Tim, anyone, please save me.*

There was no pain, just a cold feeling that started at his heart and spread outward. The ground rushed up to meet him but he didn't feel his body hit the slick stones. Even his eyes wouldn't move. All Jacoby could see was the street and a pair of shoes.

I'm dying, he thought. His vision went from hazy to grey, then reddish-black, like his eyes were shut for sleep.

Lenara. I hope I get to see you.

Chapter 63

Timori saw the barricade up ahead. The army had built a hasty barrier with sandbags, barbed wire, and motorcoaches. The soldiers were lined up, first row kneeling, second row standing, wands at the ready. They were not firing, yet.

Timori caught up to the mob and nobody paid him any mind. With the longwand in his shirt he looked like one of them. The chant was all around him, a deafening, rallying cry of *Freedom! Equality! Labour!*

It wasn't just lower-caste men who were marching, either. There were women, many of them armed, and even some of the middle caste appeared to be represented. Many wore fancier clothes, which suggested that although they hadn't been hit as hard by the depression, they were just as ready for change. Ready enough to brave the grey-clad republican army.

It was a cloudy and moonless night, but Timori could see many faces clearly thanks to the plethora of crystal lamps and torches. As he was jostled forward by the mass of the crowd, he looked for Paulo.

"Tim!" a voice shouted. It appeared Paulo had found him first. He was marching at the head of a column of NSP members – noticeably absent were both Dante and the General – and he had a pretty but tired-looking brunette beside him. She didn't appear altogether comfortable at the sight of the soldiers up ahead.

Timori nearly unslung the longwand right then, but he knew he didn't have a vantage point. He was just as likely to hit someone else in the thick of it.

"What the fuck did you do to her?" he shouted over the crowd. He tried to press through to reach Paulo's group but the surge was going forward, forcing him to move with them.

"What?" Paulo gestured to the crest of the hill, where the peak of the parliament building and the Old Temple's bell tower were coming into view. "That's the plan, dully! You made it! I left that in the stash for you!"

"No, Racquela! What the fuck did you do to her?"

"What? Racquela?" Paulo glanced at the girl beside him, then back to Timori. "No idea! Hopefully not anywhere near here!"

The heat crept up Timori's neck.

"I'll fucking kill you!"

"I can't fucking hear you, Tim! Find your way over here or tell me later. Keep your head down. You know where to meet."

Timori wanted to force his way through the throng, but he knew Paulo's cronies would stop him if they realized his intent. Not too far ahead was a boarded-up building. As the mob pressed on, Timori saw the word 'condemned' painted across the door. He squirmed and shoved his way through bodies until he reached the wall.

The marching had ceased. Timori looked ahead to see that the front ranks had reached the barricade. People were standing still, fists raised in the air, still delivering the Labour chant, *Freedom! Equality! Labour!*

The boards over the door were loose, the nails cheap and rusted. Timori pulled a board free.

"Good idea," someone next to him said. "Get a lookout in case they start shooting. You've got that fancy wand."

Suddenly there were others helping him pull the rest of the boards free, and he was ushered into a dark and dusty abandoned office lobby. Behind him, a man with a Labour arm band gave him a thumbs-up.

"For the people," the man said, remaining to guard the door.

"For Racquela," Timori whispered. He let his eyes adjust to the dark and began to search for a way up to the top floor.

"People of Captus Nove," said a voice on a crystal loudspeaker. "Disperse and return to your homes."

A multitude of cries went up from the crowd, the anger of people with grievances too plentiful to name. They were the cries of poverty, the bellows of hunger. They were the pleas for justice. The demands for equality.

Timori sneezed, stepping across a tile floor rife with mouse and rat droppings. At the back of a room filled with desks but devoid of chairs, he discovered a stairwell. He ascended.

"We have barricaded the plaza. We are aware of the situation and the representatives of Parliament will address it in the morning."

Many cries rose up then, most blaming the Republic for attacking and killing the peaceful leaders of Labour who were seeking to gain popularity through the vote. The accusation that the Republic was to blame for the shortage of food and money continued. *Freedom! Equality! Labour!* fell away, replaced by a new slogan: *Down with Castes, Down with the Republic.*

Timori had no doubt who had come up with that chant. He ascended the stairs in the dark, holding the railing so he could take the steps two at a time.

"This is an unlawful gathering," the voice called out through the loudspeaker. Whoever it was, his words seemed to agitate the crowd as opposed to calming them down. Their shouts of protest grew louder, more fervent. "Disperse immediately and return to your homes."

At the fourth and final floor, the stairs ended in a door. It was unlocked. Timori opened it to reveal an empty, single room office space – all that remained other than a thick layer of dust was a ceiling fan. Its crystal had been removed. Timori glanced at the far wall, where there were rows of windows at such a height that they could simultaneously conceal him while allowing a perfect spot from which to shoot. Pressing himself against the wall adjacent to the street, he peered out the window to see if he could espy Paulo.

Paulo was tall enough that Timori could spot him easily, pumping his fist in the air with everyone else and calling for an end to the republic.

"Disperse immediately," the voice representing the army called out again. "We will respond with equal force and will begin making arrests if you do not return to your homes."

The crowd's chant had reached a fever pitch. As Timori cracked the window and set up his wand to rest on the sill, he could see the soldiers growing restless. Members of the mob were rattling the barbed wire and some threw stones or bottles over the barricade.

"Down with castes!" the mob cried. *"Down with the Republic!"*

Timori steadied his aim. There he was in the sight of the scope: Paulo Longoro, the boy who believed he was destined to rule a Third Empire. Paulo: the boy who had masterminded the stirrings of a violent rebellion against the powers that be. Paulo: the fiend who had stolen Racquela from Timori and then nearly killed her, who had killed others without hesitation, who had probably even plotted Racquela's kidnapping.

Timori let out a slow breath and pulled on the trigger. There was an explosion of blood and a sudden cacophony of screams as the girl's chest exploded. Paulo, right next to her, had a look of shock upon his face as her body collapsed in his arms.

The pop of the longwand's shot reverberated through the street and nobody could tell where it had come from. It was the whisper that cracked the crystal. The crowd surged forward and

510

tore through the barricade, overwhelming the first row of soldiers as they fired back in fearful defence.

Timori slumped against the wall and let the wand slip from his hands. It played over and over again in his head: the red mist bursting from her heart, the shocked look in her eyes, the way she fell. He had thought green triggers just poisoned someone or froze their veins.

And he had missed.

He could do nothing but sob silently as the sounds of the street devolved into the tramping of boots, the bursting of wandshot, and the screams of the dying.

Chapter 64

Although frequented by the Noctra and other criminals, the labyrinthine network of tunnels underneath Captus Nove was much safer than it seemed. Most of the dangerous passageways in Captus Nove's tunnels had been sealed off long ago, and cutpurses didn't bother with travellers through the city's understreets. Those with money avoided the tunnels if they knew what was good for them, and those who remained were either criminals themselves or had nothing to steal. The exception was the city's engineers, but nobody bothered them. They made sure the ceilings didn't collapse on anyone, Noctra and casteless alike.

When Julio had been a teenager discovering his love for history, he'd imagined tunnels cut from pure marble, carved with elaborate depictions of life in ancient Imperial Novem. Once he'd found out they were little more than old Imperial brick foundations linked by rough-hewn passages dug out by the Occupation Resistance, his love of history had increased, but his desire to see the tunnels had diminished.

There was nothing romantic about them, Julio discovered as he checked over his shoulder. He strained his one eye to try and peer into the darkness from which they had come. Traversing the tunnels was something akin to being a miner, without the muscle strain or terrible wage.

Roberto illuminated the way ahead with a crystal lamp. Above, still audible despite layers of dirt and stone, the bells of the Old Temple continued to toll for the dead and dying. Julio also heard wandshot and faraway screams. Perhaps, Julio mused, the bells were tolling not just for men, but for the republic itself.

"They haven't rung the bells since Keeper Orvin's murder last year," Julio said to Roberto.

"What are you talking about? They ring them every year when they announce the betrothals."

"They didn't do them this year."

"Why not? It's a huge tradition."

"Dying tradition, you mean. Used to be every noble was vying for a child to get picked. Last year there were only six from Central." Julio paused to ponder the evidence. "I think something happened to the crystal."

"What makes you say that?"

"They stopped doing services at the Old Temple and they brought in the old Master of Whispers as the new..." Julio ran into Roberto's backside. His friend had stopped, frozen and staring at something ahead of them in the tunnel.

Standing at a tunnel crossroads with a wand over his shoulder was Largo Mita.

"Jova's stones," Roberto exclaimed. "The Invincible Corporal himself."

"Largo," Julio said. "Long time no see. What are you doing down here?" He figured it was work for the Noctra, but wouldn't dare suggest it to the most dangerous man he knew.

"Getting my daughter out of the temple. And don't pretend like we're still friends. You two dullards stopped talking to me years ago."

"She's...still alive?" Julio asked.

"Of course she is. The viper wants to use her, just like he did Maria. I know the hanging was faked." He scratched at his beard and lit a cigarette. "I could use a couple of veterans at my back. You even brought your own wands...what do you say?"

"Sorry," Julio said, voice shaky, "we're heading up for Drago."

"You mean Pip's bastard? What in the abyss for? He's a fucking soldier, up there shooting my miner friends just for wanting food and an end to castes...not that you two whitehands would understand that."

"I marched in the last revolution, in case you forgot," Roberto spat. "A whitehand walking beside the pickers. And Jules wasn't born rich. Don't act all fucking clear and shiny. You work for the Noctra. They're just as much about an imbalance of wealth as..."

Largo levelled his wand at Roberto. "They're redistributing and helping the lower castes, you imperialist shard of..."

Julio rushed in between them, holding his hand and hook up.

"Stop it. We've bled for each other. If we managed to put aside our political differences then, we can do so now. We both have our destinations. Largo, if we can make it back to the tunnels with Drago, I will try to come find you in the temple and help rescue Crystara."

"Jules, are you cracked?" Roberto balked.

"Our kids are the future of this nation, Rob," Julio said, holding up his hook-hand for emphasis. "History has already made its mark upon us...if we guide them, they can make the right impact. Or they can get sold on lies of glory and divine right like we were."

"She murdered the keeper!" Roberto protested.

"She was framed," Largo insisted. "He was teaching her speaking. She told me he was her friend. Abyss, she told me...she would have shot *me* in the face before him. This is a viper trick and I don't have time to wait around nattering on about history like Jules. I'm going to *make* history instead." To Julio's surprise, Largo smirked and saluted. "Arus protect you, Sergeant. Private."

Largo lumbered off down the tunnel.

"Shatters, that was..." Roberto began.

"Come on, we've wasted enough time," Julio said. He pointed to the left-hand turn at the crossroads.

"I can think of only one other time I've seen you like this," Roberto remarked, following from behind. Julio dragged his hook along the rough brick wall, feeling for ladder rungs. "You don't have to redeem yourself for anything, you know. It wasn't your fault he died...and he wasn't a very good friend, besides."

"This isn't about Pietro," Julio insisted. "I'm doing this for Ramona and Drago. And for me, godsdamnit. I have few enough friends left in this world."

"Well, you don't have to be so maudlin about it."

Julio stopped when his hook clanged upon something. He felt with his good hand to discover a ladder. Above, audible through the holes in the tunnel cover, he heard the sounds of combat.

"Are you sure you're ready for this?" Roberto asked.

Julio shut his eyes. The Parsish rushing the trenches, dying by the hundreds, Pietro's body flipping through the air, the never-ending boom of scattershot...those images and sounds would never recede. Nothing would bring Pip back, or Ramona's love, or his hand and face.

"I'm ready," he replied, ascending the ladder. The metal cover above his head was heavy, but after some grunting and sweating he managed to move it aside, letting the din of chaos and the scent of blood waft down from the plaza. Julio clambered out of the tunnel to survey the scene.

He was behind the rows of soldiers, unnoticed. Beyond the men in grey, Julio saw crowds of people pressing to get into Crystus Plaza, leaping out of second-storey windows over the barbed wire, or rushing the soldiers, brandishing wands and mining tools. The plaza itself was barren except for a cluster of high-ranking military officers and policemen, standing in a circle smoking pipes as though nothing at all was the matter. The bells shrieked through the night above it all, a haunting harmony contrasting the dissonant din below.

Just as Roberto lifted himself out of the hole in the ground, the crowd pressed through the barricade and broke the first line of soldiers.

"Hold the line!" a man with a general's epaulettes called out, right before he ducked behind the cover of a motorcoach.

Panic spread through the ranks of armed men. As the mob wrested wands from many of the soldiers' hands, true pandemonium descended upon the hill.

Julio's old training took over and he sought cover behind a marble statue of Arus. Roberto followed.

"Drago!" Julio called out. In the chaos there was no discernible reply. Julio's fear was that he was more likely to be seen as a rebel than allied with the soldiers. He craned his head around the statue to assess the situation.

From the second army line came a jet of flame, rolling over the wave of oncoming rioters. It was followed by a burst of air, knocking many off their feet.

"First rank, reform!" shouted a voice. Julio spotted Drago then, with his officer's cap and lieutenant's epaulettes. In Drago's right hand was his special-issue wand with the brown crystal trigger. Within his left fist he clutched a plethora of multicoloured crystals. They glowed in the gloom.

"Not bad," Roberto quipped. "He's certainly braver than Pip...and good with a crystal, besides."

"Still," said Julio, "we *have* to get him out of here."

Julio made the signal to advance and they left the cover of the statue to approach the second line of soldiers, many of whom were firing freely at the clusters of protesters. The soldiers traded shots with the mob, many of whom had taken cover around alleyway corners and behind parked motorcoaches. The first line had resorted to swords against pickaxes. Julio couldn't see the carnage but he could hear the bloodcurdling cries.

The clap of his hand on Drago's shoulder made the boy scream and pull his fist back to ready a punch. His face went from steely determination to relief when he saw Julio.

"Dad!" He exclaimed. "Rob! What in Jova's name are you two doing here? And how did you get past the line?"

"Tunnels," Julio said. "We have to go, Drago. That mob is going to overrun the plaza."

"What? Are you cracked? Not with me here they aren't. And this is my job."

As if to prove his point, he raised his wand and fired upon a grizzled-looking miner who brandished a woodsman's axe. The ball of metal struck the man's neck, exploding in a shower of blood and bone. Julio shut his eyes, trying to shake away old memories.

"This job is going to get you..." Julio was cut off by a rousing cry of defiance from the mob. The first line had broken again. As they picked apart the barricade, the rioters funneled and rushed for Drago's position, still chanting their credo: *Freedom! Equality! Labour!*

The soldiers closest to Drago rallied around him as the remainder of the troops and police officers were swallowed up by the swarm of combat. Julio's training truly took over then as he and Roberto overturned a nearby bench to use for cover.

"Drago!" Roberto shouted as he took a potshot. "Get down!"

In response, Drago threw a red crystal at the advancing mob, then ducked behind the bench. Julio heard an explosion and a cacophony of screams.

"I know what I'm doing, gramps," he said.

Julio popped his head up to survey the carnage. Clambering over the scattered bodies was a small group of rioters, wearing armbands that chilled Julio's spine. It was the black-and-red symbol of the NSP, the party of the Second Empire. At their head was a curly-haired lanky young man holding an unusual-looking wand. Julio's heart sank when he realized he recognized the boy from his history class. He didn't know if he could willingly shoot a student.

"They're coming," he said. "In NSP colours."

"I thought this was a Labour riot," Roberto said.

The bench exploded in a shower of slivers and chunks of wood. Julio was blown backward by the blast, sitting up just in time to see Drago spitting out blood. The boy's left arm hung limp as he stood. Across the narrowing gap between the rioters and the soldiers, Drago and the school boy raised their wands at each other.

"No!" Julio screamed. He rushed for Drago. His good hand, acting of its own accord and old, nearly-forgotten habits, fired from the hip.

For once in his life, Julio's shot was sure, blasting the boy in the gut and sending him backward into his followers. The crowd caught him and pushed him back to standing. Despite his wound, the boy gritted his teeth and returned fire.

Julio felt the wandshot like a whip across his chest and he stumbled into someone's arms.

"Oh, gods," he heard Roberto say. "Jules, no."

"Dad!" a voice cried. Suddenly Drago was there by his side, holding his hook hand. He couldn't feel it. He couldn't feel anything, really, other than a little bit of a chill. It couldn't have been that bad, he decided. The scattershot that nearly killed him had taken half his body and burned horribly for months. He was just a bit cold.

"Stop the bleeding," Roberto said. His voice sounded off somehow, like his throat was closed up.

"Dad," Drago said again.

"I'm not..." Julio tried to say, but he was coughing suddenly. When he looked down, his shirt seemed dark. Someone's hands were pushing on his chest.

"Not going to die," Drago insisted. "Shards and fucking shatters, where's a green crystal when I need one?"

"The mob," Roberto said.

There was another voice then, someone Julio couldn't see.

"Stand down, Lieutenant."

"Sir? But the..."

"That's an order."

Julio laughed, remembering something a student had told him a while ago. He had just put a name to a face. Paulo. Julio's eyes rolled in his head like he was drunk. His gaze came to rest on the curly-haired boy, who was rushing past them, clutching his bloody guts. Julio watched Paulo disappear into the sewer passage.

Despite the order to stand down, the fighting did not abate. The men with the NSP armbands had slipped past the army and were climbing up the steps to Parliament.

"Drago," Julio said, still coughing. "Be good to your mother." He watched as his legs were dragged across the stones of the plaza, though he couldn't feel it.

"Stop talking like that," Roberto said.

"Rob," Julio managed. It was getting hard to speak. "You got your empire back."

"I don't care about the empire."

Cold and tired, Julio shut his eyes. The bells of the old temple were a lullaby, a dirge.

Chapter 65

Crystara awoke with a start, shivering. Her dreams had been dark, full of bells and screams and blood. The darkness, a familiar comfort, seemed different when she opened her eyes.

She was not in the library. The previous day's events came back to her and her confusion became anger.

"Titus," she whispered. "Are you feeling better? Wake up." She went to nudge him in the darkness but her hand felt only cool marble.

He had gone.

"Ah, piss," cursed Crystara. She prayed he hadn't gone and done something stupid like try to take on De'Cadmous by himself.

Crystara didn't want to realign her ring unless she absolutely had to. There was no way of tracking Titus through total darkness, however, unless he was close enough for her to feel his mind. She whispered the ring to blue and a cool light filled the hallway.

Titus had cleared a path through the cobwebs, and she could see his bootprints in the years of settled dust. His breastplate was still where Crystara had thrown it, though she noted that a couple of the crystals had been pried out.

"Titus?" She called down the tunnel. Her voice's echo was the only reply. "Shards and shatters." She hastened after the footprints, looking for signs of Titus.

In the quiet Crystara noticed that there were muffled sounds coming from above that almost sounded like wandshot. She hoped it was a firing squad killing De'Cadomus. As if adding to that theory, she also noted the faraway ringing of the tower bells. The temple tower rang its bells only on rare occasions, such as the death of a keeper.

Crystara reached a crossroads and paused. No minds were close enough to touch with hers, and the other passageways didn't appear to have as many cobwebs. It was difficult to tell which way Titus had gone. As she peered down a side passage, her foot slipped on something and she fell, landing hard on her back.

"Ah, fuck," she exclaimed, wincing. "Shatters." She touched her shoulder blade gingerly. Nothing appeared to be broken. Another bruise she could handle. Crystara brought her light crystal down to her foot to see what she had slipped upon.

It was blood, dark and sticky and not quite cold.

"Titus," she whispered. "You were hurt worse than I thought."

"Titus!" she shouted. Her voice echoed in all directions. Again there was no reply.

Crystara spied a trail of blood that led down one of the side passages. She followed it with haste, hugging the wall so she didn't slip again. She didn't have far to go before the tunnel ended in a winding marble stair, leading up.

"I thought I was done with this fucking place," she sighed.

As she ascended, Crystara examined the blood-slick stairs and her brow creased. There were two sets of bloody footprints: the worn-down tread of heavy boots and a pair of men's shoes.

"Huh," she muttered. She doused the light of her ring and whispered it to grey. At the top of the stairs was a sliding stone wall, slightly ajar, the threshold to a familiar temple hallway. Crystara poked her head out and looked in both directions. There was not a soul in sight, but there was a trail of blood spatters leading deeper into the bowels of the temple. Crystara followed it.

Crystara heard the sounds of fighting more clearly. There were still wands being fired, the noise punctuated by shouts and screams and the bells of the tower. Crystara frowned. The priests wouldn't give De'Cadomus the honour of bells, and if they were fighting him, they wouldn't be ringing them either. Something else was going on, something...

Something brushed up against Crystara's leg and she screamed. She clamped her hands over her mouth and cursed herself for a dully when she realized it was Dusty.

"You made it out," she whispered, kneeling down to stroke him underneath his chin. He purred and rubbed up against her leg again. "I wish I could read you...or that you could tell me what's going on."

As though the cat understood her words, he padded off suddenly in the same direction as the blood trail. Crystara crept onward, following him. Dusty and Crystara rounded the bend in the hallway and Crystara froze. The massive whiteoak doors up ahead were ajar and there were voices coming from the Crystal Chamber.

She approached a door and pressed herself against it, listening to the voices.

"Just hold on, pally. You're going to survive this." It sounded like Titus.

"I'm dying, you dully." The other voice seemed hauntingly familiar, too. Crystara heard a fit of coughing.

Crystara, said a voice in her mind. *The viper comes.*

She slid through the crack in the doors and into the crystal chamber. In front of the behemoth of rock, the Great Crystal, Titus knelt over a blood-soaked Paulo, desperately trying to close a gaping wandshot wound with a green crystal. Before Crystara could even move, a voice rasped from the other side of the room:

"You should have run." De'Cadomus was brandishing his crystal sword. He took slow, deliberate steps toward Titus and Paulo. "I see Crystara was wise enough to stay hidden, or to leave you behind."

It occurred to Crystara suddenly that her grey whisper had been effective. Although Dusty had sensed her presence, nobody else had spotted her yet. She held her breath and began circling around the Great Crystal from the other side, hoping to sneak up behind the viper.

"Just let me heal him first, you soulless bastard," Titus pleaded, "and then I'll face you."

"What do I care for some kid revolutionary? I came to stop a rebellion, not assist it. Stand and face your death like a Dori was meant to."

Crystara froze. She was halfway around the crystal. *Dori?* she thought.

"And what would you know about that?" Titus asked. Crystara also heard him mutter to Paulo. "Hang on, pally. Please."

Crystara rounded the Great Crystal in time to see Titus get to his feet, whispering into his clenched fists. De'Cadomus raised his sword. The long crystal blade had gone black.

"I know more about the Dori and the Great Crystal than you could possibly imagine."

He lies, said a voice in Crystara's mind.

He would pervert us, said another.

"Too bad it doesn't like you," said Titus.

De'Cadomus swung. Titus, amazingly swift for a boy his size, ducked and rolled, getting to his feet beside Crystara. He revealed a red crystal in his open palm and a shower of shrapnel exploded at De'Cadomus. Although the metal shards seemed to pass around him, Crystara watched as another one of the viper's rings turned to white, spent. In response, De'Cadomus whispered his sword to red and pointed it at Titus.

Before Titus could react, a bolt of lightning burst from the viper's blade, striking Titus in the chest. There was an eruption of light and sound and Crystara was blown off her feet. Titus was driven against the Great Crystal, gritting his teeth in pain. His other fist opened to reveal a purple crystal, which shifted to white by absorbing the worst of the onslaught. Titus slid to the floor against the great rock.

Crystara leapt to Titus's defence, kicking the back of the viper's leg then whispering her ring to purple. There was a sickening crunch of bone as De'Cadomus's knees struck the floor and he moaned in pain, falling onto his side. Crystara grabbed his wrist and began pulling rings off his fingers.

"No!" he screamed. He rolled over onto his back, swiping his sword in a wild arc. The blade should have connected right between Crystara's eyes but instead it flew backward and the sound it made caused Crystara's ears to pop. Her purple ring fell apart and she scrambled to get away from the sword, sliding the viper's oversized rings onto her thin fingers.

De'Cadomus touched a green-stoned ring to his knee and stood, twirling the sword menacingly.

"I will have your soul, you little bitch," he threatened.

"No, you won't," said Titus, whose voice had gone deep and strange. He was standing, still touching the Great Crystal with one palm, the other outstretched and clutching the red stone. His eyes were glazed over and almost seemed to be glowing.

"Shatter," Titus commanded. De'Cadomus's blade came apart soundlessly, almost peacefully. The tiny shards landed upon the marble tile like raindrops. Meanwhile Titus's head lolled and he lost consciousness, slumping against the Great Crystal once again.

De'Cadomus uttered a nonsensical cry of rage and all of his crystals went red and orange, flinging a slew of metal and fire at Crystara. She whispered both her stolen rings to purple and shielded her face, bracing for the impact. When it was over she felt the heat of the flames singe the hair off her arms and the slivers cut into her flesh. Both her rings' crystals went from purple to white, fully spent from the onslaught.

"Hey!" shouted a gruff voice behind De'Cadomus. The viper spun to find himself face to face with a longwand.

Largo Mita pulled the trigger. The blast knocked De'Cadomus backward, but he seemed unscathed despite his robe being torn to shreds around the neck. Another of his crystal rings changed to white, leaving him with one unspent crystal.

Crystara stared at her father, wrestling with feelings of fear, shock and relief.

De'Cadomus snapped a finger and the trigger of Largo's wand shattered. Largo registered no surprise. Instead he gripped the wand by the barrel and swung for the viper's jaw. It connected, knocking teeth loose and sending a spray of blood across the room. Some spattered upon the surface of the Great Crystal. There was a sound like an iceberg breaking up as the crack in the Great Crystal spread farther across its surface.

Stop them, said a voice in Crystara's mind.

Before De'Cadomus could react, Largo had tackled him to the floor. Crystara heard the breath go out of the keeper's lungs and then Largo was swinging for all he was worth, pummelling with wild abandon. In seconds the viper's face was all blood and bruises.

"You killed Maria!" he howled. With every other word he threw a punch. Crystara couldn't even tell if the viper was still alive. "You won't take Crystara, too, you rock-kissing snake! Fucking die! Die! Die!"

Something exploded between the two men and Largo was thrown through the air. He smacked against the Great Crystal with a heavy thud. Through his abdomen was a gaping hole made by the viper's ring, which had gone white. The keeper was spent. His eyes were closed and his breathing was shallow.

Largo looked down at his torso and laughed.

"Dad," Crystara said weakly. Her father's blood smeared the Great Crystal, leaving a wide stain. To her amazement he still stood, lumbering forward, willing himself to live. Largo picked up De'Cadomus by the robes and dragged him over to the Great Crystal.

Stop him, the voice said again.

No. Free us.

The course has already been chosen, our fate set.

Not the viper.

FREE US. CRYSTARA.

She shook off the feeling of paralysis and stared at her father, a man who by all rights should have been dead already.

"Please just tell me. Why were you so cruel to me for all those years?"

Largo stared at her with a look she had never before witnessed. It was the look of regret.

"You look just like her," he said. Then he took De'Cadomus's head in one meaty palm and slapped the man's cheek with his free hand. The viper's eyes fluttered open.

"Hey. Why don't you kiss that fucking rock you love so much?" he asked. Largo slammed the keeper's face into the Great Crystal, crushing his skull.

There was a rumbling beneath Crystara's feet and the marble itself began to crack. A booming noise reverberated throughout the chamber as the cracks within the Great Crystal deepened, spreading across its surface in forked paths.

Largo fell to the ground. He stared at Crystara.

"You were the..." Then his head dropped.

"No," she pleaded. She ran over to him and shook his shoulders. "You can't die. Tell me why." She punched him. His head fell to the marble, lifeless. "I hate you, you fucking bastard!"

she screamed. "You don't get to be the fucking hero..." she sobbed.

Losing the will to hold herself up, she pressed her face into his shoulder and cried.

A choked moan brought her to her senses and she lifted her head. Paulo had crawled over to the Great Crystal, hand outstretched.

"Heal me," he pleaded.

NO.

YES. FREE US.

Crystara. Stop him.

"Paulo, wait. Don't..."

With the last of his strength, Paulo touched the Great Crystal.

It exploded.

Epilogue

"We regret to inform you that your regular morning host, Marius Ghost, will not be broadcasting today. Instead we have a special broadcast here from Crystus Hill, where the newly-appointed Chancellor of Novem will present his first address. I will now turn things over. Mr. Chancellor?"

"Good people of Novem, from the farmers who feed our families, to the miners who sweat in the earth to give us crystals and coal, to the priests who are our link to the divine, I stand here before you with a promise.

"Within the living memory of many of you were the promises of another Longoro. My father. I ask you, Novem, to stand where you are and tell me truthfully, in the sight of Jova himself, if he did not deliver upon those very promises. When you were hungry, he put the farmers back in the fields and you were fed. When you were poor, he sent the merchants abroad and you were wealthy again. When you were cold, the miners returned to the mines and there was coal again.

"We are facing a similar situation to the one my father saw nearly forty years ago. Famine plagues us. Our economy is in shatters, thanks in part to foreign powers who feel we have not yet paid in full for the Great War, despite the overwhelming evidence that the depression has affected this nation of ours greater than any other. Caste fights against caste, dividing what should be a proud and united people.

"I ask you, Novem, to bear witness to my promise. I promise to once again put food on the table of every Noven family. I vow to repair our broken economy and once again make Novem the wealthy and respected nation of trade and prosperity that it once was.

"Lastly, Novem, upon my very life I swear this: you have spoken overwhelmingly in favour of abolishing the caste system. I will make this so. Is not the shepherd just as essential as the scholar? Every man and woman has a place in Noven society, and they should all be accorded respect for the work they do.

"This shall be no chaotic redistribution of wealth, but rather a gradual series of policies that will see the lower caste rise and the upper caste step down gracefully from their place of privilege, to where all are equal. And we, Novem, shall enjoy the fruits of our labour together in prosperity.

"This last promise I make to you, Novem: Never more shall this great nation look beyond its own borders without just cause. Novem's concern is its own vitality.

"Together, we will rebuild."

Inspector Franco Martinus shut off the radio, lit up a cigarette, and slid into his leather armchair. The previous day had been one of the longest of his career and he still didn't feel fully recovered. He sipped on his glass of whiskey and pondered, letting the liquid warm his tongue and cheeks. Franco hadn't seen that kind of pandemonium on the streets of Captus Nove since the end of the Great War. It was the kind of thing that, gods willing, he would never see again.

Then again, the NSP were back in power. Franco had assumed nobody would ever show them favour again, not after everything Emperor Longoro had done, but if you gave a desperate crowd a handsome stranger with a pocketful of promises...Franco couldn't remember if there was another half to that saying or if it was something he'd made up.

Shatters, he thought to himself as he took another sip, *to think that voice on the radio is the same damn kid I was chasing.* Furthermore, the 'kid' claimed to be the son of Maximus Longoro.

As far as old Frank was concerned it was a cartload of dirt, a pretty little lie wrapped up in bows and ribbon.

The thought of ribbon stirred something in Frank's mind and he got up from his chair, downing the last of his whiskey and dowsing his cigarette. He flipped his suspenders back over his shoulders, grabbed his wallet, keys, pocketwatch, wand, and trench coat, and left his squalid apartment for the street.

The day after the revolution was abysmally quiet. People were still afraid, mostly of the military, which had assisted the NSP in achieving a coup. The police presence on the street was heightened, and Franco knew that when he returned to the precinct they would expect him to carry on as though nothing had happened.

Despite the fact that he had been a shard's length away from putting away the Paulo kid. Suddenly a criminal – a child, no less – was running the nation. Franco had given up on figuring out the world. The gods had a cracked sense of humour.

Fresh flowers were hard to find the day after a riot, but Franco knew when it was time to call in a favour. Within half an hour he was headed to the Avati Hill Hospital, bouquet in hand.

They knew him there, most of the nurses and doctors. Sometimes he brought in crooks that he'd shot in the leg, to be patched up before they stood trial. Franco flagged down one of the nurses on duty. The lady was moving at a brusque pace. The hospitals of Captus Nove were full to bursting since the riot.

"I'm a little busy, Frank," she called over her shoulder. "And I can't accept flowers. I'm married." She flashed him her wedding ring but there was some cheek to her voice.

"Don't flatter yourself, Nanci. I never bought flowers for my ex-wife either." He followed her down the emergency wing hallway. "These are for a patient. Can you tell me where to find the De'Trini girl?"

"I can, but Lord De'Trini requested no visitors, sorry."

"He'll let me in. I'm the guy who brought her here."

"Fine, fine. Third floor, private room. And could you do me a favour? When you get the chance, tell those new guys up on the hill that we are really underfunded. Public works went to dirt during the republic." She waved him off and entered a door marked 'staff only.'

"Of course," said Franco to nobody in particular. "I'm sure I'll be first in line when they start taking suggestions."

Franco made his way to the third floor of the hospital. The De'Trinis' private hospital room wasn't difficult to find. Franco just had to look for guards posted outside the door. They were big goons who looked to have about half a brain between them. Franco bet there was a private speaker inside, too, one of those types who doubled as bodyguard and healer. Franco adjusted his tie and approached the door, knocking before the guards could stop him.

The emotional turmoil coming through the closed door nearly choked him. Being an empath was handy in his line of work but it wasn't so great for his personal life. It certainly hadn't helped his marriage any.

"No visitors," said the one on the left. "Except for family."

"Little Vito Brachus, is it?" Franco said. "Not so little anymore, though, are you? Nice to see you're making something of yourself now. Sending you to the slammer for a year was the best thing that ever happened to you."

"Holy shards. Frank?" Vito eagerly shook Franco's hand, nearly crushing it. "Didn't recognize you...you've lost weight. I'm sorry. I really can't let you in. Joven's strict orders."

"Just let me talk to him. I worked with him on the kidnapping case, remember?"

Vito opened the door slightly.

"Lord De'Trini, sir? Inspector Martinus is here."

There was a pause.

"Let him in."

The room was surprisingly vacant. Joven's brother Martin was likely working with the NSP to maintain his position in politics. Joven's father had been gone for decades, but the De'Trini matriarch was there, old Astella De'Trini, praying with Jessica at a small shrine to Gitana, the goddess of healing.

Racquela De'Trini was lying upon the bed, her face wrapped up in bandages. Kneeling beside the bed was a speaker-doctor who was writing something upon a chart. About his wrist was a chain of crystals, most of them green.

"I understand I have you to thank for saving my daughter's life," Joven said as he shook Franco's hand.

"And that kid who was betrothed to her."

"So he didn't do this, then? Do you have any idea who did?"

Franco walked up to the bed and placed the flowers on the bedside table. He looked down at Racquela, who would certainly bear some internal scars even if her face healed. Franco glanced at Joven, who was wringing his hands, and Jessica and Astella, who were still praying at the shrine. The emotional cord of the room was a thin line, stretched tight between hope and despair.

At best, telling the truth would lead to assassinations and arrests. At worst, civil war.

"He got away," Franco said. "Didn't catch his face, but I swear by the Great Crystal I'm still looking."

***

Franco's first day back to the station was a waking nightmare.

It wasn't the pall of collective cigarette smoke hanging just below the ceiling, more dense than usual, nor was it the telegrams on the corner table that buzzed constantly with new reports of vandalism or another body found in the river. It wasn't even the throng of men and women in the lobby waiting to speak to a detective, or the stack of papers in Franco's office, bound and stamped with the seal of a black eagle, detailing the official imperial changes to the police department.

It was the fact that everyone knew Franco's last case concerned the NSP. Known criminals had conspired with other known criminals and were now in control of the nation.

The socialists and imperialists wouldn't give a damn. Everyone else looked at Frank like he was worse than casteless.

Frank sat down in his worn-out office chair and sighed. The grizzled, grey-moustached detective captain knocked on Franco's office door just as Frank lit a cigarette.

"Leave the paperwork," Detective Captain Mazotti suggested. "It'll keep."

Franco folded his arms. "You're not worried the new regime will come down on us for ignoring new protocols?"

"You kidding? We're up to our ears in murders and stolen property. New parliament's busy using the military to stop the whitehands from changing things back to the way they were two days ago. No way we can even *look* at regulations until half the fucking hill isn't busting down our front door."

"Okay, I'll go take statements," Franco said as he stood.

The captain shook his head. "No, Frank. Ariela's got that covered. We can only take so many cases at a time. Get some names from her lists and hit the streets. Maybe if the slammer gets full enough, these damn pickers will shut up and let us get to some important work."

"Yes, Captain." Franco stood and left his office.

"Hey, Frank." Officer Valachi was blocking the doorway. "Nice work on that NSP case."

"What do you want?" Frank blew smoke out his nostrils.

"Just to tell you that. Oh, and don't bother following up on the Largo Mita lead. He's dead."

"What a loss," Franco said with a shrug. "I have work to do." He pushed past Valachi before the man decided to deride him about anything else.

The crowd beyond the barrier glared at him accusingly, as though he was the reason they hadn't yet received justice. Franco approached Ariela's cluttered desk. A middle-aged man with a ponytail sat across from Ariela, wringing a hat in his hands.

"Ariela, hand me a few cases, would ya?"

If looks could have killed, Ariela's steely blue glare surely would have pierced Franco's flesh. It didn't help that she was friends with his ex-wife.

"I'm in the middle of taking a statement, Frank. Wait your damn turn." Ariela tossed her dark hair out of her eyes and turned back to her typewriter.

"For the love of Avari..." Franco muttered. He sat in an empty chair and smoked his cigarette, listening.

"Sorry," said Ariela. "Go on, Mister...?"

"Doctor. Ruveldi. Where was I?"

"You said you took to the sewers with your friend."

"Yeah. So we made it under the hill, behind the army. We came up to get Drago. Lieutenant Drago. Andari. But then the rioters attacked and we were stuck there. That's where Jules got shot."

"Jules." Ariela said. "That was your friend? Julio?"

"Master Julio. Vellize."

"Did you see who shot him, Sir? Doctor?"

"Yeah, I saw the kid."

"Could you describe him for me?"

"Curly dark hair. Smarmy look on his fucking picker face. Tall. Skinny. He might be dead already, but if he's not...he needs to be. I mean, shoot the army, sure. Not the veteran."

"Okay, I might need more details. Tell me what happened. How he got shot."

"The curly-haired kid was about to fire at the lieutenant. So Jules up and took a crack. They traded shots, really. Didn't see which way the kid went after that, might have been trampled for all I know. I was busy trying to stanch a chest wound. But..."

The man with the ponytail was crying.

"Take your time, Sir." Ariela said. "Doctor."

Franco looked away, staring at the crowd. A boy had climbed over the lobby divider and was approaching him, bearing a serious expression.

"Inspector Martinus?" the boy said.

"Who's asking?" said the inspector, tipping his hat up to examine the lad. There was something familiar about him.

"I'm asking," the boy said. He pushed a few dinari bills and some centima coins into Franco's hands. "I'd like to hire you to find my brother. I know he's still alive."

"You're Jacoby Padrona's brother, aren't you?"

"Yes. My name's Marco."

"What do you mean, 'still alive', kid? Was he involved in the riot? We got a stack of 'missing persons' reports the height of a Joven statue thanks to that march."

"I...I don't know. I know he hasn't come home since that night. But the last time I saw him, he mentioned he was working for you, and he had to tell Timori and Racquela something because they were in danger, and, I just have this *feeling*..." Marco blinked and tears fell to spatter his shoes. He glanced down at the wad of money in Franco's open palms, then looked up to meet his eyes.

He knows I'm responsible, Franco thought, *at least partly.*

"Yeah, I know all about feelings, kid." He sighed, knowing he was about to make a big mistake. What was one more, in a lifetime full of bad choices? He dumped the pile of money back into Marco's hands and clapped him on the shoulder.

"Kid, I'll do it for free."